KITTY ANNE]

Cattleman's Club 6

Jenny Penn

MENAGE EVERLASTING

Siren Publishing, Inc.
www.SirenPublishing.com

A SIREN PUBLISHING BOOK
IMPRINT: Ménage Everlasting

KITTY ANNE IN CHARGE
Copyright © 2015 by Jenny Penn

ISBN: 978-1-63259-374-0

First Printing: June 2015

Cover design by Les Byerley
All art and logo copyright © 2015 by Siren Publishing, Inc.

Printed in the U.S.A.

PUBLISHER
Siren Publishing, Inc.
www.SirenPublishing.com

KITTY ANNE IN CHARGE

Cattleman's Club 6

JENNY PENN
Copyright © 2015

Chapter One

Tuesday, May 27th

George Davis sighed and cracked his head from side to side as he pointedly shifted in his seat. He tried to stretch out every muscle he could as he waited outside the Dothan library in his truck for the supposedly hot and totally psychotic librarian to come out.

That was how Aaron and Jacob had described Kitty Anne Allison.

Of course, if those two idiots were to be believed, the woman was not only nuts but also scary as hell, not that GD put any faith in those knuckleheads' opinions. What the hell did they know about women anyway?

Not much as far as GD was concerned. Sure, the brothers were known to be weird. Very weird. That was a hell of a reputation to earn, given the things that went down at the Cattleman's Club. Cattlemen, after all, were not known for their normalcy.

Apparently, Kitty Anne was, or at least that was what she wanted Cole and his cousins to believe. She'd sold them all a story about how she was just a good girl who happened to be engaged to a very boring guy and wanted one last hurrah before she settled down. Of course, that was a crock of shit.

It hadn't taken GD more than two hours online to bust that barrel of lies right open. First off, there was no fiancé. Second off, Kitty Anne was apparently far from being a good girl. After all, a good girl wouldn't be trying to lure Cole into paying her for sex.

Not just sex.

Kinky, tie-a-man-to-the-bed sex, which GD didn't object to on principal, but there was something more going on here. Kitty wasn't just playing one role, but two, because she wasn't a prostitute either. What she was was friends with Rachel Allen. Rachel had something going on with Hailey Mathews, who had a bone to pick with Cole.

Hailey and Cole were at war as far as GD could tell. It was a sweaty, twisted war that was either going to end with Cole in jail or with Hailey pregnant. GD's money was on Cole. He, at least, had enough sense to figure that out before Kitty had gotten out the chains.

Instead, he'd sent his cousins in to check things out, but Aaron and Jacob weren't half as stupid as Cole thought. They'd caught the scent of trouble and were not coming back for more. Fortunately, GD didn't mind trouble…or being bound and at the mercy of a woman who knew how to make him beg. Just as long as a woman could take what she gave, she was free to have her fun. GD didn't believe there should be any limits on that commodity.

That was just the way he lived his life, with a diehard conviction that every day should be enjoyed…at some point. This was not his point. This was the point in the day when he wondered if he could have a more boring job. Watching people was only entertaining when there were people to watch.

Right then, Miss Kitty Anne Allison was a no-show.

Maybe it was time to go take a peek for himself and make sure she hadn't given him the slip. That thought was laughable, but GD rolled with it, taking any excuse to stretch his legs. After all, this wasn't a real case, and he wasn't getting paid for his time. He might as well make the most of it and get some practice in doing something other than sitting on his ass.

So he spent the next half-hour creeping up on the library. Sticking to the thickest shadows, he moved silently through the night, avoiding the overhead, security cameras and the lights. GD finally reached the line of shrubs that ran down the back of the brightly colored building. He crawled behind them up to the door that he knew was locked but doubted was alarmed.

He was about to find out.

Keeping his big body tucked up behind the prickly bush that hedged the back entrance, GD allowed only his hands to creep into the light as he made short work of picking the outdated bolt on the library's door. Then it was just a matter of holding his breath and opening it with slow caution.

Thankfully no alarms sounded.

The hinges didn't even squeak as he pulled the door open far enough to slip into a dark, narrow hall. It led down past several doors and out into the library's lobby. The whole building was shrouded in shadows except for a strip of light coming from under the break room door. The clear peals of laughter leaked out into the hall, and GD paced steadily forward until he could make out the words that formed out of the murmurs.

"How very interesting, Mr. Jackson, but I think I have a better idea…What do you think? Too coy?...Too coy."

There was only one voice doing all the asking and all the answering and only one woman GD could see as he eased back the door just enough to spy on the woman staring at herself in the mirror. He might have been struck by how crazy she was if he hadn't gone plum dumb at the very sight of her.

God but she was beautiful.

Kitty Anne's picture really didn't do her justice. While it had conveyed the strength of her features and the determined line of her jaw, it stopped short of actually capturing the spirit that animated her expression of annoyance with such a glow that he was instantly captivated. She was a Venus.

His Venus.

He'd found his one.

GD recognized that truth and accepted it without any hesitation. He'd always known this day would come. Of course, he'd been expecting it to come out at the club, because after all his Venus wouldn't be perfect if she didn't accept that he had certain sexual appetites that needed to be appeased. It didn't hurt that most of the women out at the club were built like goddesses.

Not that GD was complaining about Kitty Anne's packaging. She was definitely built right, even if she chose to dress as if she belonged in some Technicolor movie. GD eyed the bountiful curves of her breasts constrained behind a sweater tight enough to be indecent but with a collar and sleeves demure enough to be matronly.

The same could be said of her skirt. It was long enough to cover her knees but hit right at the perfect curve of her calf and stretched snugly over the luscious round rump of her ass. She looked both plush and firm, a natural vixen who managed to turn a grandma outfit into a sexy one.

She fit Jacob and Aaron's description to a T, looking just like a sex kitten all wrapped up in a lethally pure packaging. The woman obviously practiced her craft, which was just what she was doing right then as she turned back toward the TV glowing with the image of an old black-and-white movie.

GD didn't recognize it, but he could tell enough to know the movie wasn't that old. It was a noir film, one of those overwrought, overacted, highly styled movies that only crazy people watched in dark break rooms after work. Of course there was crazy good and crazy bad. He had a sense he knew which one Kitty Anne was.

"You can do this, Kitty Anne. Take a deep breath," she instructed herself as she paused the movie and turned back to her reflection. "Just look him in the eye…and smile…no teeth?"

She glanced back at the TV screen and studied the close-up of a brunette wearing long gloves and an evening gown.

"No teeth," Kitty Anne answered herself with a shake of her head and turned back to smile at her reflection, checking several more times as she perfected a slight curl of the lips that held the same sense of wicked innocence that the actress on the TV conveyed.

"Smile. No teeth. Deep breath, lift the chest and say, 'How very interesting, Mr. Jackson, but I think I have a better idea.' Oh yeah." Kitty Anne nodded, breaking out of her whisky-honeyed voice to smirk at her reflection. "That is it. Mr. Cole Jackson is going to be drooling in his sippy cup."

GD highly doubted it but couldn't help but admire the sudden display of spunk and attitude. He appreciated that it must have taken a lot of training and practice to become the kind of Venus Kitty Anne had clearly modeled herself into. It was also clear that she was as crazy and nuts as Aaron and Jacob had sworn.

* * * *

Kitty Anne sighed as she clicked off the TV and rolled the ancient media station back into the corner. It had gathered dust there for years before she'd gotten hired several months back. She had a whole bunch of old tapes and no VCR to watch them on. More importantly, she didn't have the money to buy a VCR.

That was all right.

Kitty Anne enjoyed holding her movie nights at the library after everybody had gone home. Tonight, though, wasn't about entertainment. She'd needed to practice and get herself ready for the big show that would be going down in a couple of days. *The big show…* Kitty Anne smiled as she glanced back at her reflection, not daring to admit, even to herself, that she was a little unnerved by the scheme she'd gotten herself involved in this time.

She could end up arrested…again.

Of course, Kitty Anne had never regretted anything she'd done and wouldn't this time either. It didn't matter how crazy the scheme was, she was doing this for Rachel, who happened to be her best friend and, pretty much, her only real friend. There really wasn't anything Kitty Anne wouldn't do for her, including getting arrested.

Hell, Rachel would bail her out, and in the process, Kitty Anne might actually make some new friends. After all, this time it wasn't either Rachel or Kitty Anne who had come up with their master plan. That honor belonged to the notorious Patton Jones.

Kitty Anne had liked Patton almost from the first moment she'd met her, feeling a strange kind of kinship with her almost from the start. Perhaps that was because Patton was just doing what she was doing to protect her best friend, Hailey. That was where the details got convoluted, and Kitty Anne's attention span had clocked out.

It didn't matter. She didn't need to know the rhyme or reason behind the master plan. She just needed to know her role, and she knew it well. If she got arrested in the end, then Kitty Anne would go down smiling and having fun. That was what really counted. After all, life could be so boring.

Everyday waking up and going to the same job, doing the same thing, having the same conversations with the same people, Kitty Anne had been *living* the same day over and over again. Was it any wonder that it had driven her insane?

She needed a break.

She needed a laugh. Cole and his two bungling cousins were definitely good for that. Aaron and Jacob, the cousins, they were so adorably innocent, blushing at any mention of her dominating them. That was definitely not their kink.

Cole, on the other hand, seemed to be nothing but full of perversions. Having spent enough time around enough players, Kitty Anne knew enough to recognize one on sight. Handsome, with smooth moves and quick comebacks, Cole was used to the women of the world bowing before his neatly polished boots. He was vain, arrogant, and Kitty Anne couldn't figure out for the life of her why Hailey was in love with the man.

There was no denying that she was in love with the man, even if she had basically hired Kitty Anne to seduce and humiliate him. So, really, Kitty Anne had to figure she wasn't the truly screwed-up one in the group, which was unusual, given her background. This time, though, she was among her own kind, which was just why Kitty Anne wouldn't back down.

She was going to lure Cole to a motel that operated as a known brothel. There she was going to seduce him into letting her tie him to the bed. Then she was going to take pictures, abandon him, and call the cops. Given Cole was expecting to pay for the pleasure of her company, he'd have enough cash to get taken down with everybody else.

In the end, Hailey would have her proof that Cole was a wanderer. Cole would be utterly disgraced, and Rachel would have a front-page exclusive that included pictures. That was the plan, but deep in her gut, Kitty Anne knew this was going to backfire all over her.

That was sort of what made the whole thing worth doing. There was nothing Kitty Anne loved more than trouble. One thing trouble was not was boring. There was nothing that Kitty Anne hated more in the world than being bored. So she'd done her best to scare off Cole's cousins, which hadn't been hard. Now she had a meeting with the man himself.

Cole had agreed to meet Kitty Anne for cocktails at the sleaziest dive she dared to enter, which was pretty damn sleazy, given Kitty Anne wasn't afraid of much. They'd see if the same could be said of Cole. If he played it cool, he'd meet her gaze and hold it. Kitty Anne knew that moment of silence would be her friend and prod him into taking the lead.

He'd have a come-on, and she'd counter. She'd remember to breathe deep, hold his gaze, and smile with no teeth as she purred over her words.

"That's very interesting Mr. Jackson, but I have a different idea." Then she'd slide a folded napkin across the table with an address and instructions to ask for Kitty Anne Kat. "Be there. Seven o'clock."

Then she'd get up and walk slowly away, making sure to swish her ass with every step. Matching her mental instructions with actions, Kitty Anne glanced back over her shoulder to watch her rump roll in the mirror and assure that she was getting her walk right, but instead of worrying over the swish of her hips, she froze as her gaze connected with the man spying on her through the door that was now cracked open.

It probably would have been a good idea to scream and run. Kitty Anne actually did do those two things, but she didn't flee or cry out in terror so much as bellow in outrage and swipe the broom out of the corner as she took off after the large man who thundered down the hall with a heavy-bear-like charge.

He hit the back door, and it flew open, only to snap back and smack Kitty Anne right in the face. She plowed into it, trying the same move the big man had so effortlessly pulled off, but she didn't have his girth, much less his heft. Instead of the door flying back open, Kitty Anne went wheeling backward as her nose mushroomed with an intense pain that had her cursing.

By the time it dulled down to an ache, she could hear the tires screeching through the parking lot. Kitty Anne managed to get the door open and catch one final glimpse of the pickup truck tearing out of the drive. That was all she needed.

Chapter Two

The next morning Kitty Anne woke up nice and early, spending an extra half-hour on her already hour-long grooming ritual to make sure she looked her best. She glued on individual eyelashes and picked out a royal blue dress that not only showed off her figure but also made her eyes shine.

Not that anybody bothered to notice, thanks to her never-fail-to-impress push-up bra. It worked magic, assuring that every guy she passed glanced at only one part of her anatomy. As her mother had always said, there wasn't anything a large set of breasts couldn't get out of a straight man.

She hadn't meant it as a compliment, but Kitty Anne had taken it as one. Boobs—that was her secret superpower. They were the greatest one of all. They worked on all men, even cops. A half-hour after walking into the police station with a tag number, she'd walked back out with a name.

George Davis.

All it took to find out the rest was looking him up online and realizing he hailed from Pittsview. A quick call to Rachel and there wasn't almost anything Kitty Anne didn't know about the infamous GD. As a reporter for the one-paper town, Rachel knew just about everybody, and there wasn't anybody, apparently, who didn't know GD.

He was that kind of guy. A good one, a friend to all, he'd attended almost every church in town at some point and worked hard as a private investigator. Most importantly, he was a Cattleman, rumored to be a higher-up in the little sex club all the Cattlemen belonged to. From what Rachel said, Cattlemen always came in pairs.

Cole normally teamed up with a guy named Kyle, but Kitty Anne couldn't be blamed for thinking that GD was filling in for him. That didn't seem to concern Rachel. Kitty Anne, on the other hand, was a little unnerved but didn't intend to back down.

Neither, apparently, was Mr. Davis. He showed up exactly at four that afternoon when she got off of work to shadow her all the way back to the monthly rental motel where she stayed. Kitty Anne let him stew in the parking lot as she got ready for her date with Cole and even pretended not to notice him as he followed her to the bar.

He was still waiting when she got done with Cole, who had agreed to meet her the following night at the brothel. That victory fueled Kitty Anne's growing sense of excitement, and she couldn't resist confronting GD. Besides, it seemed ridiculous to pretend as though she hadn't noticed him following her back to the motel.

Stepping out of her small car, Kitty Anne turned toward the back of the parking lot instead of toward her room and began marching her way across the asphalt to where GD had pulled his big pickup truck into a spot. She kept her chin up, her shoulders back, making every step a stomp and assuring that she looked strong and powerful. Still, she ended up feeling weak and dainty as the big man climbed down out of his truck.

He was huge…and handsome.

Not a petite girl, Kitty Anne liked her men tall and strong enough to make her feel like a woman. GD fit that bill. Dressed in a pair of softly faded jeans that clung to the powerful muscles thickening his thighs and a T-shirt that rippled with the flex of his perfectly cut chest, the man was like a walking wet dream.

A wet dream that liked to share his ladies with his buddies.

Kitty Anne's steps faltered as she felt a sudden wave of heat leave her almost light-headed. This couldn't be happening. She was always in full control when it came to men. Then again, normally her heart wasn't beating around like a jackrabbit's on a sugar rush. Hell, her palms were sweating.

Sweating!

It was gross and weird. Worst of all, Kitty Anne had a sick feeling GD knew exactly what kind of effect he was having on her. Given the smirk tugging at the big man's lip, she suspected she was wearing her thoughts on her face.

Quickly she tried to school her features into a look of disdain as she glanced back down his length, pointedly taking note of the scuff of his boots, the size of his belt buckle, and the cowboy hat that he managed to make look sexy instead of cliché. Of course, that had a lot to do with the sharp cut of his jaw. It matched the rough drawl of his accent as he greeted her with a hint of amusement lightening his deep tone.

"Evenin', beautiful." He actually tipped his hat at her in a sign of polite respect as she came to a stop before him. "Can I help you with something?"

He could help her with a whole lot, but Kitty Anne kept that opinion to herself as her inner voice snapped at her to stiffen up and not only meet his challenge but destroy it.

"Yes." Crisp and sharp, that answer whipped out of her with a strength that disguised the quiver of lust trying to weaken her defenses. "You can tell me what you were doing last night breaking into the library."

"I'm sorry, but I'm not sure what you are talking about." The twinkle in the man's smoky gaze belied the earnest quality of GD's denial and warned Kitty Anne that she was dealing with a man who had no problem lying.

"Is that right?" Kitty Anne smiled. She was going to enjoy the next moment. "You know, I can prove it was you."

"Is that right?" GD mimicked back as he imitated her smile and smugly surprised tone perfectly. "You know, I think you're going to have to."

"Fine." Kitty Anne paused to straighten up and savor the moment as she slowly revealed the ace up her sleeve. "Your license tag number is 892 GKY...*Mr. Davis.*"

"No, it isn't." GD didn't even hesitate to deny her.

"Please." Kitty Anne snorted as she stormed around him. "Why are you even arguing when all I have to do is look and see that—"

Kitty Anne shut up as she stared at the license tag hanging on the back of the truck. The vanity plate didn't even have numbers. She didn't know what the hell was going on, but that didn't change the fact that she knew what she'd seen last night. It had been his big face in the mirror. This big truck careening out into the street. It just hadn't been that tag on the back of it.

"Would you care to say it out loud for me, beautiful?"

Kitty Anne's gaze lifted and narrowed in on GD as she watched him fight back his laughter. He wasn't doing a good job of it, and damn his hide, he was even better looking when he smiled.

Kitty Anne closed her eyes and forced herself to breathe deep and focus. She was not going to be conned by either a hot body or a double-dimpled grin. Neither was she going to be undone by the infectious nature of his amusement. The man was up to something, and she wanted to know what.

"I'm not sure—"

"No." GD cut her off with a slow shake of his head. "That's not it. Come on now...say it with me....You. Are. Wrong."

"I am—"

"You are wrong."

"I—"

"Wrong."

"Fine!" Goaded into losing her composure for a moment, Kitty Anne gave into temptation and all but spat at him. "I am wrong. I am wrong, wrong, wrong, wrong! There? Are you happy now?"

"Happy?" GD nose wrinkled as he snorted. "Far from it, but we'll get there."

"We'll get nowhere, not until you answer some questions, like just who the hell are you? Why are you watching me? Why did you break into the library? And why shouldn't I call the cops on your ass right now?"

Changing gears, Kitty Anne went on the offensive, wagging a finger and advancing on him with each question. She didn't let up until she'd poked him in the chest. He glanced down to stare pointedly at her red-painted nail before glancing back up.

"I'm sorry, beautiful. I have no idea what you are talking about."

"So that's your story?" Kitty Anne pulled her hand back, finding her agitation oddly deflated by his obstinateness.

"And I'm sticking to it."

"Then let me help you out." Never one to give up, Kitty Anne was more than willing to try yet another tactic—honesty. "You're a friend of Cole Jackson's, right?"

"Guilty."

"He sent you out here to check me out, didn't he?"

"Maybe." GD shrugged.

"Maybe you like what you see." In fact, Kitty Anne knew he did.

"Maybe." The hint of amusement lightening his tone matched the sparkle in GD's eyes as he clearly waited for her next move.

"And maybe you're interested in having a little fun," Kitty Anne suggested with her own slow drawl.

GD eyed her, openly admiring her curves and sending a pleasant rush of anticipation through her veins as his gaze darkened in a look she recognized all too well. He was trying to imagine her naked, but he didn't need to paint a fantasy. She was more than willing to let him take a ride, but on her terms.

"Maybe."

"It'll cost you," Kitty Anne warned him.

"Everything always does," GD agreed easily enough, completely unfazed by her suggestion.

"Especially for a Cattleman."

That caught his attention, and GD studied her for another long moment before responding. This time his tone held a hint of hesitation. "Yeah? And what do you know about Cattlemen?"

"Just that you're willing to pay to play." Which was pathetic at so many levels, but Kitty Anne kept that opinion to herself. After all, she was trying to entice Cole to do just that. "And that you're cheap. That you guys like to split the bill between buddies. Of course, you think the money gives you a right to name the rules of the game."

"And you don't?"

"I think I'm worth more than you can afford and don't charge damn near enough for the pleasure I can show a man." That was the God's honest truth.

"I'd ask what kind of pleasure, but I'm guessing that would ruin the surprise." GD eyed her with a look that sent another flash of heat firing off through her veins. "And I do enjoy a good surprise. Tell me something, beautiful, you hungry?"

There was something about the way he asked that question that had Kitty Anne's mind churning with an image of hot, sweaty bodies writhing in ecstasy and her cunt going soft with a need to make that fantasy a reality because she was betting that there wasn't anything small about the big man.

"I might be in the mood for some meat." Kitty Anne smiled as he all but drooled over her words. "You want to go make a sandwich?"

That offer had GD hesitating as his gaze narrowed on her smile. He knew she was teasing. Kitty Anne knew she was playing fire. GD didn't take her bait, though. Instead, he just nodded.

"I'll follow."

GD agreed but didn't make a move to climb back into his truck. Standing there, he watched her walk away. Kitty Anne knew he was enjoying the sight, too, thanks to the extra little swish she put in her step. She swooshed her ass at him, a silent temptation that, maybe, if he was a good boy, she'd let him get a piece of.

One thing Kitty Anne knew for sure. This was going to be fun.

* * * *

Twenty minutes later, Kitty Anne closed her menu and looked up at the man staring back down at her in shock. The waiter had a kind of dumbfounded expression as he glanced from her to GD, who had relaxed back into his side of the booth, unable to help but smile as Kitty Anne's order grew longer and longer.

Far from thin, the girl wasn't fat either, but still, he didn't believe for a moment she intended to eat everything that she'd asked for. He had a sense he was being measured by the fatness of his wallet…or, at least, that was what she wanted him to believe. It was part of her image and her challenge, but GD didn't flinch.

Though he couldn't help but be amused as the kid cleared his throat and tried to ask politely if the lady was ordering for both of them. GD would have answered him, but Kitty Anne beat him to the punch with her snort.

"Really?" She shot the boy a look as though he'd asked the stupidest question. "Do you honestly think that is enough food for that man? Look at him!"

GD smiled, refusing to take the insult as he offered the boy a perfect response, the one that assured she'd eat every single bite of her meal or risk being discovered for the fraud she was.

"I'll just have the soup of the day with a large Cobb salad," he ordered and knew instantly that the waiter understood.

The kid broke into a quick smile, no doubt thinking that he'd gotten caught up in something personal between them and that they'd ordered each other's dinner. He'd switch the plates when he delivered them. GD would correct him then, and Kitty Anne would learn that he took all challenges very seriously.

"Right away, sir."

"That's all you want?" Kitty Anne pressed, holding up the waiter by refusing to relinquish her menu. Instead, she scowled at him and offered GD one more opportunity to retreat. "You sure you don't want a dessert, at least?"

"I'm fine, beautiful." That he was. In fact, he was enjoying himself. "Besides I believe in eating healthy."

"Oh, screw that," Kitty Anne muttered to herself as she released the menu, allowing the nervous teenager to scurry away as she took direct aim at GD's comment. "When I'm hungry, I want to eat."

"I can tell." GD could also tell that she worked out. Unable to resist running another quick look down her svelte frame, he shifted in his seat as he felt his dick begin to swell. "You are a very beautiful woman, if you don't mind me saying so."

"And why would I mind a compliment?" Kitty Anne retorted, her full and pouty lips curling into a smile that would have made a weaker man pant.

GD just shrugged.

"Because I'm guessing your fiancé wouldn't care for it." GD hesitated, letting that taunt sink in before pressing even harder. "And that you actually care for him."

"What can I say?" Kitty Anne asked, batting her fake eyelashes coyly at him. "He's rich. That makes up for a lot of failings."

She was truly impressive. GD knew there was no fiancé, rich or otherwise, and the woman had to know he probably knew. That didn't stop her from daring to not only lie to his face but to threaten him with those lies.

"And in whatever ways he doesn't measure up, I can always find another to fill in." Kitty Anne glanced up and away toward the waiter carrying back the plate of cheese sticks she'd ordered.

As GD predicted, the kid brought two plates and set one down in front of him, earning a dirty look from Kitty Anne, who actually had the audacity to pull the appetizer over to her side of the table and away from GD. That was the first sign he had that he was wrong about the motive behind her order.

The second sign was the fact that she managed to eat all six deep-fried and breaded chunks of cheese in less than five minutes. Kitty Anne wolfed through her food with an abandon that had him shifting in his seat again.

Maybe it was an act, and it was kind of funny to imagine her practicing eating, but the truth was the woman made devouring food look sexy as hell.

"So…" GD tried to focus back on the subject and not on wondering if Kitty Anne would make the same blissful expression when she swallowed a dick whole, as she did when she almost swallowed a whole cheese stick.

"You like a variety of meats, huh?"

That drew Kitty Anne's attention from her plate to him, and she blasted him with a deep, soulful look. GD could sense her weighing her options before she shrugged.

"I'm not a one-meat kind of girl." There was a grimness to that comment that held a warning he chose not to hear.

After all, GD wasn't planning on confining Kitty Anne to just his bed. He knew just who would make a perfect match to their threesome. While a lot of names came to mind, not a single one of them was worthy of his Venus. That was a problem better solved later.

"So how many meats do you keep in your pantry?" GD pressed, enjoying the frown Kitty Anne shot at him. Her strong, elegant features scrunched up with a sour expression as she rebuffed him.

"That's a rather personal question, don't you think?"

"Not given what I'm planning on doing to you," GD promised, letting the hunger sink into his voice as his gaze narrowed on the swipe of her tongue. It licked out to catch the crumbs lingering on her lips, making him tense with a need he knew she was intentionally provoking.

"I haven't agreed to let you do anything to me," Kitty Anne shot back, but she had. It was there in her eyes and the way she watched him.

"Why not?" GD cocked a brow and went for the fatal blow. "I got fifty dollars in my pocket. What will that buy me?"

Kitty Anne stiffened up instantly at that insulting question, and by rights, she should have thrown the saucer of marinara still sitting in the middle of her plate right in his face. She thought about it, but then she appeared to remember the game they were playing, and instantly, her features relaxed into a look smug enough for GD to sense that he was about to lose.

"Meet me in the bathroom in five," Kitty Anne purred as she slid over to the edge of the booth.

GD honestly thought she might meet him there, but he wasn't about to let the first time with his goddess be in the sterilely frigid bathroom at some low-rent, twenty-four-hour diner. So he stopped her before she could lift that gorgeous ass off the vinyl. Placing a hand over her wrist, he waited until those brilliant eyes settled on him before he corrected her assumption.

"I'm not looking for sex, beautiful," GD assured her. "What I'm willing to pay for is a little honesty."

"A little honesty?" Kitty Anne repeated, clearly not following.

"Why are you really messing with Cole?"

"Why are you worried about why I'm messing with Cole?"

"Because he's a friend."

That was using the term lightly. Cole was more a menace and annoyance, but he was also a lot of fun to be around. "I don't want to see him get hurt."

"I'm not going to hurt him," Kitty Anne promised with a smirk. "Well...I mean, I am going to strip him naked, tie him to a bed, and spank him, but he'll be begging for every lick."

GD blinked and burst out laughing at just the thought of what she said. It was an outrageous claim, and there was no missing the innuendo implied in her tone, but he didn't doubt that she meant what she said.

"I'll tell you what, beautiful, you pull that off and I'll pay you the fifty bucks for a picture."

"Done." Kitty Anne nodded and extended her hand across the table as if they'd struck some kind of deal.

"Done." GD played along, holding his smile until he felt her soft skin against his.

Kitty Anne might have looked strong and vibrant, but she felt fragile and delicate as he closed his fingers around hers. There was a shock of awareness with that first touch, and he felt his heart seize with an ache so powerful it almost brought tears to his eyes.

He wasn't lost alone in the moment. Kitty Anne was there with him. He could scent her response as the sweet hint of feminine arousal thickened in the air. She was already hot and wet, and the bathroom wasn't but a few feet away. So was the waiter who arrived on time to save GD from doing something colossally dumb.

The kid hesitated, waving the double quarter pounder with cheese between GD and him before Kitty Anne snatched it out of his hand. He didn't fight but shoveled another plate piled high with chili-cheese fries in front of her before turning to offer GD his bowl of soup and the salad that had clearly been pulled from a fridge not minutes ago.

Kitty Anne wrinkled her nose at it and shook her head. "That looks disgusting."

"Not a salad fan, huh?"

"Not a frozen salad." The twinkle in her eyes grew brighter as she glanced down hungrily at her burger. "Especially not when there is meat on the table."

GD smiled at that, watching with more than simple amusement as she dug into her meal. Kitty Anne ate with the enthusiasm of a starving woman. That thought struck him hard as GD considered the address Kitty Anne had listed on her license. It actually belonged to her mother, who basically lived in a tin can of a trailer. That was still better than the monthly motel rental where Kitty Anne stayed.

Librarians didn't make much, and Kitty Anne was actually worth less, which had him wondering if she spent all her money on clothes because she clearly didn't spend enough on food. He'd have to take care of that because he didn't want his woman living in poverty.

"So." GD stretched back, shifting in his seat to accommodate the massive erection he got just from watching her eat. He needed to distract himself and start figuring out a plan to get her set up better.

"You like working at the library?"

Kitty Anne shrugged. "It covers the bills."

"Well, that's a depressing level of enthusiasm."

"Work isn't supposed to be fun. That's why they call it work," Kitty Anne instructed GD with a pointed look that assured him this conversation was of no interest to her, but it was to him.

"Not if you enjoy your work," he countered.

"Really?" Kitty Anne lifted a curious brow at him. "And you enjoy yours?"

"Most of the time." That he did. "Aren't you going to ask me what I do for a living?"

"No." Kitty Anne shook her head and lifted up her glass of tea, failing to truly hide her smile behind it. "I already know. You're a PI. A dick."

"And you're my film noir sex kitten." GD didn't bother to disguise his grin as he caught and held her gaze. "I guess that makes us a perfect match, huh?"

"Except that you wear the wrong hat," Kitty Anne retorted as she glanced over at where he'd set his favorite Stetson on the seat beside him before giving GD a full once-over. "And you certainly lack the jaded detachment most of the heroes project."

"And here I was going to say the same about you."

"You don't think I'm jaded?" That clearly shocked Kitty Anne, no doubt because she put so much effort into the act.

"I think you're sweet and silly and in way over your head," GD answered honestly as he leaned forward to whisper softly across the table. "Do yourself a favor. Say no to Cole, no to your friends, and yes to me and I'll tell you anything you want to know about me right here and now."

He knew she was going to say no to him, but Kitty Anne thought about it, and that was enough for right then.

"I really don't have any idea what you're going on about." Kitty Anne waved away his comment as she began to munch her way through the massive pile of fries before her. "I like Cole. He's hot."

GD snorted and rolled his eyes at that. "And that's all that really counts, right?"

"In a lover? What else is there?" Kitty Anne paused to glance up, asking that question with a hint of honest curiosity.

"Talent?" GD suggested without any hesitation. "Skills? Creativity? Flexibility? I can think of all sorts of things that I'm looking for in a lover."

"Maybe you're just picky," Kitty Anne suggested with a hint of expectation sounding in her tone as she dared to tease him. "You limit your variety when you get too picky, but now we, at least, know why you're not married, right?"

GD tipped his head back and laughed at that, finding himself truly entertained by Kitty Anne. She really was just like her namesake—cute and funny, quick and intelligent, curious and mischievous. Thankfully, he didn't expect her to claw up the furniture, though he wouldn't object if she wanted to sit in his lap and let him pet her.

Of course, he'd feed her first because GD wasn't keen on losing a finger. He knew how cats got when they got hungry, and Kitty Anne wasn't any different. She ate like a three-hundred-pound linebacker. In all of his life, GD had never seen a man, much less a woman, put it away the way Kitty Anne did.

She could afford to eat like that he soon discovered when he asked her if she liked to work out. The answer was no, but then she admitted that she did enjoy learning different martial arts and taking dance classes and going snorkeling, canoeing, kayaking, spelunking, mountain climbing, and the list just kept going on.

"Ever tried rock climbing?" GD cut in after the waiter appeared to take away their plates and drop off Kitty Anne's sundae.

"Rock climbing requires too much finger strength," Kitty Anne complained as she swirled her spoon through the layers of ice cream, fudge, and whipped cream piled high in the tall glass in front of her.

GD watched as she pulled her spoon back out and began to lick it clean. He swallowed hard and fought back the savage pulse of lust but couldn't stop from imagining just how soft and velvety her tongue would feel stroking over his heated flesh as she licked him clean. That was just what he'd command her to do right after she finished sucking him dry.

"Rock climbing's expensive, what with all the equipment needed." Kitty Anne dipped her spoon back into her sundae. "I prefer to spend my money down at the studio working up a sweat and saving my extra cash for the fabric shop."

"Fabric?" GD repeated numbly, having a difficult time focusing as she hypnotized him once again with the slow, sensual dance of her tongue over her spoon.

Kitty Anne smirked, the sparkle in her eyes giving away not only her amusement but also the fact that she was intentionally teasing him. If GD hadn't gotten that message before, he surely did then as she straightened up and thrust her breasts out at him.

"I make all my own clothes...what do you think?"

He thought her nipples were hard and begging for a little attention. GD closed his eyes, knowing he was being toyed with but not able to deny he was enjoying the moment. Hell, there wasn't even any need to be discreet while he ogled her tits. After all, the woman was sticking them out there and waving them around.

"I think a lot of strippers spend a lot of money for that kind of rack, beautiful."

"Really? And do you know a lot of strippers?" From the glow in her cheeks to the twinkle in her eye, Kitty Anne looked ready to giggle.

"More than most women would probably deem decent."

"I'm not most women, and I think we've established that I'm not decent." Kitty Anne paused before leaning in slightly and giving a look that GD knew was going to lead to trouble. "Though, to be honest, I always wondered what it would be like to be a stripper…to be naked in front of so many strange men. Sometimes I think about that and close my eyes and then—"

Then her breasts bumped into her glass of tea, knocking over the thick, plastic cup and sending a liquid cascade of ice down over his lap. GD started hard enough to move the whole booth backward and damn near upended the table as he shot to his feet.

The couple on the other side didn't take kindly to the sudden, jarring motion, and the man yelled out a warning that cut off quite suddenly as GD turned to give him a look. He knew he was taking advantage of his size, but it didn't really impress Kitty Anne, who had fallen over laughing in her own seat.

Sighing, he left her to her giggles as he dealt with the waiter who came rushing up, and then he headed to the bathroom to try and clean up. There were not enough hand towels or time enough for him to waste beneath the hot air dryer, and he walked back out looking much like he had when he'd walked in, as though he'd peed himself.

* * * *

Kitty Anne bit the inside of her lip and tried not to laugh as GD came stalking back up to the table with a massive wet spot highlighting the very large and thick-looking bulge tenting his jeans. Her gaze lingered there as she silently tried to imagine just how big of a man he actually was.

She was betting he would be the biggest she'd ever had, and she would have him. Kitty Anne had already come to that conclusion and didn't suspect he'd put up too much of a fight…but, then again, there was always Cole. For the first time since Kitty Anne had agreed to Patton's silly plan, she wished she hadn't.

Now she had a decision to make. She could strike while the iron was hot and attempt to seduce him tonight, writing everything off to a one-night stand, or she could wait until after she humiliated Cole. That would be risky. GD might be looking for revenge right about then, and why that thought made her wet, Kitty Anne didn't know.

She knew only that it would be a shame not to get more than a night out of the man. After all, he was more than simply enticingly thick and nice to look at. He was actually a lot of fun to hang around with.

That thought lingered with her as he escorted her back to her car. When most men would have made a move, GD simply walked away, leaving Kitty Anne standing there watching him go, which only went to prove that he was up to something.

She just wasn't sure of what.

Chapter Three

Thursday, May 29th

The worst thing about getting arrested was the waiting. Kitty Anne hated waiting. It was boring. What was not boring was being paraded about in a negligee that left little to the imagination. Then there was putting up with Cole's grin, which was smug enough to make Kitty Anne itch to be nasty.

Being in handcuffs, though, she decided to shut up and behave...and plot. Cole and his buddies might have won this round, but there would be another, and next time, she'd make sure it was her that ended up smiling like the cat that ate the canary. Until then, he was Hailey's problem.

Kitty Anne had her own concerns. They'd started with being shoved into the back of a van that served as a modern day paddy wagon and dragged down to the county detention center. There she was processed, her fingerprints taken along with an unflattering picture.

Then to top indignity on insults, they'd scrounged up a female cop to do a rather probing physical search, though Kitty Anne would have sworn in a court of law it was actually a man in drag. At least she was a handsome fellow.

So was Kitty Anne's mother, who she would definitely not be calling to come bail her out. That was a show she'd rather not put on for the cops. Not to mention, with her mother's tendency toward drama, she might end up in the cell next to the one Kitty had been shoved into. She'd have to call Rachel. That is if she survived long enough to call Rachel.

The deputy shut the door behind her and abandoned Kitty Anne to a room full of pissed-off prostitutes. That probably would have tickled her mother, just as Kitty Anne knew it would have made Lynn Anne proud at how well she defended herself.

Still, there were a lot of them and only one of her.

It took a moment for the deputies to come running in. By then Kitty Anne was both exposed and disheveled, which made it a perfect time to be dragged back out of the cell and through the entire center before being informed that she was being released, but it wasn't Rachel who had come to save her. It was GD. She should have known.

He stood there waiting in the lobby, looking fresh, pressed, and very amused. He had her coat, the one she kept in the back of her closet. It so rarely got cold enough in lower Alabama to justify a full-length, wool trench, even if her mother insisted she have one. Of course the only way GD could have gotten it was if he'd broken into her motel room.

That thought unnerved her. Now he knew the truth. She was a slob, and how very unsexy was that? That thought bothered Kitty Anne more than she cared to admit, but she refused to let it show as she strutted right up to him barefoot and wearing the rags of her nightie as though she was in heels and dressed to kill, which she sort of was, given her boob was hanging out.

It bounced and swayed, drawing everybody's attention, but not GD's. Kitty Anne knew he had to be aware of her state of near undress, but his gaze never faltered from hers as he held out her coat, allowing her to step into it with a dignity that came not from a place of deep confidence but from one of well-rehearsed responses.

Kitty Anne knew how to give attitude.

So did GD.

He didn't say a word, and neither did she, as he led her out to his truck and helped up into the cab. The air inside was thick with a heavy musk that was quintessentially male. The heady scent filled her with a longing that had her eyeing GD as he paced around the hood to the driver's side.

He looked good, and now that they'd gotten over the Cole hurdle, there was no reason left not to indulge in a little second-place consolation canoodling. After all, he kind of owed her for all this trouble, and Kitty Anne didn't doubt that GD was directly responsible for the police crashing into the motel just as she was about ready to tie Cole up.

That had been a shock.

Now came her reward.

She kept that opinion to herself as he pulled out of the Dothan PD's parking lot and turned back toward the motel. Neither of them spoke. Not a single word. Not all the way back to where she'd left her car. Only once he'd pulled up behind it and parked did GD finally turn to confront her.

"So…I paid."

"Excuse me?" That wasn't what Kitty Anne had expected him to say.

After her heavy and pointed silence, she was expecting a little humility. Perhaps even some subtle groveling. The man had gotten her arrested, but instead of sounding the slightest bit hesitant, his tone was edged with a hint of demand as he repeated himself.

"I paid. Five hundred plus dollars. That should buy me a lot of play," GD stated explicitly enough to have Kitty Anne stiffening up as she caught on. Just in case she didn't, he made himself even clearer. "I figure that should buy me five honest answers to any questions of my choosing."

Kitty Anne didn't relax with that clarification but narrowed her gaze on him instead. "You do realize that you just implied that I am a liar, right?"

"Beautiful, I just bailed you out of your own sorry attempt to set up my friend, so don't even try to play that card," GD warned her, earning him an even darker look.

"Fine," she finally agreed. "You got five questions, and I'll *try* to answer them honestly."

"You'll do better than that," GD stated simply.

"Ask and we'll see."

"Like I'm going to waste my questions that easily." GD snorted. "Don't worry. I'll ask them when they're needed."

"Whatever." Kitty Anne rolled her eyes, dismissing the suggestive hint in his tone. "GD—"

"Don't."

"Don't?"

"Don't bother with whatever speech you've practiced in the break room mirror. I know all the lines," he assured her, not that Kitty Anne was certain that she knew them.

Then again, she wasn't sure what the hell he was talking about. That didn't stop GD from continuing on with arrogant presumption.

"Hell, beautiful, I wrote them. I got them memorized and the full act perfected. Watch," GD commanded as he picked up her hand in both of his. He held on to her as though she was fragile and special. That was just how she felt as his thumb rolled gently across the tops of her fingers and he stared deeply into her eyes.

"You really are a very special woman, and that's why I need to be honest with you. I want you. I want to make love to you. I want to worship you and adore you all night long. I want to make you scream and beg for more because that's what I'm good at. Relationships…I'm sorry, I'm just no good at them."

GD heaved a heavy sigh and shook his head sadly at her before going still and breaking into a smirk. "And right about then, a woman starts thinking she can reform me, but she can't because I'm hopeless, beautiful. I was built to love only one woman."

That had to be a line. It just had to be, but that didn't stop her heart from skipping a beat because he really was that good. He had her wrapped up in his spell, one he'd woven with a warm, honeyed purr. The heated suggestion lacing his words licked over her even as he all but hypnotized her with the slow, sensual roll of his thumb over the palm of her hand as he held it tucked into the heat of his own.

"See, I know," GD whispered. "I know what to say, what to do, where to stroke, kiss, lick, nick, nibble, and suck to make any woman wet enough to forget that she isn't that kind of girl. So don't even bother with giving me the speech because I am not that easy."

"Well, I am," Kitty Anne shot back before launching herself across the seat.

GD caught Kitty Anne up in his arms, holding her away from him as he laughed openly in the face of her desperation. "I'm sorry, beautiful, but being special means you get special treatment."

"Does that mean I don't get to be tag-teamed?" Kitty Anne shot back, taunting him with the knowledge that she knew his secret. "Because the rumor is Cattlemen never ride a woman alone."

"Is that the rumor?" GD's grin didn't hold an ounce of shame.

"Is it true?"

"Do you want it to be?"

That she did but Kitty Anne wasn't ready to say it out loud. So, she turned his question back on him. "Do you?"

"Oh, yeah." There was a wealth of anticipation packed into GD's slow drawl. He eyed her with a look that made Kitty Anne feel exposed in a way that went deeper than just skin.

"I thought I was special," Kitty Anne reminded him, unable to mask the husky wantonness thickening in her tone.

"And I'm going to find somebody equally special to help me worship you," GD assured her.

"Worship me?"

"All night long," GD vowed. "But not tonight."

"Not tonight?" She was still lost and confused and that was kind of the point. "Are you sure? Sure you wouldn't like to come back to my place and help me peel off the rest of this teddy?"

She asked that as she let her coat fall open, flashing just what she was offering at the big man, but damn if his eyes didn't stay locked on hers. They did start to twinkle, though, reflecting the laughter lurking in his tone.

"Yes—"

"Good!"

"—but I'm not going to," GD informed her as he reached out to tug her coat closed.

He fisted her lapels in one giant hand and lifted her across the seat with no visible effort, making Kitty Anne go weak and wet at the dominant display of superior strength. He was big, strong, and, apparently, hers.

"Make no mistake," GD whispered across her lips as he pulled her almost all the way into his lap. "One day we're going to get to all the dirty thoughts filling your head right now and to all the other fantasies you'll have come up with by then, but first, you have to pay to play."

With that he released her, allowing Kitty Anne to rear back as he smirked. "And I don't take cash, beautiful."

"And what about me?" she demanded to know. "I'm the one who got arrested."

"The one who got herself arrested," GD corrected her, but Kitty Anne wasn't interested in listening to him.

"And searched!"

"You're damn near naked. What was there really to search?"

"You don't want to know," Kitty Anne snapped, not caring for that memory at all, but it wasn't the worst. "Neither do you want to end up having to defend yourself against a whole gaggle of pissed-off hookers."

"Well, that explains the black eye."

"I've paid," Kitty Anne repeated, keeping her words crisp and succinct. "And you should see the other women."

"Tomorrow."

"Tomorrow?" Kitty Anne blinked, thrown completely off by that response. "What about tomorrow? You going to go check out the other women? Maybe put the cash in your pocket to good use?"

That drew a smile from GD but not an answer as he leaned forward to drop a sweet, chaste kiss on her brow. He leaned back in his seat and repeated himself once again, though this time with a finality that assured her he was telling her to get out.

"Tomorrow."

Kitty Anne snorted at that and heaved an aggrieved sigh as she reached for the door handle with a mutter. "Yeah. Yeah. Tomorrow. Whatever."

"And Kitty Anne?" GD called out just as she was about to hop out of the cab.

She paused to glance back at him with a lifted brow that asked the question she didn't. He didn't leave her waiting for an answer but offered her a true smile and honest compliment.

"I like your style."

It was a simple statement, one that paled in comparison to all the other more elaborate and specific ones she'd received in her lifetime, but it was the sweetest one she'd ever heard. It filled her with a strange warmth that was equal parts excitement and contentment.

"Everybody does," Kitty Anne returned, along with a smile, before she slid out of the cab and strutted up toward her car, knowing he was watching her every step.

* * * *

GD watched the sway of Kitty Anne's hips as she walked away and grinned. The woman knew how to strut. Hell, the way she'd sauntered into the lobby at the police station, half-naked and full of sass and pride, said it all. The woman carried herself with the regal bearing of a queen.

That was what she was—his queen, and he was going to need a little help keeping her in line. His queen needed two kings, though GD preferred to think of himself as a knight. Knights went into battle with an army. So, what he needed was a general that was worthy of his queen.

He still hadn't come up with an appropriate candidate. A part of GD wondered if that wasn't because he really didn't want to share Kitty Anne. If it wasn't right then it wouldn't feel right.

That reminder had GD's doubts disappearing as he considered that there was no mistaking the volatile mix of lust and want that churned within him. Neither could he deny that he felt a sense of pride that he was the one she'd walked toward, smiled for, and belonged to.

More precisely, he belonged to her.

While that might turn out to be the best spot in the world, GD also sensed it could be a very dangerous one, too, if he didn't manage to keep up. He considered that as he kept a respectable distance from her bumper, tailing her all the way home. He waited till she'd disappeared into her motel room and remained watching over her door for nearly an hour as he considered just what he was going to have to do.

He didn't like the idea of leaving her here. Though the place was relatively clean and quiet, it was far from secure by his definition. He'd have to watch over her. That decision made, GD was about ready to check into the room next to hers when his phone rang.

It was Nick.

Nick. He was perfect, a perfect match for Kitty Anne.

"Hey, man, what's up?"

"I got a problem."

"Kevin?"

"You know it." The weight of worry that sounded in Nick's tone touched GD.

The other man really did care about the kids in his care. He ran a reform school for boys. While most of the kids came out of the foster system abused or broken, Kevin had actually been sent to Nick's camp by the local sheriff right around the time a barn had been set on fire out at the Davis ranch.

It had been kind of obvious, given the kid had been carrying a gas can, just who set the fire. Unlike the rest of the boys at the camp, though, Kevin came with family. Specifically, an older brother, who had stepped in almost immediately to take full blame for anything that Kevin did. He'd also demanded a lawyer for the kid.

It had been clear then that Seth, Kevin's brother, wasn't letting the kid go down for the fire. He'd take that fall for him. Without any real evidence beyond a gas can, the sheriff hadn't had enough to arrest the kid. Now if he found out Kevin was making a habit of going back to the Davis ranch, he might change his mind.

"I'm headed to the ranch now." GD pulled out of the parking spot and out onto the highway, heading straight for the Davis brothers' ranch.

"Thanks, man."

Nick kept it simple. There really wasn't much else to say, not between them. They were tight enough to know everything that was left unsaid, like the fact that Nick was, undoubtedly, panicking despite his calm tone. Those boys out at the camp meant everything to the man.

The future wasn't going to be easy for most of them, but Kevin actually had a chance at something the rest of them didn't have, a family. He already had a brother. He could have a sister if only Seth or Kevin would admit to what was clearly obvious—they were related to Patton Jones.

Patton's mom had run off a long time ago. From all the background work GD had done with the help of the sheriff, he knew for a fact she'd gone on to have two more kids before the demons in her head finally claimed her life. Now all the two brothers had left were their sister, but neither Seth nor Kevin appeared willing to make any effort to claim her.

GD suspected Seth feared she'd fight for custody for his brother and he'd lose Kevin. What Kevin feared probably had something to do with the gas can. The only thing to do was to come clean. That was just what GD and Nick were trying to convince the kid to do.

They hadn't gotten very far.

Turning off the highway into a grassy field, GD cut across the pasture as he came up behind the Davis ranch. He didn't get too close. Instead, he killed his lights and left his truck far enough away that no one up at the main house or in the barracks would be able to spot him coming. This wasn't the first time he'd snuck onto the Davis brothers' property.

GD doubted it would be his last either, but there wasn't any need for the brothers to know about their late night visitors. After all, Kevin wasn't causing any damage this time. He was just sitting up in the new hay barn's loft, staring down at the house below and simmering with a sadness GD just didn't get.

He didn't have to understand. All he had to do was accept and try to help Kevin find a way to let go of it all. That wouldn't be happening tonight, but who knew? It might be a start.

That was the kind of optimism that GD knew caused other people to snicker at him, but he didn't care. He preferred to live in a world of hope. On the positive side, sometimes he had to spy on his friends making asses out of themselves, like the first time he'd tracked Kevin to the barn loft.

The kid had been watching Patton and the brothers play some damn game on the TV, which had Chase Davis dancing around like an ass. GD snickered as he savored the memory of the sight of his old friend actually relaxed and having fun.

Chase wasn't normally that at ease. He tended to be more pensive, kind of like the kid GD found hiding in the barn loft. Finally reaching the top rung of the ladder, GD didn't bother to offer Kevin a greeting as he crawled across the loft to settle down next to the kid. Kevin didn't bother to offer him one either. Instead, they sat there staring at the dark house until finally the kid broke down and spoke.

"They're not home. I was hoping they'd come back," Kevin stated simply, as if that explained everything.

It did, but the kid had it wrong. Patton and her men were home. GD suspected they were in the special room the brothers had built out behind Patton's studio, making sure she atoned for her sins that night. Of course the Davis brothers could discipline their woman all they wanted.

Patton would never settle down.

"I was hoping to see her again."

There was a heavy wistfulness buried in those words, leaving no doubt about what the kid wanted, but GD suspected he'd been long trained not to reach for any dream. That was a habit that would not serve Kevin well.

"She is happy," GD finally agreed. "And knowing Patton, she'd be thrilled to have a little brother to spoil."

Spoil and corrupt, not that Kevin needed the help. He was good at getting into trouble all on his own. It was almost unnerving to think of the two of them together.

"Nick sent you, didn't he?" Kevin asked, as usual refusing to respond to GD's encouragement.

"You ran out on him again, made him worry."

"I know." Kevin sighed and shifted, finally glancing over at GD to cast his big, doe-eyes up at him. "I just…"

"Wanted to see her again," GD filled in for him before reminding him of the offer GD had made the kid the first time they'd met. "You know there is a way you can do that. I could introduce you."

"No." Kevin shook his head. Just as he had every time, the kid turned GD down flat. "I don't want to meet her."

"Then why are you here?"

The kid didn't have an answer for that, but he did agree to leave with GD. They had to stop by and pick up the dirt bike he'd ridden all the way from the camp to the ranch. Kevin had left it in some brush not far from where GD had left his truck, proving that he had a knack for subterfuge, or, at least, that was what GD told him.

That broke Kevin out of his shell as he showed interest, once again, in GD's job. Despite whatever troubled past the boy might have, GD sensed that he might nevertheless end up becoming a cop one day, or possibly going into the military. Though the kid insisted he'd rather follow Seth and learn to fix cars. That was, at least, until GD pointed out that he could be fixing tanks or airplanes and who knew…maybe he'd even get to fly or drive one.

That suggestion put a gleam into Kevin's eyes that left GD comforted that he'd finally said the right thing, but the kid's mirth didn't last any longer than it took to reach the camp.

"You think Mr. Dickles's going to be mad?" Kevin cut into GD's thoughts with that quiet question as GD finally turned his truck into the parking lot that bordered the Camp D's dorms.

A refuge for boys without any other means, the camp was a self-contained community that housed nearly three hundred boys and over a dozen men, who were tasked with helping them with everything from getting their aggressions out with hard-core physical activity to helping them not only with their homework but with applying what they learned.

The camp was like a family and at the head was the father figure—Nick Dickles. He was standing there with his arms crossed and scowl darkening his brow, glaring into the headlights as GD pulled the truck up to the curb.

"Well, he doesn't look too happy, does he?" GD noted as he eased the truck toward the large man glaring into his headlights.

"He looks worried." Kevin frowned, and GD couldn't help but notice that that thought seemed to upset him more than the idea that Nick might be mad.

"I told you he was." GD pulled the truck to a stop and turned to give Kevin a pointed look. "You know people worry about things they care about."

He might only be eleven years old, but Kevin was wise enough to catch GD's meaning. The kid shot him a curt nod and hopped out of the cab. GD was slower to follow, giving Nick time to have a private word with the boy before he sent him racing up the path to the young man waiting for him at the head.

GD watched Kevin pause to have a word with Seth before the two turned to head back into the dorm. Seth glanced back at Nick, who stood there watching the boys disappear inside the large, brick building.

"That kid..." Nick sighed as he seemed at a loss for words. He settled on a cliché that had all too often been used on Nick himself. "He's something else."

"He's got a set on him to keep going back there like that," GD agreed as he slammed his door closed and stepped up onto the cobblestoned sidewalk that helped lend a fantastical air to the grounds. "But ,one day, one of the Davis boys is going to catch him and then..."

"Then *what*?" Nick demanded to know. "Everybody keeps saying, 'and then,' but I don't know what you all think is going to happen. I know the Davis brothers. They aren't going to hurt a kid."

"Yeah, but you don't know Patton."

"Actually, I remember her. Cute girl. Unfortunate name, and jealous as hell of the brothers, but it shouldn't matter if I know the girl or not. I would have thought that, given their reputations, the Davis boys would know how to manage one little woman."

"First off, she's not little anymore," GD corrected, holding out one finger and then another as he clicked off his points. "Second off, there are some women you don't manage. Some women who are as wild as the wind and you just pray to God that you can hold on."

That comment had Nick giving him a hard look. "We're not talking about Patton any more, are we?"

"I found us a goddess," GD admitted, earning a groan from Nick, but he ignored his old friend's dramatic response to step past him, heading toward the path that led up the hill to where Nick had built himself a small bungalow on a chunk of spare land. It wasn't technically on school grounds and was where Nick kept his liquor.

"Come on. You can toast my good luck, and I'll tell you about the Venus that's got me hooked."

"You do realize that Venus is a *mythical* creature, right?"

Chapter Four

Friday, May 30th

Nick crossed the camp's grounds, cutting through the massive vegetable gardens on his way toward the workshops and garages out back. He swept a critical eye over the tailored beds, making mental notes of what needed to be done. May was a crucial month in the tender development of many of their summer crops.

They had to set up nature for success if they wanted the harvest to be bountiful, which was sort of like raising kids. While some were easily led down the path to future happiness and stability, others needed a little more help to grow.

Kevin fell into the second category, unfortunately. That kid was going to give Nick gray hairs. Of course, he'd just dye them. Nick may have been a reformed rake, but he still had his vanity and his sanity. GD, on the other hand, seemed to have lost his.

As amusing as that might have been, the real joke had come when GD insisted Nick meet his Venus. The big man wasn't looking for approval. He was looking to hook Nick up. While most men would probably have been possessive and jealous of their so-called goddess, GD wanted to share his.

Finally reaching the first bay of the auto shop that Seth, Kevin's older brother, was in charge of running, Nick paused to glance around. He dismissed GD along with the big man's nutty ideas as he took everything in. Things were quiet at this time of the morning. The boys were still busy waking up and getting ready for the day.

Seth, though, was a real early riser. Normally, he used the time to work on his personal project, an old Studebaker that was all he'd inherited from his mother. Sure enough, the big tank of a car was hanging in the air on the lift, but Seth was another matter. Nick followed the heavy stench of smoke out the back door to find Seth dragging on a cigarette as he gazed up at the sky that wasn't fully bright yet.

"You know how I feel about those things." Nick spoke up loudly, startling Seth, who whipped around with wide eyes.

"Oh, Mr. Dickles, I didn't see you there." Seth explained the obvious as he stubbed the damn thing out with his boot and pocketed the butt, but that didn't diffuse the smell.

"I hope you don't let those boys catch you toking up." Nick frowned, not bothering to remind Seth that this was a no-smoking campus. "The last thing any of these kids needs is to pick up a new bad habit."

"I swear I'm quitting," Seth vowed, but that was his normal rejoinder, so Nick couldn't be blamed for doubting him.

"Yeah, right." Nick snorted and let the subject drop. "So you want to tell me what happened last night? And while you're at it, you want to clue me in as to how Kevin got the dirt bike?"

"He picked the lock to the garage and hotwired the bike."

"Smart kid." Kevin had an aptitude for mechanical things, just like his brother. "I assume you taught him those skills."

"Sometimes Mom would lock us up." Seth shrugged as if that hadn't been anything, but Nick knew the truth.

Seth's mom hadn't been an addict or intentionally cruel, but that didn't change the fact that she'd terrorized both the sons she also clearly loved. That was the case sometimes with mental illness.

"He needed to know how to get out. Otherwise…" Seth shrugged again, not finishing that thought, but Nick knew where it led.

"He doesn't need to worry about 'otherwise' anymore," Nick assured Seth before offering him a heartfelt warning. "But he might end up in jail if he doesn't learn the limits to his well-honed skills."

"I know, and I told him what happened last night was unacceptable," Seth quickly assured Nick.

"It's more than that," Nick stated softly. "It's dangerous. If the sheriff gets an inkling that Kevin's going back out to the ranch, he's going to arrest him."

"I don't know why," Seth bristled defensively. "Kevin didn't do anything."

"We both know that's not true. You know—"

"No!" Seth cut him off, not even giving Nick a chance to try and reason with him once again. "You said it yourself when I arrived here. Blood doesn't matter. Family are those people you can rely on, and I can rely on you...can't I?"

"To help you do what is best," Nick clarified, not about to be taken out with his own words. "Not what is easiest."

"You think this is easy?" Seth choked up a hollow laugh and shook his head. "I destroyed whatever chance Kevin might have had when I started that—"

"Don't."

This time it was Nick who cut Seth off, not interested in hearing him confess once again to starting the fire when they both knew he wasn't guilty of that crime. They also both knew he wouldn't let Kevin be guilty of it either.

"I'm just saying the reason Kevin needed to go buy that gas was because I siphoned all the gas out of his bike and went and set the fire."

"Yeah, I got that."

And so had the sheriff because Seth had told him the same thing the night Alex had shown up with Kevin in tow. It was obvious what had happened, who had really started the fire. Alex knew it. If he could prove it, then the shit really would hit the fan. If that happened, Nick would be there for both brothers.

"Come on." Nick nodded back through the garage toward the main building, giving up the pointless argument. "Let's go get ourselves some breakfast."

Seth fell into step beside him as they headed up to the large dining hall already filling with kids. Many called out to Nick, and he stopped to chat and linger as Seth went on ahead to get into the hot food line where the boys who had joined the culinary food track had laid out yet another delicious spread of baked goods, along with more traditional breakfast fare.

Occasionally one of the kids would come up with a recipe that was considered the special of the day. That morning it was a pumpkin-spiced coffee cake, and there wasn't a single crumb left by the time Nick managed to snatch a plate off the pile of clean ones and make his way down the line. Of course by then most things were gone, but not the coffee, and that was the most important aspect of his morning ritual.

No morning was complete without a full cup of caffeine and the unfortunate interruption of Saul Wrinkle.

"Mr. Dickles, I must have a word with you." Saul stepped up to demand Nick's attention with his normal uptight, nasal whine.

Saul was from the north, *way* north, and he sounded it. Nick had grown accustomed to the Yankee accents that dominated the New England states when he'd gone to college up that way, but most of the kids at the camp came from Alabama and the surrounding states. To them, Saul sounded like a foreigner from a strange land.

He acted like one, too, and that didn't have anything to do with where Saul was from. That was just Saul. He was a weird little dude. Strangely enough he always looked as if he'd just smelled something bad, which he might have, given the nature of the boys they worked with, but one would think he would have grown accustomed to it by now.

Saul hadn't. Not the smell or anything else. Apparently, that straw had finally broken.

"I must tell you that while I appreciate your giving me this opportunity," Saul began without waiting for Nick to even get out a basic greeting, "it has been educational to say the least."

He was talking in the past tense. That could mean only one thing. Nick was about to be dumped. He wasn't surprised. It had been coming for a long time.

"But I'm afraid I don't exactly fit in here." Saul paused, giving Nick the opportunity to deny that obvious truth and to speak for the first time.

"Are you sure you don't want to maybe give it a few more weeks?" Nick asked politely, the same question he had asked the last five times Saul had come to him with some kind of complaint.

He didn't really mean it but felt almost obliged to say it, and it wasn't like Saul was actually bad at his job. Not that he was appreciated, but English teachers rarely were and ones at reform schools were normally even less so.

Saul certainly didn't help rally the boys' enthusiasm. The truth was the man had been nothing but problems. He was always getting picked on or pranked, forcing Nick to have to discipline the boys. That wasn't something he cared to do too often.

That didn't mean Saul's departure wouldn't create a new headache. Nick would need a new teacher, somebody he could convince to come live at a camp with a bunch of boys running in all directions. It was a tall order.

* * * *

Kitty Anne walked out of the library feeling sick not ten minutes after she'd floated in feeling a glow of excitement that she hadn't felt in a long time. She'd woken up with it, a sense of anticipation filling her morning and making every one of her daily rituals new again. For the first time in a long time, she'd arrived at work looking forward to her day.

It was tomorrow.

Somewhere in her future lurked the promise GD had made the night before. The fact that she hadn't a clue to what he meant only added to the thrill tingling through every one of her nerves. That hadn't changed, but her outlook on the day had, thanks to Mrs. Diggard calling her into her office to inform Kitty Anne that she'd violated the county's employee code of conduct when she'd gotten herself arrested.

Kitty Anne should have seen that coming. She'd lived in Dothan long enough to know how fast news traveled. Considered a decent size city, Dothan was still small enough for gossip to move faster than the speed of light. Hell, it was a time-honored tradition to wake up and savor a delicious rumor to start their day, her mother included.

If Mrs. Diggard knew about her arrest, then so did Lynn Anne, which meant that Kitty Anne was in trouble. Fortunately for her, she enjoyed trouble along with a good confrontation. So she slipped on her white lace driving gloves and wrapped a decorative scarf around her head and lowered the top on her convertible to assure that everybody could see her driving past with her chin held high and no sunglasses on.

Kitty Anne even went slow as she cut through town and over the small bypass that looped around the city. Almost instantly she was embraced by the thick forests and golden fields that surrounded Dothan and made one feel a strange sense of peace. The roads that sprouted off the main highways running in and out of town were cozy, the homes tucked on large lots.

So was her mother's perfectly maintained, mid-century mobile home. The metal exterior was painted a cheery yellow and framed with the lush blossoms overrunning her mother's garden bed. The 1950s trailer was barely ten feet wide, making the gardens look even bigger and strangely more inviting, though Kitty Anne was glad not to live there anymore.

Now all she did was visit, which was bad enough, and worse was finding Candice sitting out on the back patio beneath the floral awning Lynn Anne had sewn herself. The two older women were drinking tea from leaves her mother had grown and lounging on seats she'd painted after salvaging them from the dump, not that anybody could tell.

Everything was perfect, including Candice and Kitty Anne's mother. Both women were dressed in prim floral dresses and wearing matching hats to protect their fair skin from the sun, even though they were sitting in the shade. Lynn Anne insisted that the harmful rays cut right through fabric, so two layers plus sunscreen was needed.

Kitty Anne's mom was always mindful of her skin. Her skin, her makeup, her hair, her clothes. Lynn Anne was meticulous about every detail. Strangely enough, though, she never seemed to be busy with fixing anything. A charmed life was the image Lynn Anne put forth and most people bought, but not Kitty Anne.

She knew the truth. Being perfect was hard work. Kitty Anne never really had succeeded at reaching her mother's standard, so she'd created her own and then flaunted it in her mother's face. Today was no different, and she smiled as her mother frowned up at her.

"Ah, there's my pride and joy." Lynn Anne settled her glass down as she gazed up at Kitty Anne, fooling nobody with her words. "The apple of my eye. The light of my life. The—"

"You shouldn't frown, Mother." Kitty Anne cut her off with that chastisement. It was a familiar one, though normally Lynn Anne was the one giving it to Kitty Anne, which only made the comment more obnoxious.

"You'll wrinkle," Kitty Anne reminded her as Lynn Anne's expression tightened. "And you know nobody likes a scowler."

"Neither do people like rude, little girls who sell their...*favors*—"

That had Kitty Anne laughing as she shook her head at her mother. "Trust me, Mom, I know the golden rule. Never be the one giving. Always be the one getting."

Lynn Anne lifted one perfectly arched brow in mock confusion. That was another expression she'd practiced in the bathroom mirror way back when. So was the inquisitively innocent tone she turned on Candice.

"Do you know what she's talking about?"

"I think she might be referring to the incident last night where she was parading around half-naked and cuffed," Candice answered with her normal blunt and brutal honesty. The smile she shot at Kitty Anne was all teeth.

"It was a misunderstanding." Kitty Anne shrugged. That earned her a snort from Candice and a huff from her mother.

"I really wish you would try at some point to stop embarrassing me, Kitty Anne. I have a reputation to maintain," her mother insisted as Candice nodded dourly along with her. "Just think of how embarrassing it's going to be to show my face when I go to church on Sunday. I'll be shamed."

"That's not true, Mom," Kitty Anne responded on cue as she slapped her purse down on the white, plastic tabletop and helped herself to the last glass waiting beside the pitcher of tea. "Nobody will look down on you."

"Please." Candice snorted. "It's in the paper."

"On the front page." Lynn Anne fanned herself, as if that thought had her nearly ready to faint.

"Fine, then change churches—"

Lynn Anne's gasp of shock cut Kitty Anne off. Her mother squeaked as she turned wide eyes on Kitty Anne, but Lynn Anne seemed unable to get a word out. Candice came to her aid.

"My dear child, one simply does not *change* churches," Candice informed her, as if Kitty Anne was both clueless and tactless for even suggesting such a thing. "It took your hard-working, sweet-hearted mother years to get into Oakfield, and even *more* years to work her way up to the front row. How is she supposed to sit there now, much less attend Bible study or the ladies' tea hour when her daughter has just been dragged out of the sleaziest motel, half-naked!"

"You sound like Mrs. Dillard."

"Now there is a nice, proper lady," Kitty Anne's mom said on cue. "I like her. You should listen to her."

"She fired me."

"Well, like I said, she's a proper lady. You can't really blame her for not wanting to work with a prostitute." Lynn Anne waved away Kitty Anne's comment, seeming completely unconcerned about Kitty Anne's sudden paycheck-less status, but Kitty Anne knew the truth. Behind that bland smile, her mother was plotting. Kitty Anne could hear it in her tone.

"And really, why would you want to keep that job when your other one has you up all night?"

"It's probably for the benefits," Candice answered for her. "I would think health insurance and retirement plans would hold quite a large appeal for a hooker."

"I would think she'd be able to charge enough to afford to pay for all of those things in cash," Lynn Anne retorted, sounding somewhat offended as she gestured toward Kitty Anne. "I mean look at her. If nothing else, my daughter does have very nice boobs."

"That's true." Candice nodded. "Nice enough she should be able to charge a decent amount for her services. Really, if you are going to be the mother of a harlot, Lynn Anne, you might as well be the mother of a high-priced one."

"So true."

There was a smug quality to the silence that fell between the two ladies as they sipped their tea and clearly waited for her response. Kitty Anne knew, though, no matter what she said, she wasn't winning. Not against these two. There was only one thing to do. Flee.

"Well, this has been fun." Kitty Anne forced a smile and allowed her voice to boom out loudly enough to cause her mother to frown. "We should do it again, but if you'll excuse me, I have got to go find a job."

"There really is no need to shout, honey. I'm sitting right here, and if you must run along, then go ahead." Lynn Anne waved her away with a haughtiness that assured Kitty Anne she was enjoying herself. "Candice and I have our own errands to run."

"We're going to the beauty parlor," Candice volunteered with an enthusiasm that didn't fool Kitty Anne. They were going to gossip, and her boobs would be the main topic. That and how much she should charge.

"And we're playing bridge with Amelia and Trisha this afternoon, which reminds me, did you remember to make the scones?" Lynn Anne asked, all but dismissing Kitty Anne as she strutted away.

It was hard not to turn back and inform the ladies that they weren't scones. They were cookies. Chocolate-chocolate-chip cookies to be exact and that, along with the heavy doses of brandy lacing their coffee, was the only reason they gathered to play bridge at all. So, of course, Candice had made them.

Every Friday for the past twelve years, Candice had brought the *scones* and her mother brought the liquor, and the ladies had themselves a few laughs, not uncommonly at Kitty Anne's expense. She let them have their fun and told herself that it didn't matter what a bunch of old women thought about her, but it was a little bit of a lie.

Her mood, however, improved almost instantly when she stepped out her mother's front door to find a familiar pickup idling by the curb. GD had found her.

Chapter Five

GD watched Kitty Anne strut through the grass on three-inch heels and never once lose her balance. Her hips kept perfect beat, swinging her ass with every step and making him drool. She really was a Venus. He didn't care what Nick had to say.

Though his Venus was clearly nervous. GD could see past that smile and that walk to the glitter in her eyes and flush tinting her cheeks and knew her heart was pounding as bad as his. Hell, his palms were sweaty, and that hadn't happened since he'd been a teenager practicing all his moves on Heather.

He'd had years of experience since then, but that didn't seem to matter. His breath still caught as Kitty Anne stepped up onto the side step, grabbed on to the edge of the open window, and hefted herself up until she could smile at him through it.

"Why, Mr. Davis, what are you doing here?"

That line was too smooth not to have been well practiced, and that thought had GD relaxing into a smile as he imagined her staring at herself in the mirror and perfecting the purr she put into those words. He'd practiced a few of his own, though not out loud.

"I've come for you, Miss Allison. You wanna go for a ride?"

Kitty Anne glanced over toward where her car was parked. It was blocking in the other two vehicles already piled into the driveway. He could easily guess what she was thinking.

"Why not?" Dropping back to the ground, Kitty Anne opened up the door and climbed into the cab while GD shot her car another pointed look.

"Don't you want to move that?"

"No." Kitty Anne slammed the door and shot him a smile. "Mom can drive over the grass. Trust me, it won't be the first time."

The way she offered him that assurance spoke volumes about the nature of her relationship with her mother. GD couldn't deny that his curiosity was piqued. He glanced back at the big, pink Cadillac that probably could have crushed Kitty Anne's tiny, white convertible and backed up right over it.

"I guess your mom's got better eyes than mine because I wouldn't leave anything that small parked in her rear view." That was just the God's honest truth.

"If Mom runs over my car, she knows I'll sue her."

GD barked up a laugh at that, thinking she was kidding, but the look Kitty Anne shot him as she snapped her seatbelt into its holder had him sobering up and returning her look with his own shocked one.

"You're not joking?"

"What?" Kitty Anne blinked as if he were the crazy one in the cab. "She sued me. Twice!"

"She did?" GD scowled. He hadn't found any record of that, and he'd done a pretty thorough search of Kitty Anne's mom. Pretty thorough, given there wasn't much to find.

Unlike her daughter's, Lynn Anne's file was thin and read like that of a saint. Hard-working with not even a speeding ticket to her name, she'd managed to raise and support her daughter without going into debt and all the while maintaining good and strong social ties to the community.

"You sound surprised," Kitty Anne commented as she narrowed her gaze on him.

GD could feel the wheels in her mind churning as he eased the truck away from the curb. Schooling his features to give nothing away, he waited to see if she was as smart as he suspected. She was.

"You investigated me, didn't you? And my mom, too." At least she didn't sound offended. Just the opposite. Kitty Anne sounded a little amused. "And you didn't find anything on her, did you?"

"Nope."

"That's because my mom knows where to bury the bodies so not even God himself will find them."

Beneath the cynically sharp edge of that observation, GD could detect the hint of not only amusement but also pride, proving that, whatever Kitty Anne felt for her mother, it was complicated. Complicated was interesting to him.

"So, you going to tell me where they're buried?" GD pressed as he turned out of Lynn Anne's neighborhood and back onto the highway.

"First, tell me what you found out about her," Kitty Anne pressed. "I'm curious to see how good she is."

And conversely how bad he was, but GD didn't suffer from enough pride to mind having his flaws shown. Instead of taking offense, he slouched back into his seat and cast her a quick smile before coming clean.

"To be honest, there wasn't much on her. I got a list that's about two feet long of clubs, groups, and organizations she belongs to, and I think the most controversial of them all is the Ladies for Life club."

That comment had Kitty Anne snickering. "You know that doesn't actually have anything to do with abortion, right?"

"No?" He hadn't actually. "Then what the hell kind of club is it? Is it some kind of friendship club? Or an etiquette group?"

"Please." Kitty Anne snorted with a roll of her eyes. "Don't allow the fancy title to fool you. It's more like a boozing group. Their motto is living life to its fullest, which apparently means never letting a glass run dry."

"Well, then…can I be a lady?" GD asked, sharing a laugh with Kitty Anne as she shook her head at him.

"Trust me, they'd eat you alive. Those women…they're scary."

"That's kind of hard to believe."

"Like I said, she sued me twice."

"Yeah, but you haven't said why yet."

"Slander and liable, the usual…oh, and breach of contract."

Kitty Anne shrugged, but GD wasn't buying her nonchalant attitude. She knew there was nothing normal about her and, probably, would be insulted if there were. He could also sense that she was waiting for him to ask the next question and not sitting silently because she didn't want to talk about the subject.

"So, what you say about her and to whom?"

"I didn't say anything." Kitty Anne instantly defended herself with an insulted tone GD could hear right through. Whatever she was about to lecture him on hadn't only been practiced. It had the well-worn edges of a soapbox she'd spent quite a bit of time on.

"I got arrested…the first time."

"Indecent exposure." GD nodded, well aware of Kitty Anne's arrest record. It was almost as long and colorful as her mother's social club list.

"It was a political statement," Kitty Anne retorted with a huff.

"You were caught skinny dipping." GD smirked, not only finding her indignation cute but the idea of her wet and naked alluring.

"And I should be free to be as nature and God intended if I wish. I should not be confined by the laws of man to hide what, in all honesty, all you men want to see anyway!" Kitty Anne's head had started to roll, her finger wagging as her pale cheeks bloomed with a passion that had him smiling, which only seemed to enrage the woman more.

"The only reason I have to wear clothes in public is because you guys can't control yourself."

"That and the bugs," GD agreed without pause. "Wait until you get a bite on your ass, and we'll see how quickly you're pulling on the panties."

"Please, I've been bit by bigger predators than that," Kitty Anne scoffed as her grin took on a wicked curl.

She was teasing him and testing him, needling in that way women did in an attempt to measure the depth and type of affection a man might feel toward them. Just for that, GD remained silent, knowing he was driving her nuts as her smile slipped upside down into a frown.

"Anyway," she said with a sigh, "long story short, I ended up in court with the judge asking me if my mom hadn't taught me about the dangers a naked young woman faced in public, and I responded that my mother had taught me how to bake a pie, to stitch a hem, and keep my legs crossed at all times, but I'd decided to follow her example instead of her advice. That did *not* go over well."

GD could imagine it hadn't. Judges, like mothers, didn't tend to admire flippancy. Not to mention that small towns ate up that kind of gossip. Kitty Anne certainly had fueled those fires through most of her life, but somehow her mother had come out clean and untainted by their association. That was odd.

"So she sued you?" GD asked, not exactly sure how a parent got from being indignant to litigating a child for slander.

"No, first, she came up with a plan to send me to a rehab facility. She spread the rumor that I had a little problem." Kitty Anne hesitated to smirk and shake her head before cluing him into the joke. "But given I didn't drink, I was kind of resistant to the idea."

"But you did eventually go."

He knew that. He'd seen it on her record. Kitty Anne was supposed to be a recovering alcoholic, but it made more sense that she didn't drink. She put way too much effort into her appearance and her act to give over control to something like alcohol. If she had, then she probably wouldn't have bothered with the rest of the mask that she was finally allowing him to see beneath.

"I didn't have money for a lawyer, and it was the only way to get her to drop the suit."

"Wow." GD glanced over at Kitty Anne as he slowed the truck toward a stop.

Their gazes connected for a moment, and he didn't even bother to offer her any fake assurance that he knew would only have her retreating back behind her well-defended persona. Instead, he hit her with the truth.

"That's kind of messed up."

The dark clouds that had veiled her brilliant gaze shifted with that admission, opening up her bright eyes with a sense of humor that assured GD he'd said the right thing.

"Yeah, it kind of was."

They shared a quick, knowing smile before he glanced back at the parking lot he pulled into. It welcomed members to the Disco Ball, with the ball being of the bowling variety. Kitty Anne glanced up at it and then back to him as she frowned in disapproval.

"You expect me to wear *rented* shoes?"

* * * *

Kitty Anne didn't wear rented shoes. She had her own custom pair that she'd bought back on a whim when she'd been flushed with cash. Of course she'd gone broke before she could buy the ball, but used balls were a hell of a lot more sanitary than used shoes.

Especially when one didn't even have socks.

Kitty Anne opened her mouth to repeat that thought out loud when GD surprised her by seeming to read her mind as he produced a pair of bright white athletic socks.

"They're straight out of a new pack," he informed her before shoving open his door.

Kitty Anne stared down at the socks in her hand and smiled. She really did like GD. He had a sweetness and thoughtfulness about him that she wasn't used to in the men she ran around with. Hell, he wasn't like any man she'd ever known. He even opened the door for her and held her hand in his as he led her into the bowling alley.

The innocent touch sent a shaft of pure delight up her arm, and the sensation felt more intense than it probably should have because he'd yet to touch her in any other real way. GD was moving slow, slower than a snail, but that didn't mean the attraction wasn't there. The lust, the want, they were thick in the air, making the fact that he held back all the more touching.

It also made her want to return the gesture, and she did what she always did with men, assured they won. This time, though, she threw the game out of kindness instead of her normally patronizing reasoning. That didn't seem to matter much to GD, who shot her a strange look after he won the third game in a row.

Then, suddenly, it was hard for her not to win. Kitty Anne had to put some effort into it. She knew he'd figured out what she was doing, so she changed gears and started crushing him. Of course, GD fought back, but it was too late. Kitty Anne bowled two perfect games, much to GD's amusement.

"If there was money on the table, I'd think I was just hustled," he commented as they finally called it quits.

"You should see me with my shoes on," Kitty Anne shot back with a smile that only grew as GD caught her gaze and returned the warm gesture.

"Something tells me you have an outfit to go with those shoes."

"Of course."

"Pink and black?" GD guessed.

"Yellow and white."

"Pants?"

"Of course not." Kitty Anne allowed GD to take her shoes and then her hand as he helped her up and escorted her back to the counter. "I don't own any pants."

"That's my kind of woman."

"Really?" Kitty Anne lifted a brow at that, somewhat surprised.

"Oh yeah. I've been waiting my whole life for a skirt-wearing karate master?" GD retorted.

"I'm not a karate master."

"You've been practicing since you were little," GD reminded, as if she'd forgotten that fact. "And so have I."

"Really?"

"Uh-huh." That agreement rolled out of the back of GD's throat, a slow drawl that warned her of what was coming. "And can you guess what I got planned next?"

"I think I can."

* * * *

Kitty Anne could. Just as she suspected, they ended up at her karate studio getting sweaty and physical with a whole crowd watching. More importantly, she had a lot of fun and got to put GD on his ass more than once, though, truthfully, he won most of the rounds. The man wasn't only just big. He was fast...and strangely gentle.

Every time he pinned her or took her down, he made sure she landed softly. It was that kind of attention to detail that had more than just her heart melting. She wanted him. She *needed* him, something she tried to make clear, but yet it was as though she was speaking Urdu.

GD didn't even seem to recognize she was hitting on him, but Kitty Anne knew that was a lie. All she had to do was glance down to admire the rewards of her efforts. GD was hard *all* over and had been ever since they started sparring.

While the loose fit of his karate uniform had hidden the thickening length of his erection, Kitty Anne had felt it clear as day searing her through the thin cotton more than once. He'd felt like a good ten inches and as meaty as the rest of him, but he looked more like twelve and a good deal bigger when he'd changed back into his jeans.

Kitty Anne almost felt sorry for the man as they were shown to a table at a restaurant he clearly frequented, given the hostess's reception. The cheery brunette gave GD a warm welcome along with a big hug. Kitty Anne would have been jealous, but not only did GD introduce her right away, the other woman greeted her with a smile that assured Kitty Anne whatever had happened between her and GD had happened a long time ago.

Besides, the food was too good to stay grumpy for long.

Ordering fried deviled eggs for a starter and fried chicken for a main course, Kitty Anne decided to make it an all-fry night and ended the meal with deep-fried apple fritters that had her all but drooling in her plate. It didn't even matter that GD was clearly close with more than the hostess. From the smiles he received from several of the waitresses, she was beginning to suspect that he'd ordered more than one dish that wasn't on the menu and probably been served by almost the entire wait staff.

That thought made her snicker as the one lone male waiter moved past their table. Ever alert and with eyes for only her, GD didn't miss Kitty Anne's quick little smile, and neither did he let it lie.

"What?" GD glanced back over his shoulder at the boy. "You see something you like?"

"You ever seen something you didn't?" Kitty Anne shot back, holding back the laughter as a waitress went by.

She glanced down at GD, who didn't even notice as his brow wrinkled into a frown. "And what's that supposed to mean?"

"Oh, I don't know." Kitty Anne glanced innocently around. "I'm thinking you've dined on the three brunettes, the one blonde, and the redhead behind the bar, or am I mistaken and you've just confined yourself to the actual menu?"

GD snorted at that and actually blushed at that accusation. "It's not like that."

"It's not?" Because Kitty Anne kind of thought it was. "So I'm not sitting in the middle of your trophy case?"

That had the red staining GD's cheeks darkening as he glanced about before begrudgingly admitting that she might have a point. "I'm sorry...I didn't think of it like that. I just knew you'd love the food."

"I do." Hell, the food was excellent, and none of GD's former conquests seemed to be holding any kind of candle or grudge because the service had been excellent. "And I'm not upset. We all have pasts. Mine's just not so...concentrated."

"I'm afraid that I might have made a habit of...*concentrating* my attention at all my favorite places," GD admitted forlornly, and Kitty Anne could easily guess the direction of his thoughts. She could also tell that it wasn't the women he was grieving over.

"You don't have to give up your favorite places," Kitty Anne assured him. "Just as long as I don't end up with spit in my food and you don't end up with a waitress in your lap."

"Trust me, nobody's going to spit in your food. That's not the kind of women I rolled with." GD smiled, eyeing Kitty Anne with an amused glint. "At least, I didn't used to."

"You think I would spit in somebody's food?" Kitty Anne gaped up at him, not half as insulted as she managed to appear. Not that GD seemed to care. He laughed and shook his head at her.

"Something tells me you would go even lower than that."

He said the sweetest things. They may not have known each other long, but GD really did seem to get her. Now all she had to do was convince him to take her.

She plotted her next move all the way back to her mother's house. As he pulled up along the curb, Kitty Anne was flinging her seatbelt off. By the time he had the big truck in park, she was crawling across the seat. Kitty Anne slid right into GD's lap and caught his cheeks in her hands. She stole the protests from his lips as her mouth broke over his and her tongue swept in to make her claim clear.

Or that had been her intention, but almost instantly, Kitty Anne was lost in the heady taste of his kiss. Beer, nuts, and a flavor that was even more intoxicating and unique flooded through her senses, making Kitty Anne melt down into his lap as she began to grind herself against the thick, heated length of his erection.

She could feel his heat and hardness through the layers of their clothes and didn't have the patience to remove them, even if she wished they weren't in the way. It didn't matter. The thick cream of her arousal coated the swollen folds of her cunt and soaked her panties, making the slip of lace stick to her like a second skin. It didn't offer her any protection.

Neither did her skirt, which ground roughly over her clit, making Kitty Anne pant and mew. GD grunted beneath her, his own breath sounding choppy and broken, his need as obvious and desperate as her own.

His hands settled around her waist and forced her tighter down against him as his hips picked up speed. That quickly things began to spin out of control as the frantic desperation settled in along with the pleasure that was too great for her to deny. Tipping back her head, Kitty Anne arched into each of GD's thrusts, wishing only that she could have felt his thick, hard length buried deep inside of her.

They'd get there.

Right then there were other delights to enjoy. GD seemed intent on trying as many of them at once as he could when he captured one peaked tip of the breasts she was all but waving in his face. Once again her clothing offered no protection from the moist heat of his ravaging kiss. Nibbling on her nipple right through her blouse, GD damn near had Kitty Anne climaxing almost instantly.

She would have, too if, all of a sudden, GD hadn't reversed course. The fingers biting deep into her hips hefted her upward as he dumped her on the seat beside him and shoved her across it with a denial that sounded as though it pained him.

"No!"

He ground out that denial, and it was clear what it cost him and just how close he was to breaking. Kitty Anne smiled and started to crawl back across the seat, but instead of ending up back in his lap, she ended up with a palm flattened against her forehead as he held her back with very little effort.

"I don't think so."

"Oh, come on," Kitty Anne coaxed as she lifted her chin to try and capture one of his fingers with her lips. "You know you want it."

"I do," GD admitted. "But I like my women a certain way."

"You mean sandwiched with another man?"

GD didn't answer that but just smiled and nodded toward the dash. "Open the glove box."

There was something about the way he made that suggestion that had Kitty Anne hesitating. Straightening up in her seat, she eyed his smile. He was up to something. The last time he'd looked that smugly contented, she'd ended up arrested.

"Go on. Open it."

Swallowing back her nerves, Kitty Anne reached out and did as he commanded, flipping down the plastic door to reveal a jewelry box inside. It was the size of a necklace, and her fingers began to shake as she pulled it out and stared down at the ornately engraved lid.

"Open it."

Taking in a deep breath and preparing herself for what lay within, Kitty Anne was still caught off guard when she flipped the lid up. All the tension and anticipation rebounded into sheer exasperation as she glanced up at him.

"You got to be kidding. You don't really think I'm going to wear this, do you?"

"Yep," he answered with a crisp nod. "You can go ahead and hold on to it until you're ready. I'll wait."

"And you'll be waiting forever," Kitty Anne vowed.

It was a lie, but she didn't believe in letting the truth get in the way of a good line. Besides, the man had a lot of audacity to give her a collar. She couldn't just let him get away with that without giving back some attitude.

"Oh, no, Miss Allison, I don't think I'm going to have to wait that long," GD drawled out slowly as his grin widened.

"I guess we'll see, won't we, Mr. Davis?" Kitty Anne shot back, crisping up her tone as she shoved her so-called gift into her purse. "But I do wonder what you would do if I got you a matching gift."

"You never know." GD surprised her with that comeback as he paused to look at her before he shoved out of the truck to come around and open her door. "And I hate to tell you this, but you wouldn't be the first."

Chapter Six

It took a supreme act of self-control for GD to hold back the laughter as he opened Kitty Anne's door. She pinned him with a sour expression. Her lips were pursed, her gaze narrowed, and her brow pinched with an adorable look of disapproval.

"You actually let some woman tie you up?" She picked right back up with their argument, managing to sound ironically appalled, given she had just suggested she be allowed to do that very thing.

"I don't kiss and tell, beautiful." Especially not when it was going to get him into trouble.

"Oh, you got to be kidding me!"

Kitty Anne broke away from him, dismissing GD in that moment as she rushed up to her car. There was a boot clamped down over her tire. It took him a moment to make sense of what he was seeing, but she seemed to understand almost instantly.

"That crazy old bat," Kitty Anne spat as she ripped open the note taped to her window.

She read it out loud, snarling over the words as her mother demanded five hundred dollars—cash—as a fine for blocking the driveway. It was the most outrageous thing GD had ever seen or heard, and that was saying something.

"Your mom's not serious…is she?" She couldn't be.

"Of course she is." Kitty Anne huffed, crumpling the note in her fist as she turned toward him. "I need you to take me by an ATM."

"But—"

"She needs the money."

There was a grim acceptance in those words that suddenly made everything click into place. Kitty Anne may not have made that much, but she did make more than enough to afford something more than a monthly rental motel room, but not if she were supporting two people.

"Okay then." GD nodded, silently coming to an understanding of what he needed to do. "Let's go."

Without a word, he drove her back into town, taking her by the bank, where Kitty Anne took out the cash her mother needed. GD could tell by the worried way she lingered over her receipt that Kitty Anne wasn't annoyed but anxious and knew that she had to be strapped for money. He'd have given her some, but he also knew she wouldn't take it.

No, what he needed to get her was a better job and a safer place to live. The safest place would be with him, but again, GD knew there was no way Kitty Anne would move in with him and let him take care of her. Things had to change, and they would. He'd see to it.

Laying down that silent vow, GD reached out to cover Kitty Anne's hands where they were fisted on top of her purse. After a few seconds, she uncurled one to lace her fingers through his and held on tight, allowing him to share his strength silently with her.

He didn't dare to ruin the moment by speaking, leaving Kitty Anne to the privacy of her own thoughts. She didn't need to share them. He understood how important appearances were to Kitty Anne. He also knew that the connection they shared had allowed him to slip beneath those defenses. Hell, she was technically about to introduce him to her mother.

That was actually a big step, and he took a moment after he got out of the truck to make sure his shirt was tucked in and run a hand through his hair. Still, GD couldn't help but feel a little nervous as he came around to assist Kitty Anne from the truck and follow her up the path to the front door of the small trailer.

Kitty Anne rang the bell and stepped back, shooting him little worried glances out of the side of her eye as the trailer shifted ever so slightly with movement from within. A moment later the door opened to reveal a slightly older lady dressed up in a house robe and a set of curlers.

She was tall and willow thin, the total opposite of her well-rounded daughter. Her hair was darker, too, and her features more delicate yet, there was something in the way she held herself that reminded GD of the woman beside him.

"Well, if it's not my wayward daughter and her…date?"

That was it. That was what mother and daughter had in common, a gift for the drama and the crazy. It was honestly amazing and more than a little impressive the way the older woman managed to not only look down her nose at GD but also, at the same time, rake a lecherous gaze over him, leaving no doubt of the directions of her thought.

He couldn't help but blush a little, given where Lynn Anne's gaze lingered. Never before had he so thoroughly been checked out by a woman's mother. GD wasn't exactly sure what to do or say. Kitty Anne came to his rescue, thrusting a large wad of cash at her mother and drawing the woman's gaze back toward her.

"Here's the money. Now give me the key to the boot."

"Not so fast, young lady." Lynn Anne moved quickly, blocking Kitty Anne as she tried to shove past into the house. "Let me just take a look at this and make sure it's all here."

"Mother—"

"Twenty…forty…sixty…"

Kitty Anne heaved an aggrieved sigh that ended with a glare Lynn Anne returned when she ran out at three hundred.

"You're short."

"The ATM has a limit."

"Then get your gentleman friend to pay," Lynn Anne suggested, turning a smile on him. "He can work it off."

"Mother!"

"Oh, I'm sorry," Lynn Anne apologized without a hint of remorse sounding in her tone. Her gaze lingered for a moment too long on GD before she turned back to her daughter and shocked him once again with her boldness.

"I meant to say that *you* could work it off. I mean really, what does two hundred dollars buy a man these days? An hour? A half?"

"*Mother!*"

"What?" Lynn Anne blinked innocently. "I'm just curious and trying to be supportive. As a parent, you learn to accept your child as is."

Lynn Anne imparted that bit of wisdom to GD while Kitty Anne blushed an even brighter red. "Keys! *Now!*"

Lynn Anne eyed her daughter with a smug little smirk tugging on her lips. GD held his breath as he waited to see if she pushed Kitty Anne further, but obviously the older woman had decided she'd had enough fun. Stepping back, she waved Kitty Anne in.

"On the kitchen counter."

Without a word, Kitty Anne stormed past her mother, leaving GD standing there somewhat awkwardly as the woman turned her gaze back on him. The warmth and interest that had shown there moments ago was lost now to the hard glare she pinned him with.

"So, you're the new toy, huh?"

"I think you mean boy," GD corrected her, knowing that had been no accidental slip-up.

"No, I don't." The smile Lynne Anne shot him was anything but warm. "You're a little big to be a boy, Mr…"

"Davis," GD filled in for her as he extended a hand. "George Davis."

"Lynn Anne." she responded, shaking his hand with a quick, firm grip. "I'm sure my daughter has told you all about me."

"Well—"

"Don't believe a word of what she says."

"Thanks for the vote of confidence," Kitty Anne snapped, coming up behind Lynn Anne, who turned around to defend herself.

"It's true. You go out with one guy after another, breaking hearts left and right. Someday fate is going to catch up with you," Lynn Anne warned her.

"You're exaggerating."

"Really?" Lynn Anne lifted a brow and turned back to study GD with a more studious glance than her previous ones had been. "This one looks like a nice guy. You tell him how I sued you, twice?"

"Mother."

"That's her sympathy play, cons all the good guys into thinking she's damaged and they can save her. You don't know how many men in this world want to be a hero." Lynn Anne shook her head. "It's sad really, but my girl is good. She has them grateful to be rid of her by the end of the week. Can't keep a man's interest to save her life."

"I can, too," Kitty Anne cut in defensively. "It's called dating. Things don't always work out."

That got an eye roll from Lynn Anne before she leaned in close to GD and dropped her voice into a conspirator's whisper that was still loud enough for Kitty Anne to hear.

"You want to know the truth you can come back by tomorrow and we'll have ourselves some tea."

"You want to talk about a well-practiced line," Kitty Anne muttered, a hint of jealousy darkening her words.

GD knew that he was out of his depth and it was time to retreat. Reaching out past Lynn Anne to take the key out of Kitty Anne's hand, he made a face-saving, gentlemanly offer to take care of the boot. Then he fled, or tried to. Kitty Anne's car was parked not but twelve feet or so away from her mother's front door, more than close enough for him to hear the two women whispering furiously between themselves.

"Really, Mother, must you hit on all my boyfriends?"

"Oh, please. Don't be ridiculous, and don't leave your car in my driveway."

"Then don't let Candice be so rude to me."

"Is that what this is all about? Some childish tantrum?"

"I'm not the one who booted the car!"

"You have to be taught a lesson." Lynn Anne shrugged, completely unconcerned that her daughter looked as though she was about ready to burst a vein.

GD spied on Kitty Anne as she took several calming breaths while Lynn Anne watched him work. That glint was back in her eyes, but he could see through it now. She was just as full of shit as her daughter. Lynn Anne didn't want him. She wanted to annoy Kitty Anne.

It was working.

"Where did you get that boot?" Kitty Anne finally asked after a clear pause to collect herself, but the strain still sounded in her tone.

"Candice's nephew runs a tow truck company. He brought it out."

"And how much did that cost you?" While the exasperation was clear in Kitty Anne's question, the desperation was better hidden in Lynn Anne's answer.

"Fifty and you still owe me two hundred."

"I'll bring it by tomorrow, Mom. I promise," Kitty Anne swore, her annoyance blunting any sweetness in the gesture. "Now I've got to get."

Kitty Anne dropped a quick kiss on Lynn Anne's cheek and stepped around the older woman as GD finally pulled the boot off and away. He stowed the equipment up by the house where Lynn Anne directed him. She reiterated her invitation for tea the following afternoon before disappearing back inside.

"I'm so sorry about her," Kitty Anne said almost instantly.

"Don't be."

Actually, GD was thinking that a cup of tea would be an interesting way to pass an afternoon. He didn't suspect that Kitty Anne would appreciate that thought, so he kept it to himself as he opened her car door for her. She hesitated there for a moment to offer GD up a smile that had him going all warm inside.

"You know you could follow me back to my home and we could find a better way to end this night."

GD smiled, wanting more than anything to give into the sweet rush of lust flooding through his veins, but he knew better. It wasn't time. Not yet. Instead, he dropped a chaste kiss on top of her head and whistled his way back to his truck, leaving her standing there staring after him.

* * * *

Nick was exhausted and about ready to pass out when his phone rang. It wasn't late, not by most people's definition, but it was by Nick's. He grumbled over the disruption as he reached for his phone, glancing at the number flashing in the small screen before flipping it open.

"I swear to God if Kevin—"

"This isn't about Kevin." GD cut him off.

"Oh." That threw Nick for a moment. "Then why the hell are you calling me so late?"

"Dude, it's ten o'clock."

"Yeah?"

"And you're not even thirty."

"So?"

"I got a problem, okay?"

"Uh-huh, let me take a guess. It's the Venus," Nick teased, knowing damn good and straight that he was right.

He'd been waiting for this move ever since GD had started going on about his plans for the girl. GD wanted to set him up, but Nick wasn't interested in riding shotgun into the happily ever after with some goddess. He had a camp to run. His mission to help his boys, that was what he was married to.

"I told you that mythical creatures always lead to trouble," Nick reminded the big man. "I warned you the other night. This is why I only date easy women, less drama."

"Just shut up and listen," GD shot back, sounding both annoyed and amused at the same time. "Kitty Anne got fired today."

"Uh-huh," Nick repeated, not trusting himself to say more than that for fear that the laughter building up inside of him might pop out.

As if it wasn't bad enough that GD had fallen for some naughty librarian, her name was Kitty Anne. *Kitty Anne!* Nick didn't know what was funnier, the girl's name or the fact that GD thought he'd fall in love with a woman named Kitty Anne. It physically hurt not to give into the roar of the chuckles rumbling in his chest.

"You know I can hear you snickering," GD snapped, even though Nick knew he couldn't. GD just knew him that well.

"I'm sorry, man." Nick took a deep breath and tried to push his amusement back down, but it knotted in his stomach and had his words strangling on themselves. "You were saying?"

"You just go on and laugh it up, man," GD grumbled. "I can't wait to have a laugh at your expense when you meet our Venus."

"Whatever, man," Nick dismissed GD, but the man was like a dog with a bone.

"No, it's not whatever because I need you to do Kitty Anne a favor."

"Yeah?" Nick sighed, flopping back on the bed and closing his eyes. "What?"

"Give her a job...and maybe a place to stay."

"*What?*" Nick's eyes popped open at that request. He'd expected GD to put some pressure on him but this was ridiculous. "Are you nuts? You know this is a guy-only camp. Women are a distraction, and a Venus even more so."

"Come on," GD urged. "She's in kind of a bind."

"And?"

"And…" GD drew out that word before muttering over the rest. "It's kind of my fault."

"Kind of?"

"I got her arrested, and that got her fired, and I'm sure she's good at something."

"Yeah, I can guess what." Nick snorted.

"I didn't mean *that*," GD snapped. "But since you bring it up, I'll make you a bet."

"A bet?" That caught Nick's attention. He did love to gamble. "What kind of bet?"

"I bet you can't interview the woman without fucking her."

"Oh, you are kidding me." Nick knew that GD thought he'd find Kitty Anne irresistible, but this was too much. After all, Nick had never, ever met a woman he *had* to fuck. "And what do I get if I win?"

"What do you want?"

"You know what I want."

"Dude—"

"You stole it." Nick cut off GD's groan, harping on the one thing he'd never let go.

"I won it."

"The game was fixed," Nick insisted, even though he knew it hadn't been.

"It was over ten years ago."

"I want my magazine back."

"Fine!" GD gave in with ill grace. He'd been listening to Nick complain about losing his precious magazine for years. All it was full of was a bunch of naked women. Sure, some of them had gone on to be superstar sex symbols, but a naked woman was a naked woman as far as GD was concerned. Unless, of course, they were talking about Kitty Anne.

"You want the damn thing? You can have it, but if you fuck Kitty Anne…then you get to keep her. Agreed?"

"Please, you might as well just give it to me now."

Because there was no way Nick was hiring any women. It would threaten his funding. Not to mention the effect it would have on the boys. Girls turned boys stupid, evidenced by GD's recent offer. He knew Nick couldn't hire Kitty Anne, but seemed to completely ignore that fact.

"The real problem is, how do we get Kitty Anne out to the camp?" GD muttered, ignoring Nick's comment and depriving him of the fun of antagonizing his friend. Not that Nick was one to harp.

"Didn't you say she was a librarian?"

"More like an assistant," GD corrected.

"Close enough." Especially since Nick had no intention of hiring the woman. "Saul quit, so I need a new English teacher."

"That's perfect." GD perked up at that. "And I know just how to make sure Kitty Anne gets the message."

Chapter Seven

Saturday, May 31st

Kitty Anne woke up the next morning feeling better than she probably should. After all, her life was in shambles yet again, but that didn't matter because today held the possibility of seeing GD. Just the thought of him made her smile. So did the jewelry box sitting on her vanity.

He wanted her to wear his collar. He also wanted to share her. GD had made it a challenge, a kinky one. Kitty Anne loved both challenges and kink. The best part, she couldn't lose. She either won and they got and sweaty with some other hot piece of meat, or he won and they got hot and sweaty with some other hot piece of meat. Either way, by the end of it all, she was going to get to check off another item on her fantasy wish list.

That just went to prove the game was rigged in her favor because, what GD didn't know, the idea of wearing his collar actually sent a delicious kind of thrill through her. Of course, the idea of him wearing her collar sent a whole different kind of thrill through Kitty Anne and had her laughing. All she needed now was a collar. That was going to cost money, so first she had to get a job. To get laid, Kitty Anne had to get paid.

She could only imagine what her mom would say to that thought, but it wasn't so weird. There were a lot of similarities between finding a lover and finding a job.

There was the awkward introduction phase as everybody figured out if there was an actual fit, but even if there was, that didn't mean that things wouldn't eventually become too comfortable…and boring. Then it was time to look for the next man and the next career.

Kitty Anne might have already had the man lined up, but she wasn't certain what she wanted to do next with her life. It was a big decision. So she pored over the classified ads, finally coming upon one that looked quite interesting.

A local real estate agent was looking for an assistant. The best part was that there was no experience necessary other than the ability to answer phones and use a computer. She could do those two things, and more importantly, she'd love to learn more about real estate. After all, she enjoyed watching all the house buying and flipping shows.

That was partly because she'd never actually owned a house. It was a dream she didn't expect to realize. Hell, Kitty Anne didn't even live in a real apartment. Most of her paychecks had always gone to her mother. What was left went toward Kitty Anne's greatest hobby—making her own clothes.

It was her passion, but she didn't delude herself into thinking she was anything more than a superior seamstress. Fashion, at least current fashion, was not her thing. Kitty Anne liked old clothes and her makeup and her little convertible. Besides, having to live in monthly motel rentals wasn't all that bad. She had a free pool and cable.

Still, she liked to dream and watch as other people fulfilled theirs as they bought their homes. So it made perfect sense that she would love to work in real estate. Reaching for her phone, Kitty Anne dialed up the number listed with the ad and had a pleasant conversation with a Mr. Ruggan, who invited her to come in that afternoon and meet with him.

Giddy that she might actually be able to replace her paycheck before she even felt the loss of her job, Kitty Anne began to prepare herself for the coming interview. First, she needed to pick out the perfect outfit, one that accentuated her body but in a subtle way.

It never hurt to be pretty. However, it could be disastrous to be too sexy. With that in mind, Kitty Anne went through several variations of her best separates and settled on a form-fitting sweater. Its sleeves came down to her elbows, and it had a mock turtleneck collar and was soft and pink, a nice contrast to the chocolate brown skirt that flared nicely and hit her around her calf.

She paired the demure outfit with an appropriate makeup scheme, keeping her eyes simple but with a little shimmer and her lips looking plump and rosy while her cheeks were faintly flushed. Of course that innocent, fresh-faced look required a very structured hairstyle to make sure she looked appropriately professional and not too young and misguided.

A set of heels finished the look, along with a watch, though Kitty Anne debated over whether or not to wear her cross. It was simple and on a thin gold chain, which would fit the whole image she was working for but might be a little over the top, given she had just been arrested for prostitution. She went with the fake pearls instead.

Packing up her purse, she headed out the door and toward her favorite place to grab lunch before she met her fate. A settled and full stomach would help keep her focus and concentration sharp. That was the theory, but the idea met the hard edge of reality as she pulled into her favorite diner's parking lot and found GD leaning against the back of his truck.

He was wearing a smile, and Kitty Anne knew he was impressed with himself and expected her to be, too, given they hadn't arranged to meet. Secretly she was, but she'd be damned if she'd give him the satisfaction of knowing it.

Sticking her chin into the air as she rose out of her car, Kitty Anne slammed the door and headed straight for GD. He watched her coming, and she could read the anticipation and laughter building in his gaze the closer she got. What she didn't see was his expression when she strutted right past him as if he wasn't even there. While it killed her not to glance back, she didn't dare. Of course, she didn't have to control her smile, given he couldn't see it.

Feeling the excitement sparkling in the air, Kitty Anne shoved opened the diner's door and was almost instantly greeted by her favorite waitress. Polly waved her over toward the bar where Kitty Anne normally sat so she could gossip with the older woman. She hesitated for a moment before obeying the command, fully expecting GD to stalk after her.

She should have known he wouldn't be so easily riled, much less respond with anything less than equal measure.

* * * *

GD knew Kitty Anne thought she was playing the winning hand. She was all aglow with her gloat, certain that he'd tracked her here, which he kind of had…yesterday morning when he'd followed her. Just as he suspected, she hadn't even noticed. Neither did she seem to realize that he'd moved in next door to her at the motel.

He'd had no choice in that decision. GD couldn't let Kitty Anne live there unprotected and knew better than to invite her home with him. She'd end up in his bed and he'd end up losing the battle. Then for the rest of his life, he'd be her pet. While GD was pretty certain Kitty Anne wouldn't mistreat her pets, he also feared that he'd end up dressed up in a frilly outfit wearing makeup by the time she was done with him. That was his Kitty Anne, both smart and a little ditzy.

GD, however, hadn't followed her that morning. Instead, he was there to meet the detective Chase had called in from Atlanta to solve the mystery of who'd burned down his barn. The damn thing had gone up in flames months back. Nobody had gotten hurt, but it had been a close thing.

Chase's girl, Patton, had almost bought it, and that tended to make a man thirst for things like vengeance. That was just what he and his brothers wanted. They said they wanted justice, but everybody knew that if the three brothers caught up with the arsonist that man would be in some serious trouble.

Normally that would have been fine by GD, but he suspected that, this time around, it wasn't a man they were looking for but Kevin. They didn't have any proof, but who else could it have been? Nobody far as GD could tell, which was just why he'd bowed out of the investigation himself. He'd even tried to convince the three brothers that there was no hope in finding the answers that they sought.

It had been a futile attempt, and it didn't shock him that Chase had called in outside help. Neither was GD surprised when Lana, the head of female services out at the Cattleman's Club, had called to see if GD would mind meeting with Chase's detective. He had no choice but to agree to the meeting, given not agreeing would have drawn too much notice.

So GD had picked the diner he was pretty sure was a ritual stop for Kitty Anne, given the familiar welcome of the waitress, and, sure enough, she'd pulled into the parking lot not but a minute after him. There was no denying his sense of satisfaction at just the sight of her.

As usual, the cut of her clothes accentuated the delicious curves of her body, making her look both sexy and classy. The soft, fuzzy, pale pink sweater fit her like a glove, highlighting the high, round curves of her breasts and the smooth slide of her tummy that led every man's eyes to that ass.

God had gifted her, which was really a gift to him because that ass was perfect and perfectly displayed by the cut of her brown skirt. Even better was the way that rump bounced as she walked on by. Kitty Anne moved with a mouthwatering locomotion that instantly transfixed GD and had him turning to follow, like a hound after its mistress.

He was just glad his tongue wasn't hanging out. He might have tripped over it, and it was hard enough to walk normally with his damn dick threatening to pop out the top of his jeans. GD was hard and hurting but wasn't about to be ruled by his lusts. He had more control than that.

Nick didn't.

That sucker was going down. So was Kitty Anne. Neither of them had a clue as to what was coming their way, but GD did. Nick and Kitty Anne were going to be explosive. They were both just that kind of crazy. A part of GD wished he could join in, but he knew he'd just get in the way.

That didn't mean he couldn't watch.

There was a certain thrill in watching.

That thought put a smile on GD's face as he took a booth at the back of the diner, allowing him to watch both his woman and the door.

He ordered up a healthy breakfast for him and Kitty Anne, unable to help but note that she had nothing more than a plate of toast and cup of coffee before her. GD knew she could eat more than that. Sure enough, she didn't turn down the food that the waitress brought her minutes later. Neither did she turn to offer him any kind of smile or sign of gratitude.

She just ate, and that was all he needed to be satisfied.

Actually, satisfied wasn't the word for what GD felt as he watched her devour her food. He was hard, hurting, and afraid he wasn't going to last long enough to demand she wear his collar. Those worries, though, took a backseat as a man fitting the description Lana had given him pushed into the diner.

Dylan Andrews had arrived.

He hesitated for a moment as he glanced around, his gaze finally settling on GD. GD didn't cut the guy any slack and give him any kind of nod but held Dylan's gaze as the man strutted up to the edge of GD's booth with confidence that caught the attention of the other customers, including Kitty Anne.

With her nose buried in a book, Kitty Anne might think she was well camouflaged, but GD knew she was keeping an eye on him and now Dylan as well and couldn't help but wonder what she thought of the other man. He didn't like the tinge of jealousy that followed and couldn't help but take his souring mood out on the man causing it.

"Lana wasn't lying when she said you were a pretty boy." Finally breaking the silence, GD started off with that half insult-half compliment just to see which half Dylan responded to.

"And she told me that you were the best private investigator in these parts."

"I bet she did." GD snorted, catching Kitty Anne's brow wrinkling ever so slightly and knowing just what thought was running through her head.

Who was Lana?

He'd have told her if she weren't being so difficult, but since she was, he decided to antagonize the woman instead, and he lifted his voice as he added on to his comment. "Because every woman knows I'm the best at all things."

Kitty Anne sniffed dismissively and pointedly turned the page on the book she was reading, causing GD to break into a grin despite his attempt to keep a stiff face. The woman was good, but he still intended to win this battle.

"Lana also mentioned that you were on a case," Dylan commented, drawing GD's gaze back to his as Dylan shot the blonde a pointed look. "I'm not interrupting, am I?"

"Nothing important," GD assured him, this time keeping his tone quiet enough to assure Kitty Anne didn't hear or take any kind of offense to that generically polite response. He continued on displaying his good manners as he nodded toward the opposite side of the booth. "Have a seat and tell me what it is I can do for you."

"I'm looking into the Davis brothers' barn fire," Dylan began as he slid onto the vinyl cushion that crackled beneath him. "I understand I'm not the first person they turned to for answers."

"Nope." GD glanced back at Kitty Anne, making it a point not to give Dylan his direct attention, even as he gave him the best advice he could. "But they still haven't got any answers, do they? That should tell you something, don't you think?"

"I certainly do," Dylan drawled out slowly, sounding hesitant.

He was thinking, probably figuring that whatever answers he found he wouldn't like because, if they were easy and simple, they'd have been given already. It was a testament to the type of man Dylan was that he didn't back down but tilted his chin up determinedly, clearly intent on staying his course.

He had balls, GD would give that to him, and so did the jackass moving in on Kitty Anne. Not possessive or jealous by nature, GD discovered the sick feeling thickening within him once again. He all but itched with the need to do something, but he didn't dare, knowing that not only could Kitty Anne handle herself but that she'd also be insulted if he tried to interfere.

"Still, I'd like to take a peek at your notes—"

"Don't have any." GD cut in with that lie even as he watched the man smiling down at Kitty Anne start to lose his grin. That helped GD find his, and he turned to thump himself in the head as he cast his gaze back in Dylan's direction. "It's all up here."

"So then maybe you'd care to share?"

"Sorry, man, there is nothing up there." GD shrugged, his gaze cutting back over to the man Kitty Anne had just dismissed. With a rabid kind of satisfaction, he watched her would-be suitor slink off. "After all, you've been all over the place interviewing everybody...you got anything?"

"I got an almost completely redacted police report about a kid picked up with a gas tank not but a few miles away."

Kevin.

He was talking about Kevin. That meant Dylan had all he needed to start an avalanche of bad tidings. None of them needed that right then. GD could only hope that Dylan caught that undertone as he shrugged and offered the other man all he could.

"Kid's not guilty."

That was just a lie, but there was guilt and there was what could be proven in a court of law. Kevin wasn't that kind of guilty, and that was all that counted.

"Really?" That seemed to catch Dylan off guard, and he blinked in honest confusion. "If you know the kid's not in on it, then you got to know who did set the fire."

"I have an opinion." That was about all he had because the truth was there was no proof. There was just the obviousness of the answer, but Dylan didn't have all the details yet to put Kevin's story together. GD had to stop him before he did.

So he shrugged and consigned his soul to hell as he prepared to do the worst thing he'd ever done before. None of GD's internal conflict sounded in his tone, though, as he tried one last time to avoid the inevitable.

"But then so does everybody else in this town."

"Well then, it's my opinion that it's the kid," Dylan insisted, sounding stubborn as all shit and leaving GD little choice in what to do.

"Look." GD leaned across the table as he dropped his voice down low. "I'm not saying anything, but I did notice that you didn't bother to interview Lana or those idiot brothers of hers."

"Lana's brothers?"

"Yeah, Lana talked Chase into giving them some part-time work, and idiot that he was, he didn't fire them when he changed over to his new bedmate."

Why he hadn't completely perplexed GD because, along with knowing that Lana's brothers were half-drunk more than half the time, everybody knew they were protective...and violent. Of course, Chase wasn't a choirboy, and neither were his two other brothers or any of the hands that worked on the ranch.

"What a mess." Dylan sighed.

"You're telling me," GD grumbled. Things were an absolute disaster these days. "Ever since Patton came back to town, my life has been nothing but a headache. That girl causes more trouble than Pig-Pen did messes. It's a good thing she's a hell of a lot better looking than that kid."

"Hell, she must be downright gorgeous to beat out Lana."

GD smirked at that, hearing the hint of a grudge in those words. "You haven't met Patton, have you?"

"She never seems to come by the club."

"Yeah, like those boys would let her anywhere near the club."

Just the idea made GD feel a little sick. Of course that wouldn't be his problem for much longer. He'd be resigning soon. After all, he had his special woman. He didn't need a club full of them all.

GD knew he wasn't alone in that sentiment. The Davis brothers had really been piling the responsibilities on him ever since Patton had returned home. The brothers were distracted and their biggest concern about the club was protecting Patton from it.

"The less Patton knows about the club, the safer we *all* are."

"If you say so." Dylan didn't sound the least bit interested in Patton but seemed more than stuck on Lana. "Are you sure it's not the kid?"

"Anything is possible." GD shrugged.

"It'd be a hell of a lot easier if it was," Dylan muttered more to himself than GD, but GD couldn't but pick up on those words.

"Really?" He frowned, wondering if he'd misjudged the other man. "It'd be easy for you to turn a kid in for arson?"

"No...but Lana's an old friend, and her brothers might be asses, but they're her kin." Dylan smiled sadly.

"So you're loyal to them because you're loyal to her?" GD shook his head at that reasoning. "That's just why I could never make it as a cop."

Dylan considered that for a moment, his brow wrinkling into a frown as it began to dawn on him that it hadn't sounded much like a compliment. As GD suspected, once that revelation hit, Dylan was pressing him for a clarification.

"What's that supposed to mean?"

"There is right and wrong...and then loyalty." GD had already made his choice in life.

Right was right. Wrong was wrong. The law was the law. Sometimes it was right. Sometimes it was wrong.

"And what is *that* supposed to mean?"

Dylan knew exactly what GD meant, and GD wasn't going to waste his time explaining himself. "You do what you got to. You know everything I know now."

That was a lie, but GD was a good liar. He didn't know if he was good enough to get one past Dylan, and Dylan didn't give away what he thought as he huffed off. GD watched him go with a sick feeling in his stomach. He had better call Nick and give him a heads-up just in case things got bad.

Even as he was telling himself that, GD's attention was shifting back toward Kitty Anne. She really did look pretty. He could just stare at her all day. Stare at her and smile. That was just what he did until the urge became too much to control and he found himself sliding out of the booth completely forgetting about the phone call he was supposed to make.

It was time to go play with his Kitty Anne.

* * * *

Kitty Anne felt GD coming her way but didn't dare to look up from the book she was trying to read. So far she'd managed to read the same sentence a few hundred times and still didn't know what it said. Every sense, every nerve, every fiber of her being was tuned to the big man stalking her way.

Still, she refused to openly acknowledge him. Turning in her seat and giving GD the cold shoulder, Kitty Anne knew she was being childish, but she was also having a strange kind of fun. There was a sense of excitement and anticipation to the air as each of them waited for the other to make the next move.

GD claimed it as he slid into the seat beside her and proceeded to simply stare at her. He was acting like enough of a freak to draw Polly's attention. She hurried over to assure everything was all right. Kitty Anne ignored her, too, but GD didn't. He turned to face the older woman as she asked if there was anything he needed.

"Just the check."

Offering Polly a smile as he stood up, GD didn't even glance Kitty Anne's way as he leaned to his side, invading her personal space as he fished his wallet out of his back pocket. She tilted with him, assuring GD didn't bang into her and refusing to reward him with so much as even a catch in her breath as his warm, musky scent infused the air around her.

"You can go ahead and put the rest of the lady's lunch on my tab," GD offered, causing Polly to glance in her direction and forcing Kitty Anne to either ignore her, too, or recognize GD in some basic way. That she would not do. Besides, Polly would understand.

Turning the page as though she'd actually been reading, Kitty Anne continued to ignore GD. He returned the favor, leaving Polly nervously uncertain. In the end she caved to the pointed look GD shot her as he settled back down onto his seat, his wallet now open and waiting.

"It'll be an extra three or so bucks," Polly warned him as she slid a slip across the counter. "The lady's ticket isn't printed up yet."

"That's fine," GD assured her as he pulled out a fifty and passed it along with his ticket back to her without even bothering to glance at the total with typical male arrogance. "I'm sure this will cover it."

"It certainly will." Polly's eyes widened at the sight of the generous bribe and suddenly she was all smiles. "Well, I hope everything was to your liking, sir."

"It was fine, thank you." GD paused before adding on, "You have excellent tea."

"Really?" The other woman seemed honestly shocked by that. "It just comes out of a Lipton box."

"Well, maybe it's the way you brew it because, trust me, I'm a connoisseur of *tea*."

GD stressed that last word, giving it a suggestive emphasis that might have confused Polly but wasn't lost on Kitty Anne. He was threatening her with her mother. That was a pretty serious threat.

"I'm glad you liked it." Polly didn't argue over the matter. It didn't even sound as if she cared. Of course, she wasn't in on the joke. "I hope you come back and see us again."

"Oh, I'll be around," GD assured her as he bent over once again to shove his wallet back into his pocket. Kitty Anne tipped to the side along with him, assuring he didn't bang into her.

"I got a thing for tea." GD tossed Polly a wink as he straightened back up.

"Well…we always have a pot ready?" Polly stumbled over her words, her uncertainty turning them into a question when they should have been a statement.

Kitty Anne didn't blame the older woman for getting flustered. It was hard to keep up with GD. Despite the fact that the man looked big and slow, he was slipperier than a fish and waiting for her to try and take a bite, but she didn't even flinch.

Kitty Anne didn't believe for a moment he was going to waste his afternoon hanging out with her crazy mother. He was bluffing, and she wasn't going to be suckered in. Besides, she had her own appointment to keep.

Chapter Eight

GD pulled to a stop in front of Lynn Anne's small trailer and parked by the daisy-lined curb. Somebody had laid in a set of cobblestones, assuring the flowers were protected from the sweep truck's door as it opened. The bricks and rocks looked truly old and worn instead of newly cast and led in a gentle curb along the drive and around the cheery garden beds that, no doubt, took a lot of time to maintain.

Whatever else one could say about the Anne women, they had an eye for aesthetics and drama. GD was greeted with the first as he made his way up to the door and the second when it opened to reveal a very stern-looking woman, who stood in sharp contrast to the outrageous creature that had greeted him last night.

"You came." Lynn Anne managed to make that sound so much like an accusation that GD couldn't help but smirk as he reminded her of her own offer.

"You invited me."

"Hmm." Lynn Anne drew herself up after a moment's consideration and nodded at him. "Fine. You get one glass of tea and five questions that I might not answer honestly."

GD hesitated on the step to look up at the woman in surprise because there was no way that she'd come up with that compromise by coincidence. Neither did she try to pretend it was as she snorted over his look.

"Yes, Mr. Davis, my daughter and I get along better than most people think." Lynn Anne offered him that assurance with enough of an edge marking her words to add a menacing hint to them, even as she stepped back to allow him room to pass. "Come on in."

"Said the spider to the fly," GD quipped as he shouldered his way past her and into a main room that couldn't have been more than a hundred square feet.

It was nicely proportioned, though, and appeared bright and airy. Still, when GD stepped up onto the worn carpeted floor the whole tin can of a home shifted slightly beneath his booted foot.

"You flew into my web all on your own, Mr. Davis," Lynn Anne reminded him as she shut the door. Stepping around GD to head for the little kitchenette in the back, she waved him toward the tiny, doll-sized furniture decorating the corner living room. "Please, have a seat."

He wanted to ask on what, but that felt a little too rude. Feeling very much like an elephant in a miniature toy show, GD couldn't even straighten up completely thanks to the low ceiling height. The loveseat that served as a couch for the room fit more like a chair around him. GD settled down into its floral depths, consciously aware of his bulk and size.

He was also pointedly aware that this was where Kitty Anne had grown up. Here the obvious poverty had been swept aside by a sense of taste and ability to make even used things look fresh and clean. Whatever else could be said about Lynn Anne, it was clear that she'd built a life that wasn't so much deprived as simply miniaturized.

That thought made him snicker because that was the last thing he'd say about Kitty Anne. She'd built herself a supersized persona and indulged in life with an outsized enthusiasm that made every moment a thrill. At least, that was how he felt when he was with her. Like daughter, like mother, except that, with Lynn Anne, GD was just nervous.

"So…" Lynn Anne turned back from the small kitchen tucked into the corner. It didn't even have a proper stove, but did have a burner and a mini-fridge that was big enough to hold a pitcher of tea. "Why did you really come here, Mr. Davis?"

"It's GD," he corrected her as she took one step and set the pitcher down on the tiny coffee table that was really nothing more than a tray. "And I thought I got to ask the questions?"

"Do you have any questions?"

GD considered that for the moment it took her to retrieve two glasses out of the one lone cupboard hanging on the wall. He had his answer as he watched her take that single step back to the living room.

"No. I think I got it all figured out."

"Is that right? And just what do you think you have figured out?"

"You and your daughter, you're both full of—"

"Watch your tone, young man. This is a *lady's* house," Lynn Anne declared with haughty grandeur as she settled down onto the rocking chair that faced both the windows and the small TV. GD had a feeling it was her customary seat, given the basket of needlework beside it.

"Forgive me, madam." GD tipped his head, playing along with Kitty Anne's mom's game. "I meant to say that you and your daughter enjoy a lively and entertaining relationship. And I think my first question is going to be—"

"I thought you didn't have any questions."

"—can I have some tea?"

* * * *

Kitty Anne felt a sense of déjà vu when she sailed into her apartment on high hopes, only to have them crumble beneath the weight of reality. Like always, she thought she had something good going on, only to answer the phone and find herself in a sudden conversation with her mother.

"Your boy toy stopped by for tea today," Lynn Anne stated, not bothering with a greeting.

Kitty Anne could hear the faint tug of a breath that assured her that her mother was sneaking another cigarette. A menthol, no doubt. There really was no point in nagging her about the habit. Lynn Anne didn't listen to anybody, especially not Kitty Anne.

"Did you hear me?" her mother asked, taking Kitty Anne's silence for inattention.

"Yeah, I heard you," Kitty Anne assured her. "But I'm not sure what I'm supposed to say about that. I hope you managed to keep your clothes on?"

"Oh, please," Lynn Anne huffed indignantly. "That was one time, and it was an accident."

"Yes, because you normally dance naked around the house," Kitty Anne muttered, knowing that was no accident.

Not that she believed her mother had actually made a play for her boyfriend so much as simply just trying to horrify the poor guy. It had worked. He'd all but tripped over his own feet as he fled for the door, and that had pretty much been the last Kitty Anne had heard from him.

"Actually we had a very pleasant conversation."

"Is that right?" Kitty Anne could only imagine how it really went and wondered what the hell GD had been thinking to actually meet her mother for tea.

"He's wonderfully polite and earnest. I think he would make you a perfect husband."

"Which means you really don't like him."

"Why do you say that?"

"Because you think I do the opposite of what you tell me to." Kitty Anne kind of did, but that was mostly because her mother simply didn't agree with anything she did. She saw that more as Lynn Anne's problem than hers.

"Well, you do," Lynn Anne retorted, unable to resist harping on one of her favorite topics.

"So if you're telling me to keep him, you must want to see him go."

"He's too big." Lynn Anne gave up the game and started down the list of her complaints. "He almost tipped over my trailer when he stepped in it. A man that big...you'll end up suffocating beneath him."

"Oh, please, Mother." That was the stupidest thing in the world to worry about.

"And you should see how much tea the man drinks. You're going to go broke feeding that thing."

"Yes, Mother."

"You go on and 'yes, mother' me. I know what I'm talking about. I've given birth, and you were little. That man...he's going to give you fat babies that tear you all up down there."

"Oh, for God's sake, Mother!"

"Fine," Lynn Anne snapped as if she weren't being completely overbearing. "You don't want my advice, you can pay me to shut up. Where is my two hundred?"

"I...I'm sorry, Mom." Kitty Anne felt the weight and defeat of her failure press down on her, as she had no choice but to admit to the truth. "I don't have it, but don't worry. I had a job interview today, and it went really well."

There was a long pause as silence built up into a heavy knot of tension before her mother sighed and accepted the situation. "Well, then I guess if you don't have it, you don't have it."

Far from leaving Kitty Anne reassured, her mother's words made her feel only sicker. The nausea didn't get any better when she got off the phone, only to have it ring again. This time it was Phoebe, one of her coworkers down at the library, calling to warn her that Mrs. Diggard had spilt the beans about her arrest to Mr. Ruggan.

* * * *

"You would not believe this woman," GD swore as he matched Nick's rapid pace, trailing him across the yard. "I'm telling you, man, she makes your mother look sane."

Nick snorted at that. There were few people who could compete with his mother. Thankfully, though, that was his sisters' problem. His was much shorter and a good deal more stubborn.

"She actually had me call my mom so I could find out exactly how much I weighed at birth."

Now that was weird. Nick shot him a look, but GD just shrugged and shook his head.

"I have no idea what the hell she wanted," GD admitted. "I was just hoping to get in a good word for myself."

"Please," Nick snickered. "Everybody always likes you, GD."

That was the truth. GD had been teachers' pet, homecoming king, student body president. He'd even been voted the town's most "wish I was more like him" guy. GD always seemed to have everything under control and everybody eating out of his hand. Everybody that was but the Allison women.

"No, I'm pretty certain she's not in my corner," GD insisted, coming to a stop alongside Nick as he paused to glance over the field. "So...what are we doing?"

"Looking for Kevin," Nick admitted grimly.

The kid had disappeared once again, though, thankfully, all the bikes, both motorized and manual, were accounted for. It didn't seem he could have gotten that far on foot, but Nick was still having a hell of a time finding the kid.

"You don't think—"

"No." Nick cut GD off, knowing exactly what he'd been about to ask. "I got the guys keeping tabs on him every half-hour, so he hasn't had enough time to make it out to the ranch, yet."

That didn't mean he couldn't have started in that way, which was just why Nick was headed in that direction. Thankfully, GD stopped complaining about his Kitty Anne's mama long enough to offer to help find the kid. He headed in the opposite direction, as Nick continued on the main path that cut into the woods and led miles down into the Davis brothers' ranch.

The camp backed up into the ranch, but that didn't make it close by any means. Sure enough, Kevin had given out not even three miles down the lane, taking a long enough break for Nick to catch up with him. The kid saw him coming but didn't make a run for it. Not that there was anything to run from or anywhere to run to.

He didn't even try. Neither did Kevin bother either to offer Nick a greeting as he settled down on the fallen tree trunk that the kid was using as a bench. They sat there for several long minutes before Nick finally broke the silence, asking him the question that had been bugging Nick for a while now.

"You want to tell me why you won't meet the girl, yet you keep running off to stare at her?"

Nick didn't have to be any more specific than that. They both knew that the girl he'd referred to was Patton and they both knew that Patton was his sister. That hadn't been hard to find out. Not for GD. Not for the sheriff. Both of them had known where to look thanks to what Seth had shared. Kevin, on the other hand, didn't share much.

He glanced up at Nick, blinked, and then shrugged, giving him the very answer he expected. Whatever was going on in that head of his, Kevin was keeping his thoughts deep and private. That didn't mean they were a secret. Nick figured he could reason it out.

"Fine, let me take a guess." Nick pulled in a deep breath and tried to consider the matter rationally. "Your mom must have told you about Patton and maybe you thought she had a better life and resented her? Or that she…oh, I know!"

It hit Nick with a sudden flash he almost laughed out loud at the absurdity of it all. "You thought she was a boy. Patton. Your mother never told you she named her girl like a boy…did she?"

"No," Kevin answered honestly, not nearly as amused as Nick. The kid glanced up at him with a serious gaze that had Nick's own smile fading. "Mom always said that I looked just like Patton, and I thought…"

"There was somebody out there like you," Nick filled in, realizing in that second that it was loneliness haunting Kevin.

"I hate her."

"Who? Patton?" Because that would certainly put a dangerous spin on the fire, but Nick's alarm was quickly extinguished as Kevin shook his head.

"Mom." Looking away, Kevin glanced down the lane. "She took everything away from us."

"Then take it back. Go meet your sister," Nick urged him, not bothering to argue with the kid that it hadn't been his mom who had deprived him but the disease that had control of her.

Kevin would figure that out later in life when he was old enough to appreciate the lesson. Right then, the kid shot Nick a dirty look, as if he didn't get it.

"Mom always said I reminded her of Patton, not Seth. He reminded her of his father, and I wonder…if Patton is a girl, what is it about me that reminded mom of her? Am I like her? Do I look like her? Act like her? Talk like her? What? What do we have in common?"

"Meet her and find out."

"Seth says that if she learns about me, she'll take me from him."

Nick knew that was what Seth feared. It seemed to dawn on Seth that Patton might also want to get to know him, too. Even when Nick had tried to point that fact out, Seth had insisted that it was too dangerous to take the risk.

"I think I'll just go back to camp." Kevin shoved off the log and headed in that direction, leaving Nick to follow after him.

They made the whole trip in nearly perfect silence. Nick tried to hold a conversation, but Kevin barely responded. It unnerved Nick just how quiet the kid was, making him concerned that the boy was spending too much time in his own thoughts.

He needed to find a way to break the kid out of his shell, and Nick thought he just might have an idea. Of course, he had another problem he had to deal with, one GD quickly reminded Nick of when he and Kevin finally made it back to the camp.

So, under the big man's watchful eye, Nick called up Rachel and explained that he'd thought over the argument she'd made when she'd interviewed him for the paper a couple months back and decided to consider actually hiring a woman to replace his lost English teacher.

Nick made it clear that he'd had enough of the out-of-towners who kept quitting on him every six months. He wanted a local. Sure enough, she did know somebody who might be interested in the job.

Chapter Nine

Sunday, June 1st

Kitty Anne woke up to the sound of a woman carrying on outside. Rolling out of bed, she snuck a peek out the window at the drama unfolding in the parking lot and spied GD, of all people, leaning against the railing right across from her door. His lips were curled into a disgusted smirk as he gazed down at another man trying futilely to disengage himself from a half-naked woman.

GD glanced back over his shoulder just in time to catch her spying and shot her a salute that Kitty Anne ignored as she retreated back to the bathroom, rushing to make herself presentable before he could knock on her door. She probably had only seconds, so she could forget the makeup and hope he hadn't caught a look at the rat nest her hair had twisted into overnight.

A quick brush untangled the mess but also left her hair a frizzy ball that haloed around her head. Kitty Anne pinned it down into a tight bun and wasted no time in moving on to her teeth. They were brushed and her mouth minty fresh not two minutes later, and yet there were still no sounds, other than the ones coming through the wall.

She had a new noisy neighbor. The jerk had moved in two days before and she still hadn't met him. Kitty Anne had heard him, though. He liked to listen to country rock and watched pornos until late into the night. She'd passed out hearing a woman moaning through the wall, along with the distinctive beat of porno music, which may have explained the erotic fantasies that had filled her dreams.

It was those dreams that had her more than eager as she peeked back through the gap in the curtains, but GD wasn't there. He'd disappeared.

Heaving a deep sigh that barely helped to vent her frustration, Kitty Anne unsnapped the collar she'd slipped on and turned to actually get dressed.

It was probably for the best that he'd left. After all, she had a breakfast date with Rachel. Thankfully, her neighbor left, allowing Kitty Anne to get ready in peaceful silence. She was just on her way out the door when her phone rang, and sure enough, it was GD, sounding as smug and happy as all get-out.

"Hey, beautiful, how you doing this morning?"

"I could ask you the same thing," Kitty Anne retorted coolly, not afraid to approach any issue directly. "What happened to you this morning? You chicken out?"

"Chicken out?" GD laughed out loud at that insult. "Oh, beautiful, you sound a little grumpy. Didn't you get a good night's sleep?"

"No." Kitty Anne sulked as she fumbled with her keys, trying to juggle them, her purse, and the phone as she unlocked her car and slid into the driver's seat. "My neighbor kept me up most of the night with his TV. The sad sack was listening to lesbian porn all night. All I heard was giggling and moaning."

"My poor Kitty," GD crooned, not sounding the least bit sympathetic. "Did it give you naughty dreams?"

"I'm late," Kitty Anne informed him haughtily, not about to dignify that question with a response. "So, if you have a point..."

"No," GD admitted easily enough. "No point. Just missing you."

"Oh, please," Kitty Anne huffed, masking the smile gracing her lips with an indignant tone that GD heard right through. "You don't really expect me to fall for that line, do you?"

"I think you already have."

"Bye, GD."

"Be seeing you, beautiful."

She was sure that he would. Slipping her sunglasses down from the top of her head, Kitty Anne turned out of the motel parking lot eager to start her day. What better way to start a day than with a trip to the bakery? That was just where she planned to meet up with Rachel.

Filled with sweet scents and the warm welcome of low, murmured conversations, the Bread Box seemed to have a disproportionate amount of men filling it that morning. Never one to go unnoticed, Kitty Anne put an extra *oomph* in her walk, all too aware of the gazes following the sway of her ass as she headed toward where Rachel was already seated.

"Kitty Anne!" Rachel jumped up to give her a quick hug that Kitty Anne returned before sliding into her side of the booth. "I'm so sorry about what happened with Cole."

"Save it." Kitty Anne dismissed her apology off with a wave of her hand. "I knew what I was getting into when I agreed to try and set Cole up. My arrest is on me."

"I still feel guilty," Rachel admitted, settling back onto her seat.

"You don't need to," Kitty Anne assured her, knowing that her words were pointless.

Rachel was so sweet and honest and reliable and everything else that was good and wholesome. That was what Kitty Anne admired about her. Strangely enough, though, she abhorred any hint of those traits in herself, viewing them as weaknesses to be masked and hidden, lest the world take advantage of her.

"Yes, well, I will feel much better if I can help you get this job out at Camp D because, I'm telling you, the place is *amazing*." Rachel paused to cast Kitty Anne a sly smile. "And so is the owner."

"That's...nice, but...I don't think I'm on the market." Kitty Anne took the plunge, knowing just how Rachel would react to that, and her friend didn't fail her.

"Really? When did this happen? No, screw that. Who is it? How long have you been...oh, my God! What about Cole? And being arrested? Does he know about that?"

"Yes, he knows. Technically, he helped set me up, and you know him. It's GD."

"GD! That's... Well, that..."

"What?" Kitty Anne stilled, unnerved by the frown beginning to darken Rachel's brow. "What's wrong with GD? I thought you liked him. You had nothing but good things to say about him before."

"I do like him," Rachel insisted. "Everybody likes him, and that is sort of my point. He has a way with women. They are always falling for him, and because he's such a gentleman, they think he's falling with them, but a few weeks later, he's always on to his next conquest."

That really wasn't news. GD himself had pretty much assured her he knew all the lines, just as he'd assured her he wasn't feeding her any. The real question was whether or not she trusted him. The truth was she did. It really wasn't a matter of choice so much as simple instinct.

"Nick, on the other hand, would be perfect for you," Rachel swore as she leaned in across the table. "Trust me, you'll like him."

"Rachel—"

"I mean, seriously, he dedicates his life to helping children…how sweet is that?"

"I—"

"And I swear, he's not a dork. He's hot, like…I don't know, like…he's *hot!*"

Kitty Anne didn't even respond to that, just shot Rachel a look that had her caving.

"Okay, okay. The truth is it would be really great if you get this job because…" Glancing around at all the men surrounding them, Rachel leaned in closer over the table and dropped her voice lower. "I need some help on a story I'm working on."

"What story?" Kitty Anne copied Rachel and tipped forward as she pressed for the juicy details. "Abuse? Neglect? Prostitution? Because I know about Nick Dickles."

Everybody knew about Dickles. He'd gotten a full ride to some uppity college in the north. He hadn't managed to get a degree, but he had managed to get arrested for running a prostitution ring. Maybe he was back to his old tricks.

"Don't be sick," Rachel snapped, appearing to read her mind. "He's reformed."

"Uh-huh." Nobody was ever truly reformed as far as Kitty Anne was concerned.

"Look, the story isn't about him. It's about a guy who works out there. Seth Jones."

Rachel paused as if that was supposed to mean something.

"Yeah?" Kitty Anne prodded her along because that name meant nothing to her. "And?"

"I think he's Patton's brother."

"What? Why?"

"Patton's mom ran off and left her when she was little," Rachel explained as if Kitty Anne didn't already know that story. Her mother's abandonment, her father's murder, everybody knew about Patton's tragic origins. "Nobody knew what happened to her mom, but I've done some work, and it looks like the woman settled down in Louisiana."

"Why did she leave?" Kitty Anne didn't know why she cared, but her curiosity was caught.

"I really don't know, but she did have a kid." Rachel paused to frown as she admitted that things didn't completely add up. "Though the name on the birth certificate is Kevin, and he'd be eleven."

"I thought you said this guy was *working* out there," Kitty Anne reminded her, wondering if she'd misunderstood something. Apparently not.

"I know it doesn't all add up, but that's why I need somebody on the inside to get me the real scoop," Rachel stated with a pointed look. "I can't get it because…"

"Because?"

"Adam and Killian have a history with Nick. They're friends and if I spend too much time out at the camp, Adam and Killian will become suspicious.." Rachel shrugged, though Kitty Anne suspected there was a lot more to that story. "So, I need a little help."

"Let me get this straight. You want me to go out there and befriend this Seth guy and what? And find out if he knows about Patton?"

"Or maybe he doesn't know," Rachel countered. "That's what I need to figure out."

"And once you do?" Kitty Anne asked. "You going to tell Patton?"

"Of course. What would be better than a story that put a happy ending to the little lost girl without any family?"

* * * *

Nick absently listened as Kitty Anne prattled on at the other end of the phone about her work experience, focusing most of his attention on the pair of scissors he was swinging around his finger. With a snap of his wrist, he sent them flying outward, embedding them in a wall that already had several deep holes sliced into the drywall.

"That's fantastic." He spoke on cue as she fell silent. He didn't need to think about his words, already having them basically scripted for him by GD. "You sound like an ideal fit, so I think maybe the best thing is for you to come on out to the camp and see if things continue to flow as smoothly."

And so he could prove to GD that Venuses didn't exist.

"That would be great!"

There was no denying the enthusiasm filling those words, and Nick cringed, unable to escape the sour bite of guilt her happiness filled him with. From what GD had said, the girl was in a desperate situation. It probably wasn't right to waste her time or money on the gas, but he'd made a bet with GD. So, Nick would just have to reimburse her for the fuel because he didn't back out of bets.

"Tomorrow would be—"

"My schedule's packed tomorrow." Nick cut her off, not about to waste her time by dragging out this situation. "It'd be best if you came out today."

"But…but, it's Sunday."

Meaning she wasn't ready to be interviewed. Nick had spent enough time around enough women to know how to translate what they were really saying. He'd spare her the effort and himself the extra temptation.

"I really must insist, Miss Allison. After all, flexibility and adaptability are two important traits necessary for this position."

"Well, if you insist…"

"I do."

"Very well then."

Not sounding half as exuberant as she'd been moments ago, Kitty Anne agreed to meet with him just two hours from then. That might not have given her all the time she wanted to get herself together, but it gave Nick all he needed to get a workout in with some of the older boys on the obstacle course before checking in to assure that dinner service was on schedule and that the chapel was being prepped for the Sunday sermon that Father Lopez came out once a week to give.

Nick caught a quick shower before dressing in his preppiest outfit and was all but ready to walk out to go wait for GD's Venus when he opened the door and found the big man standing there with an expectant look alighting his face and a fist raised to knock.

"What are you doing here?" Nick stepped back, caught completely off guard by GD's sudden appearance.

"I've come to watch you go down." GD paused as if considering his words and hearing the double meaning in them. His grin widened just as Nick's scowl deepened.

"And just what do you think is about to happen?"

It seemed impossible, but GD's smile actually grew larger. He didn't answer, though, but just shook his head.

"It's a job interview," Nick reminded him, exasperated by the big man's attitude. "Nothing is going to happen."

"Uh-huh."

"I mean it."

"Sure thing." GD nodded.

"You can't possibly believe that anything is going to happen here."

"I'm going to go hide and spy on you." With that GD turned to go, but paused to throw back one last warning. "Don't let Kitty Anne know I'm here."

"Why the hell not?"

"Because then she'll figure out my plan," GD shot back, a "duh" sound in his tone as if Nick were the crazy one here.

"You have a plan?"

"Of course."

"Well, tell me, because I can't figure it out."

"It's simple. It's you, me, and Kitty living happily ever after."

That gave Nick pause. Forgetting that the idea itself was insane, he wasn't exactly sure how setting Kitty Anne up with Nick and then spying on them accomplished that goal. He just didn't know how to ask that question, so he went with a simple statement.

"I don't get it."

"It's simple," GD insisted with a hint of annoyance. "You're about to get taken out. From here on out, you're going to be Kitty's pet. Trust me, you don't want that woman in charge. She's nuts."

"*She's* nuts?" Nick wondered if GD was listening to himself. Apparently not.

"That's what I said. She's crazy. I'm sorry, I can't have crazy in charge. That means it's up to me to be the enforcer of the relationship. To be able to command, I have to be respected."

"Uh-huh."

"So, I'm holding out on her."

Again Nick was left dumbfounded by GD's logic. It was almost laughable. From the things he said to the way he looked, GD proved that somebody had gone insane, but Nick didn't think it was Kitty Anne.

"Whatever." Nick sighed, accepting that he was just not going to understand GD's reasoning no matter how much he tried to explain it. "I won't tell her. Go and hide if that's what you want."

All the big man was going to do was get a peep show of Nick asking his Venus a bunch of questions. Then he'd get to watch Nick turn her down, which would at least give GD a chance to console the woman and save Nick from the task himself.

That would be a relief because he was actually quite busy that day and didn't have a lot of time to devote to GD and his games. So Nick was out waiting exactly at two forty-five to watch Kitty Anne pull her small convertible into the parking lot. The woman was punctual, a trait Nick appreciated.

He also appreciated the length of her legs as they scissored out from behind the door that was thrown open seconds later. They were long, golden-tan, and disappeared beneath a hem that was way too low. The length of her skirt might have been demure, but the way the fabric clung almost indecently to the voluptuous curves of the woman's ass and hips was anything but modest.

The same could be said of her sweater. The soft blue fabric molded itself to her like a second skin, revealing the smooth dip of her waist that only highlighted the heavy mounds of her breasts. Nick's gaze lingered there as he admired the way her generous curves bounced and swayed as she straightened up.

Then she turned toward him, and for the first time, Nick took in the full package, and he knew. He was in trouble now.

* * * *

Kitty Anne took a deep breath and told herself to remember to focus. She needed this job...that is if it came with room and board because the drive out was way too long to make every day. According to Rachel, there were dorms that she believed both the kids and the staff stayed in. As long as they were separate, then everything was good by her because she didn't plan on...on...

Every thought in her head vanished as she looked up to take in the sight of the man who was waiting politely by the curb for her. He was perfect. Tall, thick, with a dark head of hair and a set of eyes that sparkled with a mischief that sent a thrill racing through her.

Instinctively Kitty Anne knew he was more than a match for her. There was just something about him that she couldn't explain, but she knew he was the hero to her heroine. He was certainly dressed the part, all dapper in his dark slacks and pressed shirt. His clothing only highlighted the lean strength of his body and had her imagining just how good he'd look naked.

It was wrong.

It was sinful, as Mother would have said, but Kitty Anne didn't care.

Drawn toward the man by a magnetic pull that held her hypnotized, it was a miracle she didn't trip over her own feet as she stepped up onto the sidewalk. The quivers in her stomach warned her that she would not find salvation by treading closer to the flame, but she couldn't help herself.

All Kitty Anne could focus on right then was the sheer perfection of his features. His jaw cut a hard, rugged line that matched the strong arch of his brows. With his gray eyes stormy and steaming, he fairly smoldered with an inner heat that warmed the very air around him.

The heavy scent of musk and lust thickened between them as Kitty Anne stepped up onto the curb, leaving her feeling drunk and a little dizzy. Her knees wobbled, her stomach churned, her heart raced, and she felt both sick and excited all at once. She wanted him, wanted him with a depth of hunger that probably should have frightened her, but she was too distracted by the need to worry.

"Miss Allison, I presume." Nick finally broke the heated silence, his words licking over her with a husky purr that had her own voice dropping into a seductively breathless whisper.

"And you must be Mr. Dickles." Kitty Anne held out her hand in a reflex that had her breath catching and her whole body tightening with an intense rush of longing as his warm, callused grip tightened down around her.

Instantly an ache filled her as she imagined just how good his hands would feel sliding all over her body, skin-to-skin. Just the thought had her tingling with an awareness so blindingly bright she jerked backward as if he'd shocked her with pure electricity. Her eyes rounded with the sensation and crashed into his, holding his gaze as she realized she was not lost alone in the moment.

Nick was there with her, too, leaning in toward her as if he wanted to say or do something more. She ached for more, ached for the feel of those lips against hers, to feel them move down her body, to have him touch her, hold her, take her in a sweaty, writhing—

"Um...maybe we should go to my office," Nick suggested, jerking backward mere seconds before his mouth would have brushed across hers in that first, tantalizing taste, but he denied her and himself.

"Yes, your office," Kitty Anne repeated as she tried to shake off the spell weaving its way around her.

It was a futile attempt. The hunger and want clung to her, an insatiable need that she feared would drive her to the brink of insanity if it wasn't indulged. Indulged? She wanted to drown in the delicious warmth curling through her, but that wasn't why she was there.

Grasping for the frayed edges of her self-control, Kitty Anne pulled herself together as she straightened up. She needed a job, not a man. She reminded herself she already had one of those...sort of. It wasn't as though the man had gotten her a ring or anything. No, he'd gotten her a collar, and God only knew how many of those he'd given out in a lifetime.

What Kitty Anne did know was that they'd gone out only twice, far from the amount of dates needed to establish a relationship as serious, much less monogamous. If all of that were true, then why did she feel so guilty? Because she knew the truth. There was something special between GD and her, but there was no denying her response to Nick either.

Barely paying any mind to the world around her, Kitty Anne followed Nick blindly, attuned only to the feel of Nick's palm resting on the small of her back as he guided her forward through the lush gardens surrounding them and toward the large Spanish-styled buildings rising up behind them.

Beside her, Nick stared down at his feet, frowning at them as if they'd offended him in some way, but Kitty Anne knew the truth. He was making sure he didn't trip over them, and that small sign of how affected he was by her presence made her realize Nick was more than simply devastatingly handsome.

He was adorable.

So damn cute she tripped over her own feet as she stared up at him instead of watching where she was going. Like a true gentleman, he caught her by the arm, helping her to straighten, even as his touch threatened to have her melting into a puddle at his feet.

Kitty Anne felt her cunt swell, growing soft and wet with the same need that had her nipples puckering into hard points beneath her sweater and drawing his gaze downward.

Nick's eyes lingered there, making her breath catch and breasts lift as his gaze darkened and his fingers tightened around her arm. Kitty Anne wouldn't have denied him if he'd tried to take her right there in the middle of the path. She wanted him that bad. As if he read the thoughts racing through her mind, he growled and started back down the path at a fast clip as he all but dragged her behind him.

Kitty Anne nearly had to skip to keep up, but she didn't offer a complaint, in as great a rush as him to find a bit of privacy. It didn't even dawn on her that he led her up a steep hill to a small cabin and not his office.

He shoved open the door to the small bungalow and pulled her into the warm, masculine confines of a small living room. The door slammed back into its frame as her purse hit the floor, and suddenly she was in his arms, Nick's lips crashing down over hers as the dam holding back the need snapped like a twig in the wind.

Chapter Ten

Nick didn't know what he was doing. He was out of control, but he didn't care. All that mattered was the sweet, addictive taste of Kitty Anne's kiss. Like a fine wine, but with the deep punch of an aged whiskey, she was delicious. It took only one drop of that heady ambrosia and he was drunk on the taste of her, the feel of her, the intoxicating scent of female arousal thickening in the air.

Nick had never felt like this before.

He must be crazy.

Late-onset insanity was all that explained his response to Kitty Anne. He'd never felt like this, reacted like this to any woman ever before. Who would have thought that he would now?

Normally Nick liked short women, thin ones who understood the chic, sophisticated style of an urban elite, but Kitty Anne was far from that modern benchmark. She was tall, curvy, and dressed like a bombshell from a bygone era. Bold, that was the best word to describe her, and as a general rule, Nick preferred his women to be a little more aristocratic.

He doubted Kitty Anne even knew how to pretend to be that reserved. She fought for and won control of the kiss, her tongue dueling with his and firing up Nick's passions to levels that had him ripping at her clothing in desperate attempt to get to the soft skin beneath.

Not to be outdone, Kitty Anne fisted her own slender fingers in his shirt and tore it open. Almost instantly, she buried her hands beneath the shredded edges and raked her nails straight down his back, making him arch and break free of her kiss to cuss and gasp as the blood rushing through his veins began to boil with a searing heat.

He needed her.

Needed her now, but he was held spellbound as that hot, wicked mouth of hers began to nibble and lick its way right down his chest and over the corded muscles of his stomach toward where her hands were fumbling with his belt. Nick didn't help. He didn't need to. Kitty Anne managed to rip the leather strap free of the buckle and all but tore his zipper clean off as she freed the throbbing length of his erection to the heated grip of her fingers.

Those naughty fingers curled around the aching width of his dick and measured him with several smooth strokes, pumping him until he was painfully hard and flushed. Nick was all but ready to beg for mercy as the perfect pout of Kitty Anne's lips parted and dipped down over the weeping head of his cock. Flared and swollen, it pulsed in angry demand as she dared to tease him with several skittish licks that ended in a perverted spanking as her wickedly large tongue snaked out to pat his head like a dog, causing Nick to growl like one.

The feral urge to take control nearly overwhelmed him and would have if Kitty Anne hadn't turned his snarls into howls as she took him deep, allowing that tongue of hers to lead the parade. It whirled around the length of his cock, followed quickly by the tight, velvety squeeze of her lips.

Kitty Anne took him all the way down her throat, fucking him deep and allowing her hands to warm the flesh she couldn't reach. Nick's dick swelled and pulsed, happier than it had ever been, along with being thicker and longer than he'd ever grown. She sucked him like a pro. Hell, she sucked better than one.

Nick would know.

It was too much. He was being tormented by the pleasure building into a pounding throb that echoed straight out of his balls. The sweat gathered along his shoulders and trickled down his back as he flexed every muscle and strained to hold back, not wanting to waste even a second of the rapture starting to rip through him, but then the damn woman stole the very will from his bones.

Closing her fingers around his balls, she began to expertly roll and squeeze them, milking the release straight from his tender sac as she fucked him with a speed that had him damn near hyperventilating. His breaths shortened into desperate pants as the world condensed before him, becoming defined only by the warm, moist pull of her lips until finally he snapped.

"Shit!"

Nick came. He came harder than he'd ever come before, hard enough that actual lights sparkled in his eyes and he found himself wobbling on his feet as the world spun around him. Then he was going down, falling backward onto his ass. For a second, he'd thought he'd really lost it, but then Kitty Anne crawled up over him, pinning him down as she mounted him like some kind of stud, and Nick realized the woman had actually knocked him over.

She wasn't waiting for him to take her. Kitty Anne was taking him, as if he was capable of going for another round seconds after having shot a full load. Damned if he wasn't. Nick didn't know what kind of spell Kitty Anne had woven around him, but she was better than Viagra.

He was the luckiest son of a bitch in the world.

That thought echoed through Nick as Kitty Anne lifted her skirt high enough for him to catch a glimpse the pearly pink folds of her pussy, swollen and parted in welcome. He didn't know what had happened to her panties, and he didn't care as she levered herself up over the flushed, rounded head of his cock.

Before she could lower herself down onto his turgid flesh, Nick decided he wanted a taste of that cunt. Latching on to Kitty Anne's waist, he took control of her and the moment as he jerked her up over his face. The heavy folds of her skirt enshrined him as she squealed and released the hem, trapping him in a cocoon of warm cotton and the sultry scent of a ripe pussy ready to be eaten.

She was dripping wet, and he stuck his tongue out to catch a drop of her honeyed cream, savoring the rich flavor that was distinctly hers before giving into the savage need to bury his face between her softly rounded thighs and claim the pussy that now belonged to him.

* * * *

GD snickered as he peered through the window and watched Nick finally take control of the moment. He had to fight for it, though, because Kitty Anne wasn't giving in. Not an inch. It was just like he predicted.

Nick was going to end up at her beck and call, but not GD. Crazy wasn't going to command him. He'd meant what he said to Nick. GD planned on living happily ever after. That meant that somebody had to be in charge. Clearly that somebody was him.

It wasn't going to be easy, but Kitty Anne was worth the effort. So, despite how much fun it would have been to walk right into Nick's bungalow and give Kitty Anne the dick she was begging for, GD held back.

That didn't stop him from thinking about it. He didn't have to wonder how she'd respond to that if he went in and took her right then and there. She'd melt all over him and give him some good-fashioned sass that would have him riding her hard and fast. God, he wanted to give it to her just like that and probably would if he didn't have to busy himself elsewhere.

That was just what he did, tracking Alex back down as he hung out playing video games on his tablet with his cruiser hidden by a patch of trees off the main highway. Normally that was where cops sat to catch inbound speeders, but today, the sheriff was simply hiding. From who was the real question, but he didn't get the chance to ask before Alex was snapping his own question at GD.

"How'd you find me?" the sheriff demanded to know as GD pulled his truck to a stop so that his window lined up with Alex's. "I haven't told anybody where I was."

"I told you years ago, man, I am the *best* at hide and seek," GD shot back, reminding him of when they were kids playing in the neighborhood because that was just how far back GD and Alex went.

Back then, of course, they'd been both competitors and friends. The years hadn't really changed much. The antagonism that had existed when they were boys was so engrained into their relationship that they still bickered as much as they conspired.

"Oh, please." Alex rolled his eyes. "Who said I was hiding?"

"Oh, please," GD shot back obnoxiously as he rolled his eyes in an exaggerated imitation of Alex's less-than-believable denial.

"Well, you're in a good mood," Alex muttered, now playing the offended role as he glared over at GD. "Is there a reason you are visiting it on me?"

"Is there a reason you're antagonizing Heather with Gwen?" GD shot back, referencing that morning's drama at the motel. "After all, I backed you with Heather. I think I'm owed an explanation."

"It's like I told you earlier. I was just proving a point," Alex insisted.

"Bullshit." GD refused to believe that Alex was that stupid. "Something is up…and if it isn't, then you are the stupidest shit around because you got something good with Heather, and Gwen…that woman is dangerous."

Psychotically so, given she'd actually walked right into Alex's house uninvited and crawled into his bed while he was sleeping, which was not a normal thing to do. Despite her denials and her pleas that it was all a misunderstanding, GD sensed that she'd been up to more than any of them knew.

"She asked to speak with me." Alex shrugged that admission off and popped a quick, arrogant smile. "The woman's tore up…who can blame her?"

"Oh God." GD sighed, rolling his eyes for real that time. "You can't actually believe that."

"What I *believe* is that you had some kind of conversation with Chase's little mutt-faced boy, and now that idiot's made my life a living hell," Alex shot back, switching topics in a clear and desperate attempt to turn the tables on GD. There was only one problem with Alex's plan.

"I have no idea what you're talking about. What dog-faced boy?"

"That detective…Dylan."

"Man, it's not like I swing that way," GD started with that qualifier, "but, really, we should both feel lucky he isn't looking at our women."

"You have a woman?" Alex cocked a brow at that. "No, wait. I don't care. I'm still mad that you sent that Ken-doll after me."

"I didn't send him after you," GD scoffed, irritated by that accusation. "I sent him after Lana's brothers."

Apparently that hadn't worked out.

"Yeah, well, I guess he's got his loyalties." Alex sighed and glanced around. "And now I got Chase tearing up the county looking for me."

"So that's who we're hiding from." That made sense.

Not only was Chase willing to make his point using his fists, he had the money and the power both at the club and in town to make anybody's life hell, but he especially could make an elected official's life completely miserable. More than that, nobody got elected if Chase didn't back them.

That gave him rights most citizens didn't have, like the right to possibly beat the crap out of the sheriff. GD understood why Alex didn't want to put that one to the test. The problem was that the only thing really standing between Kevin, Seth, and the tragedy of a lifetime was Alex.

So far he'd held strong, refusing to believe Seth's confession. Chase might not leave the sheriff much choice, though, but arrest him. The eldest Davis brother wanted somebody in prison. GD didn't think he'd care if it was Seth or Kevin.

Patton might.

"So?" GD pinned him with a hard look. "What are you going to do?"

* * * *

Kitty Anne didn't know what the hell she was doing, and she didn't care. The scream that caught in her throat never made it past her lips as she strangled on her own breath. She was searing hot and going down in flames that licked out of her cunt, driven by the ravenous plundering of Nick's velvety tongue.

With mischievous delight, it danced up the weeping walls of her sheath, massaging her quivering muscles as he teased her with gentle licks and flicks. Those taunting caresses that never quite went deep or hard enough did nothing more than cause her to twist and mew as she strained beneath the rapture twining through her. It wound through her muscles until she was strained and tense, all but sobbing for more.

He gave it to her, allowing his hands to fist in the folds of her skirt and lifting them out of his way as his callused fingers tightened around the soft flesh of her thighs. His grip was hard, his touch rough and savage as he gathered the thick cream slickening the insides of her thighs up on the tips of his fingers. He slid them back down the crease that led from the weeping folds of her pussy to the forbidden entrance hidden between the plump cheeks of her ass.

She'd never been taken there, never even been touched, but there was no stopping Nick. Kitty Anne's breath caught on a cry as he screwed first one and then the second finger deep into her tight channel, making her whole world burst with a searing blast of pained pleasure as he added a third finger in a dark forewarning of just how many ways he planned to take her, to use her.

That thought had Kitty Anne almost coming, and then she was as he pressed down from behind on the same sweet spot that his tongue rapped deep inside her cunt, unleashing a euphoric wave of ecstasy that had her whole body spasming with the hard pound of her release...or perhaps it was Nick's cock. Kitty Anne didn't know.

She lost track of time and space as the world spun around her, and suddenly her cheek was being pressed deep into the soft carpet beneath her, the cool air fanning over her ass as a set of hands gripped her hips hard and tilted, opening up her cunt to the thick cockhead pressing down between the swollen lips of her pussy. Then he was filling her with his thick heat, making her muscles stretch wide as he slid slowly into her.

He took her with a steady determination that allowed Kitty Anne to savor every second. As his balls banged against her, Nick stilled, holding steady until she milked his length with a tight, intentional pulse of her sheath's walls. His response was instantaneous as he began to pound back and forth inside her, riding her with a reckless abandon that had Kitty Anne sobbing into the carpet as her pleasure grew so wickedly intense her whole body throbbed with it.

Then she felt his fingers pushing back into her ass, and that was all she needed, just that little bit of extra fullness, that slight pinch of pain, and she was coming harder than she ever had before. Spasming with the uncontrolled ripples of her release, her muscles gave out, and she crashed down onto the floor, but Nick wasn't done with her.

* * * *

Not by far.

In fact, in those seconds, Nick didn't know if he'd ever be done with Kitty Anne. The intensity of the pleasure, the sheer heavenly delight of fucking his sensitive length down the rippling walls of her cunt, everything about the woman was perfection.

As he gave himself over to his release, he knew that he was also giving himself over to Kitty Anne as well. She was his mistress, his love, his everything. She was his Venus, and GD was never going to forgive him...or maybe he would. After all, the big man had set this all up. Why was a question Nick would deal with later.

Right then all that mattered was the burning drive to pound his hips forward in a mindless, endless need to fuck. It would be so easy to give in, but this was no way to take a woman—half dressed, on the floor, feet from the door. He'd treated hookers with more respect, but Nick's defense was simple.

Kitty Anne drove him that wild, that crazy. Even now, as the insatiable need still churning within him had been blunted, Nick found it took all his strength to do what was right and take care of his woman, but he managed.

Forcing himself to release Kitty Anne long enough to regain his feet, Nick knew she hadn't actually passed out, though she was puddled on the floor much like a jellyfish washed ashore. She barely managed a moan and a wiggle when he pulled free of her tight sheath. She didn't even bother to open her eyes as he picked her off the floor and carried her to his bed.

There, Nick took the time to finally strip her completely free of her tattered clothes and admire the beauty of his Venus. She was plush and soft and so inviting he couldn't help but touch.

While he'd meant to only climb in and join her for a quick nap, Nick found himself stroking his hands over Kitty Anne as she began to slowly twist and turn. Arching into his hands, her wide, beautiful eyes blinked open to reflect all her longings and doubts.

He didn't have to wonder at what had her worried. Nick just knew.

"I don't have any diseases," he said, offering her that assurance. "I never have done this before without protection."

"Me neither," Kitty Anne whispered, a smile curling at her lips. "I'm on birth control."

"Then I guess everything works out."

But when he dipped his head to seal that vow with a kiss, Kitty Anne planted a hand on his chest and held him back.

"I want you to know I would never sleep with a man to get a job." Clear and sincere, her words were a sharp contrast to the husky want still thick in her voice.

"And I'd never give a job to a woman just because I slept with her," Nick swore as he slid his hand up her calf and around the curve of her thigh as her legs shifted, opening her cunt to his touch.

"So we're agreed then?" Kitty Anne asked, and Nick accepted her invitation, stroking his fingers over her plump, wet folds. He eyed her smooth mound remembering just how delicious she tasted.

"You want the job?"

"Yes," Kitty Anne whispered, accepting more than just his offer for employment.

"Then we're agreed."

Brushing her hand aside, Nick bent down to seal that vow with a kiss, one he laid right across the plump folds of her pussy lips as he gripped her thighs tight and forced them wide, opening her up for a true devouring.

Chapter Eleven

It was dark the next time Kitty Anne became fully aware of the world around her, and it took a moment for everything that had happened to hit her. The second she shifted, though, she felt the twinge of so many sore muscles and the buzz still vibrating through her from so many climaxes.

That had been fun.

It had also been wrong. That probably shouldn't make her smile, but there was no taming the curl of her lips as Kitty Anne stretched out in Nick's big bed. The blanket and most of the pillows were strewn about the floor, along with the remnants of her clothes, which was a testament to how good things had been between them.

That still didn't change the fact that what had happened was wrong. Kitty Anne was going to have to deal with that at some point, but not right then. First, she was going to get cleaned up because she couldn't deal with serious issues when she was a mess. That was just what she felt like right then—sweaty, sticky, and disheveled.

A hot shower and a good scrubbing helped to loosen up her tight muscles. It also helped to clear the last vestiges of erotic euphoria from her mind, leaving her no place to hide from the truth nagging at her nonstop.

She really had done something wrong. She felt guilty, and a little sick from it. There was only one way to soothe those nerves. She was going to have to confess. Confess to GD that she'd made a mistake, which she must have done because nothing else explained her actions.

Still, no mistake had ever felt that good, and Kitty Anne really couldn't bring herself to regret what had happened with Nick. The man was a stud. In all ways. In all things. And she wanted him again. Something warned Kitty Anne that would never change.

Maybe it was time to actually talk to the man and discover whether there was anything between them beyond explosive chemistry. That might be hard to do, given she didn't have any clothes left to wear. Fortunately, Nick had a closet full of shirts that were warm, soft, and smelled just like him, like heaven.

She responded almost instantly to the heady scent, going soft and weak and wanting Nick all over again. It was like a sickness, like a disease, and she tried to shake it off, but it was impossible, which made the guilt eating at her only all the more acidic.

That didn't stop Kitty Anne's mind from wandering as she took in all the clothes hanging before her. Nick had style, and he wasn't a small man by any measure. He was large, and thick...in a lot of ways... Kitty Anne blinked and threw off the dirty thoughts that had started to flood her head and all the memories that had fueled them, along with the equally naughty thought that Nick was big but not nearly GD-size.

Clearly talking to the man wasn't actually going to be a good idea. She probably shouldn't even be in the same room as him. Kitty Anne needed time, and distance. So, maybe, a conversation wasn't the best idea. Fleeing sounded more on par with the moment. She'd need to be wearing more than a shirt for that.

Thankfully Nick wore boxers, and her ass was big enough to hold them up. A belt helped. She had to knot it, though, which looked absolutely ridiculous. It looked even stranger when she lowered the shirt back down. The cotton bulged with a distortedly aligned protrusion that looked as though she might be in transition. The only question was, which way was she going?

The short-term answer was to the living room to find her purse, but when Kitty Anne crept into the living room to find her purse and her keys, she found Nick instead. He was slouched in the frame of the back door that led out of the kitchen just off the living room.

He had his back to her, and she probably could have made it out the front door, but Kitty Anne got distracted by how damn sexy Nick looked standing there wearing nothing but a pair of jeans riding low on his hips.

His back muscles bunched and flexed as he pinned a phone between his ear and shoulder while he lifted a bottle of beer up to take a deep gulp. His arm bent, his biceps bulged, and Kitty Anne went weak in the knees, completely forgetting she was on a mission as the want and lust boiled anew in her veins.

That was her man, and she wasn't going anywhere.

* * * *

Nick cracked his neck as he listened to GD gloat on the other end. The man was having too much fun, but then again, he hadn't heard the decisions Nick had come to. He probably wouldn't be laughing for too much longer, or he might be. GD was a weird fucker.

"Yeah, yeah, yeah." Nick sighed, agreeing with everything GD said. "You were right, okay? Now I got to give the woman a job, and where am I supposed to put her?"

Camp D was a boy's only refuge. No women allowed. He couldn't just install Kitty Anne in a classroom and call her mister. The boys were bound to notice she was a woman…and what a woman she was.

"Well, put her in your bed," GD retorted as if that answer wasn't obvious. "Isn't she there now?"

"Yes, she is, and I'd like to keep her there, but you know how women are. They complicate things."

God did they ever, and Kitty Anne was set to blow his life apart. The last thing Nick had imagined was that he would fall in love. It seemed impossible to believe that it would be at first glance, but there was just no denying the evidence. Hell, he'd slept with enough women to know the difference between a good fuck and a special one. At least, he did now.

"Trust me, Kitty Anne likes to complicate them more than most," GD warned him as if Nick hadn't already figured that much out.

"I'm not blaming this one on her, big man," Nick shot back. "You're the one who set me up, and now look at me. I'm already whipped, and I haven't said more than five words to the woman."

He knew GD would laugh at that. Hell, that was partly why Nick had said it, but he wasn't lying. That morning his life had been simple, busy but simple, and now…

"My damn dick won't settle down for nothing," Nick muttered over that complaint, staring down at the growing bulge in jeans. That was what happened when he just thought about the woman.

"I swear, I'm not going to be able to hold a whole conversation with the woman for months at this rate, and how am I supposed to get any work done with her around? Huh? This is all your fault."

"Yeah, yeah, yeah," GD shot back obnoxiously. "You said that already."

"Oh, go fuck yourself, GD," Nick grumbled without any real heat. "And enjoy it because I'm not giving Kitty Anne back. You sent her to me, and I'm keeping her."

"So am I."

"Yeah, I know. You want to be the head chef in the kitchen." Nick rolled his eyes. He'd let GD do all the cooking if he wanted and would call himself lucky to be Kitty Anne's lapdog instead. "But, let me tell you something, letting crazy have her way has some advantages."

Some very pleasant ones.

"Which is just why I'm the one who is going to marry her," GD shot back, bringing an instant frown to Nick's brow.

"What? No, way." Nick wasn't going to be Uncle Nick to his own kids. "I'm going to marry her."

"So now you're going to marry her?" GD snorted, but amusement colored the sound, not disbelief. "I thought you had barely said five words to the girl?"

"And aren't you glad for that?" Nick shot back. "After all, I could ruin your chances with the girl just by telling her you're working an angle."

"Please," GD scoffed, sounding smug and unconcerned as he assured Nick, "Kitty Anne already knows. I already told her that I had plans for her."

"What? Holding out on her?" Nick bit back a snort at that stupid idea. "You don't think you are being a little stubborn?"

"Stubborn?" GD sounded honestly surprised by that word. "I'm not stubborn."

"Oh, come on. You just don't want to admit you're in love with the woman." Nick could understand that. He was still having a hell of a time accepting it, too.

"I'm not afraid of anything," GD dismissed Nick's argument. "I know I'm in love with the woman just like I knew you'd fall, too."

"Yeah, about that, I'm curious to figure out how you knew I'd fall in love with the girl."

"I bet you are." But GD was clearly not going to tell him. Smug bastard, he thought he was the only one with any insight.

"And I bet I can guess what you're really up to with Kitty Anne."

"Go for it," GD challenged him, and Nick never turned down a challenge.

"Okay, fine. I will." Nick paused to consider the matter. "Let's see…your story is you met this girl and fell for her in an instant. Then after a day or so, you realize that I'd fall for her, too, so you got me calling her friend to set her up to come out here, hoping I'd end up fucking the woman unconscious, which I did do."

Nick paused, finding himself distracted by that memory. It was a good one…best damn one of his life, but he could be making more—

"And what does that get me?"

"Huh?" Nick blinked, needing a second to remember what he'd been saying. "Oh yeah. It gets you guilt. Kitty Anne's going to feel bad about betraying you, and you're planning on milking that for something."

"Not just something, man. It's going to be the best damn night of either of our lives," GD vowed.

"Then don't hold me in suspense."

* * * *

Kitty Anne wasn't in suspense. She was stunned, and she stumbled back into the bedroom as she tried to grapple with all that she had just overheard. GD loved her? Nick wanted to marry her? Had she fallen down some kind of rabbit hole?

Obviously she had because Kitty Anne didn't know on what planet GD's plan made sense. He refused to sleep with her himself, but then he set her up to go all orgasmic over his friend? She should probably be pretty pissed about that and would have if it had been a joke.

Kitty Anne didn't think either of the men was laughing at her, though. From the confusion that she'd heard in Nick's tone, she sensed that they were as overwhelmed by the situation as she. Of course, she hadn't complained about where to *put* him. Neither had she manipulated the situation like GD had.

Whatever else could be said about the situation, one thing was clear. Her men were running wild, and it was time to remind them of just who was in charge. With that in mind, she stripped back down to nothing more than Nick's shirt, which she left unbuttoned.

Of course, she needed the proper hair to go with her look. So Kitty Anne slipped back into the bathroom and brushed her tresses until they poofed up, giving her a wild, lioness look. Makeup would have helped, but she'd washed all hers off already. Obviously Nick didn't have any. She did have some in her purse, which was in the living room. Thankfully, Nick was still leaning in the back door, arguing with GD.

"No fucking way," Nick snapped, sounding honestly outraged as Kitty darted out of the bedroom. "You want to bring all that shit out here, you're going to be moving into the dorm."

That comment caught Kitty's attention, but she didn't hesitate to snatch her purse up.

"My cabin *isn't* that big," Nick complained as he began to turn and almost caught Kitty scurrying back into the bedroom. She knew she was safe. She heard his beer bottle thunk into the garbage can as Nick continued on bitching. "Equal my ass. Have you fucked her?...Uh, huh. You know what that makes you? Boyfriend number *two*!"

Kitty Anne rolled her eyes at that comment and hurried back into the bathroom to work on her face. Like any good, self-respecting woman, she carried with her enough makeup for a morning-after look. Of course, what she really needed was a nighttime look, but Kitty Anne worked with what she had. All the while she kept an ear out for Nick as he continued to argue with GD.

"No! I don't care if you saw her first. I did her first. I'm boyfriend number one....Whatever. Just tell me how much closet space I'm going to lose because something tells me Kitty Anne comes with a lot of clothes."

That she did, and she couldn't help but smile that he already knew her well enough to have figured that much out.

"No, I don't mind."

Kitty Anne could hear the sigh in his voice through the wall. It made a lie out of his words, but she didn't take it personally. While his little bungalow was ideal, it was ideal for only one person or one vain person. The bathroom, the closet, they were about to become hers. Then they were going to have a discussion about a lack of a tub.

Stepping back to admire her reflection, Kitty Anne pushed aside all her concerns about housing and refocused her attention on the seduction she had planned. She looked ready for love, too. With her smoky eyes, her bedraggled hair, and her pouty lips, all she was missing was some sexy lingerie, but Nick's shirt worked.

Crawling back into the bed, she left it as messy as she centered herself in the middle of the mattress. Kneeling there, she fussed over the shirt until she got it to lay just so that the sides of her full breasts were showing and the shadowed valley between her legs was barely visible. Then she waited, silently practicing all the conversations she could end up having with Nick once he got off the phone with GD.

"Listen, I don't care what tricks you know or what kind of toys you have access to out there at your perverts' club. I am boyfriend number one...Number one! You know it. After all, you got your little peep on, didn't you? You see her mount me?...Yeah, that was hot."

Kitty Anne's eyes narrowed at that compliment, though it wasn't what caught her attention. Her focus, instead, was on what else Nick had revealed. So GD liked to get his "peep on." She could guess what that meant. If he wanted to see a show, she'd be glad to give him one.

"Think of it this way. At least you don't have sleep at that motel tonight...You really think she's *that* oblivious?...Now that's just cruel. I'm sure she's not a ditz."

A ditz? A ditz! GD was going to pay for that one. Nick, on the other hand, had just been promoted to boyfriend number one in her mind. He only solidified his position with his continued defense of her.

"Listen, I may not have had any kind of real conversation with the woman yet, but I think you are underestimating our woman, and she's going to make you pay."

That she was.

Kitty Anne was already plotting how. One thing was for sure. She wouldn't be wearing his collar anytime soon. She sure as shit wasn't going to feel the least bit guilty over what came next. It started when Nick finally said good-bye to his buddy and came strutting back into the bedroom.

As good as he looked in clothes, he looked a hell of a lot better out of them. Kitty Anne raked a gaze down his long, muscular frame, feeling her stomach quiver with the thrill of lusty excitement. Hell, even his feet looked sexy. Now she just needed to get him out of his jeans.

She had a plan for that.

Nick came to a stop, and she could almost see the questions run through his head as his gaze narrowed on her with heated intent. Kitty Anne knew he was wondering if she'd overheard his conversation, and at the same time, she suspected he didn't care.

What he cared about, what his eyes lingered on, was the part in her open shirt. Kitty Anne smiled, pleased that her plans were working as anticipated.

"Hello, Mr. Dickles." Kitty Anne gave him that husky greeting as she settled her palms down on her knees, brushing the tails of her unbuttoned shirt to the side and drawing his gaze downward.

"Miss Allison." Nick tracked the slide of her palms as they started slowly up her thighs.

"I think it's time we had a conversation, don't you?"

"Depends on what you want to talk about." Nick's tongue snaked out to wet his bottom lip before his teeth bit down into it, his entire focus trained on the fingers that had finally reached the swollen lips of her pussy.

Kitty Anne didn't hesitate to brush them open and treat herself to a teasing stroke across her clit. Neither did she bother to disguise the pleasure her own touch gave her as she arched and moaned, unable to resist repeating the caress once…twice…three more times before she remembered she was on a different mission right then.

Releasing her molten flesh, Kitty Anne drew Nick's gaze back toward hers as she lifted her fingers up to her lips to suck them dry and make him pant.

"I need to confess something."

"Yeah?" Nick swallowed hard, barely appearing to have heard her. "What's that?"

"I'm in love with another man."

That did have Nick glancing up at her, a look of uncertainty crossing his features before they settled into a gruff scowl. "Really? Because you have an odd way of showing it."

"That's not my fault." Kitty Anne batted her lashes just as she'd always practiced in the mirror and crawled forward with a pout. "He's…not capable of satisfying my needs."

That put the sparkle back in Nick's eyes and brought the smirk back to his lips. "Is that a fact?"

"Hmm."

Kitty Anne shrugged, not about to go too far out on that limb. After all, at the end of this, she was going to end up at GD's mercy, which made it wise not to push the big man too far. Instead, Kitty Anne turned the subject back toward where she wanted it to go.

"But you can." Kitty Anne smiled up at Nick. "In fact, you're in no position to deny me."

"Is that right?" If Nick's grin grew any wider, he'd be laughing outright at her.

"You'd be amazed at what I would dare." That wasn't a lie. "So, this bungalow…it's mine now, and if you want to share it with me, you had better be a good boy and keep me *very* happy."

Kitty Anne whispered that demand against Nick's lips as she dared to press her naked length against his in a wanton caress. "And there is something I really, really want."

"And what is that?" Nick growled back, his hands branding her waist as he dragged her even closer, flattening her breasts against his chest and making the hard points grind against him.

"You, on your knees." Kitty Anne pulled back to smile up at him as her fingers twined through his hair, directing him to obey her command. "It's time for you to earn your keep if you're going to be spending the night because now…I'm the Kitty in charge."

Chapter Twelve

Monday, June 2nd

Nick woke up to the heavenly feel of Kitty Anne's tight little cunt pulsing up and down the hard, aching length of his dick. He'd been dreaming about her, about fucking her, and now he knew why.

Cracking open his eyes, he caught sight of Kitty Anne flexing and smiling above him. She was taking her time and savoring every stroke. It didn't matter to her that she was driving him insane. That was just what he must have been—crazy—to allow her to tie him to his own bed, but he had. He was still bound, unable to do much more than eye the puckered tips of the large tits bouncing up and down as she fucked him with an even and measured rhythm.

Kitty Anne could go for a good hour like this. Nick knew that from experience and had no problem with her doing all the work. Hell, it was actually one of the sexiest things about the woman. All he had to do was lie back and enjoy.

That was just what Nick did as Kitty Anne rode him until they were both straining and sweating with the need for a release. A release that Kitty Anne denied him as she slowed to a stop. Nick grunted his annoyance and forced his gaze up from the hypnotic bounce of her breasts to catch her smiling down at him.

"Do you want me to untie you?"

He didn't really care, but he could tell that she had hoped to drive him crazy enough to revert back to the rutting madman he'd acted like last night. That was clear from the way she taunted him as she stretched across him to reach for the tie she'd used to bind his wrist to the bedpost last night. Her tits dangled mere inches from his lips and that was no accident.

It was a challenge.

The second he had his freedom he proved that to Kitty Anne, rolling her over and pinning her wrists to the bed with one hand. His hips began to pick up speed, pounding into her hard and fast as she cried out and arched upward, meeting him thrust for thrust.

He rode her right to the peak of the pinnacle, and Nick felt Kitty Anne tightening all around him with her impending release. It would have been so easy to ride that wave with her, but he had a point to prove. So, he gathered his strength and forced himself to come to a complete stop, sending Kitty Anne into a writhing, frenzy. A fit that lasted a good minute before she calmed down enough to glare up at him with naked irritation.

"You having fun now, sexy?" he teased her, knowing she was. "I'd point out to you I'm on top, and that makes *me* in charge."

He emphasized that point with a hard thrust of his hips as he once again took up a rapid pace that had her squealing and flushing with an impending release that he denied her. That time her tantrum lasted longer, and Nick didn't even wait for her to finish before he reared up onto his knees and jerked Kitty Anne onto his lap.

Staring down at the delicate, pink lips of her pussy parted around the hard, dark length of his cock, Nick felt a strangely primitive and slightly feral sense of satisfaction flood him. It took almost all of his self-control not to start fucking her again while he watched. They'd get to that, but first, he still had a point to make.

"You with me, sexy?" Nick asked, waiting patiently until Kitty Anne caught her breath enough to growl at him. He took that as a yes. "Good. Now let's be clear about something. This is *my* camp. I'm the boss. You're…"

Nick hesitated, looking for the safest word as Kitty Anne's gaze narrowed on him.

"Well," she demanded, "what am I?"

"Mine."

That brought a smile to his Kitty Anne's lips. "Only if that makes you mine."

"I think we have a deal."

Reaching down to brush back the swollen folds of her pussy to reveal the puckered bud of her clit, Nick smiled and dared to trap the sensitive little bundle of nerves beneath the callused tip of his finger. He gave it a twirl, eliciting another squeal from Kitty Anne as her eyes widened and her whole body lifted with the motion.

Nick didn't stop with just one roll. He kept it up, tormenting Kitty Anne until she'd lost the ability to plead or cuss, much less speak. Her breath heaved in with ragged pants that drew his gaze to the full, lush globes of her breasts. He couldn't resist taking a taste of the pebbled tips crowning her heavy curves.

Kitty Anne's response was instantaneous. She began to buck and fight him for control. Nick let her have it, allowing her to rear up and topple him over as she fell with him. Then all he had to do was lie back and enjoy the show as Kitty Anne rode him with a sexy abandon that had her cunt pistoning up and down his length. The walls of her velvety sheath pulsed with a rhythm that sucked the release right out of his balls.

Nick felt them swell and the searing heat shooting down his shaft and gave himself over to the rapture rushing through him. It sent him catapulting into a universe of bright colors and intense satisfaction. Hell, there was even a hint of contentment to his release, which just went to prove he was done for.

He probably could have and should have bemoaned his fate, but it was hard to feel bad about what destiny had gifted him with when Kitty Anne was passed out sweaty and naked on top of him. The woman might be dainty looking, but she could snore like a man three times her size.

Nick smirked, knowing Kitty Anne would be upset to learn about that unladylike behavior. That was just why he wouldn't tell her. GD probably would. Sighing over that thought, Nick couldn't help but replay his conversation with his friend last night.

The man was crazy, and Nick wasn't convinced that Kitty Anne would end up playing the role GD had assigned her. After all, she didn't appear even the slightest bit racked with guilt. Instead, she'd been bossy and demanding, claiming his bungalow for herself and ordering him to satisfy her in every dirty way she could think of…which actually wasn't all that dirty.

He'd never tell her that, though.

Nick preferred to show her, but even that would have to wait because he was running late. Managing to slip out from under Kitty Anne, he ordered up a breakfast and some small clothes from the junior laundry center. By the time he'd finished showering, they'd arrived, brought over by one of the older boys.

Nick thanked him and then went to wake his Kitty Anne.

* * * *

Kitty Anne didn't want to wake up. She was tired and deliciously sore, but Nick arrived, carrying a bribe. He plunked down a tray that smelled like her two favorite things in the morning—bacon and coffee—just inches from her nose.

"Time to rise and shine, sexy," Nick called out, reaching out to force Kitty Anne to roll over and assure that she did, indeed, wake up. "We got breakfast to eat, and then I got a camp to run, so we need to go ahead and have that talk we've been putting off."

Kitty Anne frowned up at Nick's cheery smile and sighed. "Fine."

Wrapping the sheet around her, she reluctantly sat up as Nick whisked the tray of delicious smelling foods off the bed and informed her that he'd be waiting with whatever would be left of breakfast if she didn't hurry up and join him in the other room. Kitty Anne rushed through her morning rituals, not even bothering with most of them.

She did take a moment to use the facilities and wash up before strutting into the living with an intentionally regal air to counter the sheet she had wrapped around her like a towel.

"I'm not having any conversation until I have at least five sips of coffee," Kitty Anne declared before Nick could even completely finish rising out of his seat to greet her.

Whatever he had been about to say remained unsaid as he pointedly closed his mouth and reached for the coffee pot. Kitty Anne settled down in the chair stationed to the side of the couch and accepted the cup Nick passed her. Five sips later, she felt more centered and finally met his gaze.

"So…"

"So," Nick echoed, appearing to be at a complete loss for words, too. "You're really good in bed."

"Thank you." That was one of the nicest, and most direct, compliments she'd ever received, and she couldn't help but beam a smile at him. "I was quite pleased with your performance as well."

"I aim to satisfy."

"And you did."

"Good."

That strange awkward silence descended over them as Kitty sipped away at her coffee and waited for Nick to find something to say. After all, he was the one who looked as if he had something to say. Whatever it was, it was taking forever to get it out.

"So…about this man you're in love with—"

"Oh, I wouldn't worry about him." Kitty cut him off with a wave of her hand.

"Really?" Nick scowled as he heaved a deep sigh. "You know that's not reassuring, right?"

"It's not?" Kitty Anne blinked innocently. "Well, what would reassure you?"

That threw Nick off, and she saw him hesitate. The correct answer would be to get rid of the other man, but that wasn't really what he wanted. Not him. Not GD. Certainty, not her. She was looking forward to having both GD and Nick at her beck and call, serving *all* her needs.

"I was warned about you, you know." Kitty Anne spoke up as Nick continued to silently flounder.

"Really?" That appeared to pique Nick's interest. "By who?"

"Rachel Allen."

"Rachel? I've never been anything but nice to Rachel," Nick huffed as if he were offended even though he didn't sound it.

"And Heather Lawson," Kitty Anne continued on as if Nick hadn't objected. "She said you were hotter than the sun."

"Well, that just proves she has good taste." Nick flashed her a grin that faded right back into a frown with Kitty Anne's next revelation.

"Rachel said you were quicker than quicksand."

"Reporters, they're paid to embellish."

"I don't think there is much about your reputation that needs embellishment," Kitty Anne assured him dryly. He had proven to be the stud everybody knew him to be, but Nick might take her comment in a different way.

He reared back and she didn't think there was anything fake about the indignation that had stiffening up. "And what is *that* supposed to mean?"

Kitty Anne stared at him in amazement, shocked that he had the audacity to act offended. Maybe he had forgotten, but neither one of them had that right anymore. Just in case he had forgotten, Kitty Anne reminded him of that fact.

"It means I'm not the only one in this room who has been arrested for prostitution."

"I was not a prostitute," Nick defended himself instantly, but did pause before reluctantly admitting, "I was in charge of the prostitutes, and really they were classy. So it's not like I was arrested in some cheap motel."

"And it's not like I was really going to have sex with anybody," Kitty Anne snapped back. She was ready to go full bitch mode now, but Nick undid her with a simple response.

"Except for me."

That put the smug in Nick's smile as he settled back against the couch with an arrogant tilt of his chin. "Can't deny that."

"And quicker than quicksand," Kitty Anne added on, biting back her own grin as he frowned at that comment.

"That may be an exaggeration."

"Says the man who had me on all fours within ten minutes of meeting me."

"Says the woman who sucked the sanity straight out of me through my dick within five minutes of meeting," Nick shot back.

"Something tells me you weren't that sane to begin with."

"Takes one to know one."

That time Kitty Anne couldn't control the tips of her lips, and she felt them curling upward. "I'll take that as a compliment."

"I think you should," Nick agreed easily before leaning forward with a growing seriousness. "Because I mean what I say. You're crazy. Crazy, wild, undisciplined, and mine, which means we have a problem."

"We do?" Kitty Anne arched a brow as Nick nodded.

"Yes, ma'am, we do. See, Camp D is already full-up on crazy, wild, and undisciplined boys all around. You add a woman to that mix...bad things are bound to happen."

"That's the most sexist thing I ever heard."

"And the God honest truth."

Kitty Anne could tell Nick meant what he said, but that didn't make any sense. "Then why did you hire me?"

That stumped him, which only made the answer more obvious. Nick recovered badly, too. With a grunt and a wave of his hand, he dismissed both her question along with his own concerns.

"We'll work it out."

"Uh-huh." Kitty Anne didn't blink, but pinned him with a look that had Nick squirming within his seat in seconds.

"Look, it's just that the camp is everything to me." He wasn't lying. She could sense his desperation. It sounded in his tone as he all but pleaded with her. "You know, when I was younger, I lost my parents. I bounced all around with different relatives and that's kind of where these boys are. I don't want them to end up where I ended up, because trust me, jail is not fun."

That she knew. That and she'd really lucked out, because Nick was not only sexy as hell but also sweet as sugar. Kitty Anne just wanted to lick him all up. Licking her lips and eyeing him like a tasty treat, she did consider the merits before he caught her look and frowned.

"Don't stare at me like that. I don't have time for any more funny business."

"Funny business?" Kitty Anne laughed at that. "You're calling sex with me, funny?"

"No. No! I didn't mean it like that."

"Uh-huh."

"I swear it." Nick crossed his hearts and joined his hands in a prayer as he batted his long lashes at her. Kitty Anne could sense the laughter lurking in the twinkle of his eyes.

"And I swear not to cause problems at your camp," Kitty Anne swore. She reached out to cover the hand resting on his knee and laced her fingers through his. "I understand how important this place is for you and I wouldn't want to ruin that."

"I know." Nick gave her fingers a quick squeeze. They shared a quick smile before he nodded at the food. "Your breakfast is getting cold."

Kitty Anne smiled as her stomach rumbled. She was hungry and didn't even try to pretend like she wasn't. Digging in with her normal fervor, it took Kitty Anne a moment to realize that Nick was watching her with a strange look. Actually, he was staring at her like he was fascinated, which was sort of the way GD watched her eat. Maybe it was a weird fetish that they shared. Whatever it was, it kind of creeped her out.

"What?" Breaking down, Kitty Anne paused to confront Nick, who just blinked and parroted back her question.

"What?"

"Why are you staring at me like that?"

"No reason." Nick shrugged.

"Uh-huh."

"Don't start that."

"Start what?" Kitty Anne blinked innocently back at him.

"Oh, I see." Nick smirked.

"What?"

"Nothing."

"Uh-huh." Kitty Anne smiled and waited, but Nick didn't take the bait this time.

Instead, he finally turned his attention toward his breakfast. The next several minutes passed in compatible silence. It was only when she'd plowed through more than half her plate that Kitty Anne finally slowed down and really started to focus on the delicious meal before her.

"This is really good," she commented as she glanced over at Nick. "Where did it come from?"

"What?" Nick paused to meet her look and lift a brow at her. "Don't you think I made it?"

"The kitchen is not dirty and neither are you," Kitty Anne shot back. "So, where did it come from?"

"The culinary students," Nick answered succinctly, only to quickly follow it up with a better explanation. "The camp is part orphanage, part school, and as a school, we have several trade programs along with after-school and summer programs for kids in the surrounding area."

There was something in his tone, in the way he spoke that assured Kitty Anne that Nick could go on about his camp for hours. He was holding back. Maybe because he didn't think she was interested, but the truth was Kitty Anne was fascinated.

"You really love this place, huh?"

"It's my dream," Nick stated simply. "I spent every day in jail planning this place. It's what kept me sane and gave me a sense of purpose."

Kitty Anne smiled at him, admiring that kind of dedication and passion. She wasn't sure she had it in her. She never really stuck with anything. As if reading her thoughts, Nick frowned over at her.

"What about you? Don't you have a dream?"

She did. One that lingered.

"I want a house," Kitty Anne confessed with a whisper. "A southern cottage with a wraparound porch and a white picket fence."

"Then you'll have it," Nick vowed without hesitation.

"I want lots of ornate lattice work."

"And a red tin roof?"

Kitty Anne smiled. He could read her mind, except Nick had forgotten a detail. "With a roof-top deck and a swing set so I can feel like I'm flying into the stars when I pump my legs."

"Done."

"You are so full of shit." Kitty Anne snorted.

"You don't even know me."

"I know you're quicker than quicksand," Kitty Anne shot back, all but daring him to say she was the same.

"And you're hotter than the sun," Nick returned, fighting back a smile that quivered at the edges of his lips.

"Then I guess you better watch out and make sure you don't get burnt."

"Sorry, sexy. The danger just makes it more fun."

On that, they agreed. Kitty Anne couldn't deny it. "So? Where does that leave us?"

"With you packing up your stuff and moving in here," Nick stated as if that were the obvious answer.

"And what about your stuff?"

"What about it?"

Kitty Anne smiled, feeling like a cat about ready to take down the canary. "I think I already explained this to you last night. I'm claiming this bungalow, and under its roof, I'm in charge. You want to stay here? You got to earn your keep."

* * * *

GD frowned as he watched the motel parking lot below. He was waiting for Kitty Anne to return home. She was due to arrive at any second. He had a surprise planned for her, which was just why GD was peeking around from behind his curtains.

His phone buzzed in his pocket, distracting him from his mission. It wasn't Nick. He'd already called to say that Kitty Anne was on her way back home to pack up her stuff. That was when he'd corner her. There would be tears, no doubt, and begging. He'd give in, eventually. Then he'd collar her, gift-wrap her, and return to the camp so that he and Nick could have some fun.

That was the plan, even if Nick didn't believe in it.

Alex would have, GD thought to himself as he saw the sheriff's name flashing on the cell phone's screen. Of course, the sheriff was a little crazy, so that might not have been the best endorsement.

"Hey, man." GD grunted out that greeting as he flipped the phone open and lifted it to his ear, his gaze returning to the parking lot below. "What's up?"

"We're having a party." Alex sounded excited by that fact. "A barbeque for Taylor and Ralph. You in?"

"Always." GD did not turn down free food. Neither did he miss a chance to hang out with his friends. "Can I bring a date?"

"As long as you bring some beer with her."

"How about some tea and potato salad?" GD suggested instead. Not much of a drinker to begin with, he wasn't about to get soused and let Kitty Anne take advantage of him. She would. He didn't doubt that.

"Whatever you want." Alex didn't sound concerned. "Just don't mention this to Heather. It's supposed to be a surprise for her, too."

"Uh-huh."

"What?"

"I didn't saying anything." GD was thinking it, though, and Alex knew it.

"There is nothing wrong or unusual about surprising a girlfriend with a little get-together to celebrate her family coming back from vacation," Alex insisted defensively.

"Girlfriend?" GD smirked at the use of that word. "Has Heather actually agreed to that?"

"Shut up."

"That's a no."

"You know what? You're uninvited!"

"Uh-huh."

There was a deep moment of silence where Alex accepted he couldn't win this argument, and GD silently gloated over having won. It ended with a sigh as Alex pointedly changed the conversation.

"So? Who you bringing?"

"Gwen."

"Good-bye, GD."

GD flipped his phone closed, unable to help but laugh. Alex was so easy to annoy and so much fun. Kitty Anne was going to love him, and, hopefully, she'd get along with Heather. He and Heather had been friends from the cradle, and he couldn't imagine that she wouldn't be a part of his life, but he knew things were changing. She had Alex and Konor now, and he had his own personal Venus.

Better yet, she'd arrived.

Retreating back into his room as he caught sight of Kitty Anne's little convertible pulling in below, GD felt the anticipation thickening in his veins as he listened for the sound of Kitty Anne in the adjoining room.

Chapter Thirteen

Kitty Anne entered her room and started talking as loudly as she could as she headed straight for the remote. Laughing and giggling and murmuring throaty come-ons to nobody, she clicked on a porno and turned it up loud before jumping on her bed. She began to thrust her hips back and forth, swinging her whole body and the mattress until the headboard began to bang against the wall as she moaned and squealed.

Sure enough, her phone rang within seconds. It was GD, and Kitty Anne could easily guess what he wanted. That was just why she ignored his call and picked up speed, all but screaming now as she thanked God and begged for it harder. A second later, her cries sharpened into real ones as she all but fell off her bed in shock as GD walked right in.

She knew he'd picked the locks before. After all, that was how he must have gotten her coat, but still his sudden seething appearance caught her off guard, and for just a half-breath, Kitty Anne wondered if maybe she'd pushed him too hard. It clearly took GD a minute to figure out that she was alone and screwing with him.

"Is this some kind of joke?"

"And where the hell did you come from?" Kitty Anne shot back in just as outraged a tone, even if her indignation was fake and his was very real.

"I thought…" GD's voice faded away as a scowl darkened, and Kitty Anne knew just what he was thinking and what he'd been about to say.

"What?" she demanded to know, seizing the moment to advance on him. "You thought I was with another man? That I would betray you like that?"

Now she had him cornered in his own lie because he not only thought it he also knew it, but he couldn't admit to that without revealing more than he wanted. That just pissed him off all the more. Kitty Anne could see it in the flush staining his cheeks and decided to put him out of his misery.

With a sudden reversal in attitude that left no doubt that she was acting out a role, Kitty Anne threw herself into GD's arms. She knew she shocked him as she burst into loud, overly dramatized wails. Almost instantly, she began begging for his forgiveness.

"Oh, GD, I've made a horrible mistake! I don't know how you'll ever be able to forgive me…but I *have* betrayed you." Kitty Anne looked up at him longingly as GD caught her in his arms and glared down at her.

"I didn't mean to do it, I swear! It was just…one of those things, but"— Kitty Anne jerked back with a sudden sniffle and dared to furl her brow into a scowl as she glared up at him and declared—"this really is all your fault!"

"What?" GD blinked, clearly reeling in confusion as he tried to keep up with her sudden shift in attitude.

"A woman has needs after all." She took a deep breath and let it out with a dramatic sigh and relaxed her expression into one that, hopefully, gloated with enough smugness to leave him in no doubt as to the sincerity of her words.

"And your friend Nick really knows how to satisfy them all…so, I guess I really owe you a thanks, don't I?"

GD stilled at that before groaning to himself. "Oh no."

"Oh yeah." Kitty Anne's tone tightened over those words as her gaze narrowed dangerously on him. "I know all about you and your buddy Nick's plan to make me feel guilty enough so I would…what? Wear your collar?"

"And let me do anything I want," GD drawled out hopefully.

Kitty Anne had to bite back a smile at that look, not interested in giving in just yet. "I could. In fact, I would have if you hadn't played this stupid trick, but now…I'm not sure I can trust you."

"That's rich, given I wasn't the one you were sweating up the sheets with last night," GD reminded her.

"So?" Kitty Anne shrugged. "I'm not actually under any obligation to be faithful to you. We had no agreement."

"It was unwritten," GD insisted without any real attempt to back that opinion with even a hint of indignation.

In fact, he was watching her with a glint twinkling in his eyes that reminded her of Nick. The two of them, they were as slippery as eels. She was in so much trouble, but that didn't mean she wouldn't go down without a fight.

"Then get a pen and a piece of paper, big man, because I'm changing the rules," Kitty Anne shot back. "Now there is only one. It says I'm in charge. You want in my bed? Then you better earn your keep."

"Is that right?" GD took a bold step forward, crowding into her personal space as he glared down at her in a blatant attempt to intimidate her. "And just what kind of payment system did you have in mind?"

"Nick's building me a house." Kitty Anne couldn't help but giggle as she pressed in against the hard, heated wall of his chest. "And he made me come harder than any other man ever has."

"That's a pretty low bar to set," GD whispered as he dipped his head, his lips brushing against hers in the softest of caresses before he lifted his head and stepped back. "But you're not wearing my collar, and I don't play with toys that aren't mine."

"So it's like that, huh?" Kitty Anne smiled. She did like a challenge.

"Yep. Just like that."

"You do know that I'm moving in with Nick, right?" Kitty Anne wanted to make sure she had the rules of this game right before she finalized her agreement. "We're going to be having sex…and lots of it."

"I imagine so."

"And that doesn't bother you?" If it didn't, that might bother her more than a little, but GD soothed that worry away before it could burrow deeper into her heart.

"Nick is different," GD stated softly. "He is part of us…and make no mistake. There is an us."

"Really? And are there any other people who are a part of us? Like, maybe, another woman?"

It was hard as hell to get those words out and impossible to make them sound unconcerned. GD's smile assured her that he heard the difference.

"And would you care? I'm using one of my payment questions," he quickly added, cutting off her answer before she could tease him with it. "You have to be honest."

No, she really didn't have to be, but she was anyway. "Yes, I care."

"And if I told you I was only interested in you, would you believe me?" GD pressed.

"Yes." She really would.

"Then you trust me?" GD pressed, and Kitty Anne knew just where he was headed.

"Yes." She really did.

"Then prove it," GD growled as he stepped back into her personal space. "Wear my collar."

Kitty Anne lifted her gaze to meet his and knew that he wouldn't be straying. That gave her the strength to let him go. Slinking backward, she slipped free of the oversized sweats she was wearing. They pooled on the floor as she faced GD.

"Make me," she dared him, all but certain of what he'd do.

* * * *

GD raked his gaze over Kitty Anne, savoring the sight of her lush, naked curves and knew what he had to do. It was going to be harsh and brutal. In the end, he wasn't even sure he knew that he had the strength to see his plan through, but that didn't stop him from reaching for his belt buckle as he stepped forward.

"On your knees, beautiful. It's time to convince me to see things your way."

That dark growl should have had her concerned, but Kitty Anne just smiled and sank gracefully to her knees. Then she spread them, opening up the plump folds of her pussy in a silent invitation as she clasped her hands behind her back and thrust her breasts forward.

"Like this?" Kitty Anne asked as she parted her lips, letting her tongue swept out to coat them in a glossy sheen that made GD's dick swell.

"Yeah, beautiful, just like that," he murmured as he fumbled with his zipper.

He was in a rush and could feel his self-control slipping away. A release, that was all he needed, just a break from this maddening lust, and then he'd be able to think straight. Freeing his aching length helped a little. Stepping up to fist his hand in the silky tresses of Kitty Anne's hair and forcing her head down over his dick helped a hell of a lot more.

GD breathed out with a rush of satisfaction as Kitty Anne allowed her tongue to roll around the thick length of his cock, warming him with her velvety caresses before engulfing him in the sultry heat of her kiss. With slow deliberation, she tasted her way down his shaft, making sexy little noises that quickly began to drive him insane.

She was enjoying herself, enjoying him, and that was just the hottest thing in the world. Kitty Anne's obvious delight fed his need, making his fingers tighten around her head and forcing her to go down, all the way down. She swallowed every last inch he fed her, taking him to the back of her throat and then down it as her tongue continued to spiral around him, intensifying the tight, moist constriction of her mouth as she pumped her head back up against his hand before sucking him back into the heaven he'd just discovered.

GD allowed her free rein to set the rhythm, and Kitty Anne didn't leave him disappointed as she set about enthusiastically sucking on his dick as though he was the best tasting treat she'd ever indulged in. She sure as hell was his because he couldn't remember a blowjob that had ever felt so damn good.

The heat building in his balls with every stroke of her tongue and pump of her lips flamed outward, warming him to his very soul and filling him with a delicious thrill that tickled up his spine. GD knew he was close to coming.

Kitty Anne's hands appeared to help him over the edge. She caught the tender sacs of his balls up in an exciting grip that had him taking control once again. GD forced her into a frantic pace that matched the wildly escalating pound of his heart. Then he was coming, hard and deep, in a release that sang through him as Kitty Anne pulled back and allowed the liquid proof of his climax to spray out over her chest until the heaving mounds of her breasts were coated in the white glisten of his seed.

In a move that he wanted to believe she could have learned only watching porn, Kitty Anne rubbed his cum all over her breasts as she gazed up at him with a hunger that she didn't even bother to disguise. Just in case he didn't get the message, she plumped up her breasts and lifted them high enough for her to dip her chin and try to lick them clean.

GD bit back a smile, knowing exactly what she was trying to do and wanting her to believe it was working…because, in a way, it was. She had already won. He had fucked her, and now he was going to punish her for making him break his promise.

"On the bed, now!"

* * * *

Kitty Anne thrilled at the snarl in GD's command and all but tripped over her feet as she rushed to the bed. He didn't even have to tell her to lie facedown. She assumed the position she suspected he would like the best and kept her knees bent and spread wide with her ass held high and the cool air caressing the heated lips of her pussy.

They were swollen and wet. She felt the arousal all but dripping off of them and slickening her thighs as GD paced slowly forward. He disappointed her, though, when he didn't immediately mount her like Nick had but, instead, paused by her nightstand.

A second later it dawned on her just what he was going for, but it was too late. GD had found the big, purple dildo she kept stored there for those nights when inspiration took hold. She didn't know what he intended to do with it, but she knew from the wicked curl of his smile that it wasn't good.

"Maybe we—*Ahhh!*"

Kitty Anne let out a squeal as GD smacked a palm across her ass, setting the rounded cheek to bouncing as it flushed with a heat that seared straight up her spine in a deliciously decadent whirl.

"I didn't tell you to move or give you permission to speak, beautiful," GD warned her. "Now you rest that cheek down against the mattress and stick that ass into the air because I'm going to give you the fucking of a lifetime."

"With that?" Kitty Anne snorted, unimpressed by his vow. She'd fucked that dildo enough to know that it was no lifetime lover. It was just good enough, and GD was better than that.

"I'm sure you have something else you could give me," Kitty Anne all but purred as she glanced pointedly down at GD's thick cock. It was still hard and ready to go again.

"I would," GD agreed as he leaned down to whisper in her ear. "But you see, I have this problem…apparently I'm not capable of satisfying your needs."

Those words echoed ominously through her head, and she recognized them almost instantly as her own. "Uh-oh."

"Don't worry, beautiful," GD consoled her, even as he reached a hand behind Kitty Anne to trace the enticing crease of her ass down to the slick folds of her cunt. His thick, blunt fingers rested there, a warm weight as he hesitated to offer her one last warning. "I don't hold grudges…I just get even."

He proved that point with the sudden, rough capturing of her clit. Pinning the poor, sensitive bud beneath the heavy weight of his thumb, GD began to massage the little bundle of nerves and make Kitty Anne whimper and mew as her whole world exploded with a sudden frenzy of sensation.

He became only more demanding from there. Kneeling down behind her, he used his own massive knees to force hers wider and open her completely up so he could watch as he fucked her favorite dildo deep into her cunt. Like an old, familiar friend, the hard plastic stretched her muscles enough to fill her with a delightful sense of fullness, though today it was a paltry thrill compared to the one Nick had introduced her to when he'd claimed her body as his.

That was just what Kitty Anne taunted GD with as she wiggled her ass and dared him to do his worst. Just as she'd hoped, that taunt broke through his control and had him going all the way down to the mattress as he slid beneath her. A second later he was pulling her down, capturing her cunt in an open-mouth kiss as he took command of the dildo once again.

This time he pounded the hard plastic into her with a strength and speed Kitty Anne simply didn't possess but, God, did she wish she did because the pleasure racing up her spine was intoxicating. It had her buzzing with a thrill that made every one of her muscles tighten with a rapidly building need that had her crying out for more.

He gave it to her, his tongue dancing over her molten flesh in an erotic teasing that was ticklishly delicious and focused on her clit. Fizzy bubbles of pleasure popped all along her spine as he twirled and pumped the little bud in beat with the hard plastic pillaging her cunt.

Kitty Anne couldn't help but laugh and thrust her pussy back down onto GD's tongue even as her sheath began to pulse with the first quakes of her release. They built into towering waves that crashed over her and had her crying out, both in ecstasy and despair as GD whipped the dildo free of her cunt, leaving her clenching down on nothing but the air.

A second later her world ripped apart as a shaft of pure, white-hot rapture shot straight out of her ass and up her spine as GD pumped her dildo right into her rear. He didn't ask. He didn't tease. He simply set up a rhythm that matched the relentless thrust of his tongue as it licked up the walls of her sheath and drove her release up another notch.

It was all too much. The pressure, the pleasure, the hint of pain, it all whirled together into an intense sensation that left her sobbing as her climax blossomed into a tiered mushroom that bloomed big and bright before caving back in on itself. Kitty Anne collapsed with it, every muscle in her body vibrating as she melted into the bed and allowed the exhaustion to claim her.

* * * *

GD stared down at Kitty Anne and listened to her snore. That hadn't gone the way he'd anticipated. Not almost from the beginning, but things had generally worked out to a draw between them, and he could live with that. At least for now because he had to get going.

After all, he had a few meetings this afternoon and hadn't planned on getting so badly sidetracked. In fact, he hadn't planned on spending any real time with Kitty Anne. She was supposed to have confessed, which she actually did do. He was supposed to have huffed off, leaving her to stew, but as usual, GD had gotten distracted by the sheer joy of being near his Kitty Anne.

He enjoyed playing with her, which was just why he tucked her under the covers with the dildo still buried deep in her ass. GD even paused to pen a note, warning her to keep it there until he caught up with her later and took care of the matter himself, not that he expected to actually have that chance. No doubt, Kitty Anne would have a fit over that note…or, maybe not.

GD debated the matter for the better part of the rest of the day as he headed out to Alex's barbeque. He didn't bother to wake and ask Kitty Anne if she wanted to go, knowing instinctively that she'd cause trouble simply as way to mess with him. She could meet his friends once she'd settled down a bit.

The party might have been fun, though Heather looked a little harried, but GD had more work to do. This time out at the club. He met up with

Slade Davis to go over the activities planned for the coming weeks and to discuss any issues with members or membership that had come up since they'd met two weeks before.

That was a long, tedious meeting, one he needed a drink to recover from. A stiff one. Unfortunately his ass had barely settled down onto one of the round, wooden stools that lined the bar in the men's den before he was thunked right between the shoulder blades by a rather pissed-off raven-haired beauty. GD turned to confront Lana, barely taking note of the woman's complete lack of clothing. That was pretty much the dress code for the women at the club.

Of course, Lana was above all those rules. As a co-owner and director of female services, she was the queen in a house full of kings. That thought had him thinking of Kitty Anne again. She could hold her own against Lana, but he'd be damned before he'd let his little Kitty Anne strut around naked in front of all these hound dogs.

"Did you tell Dylan that my brothers set that damn barn fire?"

GD sighed as he turned back to his drink, daring to irritate Lana even more by taking a fortifying sip before he confessed to the truth. "Yep."

"GD!" Lana's fists clenched at her sides, and if she'd been Kitty Anne, she probably would have thrown one of them, but Lana was more dignified than that.

"I had no choice." That was as far as he was willing to go when it came to an explanation, though GD knew that was not nearly far enough to satisfy Lana.

"Why not?"

"Can't tell you."

"GD!"

"*GD!*" He mimicked the high-pitched demand in her tone before casting Lana a smirk. "You can yell at me all you want, but you can't deny that your brothers had motive and opportunity."

"And if they were guilty, Alex would gladly have arrested them," Lana shot back.

"If you haven't noticed, Alex is a little busy these days," GD muttered as Lana slid into the seat beside him and hailed the bartender for a drink.

"I noticed our esteemed sheriff is hiding from Chase," Lana shot back. "So you see, your ploy didn't work."

"Then why are you here yelling at me?"

"I'm not going to let my brothers go down for this," Lana stated simply, giving him a familiar look.

She meant business, not that GD knew what she was really threatening. After all, when Seth had made a similar proclamation with the same damn glint in his eyes that was in Lana's right then, he'd intended to go down for his brother. Something told GD that Lana wouldn't be making that trip.

"You want to go broke defending those two…be my guest." GD shrugged, assuming that was what she meant. "I don't know why you'd waste your money. You've let them go down before."

"For petty shit," Lana corrected. "We're talking arson and attempted murder, here. You know what kind of sentences those carry?"

Hefty ones, but they had a saying for that. "Don't do the crime if you can't do the time."

That annoying cliché earned him a dirty look as Lana ordered up a second round for him and a first round for her. He could tell this was going to be a long argument.

Chapter Fourteen

"I got a job!"

Kitty Anne also had a sore ass and permanent blush, but she kept that information to herself as her mother lorded over her threshold like a gatekeeper with her hand out for the toll. Slapping the two hundred dollars she wouldn't be needing now to pay next week's rent onto her mom's palm, Kitty Anne was not shocked when her mother greeted both her bold declaration and her peace offering with nothing more than a skeptical scowl.

Lynn Anne took the cash and quickly counted it. Once she was sure Kitty Anne hadn't shorted her, the cash disappeared into the folds of her floral skirt. Only then did she bother to respond to Kitty Anne's happy announcement.

"Where?" Lynn Anne eyed her with a sparkle in her eye that assured Kitty Anne her mom was pleased. "The nudie bar?"

"Oh, for God's sake, Mother!" Kitty Anne huffed and rolled her eyes, but she had to force the annoyance into her tone because she was feeling so damn good even her mother couldn't ruin her mood.

She had not one but two amazing hot men at her attendance. More than that, Kitty Anne was going to have them both at the same time. That was after she won her little battle with GD. That thought spread a grin across her face she couldn't seem to control.

"Don't mother me," Lynn Anne shot back, clearly affronted by Kitty Anne's smile. "Do you know the social embarrassment I've had to put up with all this week?"

"It's only been a couple of days."

"It felt like a week!"

"Yes, Mom." Kitty Anne held up her hands, not wanting to argue over the issue. "I'm sorry you've been suffering, but now you can go tell all your snooty friends that I'm working in a charitable capacity out at the prestigious Camp D."

"Camp D!" Lynn Anne gasped in overly dramatized horror. "You can't possibly mean that prison for runaways and ragamuffins."

"I don't think they call them ragamuffins anymore." Actually Kitty Anne was pretty certain of it, even if she wasn't all the way up to date on current slang.

"They're heathens!"

"Mother—"

"Criminals!"

"Why don't you come out to the Camp—"

"Are you kidding me?" Lynn Anne reared back as if Kitty Anne had actually threatened her. "Is this your plan? Kill me for the inheritance?"

"What inheritance?"

"What do you mean, what inheritance?" Lynn Anne shot back as if it wasn't obvious. "What about my trailer? My figurine collection? My spoons! Some of those are worth real money. At least, two are worth about fifty dollars."

It took every ounce of self-control Kitty Anne possessed not to laugh in her mother's face because she knew Lynn Anne wasn't actually kidding. Kitty Anne managed, somehow, to swallow back every snotty, obnoxious, and disrespectful retort that came to her mind and settled on her default response.

"Yes, Mother."

"Oh, don't 'yes, Mother' me!"

"I'm sorry, Mom. I won't agree with you in the future."

"Well, now you're just being bratty," Lynn Anne huffed.

"Well, what am I supposed to say?" Kitty Anne asked. "I swear to you the boys are not dangerous, and the camp is more luxurious than any place you've ever been to."

"I doubt that." Lynn Anne drew herself up proudly as she reminded Kitty Anne of the only two trips she'd taken in her entire life. "I've been to both Graceland and Rock City."

"I have my own bungalow," Kitty Anne taunted her, knowing just what to say to have her mother marching back across the living room to get her purse.

"This I got to see to believe."

Fifty-three minutes later, Lynn Anne was staring at the closet full of male clothes and casting a brow in Kitty Anne's direction. She'd known this moment was coming. She'd sensed it from the moment they'd pulled up under the flowered arches that had welcomed them to Camp D. She'd made a mistake. She shouldn't have brought her mother here because Lynn Anne was in love and getting rid of her was not going to be that easy.

"Is there some kind of change you wanted to tell me about, young…um, lady?" Lynn Anne turned back to offer Kitty Anne a sly look that had Kitty Anne rolling her eyes.

"No, Mom, those aren't mine," Kitty Anne assured her as if it actually needed to be said.

"Obviously." Lynn Anne rolled her eyes as she closed the closet doors and moved on to the bathroom.

"They belong to the owner of the camp, Mr. Nick Dickles." Kitty Anne continued her explanation as if her mother had asked.

"I see."

"Technically this was his place."

"Mm-hmm."

"But he's lending it to me because there's no place for me to stay on the camp's campus."

"Uh-huh."

"He spent time in prison." Kitty Anne paused, but her mother didn't even blink as she surveyed the efficiently laid out bungalow. "So…we have *that* in common."

"Yes, well, sex does seem to be quite a marketable skill for you, my dear." Her mother tossed her a bright smile with that cheery encouragement.

"Hey, Kitty Anne, you want to join me for a—well, hello there." Nick came to an abrupt stop, right along with an offer Kitty Anne knew would have been more entertaining than watching her mother admire her new home.

"And you must be the infamous Mr. Dickles." Lynn Anne didn't introduce herself or extend a hand. Instead, she circled Nick, pointedly looking him over. "Well, at least you're normal sized."

"*Mother!*" Kitty Anne gasped, truly mortified and wondering if there would ever be a day when her mom didn't embarrass her.

"What?" Nick asked, glancing between Kitty Anne's blush and Lynn Anne's smirk. "What is going on?"

"Are you going to marry my daughter?" Lynn Anne demanded to know, pinning Nick with a pointed look that should have had him worried, but the damn man just grinned and relaxed.

"So you're the mother." Nick returned Lynn Anne's scrutiny and gave her a once-over but with a far less inappropriate eye. "I was warned about you."

"Lies." Lynn Anne drew herself up self-righteously and jumped to the wrong conclusion. "My daughter tells nothing but stories. Now answer my question, young man. Do you or do you not intend to treat my daughter with honor?"

"I swear to you, Mrs. Allison, that I plan to honor your daughter as well as treat her to the kind of loving care she deserves," Nick declared nobly, managing to make Kitty Anne's heart melt, even if his words had less effect on her mother.

"That's what they all say." Lynn Anne sighed. "So few actually mean it, but if you do, then you'll understand why I have to move in here."

"*What?*" Kitty Anne almost fell over at that proclamation, and she responded without thought. "No!"

"Yes." Her mother rounded on her with a cliché that Kitty Anne knew she didn't believe. "A man does not buy the cow if he's getting the milk for free."

"That is the stupidest thing I have ever heard, and you're not moving in here to protect me." Kitty Anne knew the truth. She knew her mother. "You're just jealous of my bungalow."

"Um...excuse me. Technically, it's my bungalow," Nick tried to interject, but neither woman paid him any mind.

"You always think the worst of me, but I'm doing this for your own good." Lynn Anne wagged a finger at Kitty Anne. "You're reputation is already in tatters. You can't live out here with all these men without a chaperon."

"I'm an adult woman, and it is the twenty-first century," Kitty Anne declared, taking her stand. "I can do whatever I want. I'm in charge here!"

* * * *

"You are kidding me, right?" GD asked hopefully, though the look on his face said he already knew the answer to that question. "You really let Kitty Anne's mom kick you out of your own home?"

Nick sighed. He wasn't thrilled about the current sleeping arrangements either. "I don't know how it happened. All I know is that woman scares me."

"That's because she's scary," GD agreed. "But that's not why you let her take over your house. You did it for Kitty Anne. Go on and admit it."

"I—"

"—am whipped," GD finished for him with a laugh.

"I am—"

"—whipped!"

"I—"

"Pussy whipped!"

"You're just jealous," Nick snapped back, irritated by GD's laughter. "Because you haven't had a taste of that."

"I could have a taste whenever I want," GD assured him. "At least, I'm not living in a dorm with three hundred boys."

"Yeah? And at least I'm living not ten minutes from Kitty Anne's front door." Nick had every intention of taking advantage of that fact.

"You mean Lynn Anne's door," GD corrected him. "Because you got to get passed mommy first."

That gave Nick pause as he considered that he should have arranged for Kitty Anne to meet him tonight after her mom had passed out, but he hadn't had a chance to have a single private word with her since Lynn Anne had showed up. That woman was something else.

"I don't know how she did it. I went back to work and before I even reached my office, she had half a dozen boys packing up my stuff and...well, look at it. My entire world reduced to boxes while dollies are now decorating the arms of my leather sofa!"

"The woman is evil." GD nodded as he sipped the root beer Nick had gotten from the vending machine at the end of the dorm's hall.

The thing didn't operate on cash but on tokens that the boys earned from exercising. It was a good system. They were good boys. Still, Nick would rather have been spending his nights with the plush comfort of Kitty Anne's curves than in a small bedroom that served a young boy's needs than a grown man.

There were actually full-sized apartments on each floor of the dorms. There were two, one at either end of the long hall. That was where staff normally stayed, allowing them to have both private space and keep an eye on the kids. The apartments were also all full, except for Saul's, but that unit was being cleaned and prepped for the next teacher.

The one Nick still had to hire.

That problem paled, though, in comparison to the other one he was facing.

"Lynn Anne has got to go."

"She's going to be the mother-in-law from hell."

"Oh God." Nick breathed out at that comment. He hadn't even thought about that. "You think maybe we could bribe her into leaving…like with a small condo down along the coast?"

"Good luck with that," GD shot back, sounding far from excited about that idea. "Something tells me that, despite all the attitude and antagonism, Lynn Anne and Kitty Anne are tight. Real tight."

Nick heaved a sigh at that, having to silently agree that he sensed the same undercurrents between Kitty Anne and her mother. After all, Kitty Anne was the one who'd brought her out there in the first place.

"Then I better plan on building two houses, or something tells me she's going to be living with us."

"Man, what is with these houses?" GD glanced up, pinning Nick with a pointed look. "You really planning on building them?"

"I got the land and it's not like I can move. I need to be near the kids." Which was just why Nick had bought the hill next door.

It was perfect and, given it wasn't on school grounds, he could even have a drink every now and again. That was a treat he shared with his staff. Kitty Anne, though, would be a private treat that shared his bed…and GD's.

"Kitty Anne wants a metal roof and wraparound porch with a lattice." Nick glanced up to share a look with GD. "You got any requests?"

"A gym."

"We got one here at the school."

"Not for us. For Kitty Anne." GD paused to offer Nick a toothy grin. "Or didn't you notice just how limber the girl was?"

"Trust me. I noticed." He'd like to be doing a lot more than that right then. "But we're talking about the house. So focus."

"Fine," GD grumped. "I want an office. If I'm going to live out here, I'm going to need a place to work...but I think I'd like for it not to be attached to the house. Maybe, I'll get a shed or something."

"You want to work in a shed?"

"Why not?" GD shrugged. "Put a light in it, cut a hole for a window and another for a window AC unit and I'll pee out the back door."

While that last bit might have made some people think GD was joking, Nick knew he wasn't kidding. The bastard really would pee out the backdoor. Nick would let that be Kitty Anne's problem. After all, GD's idea had some merit.

"Fine. Whatever. Go buy yourself a shed."

"Really?" GD frowned, eyeing Nick as if he were sick. "You don't mind if I go buy some nasty, used, redneck shed and plant it in your perfectly manicured yard."

"My yard is not manicured." Nick snorted, thinking of just how messy his yard had gotten lately. Between the heat and the camp overflowing with summer camp students, he hadn't had the time to keep up with simple maintenance.

"Please." GD snickered. "I've seen you on your knees next to the mailbox cutting the grass with scissors."

"So?" Nick really didn't get what was funny about that. "What am I supposed to do? A weed eater string would mar the wood post for the mailbox, and I can't just let the grass run wild."

"No, of course not," GD agreed, but Nick could hear the laughter in his tone.

"I really don't get what's funny here."

"And *that* is what is funny."

"Whatever." Nick dismissed. "You want to sit here and laugh at me or do you want to go see if we can liberate Kitty Anne from under Lynn Anne's watchful gaze."

"Well, if nothing else this should be entertaining," GD suggested as he followed Nick out of the dorm room and started down the hall with him. "Of course, you've got a logistical problem...no place to take the woman after you've absconded with her."

"Absconded?" Nick repeated, raising a brow at GD's sudden use of a big word.

"Would you prefer abducted?"

"I'd prefer it if you'd hush up and let me think," Nick shot back as he slammed open the door at the end of the hall.

It led out onto a large balcony. There was a long flight of stairs to the right. All dorms had to have extra entries and exits in case of a fire. These steps, while attractive, were built just for that purpose. They were wide and gently slopped downward, allowing both Nick and GD to all but race down them side-by-side.

Too soon, they reached the ground. Nick still didn't have an answer to the question plaguing him. Where were they going to take her?

Alex and Heather had already scandalized enough kids with the show they'd put on at the obstacle course just a week or so back. The obstacle course, now there was an idea.

It was completely encased in a thick wall of shrubbery that hid an even thicker wall of cinderblock. That made it nice and private, not to mention it was on the other side of the campus from the dorms, so they'd be far away from the kids, who should all be bedding down for the night. Even if one or two of the kids managed to skip out, they wouldn't make it into the obstacle course.

It was gated with a separate security system. Those were the requirements of the insurance company. They hadn't been particularly thrilled by the idea of the large obstacle course and had, ironically, made Nick jump through a number of loops before agreeing not to revoke his insurance.

Nick was betting that Kitty Anne would enjoy jumping through some loops. In fact, he bet she'd love it.

* * * *

Kitty Anne lay stretched out on the small couch she'd bedded down on and listened for the telltale sounds of her mother's deep-chested snores that assured her Lynn Anne had sunk far enough into her dreams that not even a grenade would have awakened her. Conversely there was no way any normal human being could sleep through the racket her mother was making.

That explained why Lynn Anne was with Mr. Whellon. That man was half-deaf and ugly to boot. He was rich, though, and Kitty Anne suspected that was what her mother found most attractive about the man. There really was nothing else to recommend him, and he had a wife, who was known to be ravenously jealous. Of course anybody who knew Mrs. Whellon couldn't blame Mr. Whellon for looking for affection elsewhere.

The woman was cold, bossy, and all-around unpleasant...not that Kitty Anne's mother was much different. So maybe Mr. Whellon had a type. Of course, Lynn Anne didn't boss Mr. Whellon around. No, she bossed Kitty Anne around. For some sick reason she couldn't explain, Kitty Anne let her.

So had Nick.

Kitty Anne knew he was just as confused as she was about how it was that Lynn Anne came to be the one sleeping in his bed. Somehow her mother had managed to cast Nick off to the dorms and demote Kitty Anne to the couch. She did it all under the guise of protecting Kitty Anne's honor, but they both knew that was a lie.

Her mother wanted something. The only question was what and Kitty Anne suspected she knew the answer—Nick's money. It was clear that Nick had done well for himself somewhere along the line because the campus below did not only appear large, it appeared perfectly tailored. There was just something about the design of it all that reeked of wealth.

Lynn Anne was attracted to wealth, but Kitty Anne wasn't going to let her mom use Nick like that. While she'd always taken care of her mother and always would, there had to be limits. Limits that one day she hoped she had the strength to enforce.

That day had not been today. Today, Kitty Anne felt like she'd regressed. Feeling very much like the teenager, all giddy and silly over her new boyfriends, Kitty Anne had embraced the regression. Why not?

If her mother wanted to treat her like a virginal child then she'd act like the wild one she'd actually been and sneak out of the house. Sneak out of the house to infiltrate an all boy's school in search of the hottest guy on campus? Just the thought kind of thrilled her. It added a forbidden element to her plans.

That was just why Kitty Anne had gone to sleep wearing a set of sexy black sweats and tank that clung to her body. She'd put her hair up into a ponytail but had been forced to forgo, making herself up more appropriately. After all, one did not wear makeup to bed.

At least she had shoes. Kitty Anne had planned accordingly, tucking a pair of sneakers beneath the couch, and thankfully, her mother hadn't noticed them on her final inspection before bed. Otherwise, she'd have put them in the closet, as was appropriate. After all, everything had a place, and everything was put in its place according to Lynn Anne.

Everything that was but Kitty Anne, who slunk out from beneath the covers and tiptoed across the floor to the front door. She was careful to grip the bells her mother had hung on the back of the door in a tight fist, assuring they didn't ring as she removed them and placed them silently on the little table that served as the entryway's counter. Then out the door she went.

Kitty Anne couldn't help but smile as she felt the cool night air crisp against her cheeks and the rough cement beneath her feet. It was as though she'd been transported back in time to her teenage years when she used to sneak out of her mother's trailer, normally to go run off and meet some boy. Tonight, though, she was older and felt the weight of her maturity as she considered how much trouble she might cause if she went down the hill to sneak through the boy's campus.

Being led around was one thing, but Nick had made it clear when he came to get her and her mother for dinner that women weren't really allowed on the campus. Nick was making an exception for meals, but also made it clear that they would be escorted to the dining hall for everyone.

Her mother had scoffed at his attitude, and Kitty Anne had a suspicion she was going to get kicked off of the campus. She certainly had appeared like she was trying to all through dinner. That had been an interesting experience, watching Lynn Anne eating with well over two hundred boys surrounding her.

Her mother had been torn between lecturing Nick about proper child-rearing techniques, snubbing GD, and correcting any boy that came too close to her about proper manners and how to treat a lady. It had been a long meal, and Kitty Anne hadn't even gotten a chance to ask GD why he was there, though she could guess.

He was up to no good. No doubt he'd arrived to see if she'd obeyed his outrageous demand and left the dildo in. He should have known better, and he probably did, which only meant it was time for her to be punished.

Normally, Kitty Anne wasn't much into those kinds of games but couldn't deny the wicked thrill that had her tense and eager at the very idea of GD dominating her, especially if he planned on doing it in front of Nick.

Nick was such a sweetie. It was almost cruel to unleash her mother on him. He was simply no match for Lynn Anne. Not that Kitty Anne believed for a moment her mother had vanquished either him or GD when she'd firmly told them good night over an hour ago and slammed the door to Nick's bungalow in his face. That had been a priceless moment, though not worth having to put up with her mother's traditional lecture. Lynn Ann had a beauty routine that took nearly two hours to complete. It ended with twelve hours of sleep, which meant the lights were out by nine, even though the sun was technically still up.

Who the hell could sleep when there was light still shining through the windows?

Not Kitty Anne. There was a reason why she preferred to live in a monthly suite at the motel than at home in her old bedroom.

Her mother was nuts or, as Lynn Anne would have said, two peas short of a pod. That right there made no sense, which went to prove Kitty Anne's original point. She didn't question whether her apple had fallen far from that tree, even as she began climbing the magnolia that draped over Nick's bungalow.

It had nice thick branches and fat leaves that hid her from sight even as she heard her men come grumbling down the path that led up from the dormitories down at the bottom of the hill. Soon enough they'd be right below her and Kitty Anne planned to drop down and give them the start of a lifetime. She knew that was a little childish, but it would also be funny.

"Will you *stop* that?" Nick's complaint weighed heavy in the night air, drawing Kitty Anne's attention to the two supposed knights in shining armor who had arrived to save her.

"Stop what?"

GD sounded innocent, but even from a distance, Kitty Anne could tell he was full of shit.

"Making that infernal racket."

"I'm whistling a tune."

"I don't think you know what a tune is," Nick muttered, and Kitty Anne had to agree.

She'd noticed that GD tended to like to whistle, but he couldn't hold a tune or follow along with one. Unlike Nick, though, Kitty Anne had found it kind of an endearing trait. Of course, her opinion might be a little colored by the lust that filled her whenever he was near. Nick, on the other hand, sounded far from entranced as he continued to pick on GD.

"And don't think I don't know what tune you're *trying* to whistle. This is not a death march," Nick informed him haughtily. "There is no need for you to whistle your own whacked-out rendition of 'Taps.'"

Kitty Anne smiled at that complaint as she slid along the shadowed curve of the bungalow until she could spy on the two of them marching across the yard toward the back of the small apartment. They were easily visible in the moonlight and were making no attempt to approach with any kind of stealth, not even bothering whispering.

"So you say, but I wouldn't test Kitty Anne's mom. That woman is scary," GD grumbled as their footsteps began to shuffle through the yard.

That Lynn Anne was, and Kitty Anne knew her mother would take that observation as a compliment because the truth was Lynn Anne was all bark. It was Kitty Anne they had to watch out for because she was planning on taking a bite or two. That thought had her grinning and scheming as GD pressed Nick for a plan of action.

"Well?" GD prodded as they came to a stop a couple of yards from the bungalow. "You got *any* idea of how to break Kitty Anne out of there?"

"I was hoping something would come to me..." Nick admitted slowly, not completely finishing that thought.

"And?"

"I was *hoping*," Nick stressed, shooting GD a dirty look easily visible in the bright light of the night as they stood out in the open.

Kitty Anne, on the other hand, kept to the shadows as she began to shimmy down the tree. She had every intention of coming up behind them and giving both men the start of their lives. Just the idea had her biting back giggles.

"You know, you could help here," Nick complained.

"Why?" GD snorted. "When it is easier and more entertaining to watch you come up with...nothing?"

"Okay, fine. I'll pick the lock."

"Something tells me that Lynn Anne is the type of mother to put bells on the doors," GD warned him, proving that he understood Lynn Anne pretty damn well. That probably explained why she'd been so against him. Kitty Anne's mother didn't want to be understood. She wanted to be believed.

"Then the windows," Nick retorted indignantly as he started forward.

"Don't try the one in the bedroom," GD warned him as he shuffled after the other man, seemingly completely unaware of Kitty Anne bringing up the rear.

She'd have announced herself, but it was kind of entertaining to watch the two friends plot their way through what was clearly supposed to be an abduction. Master criminals, they were not.

"I could do the one in the living room," Nick suggested. "But I got stuff under it."

"Stuff?"

"I could throw a pebble or something at Kitty Anne through the bedroom window." Nick perked up with that idea, but Kitty Anne found it lacking in a serious way. Thankfully, she had GD to echo her complaints.

"You're going to throw a rock at a woman and expect her to respond warmly?"

"Maybe it will hit her mother." Nick snickered at that thought, but GD wasn't as impressed.

"You really have lost your touch."

"Well, you know, it's been a while," Nick snapped.

"Really?" GD paused to shoot Nick a curious look. "Define a while? Are we talking weeks, months…*years*?"

"More like a year," Nick corrected, taking instant offense to GD's snicker. "What? I've been busy."

"Apparently not."

"Don't be a dick."

"I guess you really owe me a thank-you for sending Kitty Anne your way, huh?"

"I'm going in through the window in the bathroom," Nick declared, ignoring GD's smug question.

"Dude, man, you'll never fit through that one. It's tiny," GD pointed out, his smile fading into a frown as he considered the bungalow before them. "In fact this entire thing is tiny. Why didn't you build yourself something nicer?"

"It's all I really need." Nick shrugged as he started around the side of the building back toward the back once again. "Hell, it's like ten times bigger than my cell in prison, so why waste the money on extra space when the kids needed it more?"

That said a lot about the man, and Kitty Anne couldn't help but be warmed by this words. Nick would make a great father. GD...he probably would make some big babies. Hopefully not twins.

"You know, you should have just told her to meet us out here," GD suggested, sounding all too rational and superior. "That would have been the intelligent thing to do."

"And when would I have gotten a chance?" Nick shot back. "Lynn Anne wouldn't even let me sit next to Kitty Anne at dinner!"

"No," GD contradicted him instantly. "Kitty Anne wouldn't let you, because she's the one who is letting her mom run wild."

That put a frown on Kitty Anne's face. Clearly, GD didn't understand her mother if she thought Kitty Anne had any control over the woman. The only thing she could have done is thrown her out, called the cops, and had them arrest her or something. That was ridiculous. After all they were talking about her mother.

"You know how to pick that lock?" GD asked after a few moments of silence.

He was back to eyeing Nick with a smirk and twinkle of amusement glinting in his gaze. Kitty Anne could see how this was going to go and considered that it was time to announce herself.

"It's not locked." Nick shot back, along with a waggle of his brows as he reached out to shove it open.

"That's because it's alarmed," Kitty Anne warned him, but it was too late.

She got what she wanted. She startled the crap out of both men. At the very sound of her voice, Nick jerked, his hands banging into the window and setting off the piercing wail of the motion sensor her mother had taped to all the windows.

All three of them froze for a second, but the light bursting on in the bathroom jarred both men out of their stupor. Before Kitty Anne knew what had hit her, she was being tossed over GD's shoulder as he and Nick raced back across the yard. In the distance, from behind, she heard her mother hollering out the window at them.

* * * *

GD heard Kitty Anne laughing and her mother shouting out antiquated terms at them, like "heathens" and "scoundrels." It wouldn't have shocked him to turn around and see Lynn Anne trying to fit her way through the small window to chase them down, but thankfully, she had a little more sense than that.

That didn't mean they weren't all going to pay a heavy price for tonight's escapades. So they might as well make them worth it. That was just what GD had in mind as he carted Kitty Anne into the obstacle course that Nick had prepped for a little evening entertainment.

GD had to give it to him. Nick had managed to make a muddy, rough-hewn course look like a fantasy with all the torches casting a flickering glow across the enclosed field. The wall had been an insurance necessity, but tonight it provided an intimate privacy GD and Nick had every intention of taking advantage of right along with the woman flung over his shoulder.

GD lowered Kitty Anne back to her feet before the arched, ancient-looking entrance to the obstacle course. She barely noticed the architecture, much less bothered to look around at where they'd carted her off to. Instead, Kitty Anne checked her hair with a quick hand before striking a pose with her hip out and her lip curled in a saucy look he knew she had to have practiced. It was just too perfect, as was the purr in her tone.

"Well, if it isn't my two Prince Charmings." Kitty Anne shook her head at both him and Nick, who was breathing a little hard beside GD. "You two are really slick. You know that?"

"And look at you," GD growled back, raking a gaze down Kitty Anne's svelte form. "You're all dressed up for the occasion."

"And here I thought you'd want me undressed for it," Kitty Anne shot back, quick as ever. "Of course, I might be a little more undressed than you demanded."

GD knew exactly what she was referring to, the dildo he'd left stuck in her ass. He already knew she'd taken it out, but the fact that the woman could tease him about the matter while smiling suggestively at him just went to prove that Kitty Anne really was a custom-made Venus just for him...and Nick.

"Oh good God, no." Nick made a face as he shook his head at her. "I'd hate for you to get rope burn in the wrong place."

Kitty Anne's mouth opened on a retort that went silent as Nick's words hit her. "Excuse me?"

"Take a look behind you." GD nodded over Kitty Anne's shoulder, causing her to turn slowly around to take in the romantically lit obstacle course.

"Oh my," Kitty Anne whispered as she strolled slowly forward. "What in the world is this?"

"In one word? Fun," Nick assured her as he stepped up to take her hand. "Please, allow me to escort you, madam."

"Why certainly, sir," Kitty Anne returned, matching his polite diction with the similar southern drawl that was slightly overemphasized, no doubt for effect.

GD followed after them, listening with half an ear to Nick explain how they'd held a competition that included the boys learning enough about history and engineering to help design and build the course before them. Then they'd run it in a rite of passage that had taken them from boyhood to manhood, or that had been the story.

Kitty Anne certainly seemed to eat it up, and she was all too eager to give the course a try, or as much of one as they could in the dark. The shadows made everything harder and, just as Nick had promised, more fun.

Kitty Anne held her own as they competed against one another, surprising GD with both her strength and her flexibility, as well as turning him on with the promise of such limber stamina. He really had to get his collar on her because he just wasn't going to survive a long wait.

And why should he wait?

All he'd vowed was not to fuck her. Technically it could be argued that "fuck her" meant sticking his penis into her vagina. That didn't mean it couldn't be stuck other places. Just like earlier today, that left a whole lot of options open, but GD moved too slowly. Nick cut him off, advancing ahead of both GD and Kitty Anne as they all climbed down the heavy cargo net draped over a fifteen-foot wall. Nick reached the bottom and caught Kitty

Anne within the net, using the thick rope to bind her wrists as she giggled and squirmed, teasing him with breathless questions about just what he planned to do.

Nick didn't answer her. Instead, he showed her…and GD.

Chapter Fifteen

Kitty Anne's heart caught in her throat as Nick pinned her back into the rope webbing. He smiled down at her, and her cunt clenched, weeping because she knew that look. He was hungry, and she was his snack, his ready and eager-to-be-eaten snack.

"Did you want something?"

Daring to taunt him with that teasing question, Kitty Anne wrapped her hands around the ropes and clung to them as she arched upward against the hard wall of his chest. The pointed tips of her nipples caught on her bra as they ground into his heated strength and she couldn't help but moan and repeat the electrifying caress.

"I think it's you, sexy, who's looking to get something," Nick growled out, his tone as dark and deep as the wicked intentions gleaming in his eyes. "I'm the one who is looking to give it."

"I won't argue with that," Kitty Anne assured him. "I'm willing to play the virginal sacrifice if you're interested in being my rampaging barbarian…with a buddy."

All but purring in anticipation over her words, Kitty Anne shifted her gaze as GD dropped down onto the platform beside Nick. She hadn't forgotten about him. In fact, a part of her had felt deliciously naughty coming on so boldly to one man in front of another, especially when she was planning on fucking both men in the very near future.

"Prove it. Strip." Nick stepped back, releasing her and giving her the freedom to obey or flee.

"Sacrifices don't heed any commands," Kitty Anne informed both of them as she slid free of the ropes and down onto the same wooden platform they stood on. "Because savages don't make any. They simply take what belongs to them."

There was a second of mutual understanding about what she was all but daring them to do, and then GD lunged forward, but Kitty Anne was quicker. She managed to duck under Nick's arms and fly back up the cargo rope ladder behind her before either man could catch her. Then she was sailing through the air as she grabbed onto a set of handlebars and stepped off the platform to ride a tension line all the way back down to the ground and straight into Nick.

He was waiting for her, but she caught him off guard with some fancy moves that had him on his ass before he could even figure out how she'd managed that feat. Kitty Anne wasn't lingering around to explain things to him. She was running, flying through the mud to reach the log roll, but before she could test her balance and dexterity, she found herself being swooped up as GD caught up with her.

He lifted Kitty Anne right off her feet without ever missing a stride. Cradling her in his arms, he leapt up on the first log, which was actually big and padded instead of wooden. It rolled just the same, and suddenly Kitty Anne found herself dangling in the air, feet above a mud pit as GD jumped from log to log effortlessly.

He was showing off, and Kitty Anne couldn't help but think that if he were a peacock he'd have his feathers spread now. Such a display just for her benefit deserved a reward of some kind. So Kitty Anne shrieked with dismay and played the role of the frightened damsel as she turned to wrap her arms around GD's neck and cling to him.

Not shockingly, they made it safely to the other side, where Nick was waiting for them, but apparently, GD wasn't in the mood to share, at least not authority. Instead, he held on to Kitty Anne as he eyed Nick and issued a thinly veiled warning.

"To the victor goes the spoils, man. To the loser goes nothing."

"Wouldn't I technically be the loser?" Kitty Anne interjected, not wanting them to fight, especially not over her. This would never work if they did.

"No, sexy, I think you're the spoils," Nick corrected her before turning a calculating look back on GD. "Of course, I'm a little more than the loser. Aren't I, big man?"

"I don't know." GD shrugged, but there was a sparkle growing in his eyes that reassured Kitty Anne they were simply messing with her. "What do you think you are?"

"I'm a tool."

A bark of laughter shot out of Kitty Anne at that comment. She didn't mean to laugh. It just happened. It wasn't appreciated. That much was clear from the dirty look Nick shot her.

"Not *that* kind of tool."

Nick's gaze shifted back up toward GD's, and Kitty Anne felt a trickle of unease dance down her spine as they shared a look. This was definitely planned, and she'd walked into some kind of trap. She had a pretty good idea of what kind. Even if she hadn't, GD made her position perfectly clear as he nuzzled his lips up alongside the curve of her ear and whispered into it.

"More like the kind that's a little more flexible and whole hell of a lot more useful than a dildo...which I'm assuming you took out?"

"You didn't really think I was going to walk around like that all day, did you?" Kitty Anne shot back, the scoff clear in her tone, but GD didn't look as though he was joking.

Neither did he respond as he finally released her. Allowing her legs to slide down until her feet touched the ground, GD caught her wrists as they followed suit, slipping from around his neck. With his hold, he forced her arms high above her head, making Kitty Anne's position clear—she was captive. GD was master, and Nick...Nick was a tool.

"Rip the clothes from her body," GD commanded.

"Then I won't have anything—Hey!"

Kitty Anne's complaint turned into a shriek as Nick did just as GD demanded. He closed in on her, making short work of tearing through her sexiest workout outfit, despite Kitty Anne's attempts to get away. There was no escaping, not with GD's firm grip leashing her in place. The fact that it took him only one hand turned her on almost as much as the erotic thrill of being stripped for their pleasure, a pleasure they intended to claim out here in the middle of the night.

Just the thought had her flushing with a wicked thrill as the sultry night's air caressed her heated flesh. Her breasts felt swollen and heavy, her cunt soft and wet, and with every fiber of her being, she ached. She wanted this, wanted them, and there was no point in fighting it anymore.

Not that she really put much effort into the fight in the first place, but Kitty Anne did stop wiggling about. Going still, she pinned Nick with a grin as she arched her back and thrust the pointed tips of her breasts upward.

"See anything you like, Mr. Dickles?"

"Don't taunt the man," GD cut in. "This is my show, beautiful. I'm in charge here."

"See?" Kitty Anne shot Nick a smirk. "I told you he couldn't satisfy my needs...at least, not without assist—*ahhh!*"

Kitty Anne started when GD's palm cracked over her swollen folds, squealing with the sudden, shocking explosion of the stinging heat that shot out of her cunt. She twisted with the searing pleasure that ripped through her. It was deliciously wicked and wrong, and she wanted more.

"—assistance," Kitty Anne finished when she finally caught her breath, refusing to be cowed and hoping to be punished. "You should have seen what he had to use earl—*ahhh!*"

That one was better because this time she had her legs open, and her hips arched, assuring that the intimate flesh of her pussy was vulnerable to the sharp crack of his palm. The intense rush of searing rapture had Kitty Anne panting hard as the buzz flooding through her lasted a little longer that time.

"—ly, early! *Ahhh!*"

Kitty Anne squealed as, this time, the hard curve of his palm ground down over the sensitive bud of her clit. That little bundle of nerves had swollen with a rush of heat that magnified a thousand times in that second, causing her cunt to melt and the thick cream to drip down her thighs. The air thickened with the scent of her arousal along with her cries as GD spanked her again, paddling her pussy until Kitty Anne was weeping with the pressure that built up inside her.

She needed a release. She needed to be fucked. That was what she begged for, but GD didn't have that kind of mercy in him, and Nick...Nick was a tool. He did just as GD commanded.

Plumping up her breasts in either of his hands, GD dared to release her, but Kitty Anne didn't interfere as he ordered Nick to take a taste. Instead, she wound her arms back around GD's neck, keeping them up and behind her head as she offered herself up to Nick while his mouth descended over her breasts.

Feasting on the hard, puckered tips of her nipples, he licked and nibbled his way from one peak to the other. The velvety caress of his tongue teased and tormented, even as the hard ridge of his teeth scraped down over her sensitive tits in a dark warning. Kitty Anne's breath caught as the pleasure and anticipation twisted into a need that GD answered. His callused fingers captured her tips in a rough caress, starting a war between him and Nick.

They fought over her flushed flesh, making Kitty Anne moan and writhe in sensual delight. She felt sexy and beautiful, worshiped and adored and, more than anything, hungry. Giving in to the primal instincts flaming to life within her, Kitty Anne twisted away from both Nick's kiss and GD's touch as she turned in the big man's arms before slowly sinking down to her knees.

Kitty Anne caught and held his gaze as she reached for his belt buckle, silently daring him to order her to stop. He didn't make a sound, didn't even seem to breathe as she pulled the leather straps of his belt apart and eased the metal tab of his zipper downward. The thick length of his dick eagerly fell into her palm, having already outgrown the seam in his boxers.

She smiled, but before she could dip her head and take a taste of her treat, a set of hands clamped down around her ankles and jerked her backward. Nearly falling on her face, Kitty Anne caught herself and ended up on all fours, which was apparently just how they wanted her.

"That's better," GD growled down at her as he reached out to fist a hand in her hair. "That's the way it's supposed to be with the big dogs in charge…not little kitties."

She had a response to that. Kitty Anne just didn't get a chance to get it out before Nick struck once again. Shifting his hold to her thighs, he shoved them wide open and bent down to cover her cunt in an openmouthed kiss that had her gasping.

"You make me come before he makes you come, beautiful, and you can have two dicks for dessert tonight," GD vowed, tantalizing Kitty Anne with the very idea of having both him and Nick.

It sent both a shaft of excitement and a curl of apprehension through her. She was still a little sore from the toy, and it was barely half the size of either of her men, but Kitty Anne didn't think she had to worry about that.

Not with Nick's kiss lingering over the lips of her pussy. He teased and tickled her as he tried to suck the cream from her heated folds before parting them to devour the sweet inner flesh of her cunt.

Kitty Anne moaned over GD's cock as she began to return all the pleasure Nick fed her as he fucked his tongue into the tight clench of her sheath, teasing her with just a hint of what it would be like when he took her for real. She treated GD to the same as she sank down over his cock, keeping her lips puckered and tense as she sucked his sensitive length as deep as she could go.

Then she swallowed and earned a few moans of her own. That guttural noise pleased her in ways that the tongue fucking deep into her clinging depths never would be able to. The sounds of GD's pleasure fueled her own, making Kitty Anne frantic as she devoured his dick, fucking him fast and deep and challenging Nick to keep up.

He didn't have a problem with that. Abandoning her sheath, he trapped her clit beneath the soft, velvety weight of his tongue and began to torment her with a whirlwind of quick strokes and long, suckling nibbles that had her losing rhythm as her focus splintered between her delight in the taste and feel of GD's meaty cock and the rapturous heat pounding out of her clit and sending her blood boiling through her veins. She was burning up from the inside, and there was no holding back the release as she came in an ecstatic rush.

Her cunt pulsed and wept, desperate for the hard feel of a cock, and Nick didn't deny her. Slamming into her from behind and screwing a squeal right out of Kitty Anne, he didn't hesitate to start fucking her with a hard, fast rhythm that matched the one GD set as the hand buried in her hair took control of her motions. He began pumping her up and down his length, racing her to the finish line.

This time Nick stopped short, leaving Kitty Anne hanging, even as GD's shout of fulfillment ripped through the night with the same force of the release that shot out of him. She was forced to swallow quickly or take another bath in his seed. As hot as that had been, there wasn't a shower convenient this time. Besides, he tasted delicious, and she couldn't help but savor her victory.

Lost in the moment, she forgot all about Nick until he shifted. Slowly he began to drag the thick length of his dick down the aching walls of her sheath. Her pussy pulsed and clenched in a desperate and vain attempt to hold him captive. Even as she failed, Kitty Anne caught her breath in anticipation of him pounding himself back deep into her, but instead, the rounded head of his cock stretched the entrance to her cunt wide before he popped free, leaving her empty and annoyed.

Throwing off GD's hold, Kitty Anne glanced over her shoulder, but before she could demand an explanation from Nick, he fucked two thick fingers back deep inside her. They were a paltry offering, but there was something strangely erotic about watching him watch as he pumped his fingers in and out of her cunt.

He teased her sensitive walls with a quick caress as they gathered up the creamy proof of her arousal and retreated, leaving her feeling achingly empty once again and all too aware of the sticky path his fingertips left as they traced the crease that flowed from her cunt to her ass.

Kitty Anne whimpered as he teased her opening, much as he had done the other night. Just like then, he pressed past the clenched ring of muscles guarding her entrance and stretched her wide enough that the pleasure and pressure blurred into an intense ache that had her arching into his touch.

"Tonight, beautiful," Nick whispered as he twirled his fingers, making her mew for more. "Tonight, this ass is mine."

"Promises. Promises," Kitty Anne panted out, daring to taunt him with a smile. "Besides, you're too late. GD already claimed my ass…isn't that right, stud?"

Turning her attention on the big man, who was carefully pumping his thick dick. He was clearly stroking himself back up to full-size, and Kitty Anne couldn't help but tease him, too, as she eyed his meaty erection.

"You need some help with that?"

"I think I got it," GD grumbled as he cast a smoldering gaze in her direction. "Thanks."

There was a wealth of meaning buried in that one word, making it something far from a simple expression of gratitude. Instead, it sounded like a warning, but Kitty Anne didn't have time to guess at the threat, not with Nick sliding his cock between the cheeks of her ass. With slow strokes, he pumped himself up and down her crease, taunting her each time with a gentle press against her forbidden entrance before finally allowing his cock to slip farther down to lodge against the aching opening of her cunt.

It wasn't the dark fantasy he'd promised her, but the feel of Nick sliding slowly into her sheath had Kitty Anne's toes curling with the kind of pleasure she'd grown addicted to over the past day. He felt so good, and so did GD as he stepped up to press Kitty Anne backward until she was forced up onto her knees with her back settling against Nick's chest.

The new position had her cunt constricting around Nick's dick and left her gasping for breath. She wasn't given a chance to find it as GD's hands lifted to capture her breasts as Nick slid one hand down between the press of their bodies to plunder the molten folds of her pussy. He pinned her clit beneath the heavy weight of his thumb. Together they tormented her, driving Kitty Anne to the peak of a release with just their touch.

The world faded away until only the pleasure whirling through her existed. It grew more intense by the second as Nick slowly began to shift. He fucked her with even, measured strokes as GD's head dipped as he rained heated, little kisses all down over her breasts before taking a gentle nibble at her nipple.

Kitty Anne squealed and bucked, fucking Nick back as she gave over to the primitive urges taking command of her muscles. They were fed and fueled by the feel of the two men holding her tight between them. Kitty Anne was surrounded by their heat and hardness, and for the first time, she actually felt small and delicate and wondrously vulnerable.

Then all she felt was wondrous as her climax claimed her, making reality sparkle with a rapturous sheen that had her laughing even as she convulsed with the pleasure. GD held her close, his lips capturing the cries that fell from hers as she gave herself over to her release.

Kitty Anne returned his kiss with wanton abandon, drinking in not only his taste but his desire, too, as he pinned her close and held her steady while Nick slowly pulled free of her body. She knew what came next, could feel GD's excitement as his palms spread over her ass and pulled her cheeks apart for Nick, whose flushed cockhead was leaving a searing and sticky trail as it slid back up to the clenched entrance to her ass.

Her breath caught as she instinctively clenched, making his invasion all the more intense as Nick forged inward. Sliding slowly deeper, he stretched her barely-used muscles wide, making Kitty Anne mew and clutch desperately at GD. His lips lifted to catch the tears that began to gather along her lashes before they could fall.

He held her close, whispering incoherent bits of comforting clichés as Nick continued to claim her in the most feral of ways. It would have helped, though, if the two of them would have allowed Kitty Anne to kneel down and wiggle through the electrified fizzles of delight singing through her, but instead Nick and GD kept her upright and strung out with a pressure building inside of her. Kitty Anne almost feared what would happen when it finally snapped free.

"Relax." GD growled out that command as if he could force her to obey.

He was smarter than that and reached down to cup her cunt and tease her clit. Nick had abandoned her pussy to hold on tight to her hips, trying to control Kitty Anne's reflexive motions as the need and want twisted through her with an intensity that was fed only by the pleasure of GD's touch.

His big, blunt fingers stroked over her sensitive flesh in a gentle caress that had her melting as her body began to adjust to Nick's invasion. Settling the full length of his erection deep into her ass, he hesitated, giving Kitty Anne the time she needed to adjust to the thick, hard feel of him.

In fact, Nick didn't move until she twisted hard in his hold, trying to break it and the leash holding back the savage roar of ecstasy gathering deep within her. Only then did he give in to the need already pounding through her veins and begin to move, much to Kitty Anne's delight.

She was still tight, but not painfully so.

Now, instead, the pressure that bloomed through her held a tantalizing edge, one that had her shifting beneath Nick and gasping over the pleasure those little motions sent spiraling up her spine. Those thrills grew in intensity as Nick began to gently sway, lending a beat to the delight fizzling through her.

It burnt away the last shreds of her doubt, along with any hint of reservation, leaving Kitty Anne at the mercy of her own feral lusts. They drove her forward into the storm as her hips flexed with a desperate franticness that had her fucking Nick back with the same ferociousness with which he rode her...not that he was really riding her.

Their position allowed for only so much motion, but Kitty Anne knew how to fix that.

Shoving GD backward, she caught the big man off guard and sent him crashing onto his ass. Kitty Anne was on him in an instant, bending over and pinning him to the ground, even as she offered her ass up to Nick. He pounded into her with a force that had her mewing as the pressure bloomed out of her pelvis in a glorious frenzy that only fueled her need for more.

She wanted everything. She wanted it right then, but there was no way either man would give her the room to crawl up GD's length and claim the deliciously thick cock bobbing beneath her nose. That didn't mean she couldn't enjoy having him another way.

Smiling with that thought, Kitty Anne cupped her breasts and caught the heated length of his dick between her soft curves and angled his weeping head right up to her lips. She treated him to a sensual massage as she dipped her lips to suck and nibble on his swollen head as though it was a lollipop she couldn't get enough of.

GD grunted, straining visibly as the sweat built up along his brow, but he let her run free, enduring the sensual torment. He had to know his resistance just drove her to push him even harder. That was just what Nick was doing—pushing even harder. He was pushing in all the right places, too.

Kitty Anne had never even dared to dream that it would feel so good to have a man fucking her ass with the kind of abandon Nick had given himself over to, but each hard thrust lit her up with another round of electric thrills. They came brighter and faster until the shine blinded her to all else. The whole world faded away, and only distantly did Kitty Anne sense Nick picking up speed until he cried out and whipped himself free of her body.

A second later Kitty Anne felt the heated proof of his release rain across her back as Nick continued to pump his pulsing length up between the cheeks of her ass. That warmth was matched by the spray raining down over her chest as GD grunted out his own words of satisfaction. Together, both men claimed her in the most primitive way two men could mark a woman as theirs…well, maybe, not the *most*, but they'd get to that, eventually.

Chapter Sixteen

Tuesday, June 3rd

The next day dawned bright and frigid for Kitty Anne as she woke to a mother who was barely speaking to her, not that Lynn Anne needed words to express the thoughts in her head. The glare she beamed in Kitty Anne's direction said it all. Still, that was nothing compared to the intensity of the scowl she pinned on Nick when he arrived to escort them both to breakfast.

The real kicker, though, was when Nick reached for her hand, only to have his knuckles racked by a stick Lynn Anne had shoved up her sleeve. The hit shocked both Nick and Kitty Anne into a momentary stupor as her mother explained that Nick had, no doubt, gotten more than a handful the night before and that was all he would be getting. With that proclamation made, Lynn Anne ordered Kitty Anne to move it, pointedly placing herself between Kitty Anne and Nick.

That probably was when Kitty Anne should have objected, but this was her mother, and it was hard not to obey direct commands. Besides, Kitty Anne reasoned, Lynn Anne had lost a major battle last night. It was to be expected that she'd try to pick new ones that morning. Her mother was looking for a way to irritate her, and Kitty Anne wouldn't give it to her.

At least, she tried not to, but it was hard with Lynn Anne pushing Kitty Anne at every turn. She shadowed her daughter's every move, commenting and criticizing Kitty Anne, the camp, the boys, the very air itself. Nothing was spared her foul critique. Typically, she ruined everything, making it hard for Kitty Anne to focus as Nick showed her the classrooms. None of them would be hers, at least not permanently.

Nick was apparently making special arrangements for her. Kitty Anne didn't ask what and he didn't elaborate except to explain that she could use Saul's room until everything was settled.

She wouldn't be working with more than one kid at any time.

Her job over the summer was to assure that they didn't fall behind when it came to reading and writing skills. He didn't talk about during the school year and Kitty Anne could all but sense Nick's nervousness. She had a feeling he didn't expect her to last that long. At least, not as a teacher.

Kitty Anne suspected she was more of a placeholder.

All of the boys had been tested when they arrived at the camp, and not shockingly, many were behind their grade level when it came to core academic subjects. Nick explained that to maintain state and federal funding the boys were tested every year and always needed to be progressing. Fallbacks could, and would, endanger the camp's accreditation.

Fortunately there was another English teacher, who went by the moniker Dr. J, who would help her settle in and figure out the program. Kitty Anne was very relieved to meet him. Needless to say, her mother wasn't. She made as many snide comments as a person possibly could while Dr. J explained how the boys were all to be given assignments that they worked to complete, and based on her judgment of their success, they'd be awarded points that they could use like currency at the camp.

Basically they bribed the kids to learn.

The boys could do all sorts of things with their points, like "buy in" to activities or "purchase" food. They even were allowed to sell their points to each other. According to Nick, they mostly paid another kid to do a chore for them, though sometimes they paid for services like fixing something.

Learning to fix things was sort of a big deal at the camp, Kitty Anne quickly discovered. The kids were all learning trades, though they were masked as activities. There were traditional woodshop, auto shop, and landscaping groups, but there were also computer labs dedicated to teaching everything from how to program to how to use computers to design all sorts of things. They even had a 3D printer.

There was an actual literary club, mostly dedicated to what Nick called graphic novels but were just comics. She'd never been much of a comic person but would now be the advisor to the club, which should prove interesting, though probably not half as amusing as watching her mother's eyes bulge out as she took in the big-breasted, half-naked heroine drawn in scene after scene of the homemade comic one of the kids had done.

Truthfully, the kid had talent. So did her mother. Lynn Anne was gifted with an affinity for drama and actually clutched her chest as she dropped the comic and gasped theatrically.

"Well, that is just filth!" she declared with such rigorousness that Kitty Anne couldn't help but snicker. Nick wasn't laughing, though.

He'd been tolerant of Lynn Anne to that point, but she had apparently pushed too far this time, and he stepped forward to come between Lynn Anne and the thirteen year-old artist she'd just insulted.

"I have to remind you that you are the guest here, Mrs. Allison, and it isn't appropriate for you to speak in such a manner to one of my kids."

"*Excuse me?*" Lynn Anne blinked in innocent horror as she stumbled back like Nick had actually threatened her.

"These boys put a lot of passion and attention into their work, and the only thing filthy in here is *your* attitude."

"Well I never!" Lynn Anne declared as she lifted up her skirt and swept it aside to storm out of the room as if she were some kind of matron of the ball making a grand exit.

Kitty Anne watched her go. While she was impressed that Nick had dared to stand up to her mother and touched that he had done so for the kids, that didn't change what their future held.

"We're going to pay for that," Kitty Anne muttered, knowing in her gut that her mother was off to claim revenge.

"You don't think she just might leave?" Nick asked hopefully, but Kitty Anne couldn't let him cling to that delusion.

"Sorry," she apologized as she shook her head. "The more insulted she feels, the more likely she is to dig in."

"Great."

God only knew what trouble Lynn Anne intended to cause, but the day did go much smoother from there. Nick left Kitty Anne with Dr. J, who stayed with her as the boys started to trot in for their tutoring sessions. Up to date on what most of the boys were doing, he helped catch Kitty Anne up. She was thankful for his assistance.

She'd never really dealt much with children and was a little unnerved by many of the boys' blatant interest. It soon came to her notice that she was the only woman on campus, she and her mother that was. She was dutifully informed by more than one kid that Nick preached on how women distracted men from accomplishing their goals.

She could have, and probably should have, taken exception to those comments. Dr. J had been quick to explain that most of the boys there were easily distracted by the opposite sex. Kitty Anne understood. She wasn't much better.

All day, thoughts of Nick and GD and the things they'd done out at the obstacle course had her flushing with a warmth that had nothing to do with the afternoon summer's sun. Kitty Anne couldn't help but wonder how she was going to escape her mother when the sun went down...and just what kind of decadent delights Nick and GD had in store for her that night.

They better have something planned because she wasn't putting up with her mother without getting compensated. That worry faded away when the lunch chime rang. Nick reappeared to escort her across the campus to the dining hall with Dr. J in tow. The three of them chatted easily, though they broke apart when they reached the glorified cafeteria.

Nick got called away seconds after Dr. J took off down the hall to use the facilities, leaving Kitty Anne, for the first time, on her own in a sea of males, both young and old. There wasn't another woman in sight, including her mother. Kitty Anne didn't know if Nick had simply failed to send somebody to retrieve Lynn Anne or had spared them all her ill humor by sending a lunch down to her at the bungalow.

As glad as she was that her mother wasn't around, she'd have to check to assure her mother didn't starve. There really shouldn't be any threat of that given the amount of food the culinary track students put out with every meal. Kitty Anne couldn't deny that she was impressed, not simply by the volume of food they prepared but also by the fact that it all got eaten. Where those kids put it away she didn't know because there certainly weren't very many portly ones. They actually seemed to come in only three different sizes—young, teen, and old.

Kitty Anne gravitated toward the old ones clustered around the back tables, seeking refuge among the adult males and assuming that it would be less awkward to eat with them. She was wrong. They grew quiet as she approached, their gazes lifting as they watched her with a speculative curiosity that had her cheeks warming.

They knew.

They *all* knew.

Maybe not exactly how she'd spent last night but they had the general idea, and Kitty Anne could sense just what they thought about that. Without even giving her a chance, they'd already relegated her to the role of the boss's girlfriend...probably the ditzy, slutty, boss's girlfriend. That thought had her sighing as Kitty Anne consoled herself with the assurance that they, at least, knew who had the power.

They'd probably kiss her ass for it. If that was the role they wanted to cast her in, then that was the role Kitty Anne would play better than any other girlfriend ever had. First, though, she had a different mission to accomplish.

Narrowing her gaze on the lone guy sitting at the end of the last table, she watched Seth Jones chomp down on his sandwich and wipe his lips with his napkin without ever once taking his eyes off the magazine he had propped up in front of him. Kitty Anne could see the classic car featured in the photo display as she took the seat beside him without bothering to ask if he minded.

Seth glanced up, surprised by the sudden motion but not annoyed by it. Instead, he smiled and offered her a nod.

"Good afternoon, Miss Allison." He offered her that polite greeting as he displayed the same manners he had when Nick had introduced them earlier.

It was those manners that made it hard to believe that he was related to Patton, who was way too excitable to be polite. She also wasn't half as skittish as Seth appeared to be as he rushed to fold up his magazine and scoot his chair over to assure she had space.

"Thanks, Seth." Kitty Anne smiled, stressing the use of his first name as she set her tray down on the table. "And I believe I already told you that it's Kitty Anne. Miss Jane just sounds so...old maid, don't you think?"

"No. No. Of course not," Seth vehemently denied with a shake of his head. "I didn't mean to imply any such thing."

"I know." Kitty Anne could also figure out from the blush staining Seth's cheeks that he hadn't spent much time around women either. "Don't sweat it. I was just teasing. So...what are reading about?"

"Cars." Seth shuffled his magazine about nervously as he looked shyly over at her. "I don't imagine that's a very interesting subject to a woman like you."

"Like me?"

"Pretty," Seth qualified.

"You say the sweetest things," Kitty Anne murmured.

He was young, yeah. He could barely be but about twenty. Still, the promise of the man he'd finish growing into was there. Tall and lean and a little gawky right now, Seth would soon fill out. Those sweet-boy features, which were slightly blunted from his youth, would sharpen into a look that would be a lot more dangerous to the female population.

Then, of course, there were those eyes. So clear, so deep, so violently violet, they trapped a person within their depths and made it hard not to get lost in his gaze. Kitty Anne managed, though, finding herself strangely unaffected, probably because her heart already belonged elsewhere.

"Actually, I like cars." Kitty Anne smiled, hoping that didn't sound as weird coming out of her as it had felt. "I admit I don't know much about them, but…I like pretty ones."

She knew how that sounded, just as Kitty Anne knew how Seth would take it. Sure enough, that giggly answer put him at ease.

"You want pretty, you got to go back to the classics," Seth informed her, grumbling over what sounded like a well-worn complaint. "Modern cars are all plastic and soulless."

"You sound like my mom."

"Your mom?"

Kitty Anne could make out the faint echo of fear in Seth's tone as he repeated those two words, and she could easily guess why. "Left an impression, didn't she?"

"She was lovely."

"And you're lying." The last thing Kitty Anne would ever say about her mother was that she was *lovely*. Feisty was more like it.

"Your mother is not that bad," Seth quickly assured her, continuing on before Kitty Anne could tell him to save the lies. "You should have met mine."

She couldn't have asked for a better opening but tried to play it cool, not wanting to startle her prey. "Your mother was a character, huh?"

"She had…some issues."

There was a world of possibilities hidden within Seth's hesitation, but Kitty Anne didn't get a chance to try and explore them. Before she could press him for more details, Nick appeared by her side, yanking a seat out and plopping down his tray as he slumped down with a sigh.

"I swear, one day I'm going to go through that line when there is actually still food left in it," Nick huffed as he eyed Kitty Anne's plate. "Hey, you got two bread puddings!"

"Get back." Kitty Anne smacked his hand with the back of her spoon as she guarded her tray. "That's my pudding."

"Ah, come on, don't you want to give me just a little?" Nick asked, giving her a big puppy-dog eyes look as he outright begged. "Just a tiny taste? Hmm? I've been a good boy, haven't I?"

"Oh, stop embarrassing yourself." Kitty Anne shrugged his chin off her shoulder when he rested it there to blink up pleadingly at her. "It's just bread pudding."

"Please?"

"Fine."

"You're the best." Nick swiped one of the small bowls of bread pudding off her plate while dropping a quick kiss on her cheek.

"And don't you forget it," Kitty Anne shot back, but her attention was caught by the boy approaching the table.

He looked very, very familiar. Kitty Anne all but froze as the kid skirted around the table to stop and talk to Seth about needing help with some math homework. Math, apparently, wasn't Seth's subject, but he promised to help. That was just what brothers did for each other, and there was no denying their relationship or the brilliant color of their eyes.

Patton didn't just have one brother. She had two.

Rachel was going to flip.

* * * *

Nick didn't like the way Kitty Anne was eyeing Seth and Kevin. He could all but sense the excitement gathering within her. That couldn't be good. Something was definitely up, and he could take a guess as to what, or more likely who. Nick was pretty sure the answer started with Rachel.

Rachel was a mischievous one. She was the one who had dragged his Kitty Anne into that insanity down in Dothan. Now, clearly, the little reporter was using his woman to do her dirty work again. That meant the real question was what was Rachel after.

There was one way to find out that answer. He'd have to interrogate Kitty Anne. Nick had never interrogated anybody, but it sounded like fun, the kind of fun GD would want in on. It also sounded like the kind of thing that would go better if it was planned and prepped ahead of time.

That was just what Nick headed back to his office to do after he dropped Kitty Anne back off at her classroom after lunch. He didn't make it, though, before Mr. Selvage caught him in the hallway. Selvage was the academic administrator, and as such, it was basically his job to annoy Nick with details that he'd often like to avoid, which was just why Selvage was there that day.

"Mr. Dickles, we need to have a word about that woman you hired." The tall, lanky man stepped up to block Nick's way as if he weren't a hundred pounds outmatched.

"That woman happens to be my fiancée," Nick returned with a dark enough glare that Selvage should have been intimidated, but nothing fazed he man, which was one of the reasons Nick had hired him in the first place.

"Oh good. Then can she just be that?" he asked hopefully. "Because if you hire one woman, then you have to hire a whole bunch more. It's none or a ton, your choice, but whoever you hire, they have to be qualified first!"

Nick had known this was coming. It'd been a bit of insanity to actually hire Kitty Anne, but he had to keep her close, and he knew she wouldn't let him keep her any other way. Selvage was just going to have to find a loophole.

"Kitty Anne's qualified," Nick insisted. "It's English, and she's been speaking it her whole life."

"*That* is not the point," Selvage shot back in that stiff tone that assured Nick the man was not amused. "She is not certified to teach in this state or any other state."

"Then what about hiring her as a tutor?" Nick was pretty damn sure there were no regulations regarding tutors. "That could work, couldn't it?"

"Except for the fact that you still need to hire another teacher," Selvage stressed. "We need two English teachers, given the number of boys in attendance, or we're in violation of the state's ratios.

"And if you do that, then you need more money." Selvage rushed to talk over Nick when he opened his mouth to tell him to go hire another teacher. "You'll be creating a position for your fiancée, and that is not in our budget."

"Fine!" Nick snapped, knowing he was not going to win this battle. "Then we won't hire her, but just don't tell her, okay?"

"Don't tell her?" Selvage blinked in confusion. "I don't even know what that means."

"It means don't tell her," Nick repeated. "I'll pay her out of my own pocket, and we'll just hire another teacher. Okay?"

It was not okay. Nick could tell, but Selvage was now the one who had to admit to defeat. He did so with a curt nod before he turned and stormed off. That was not the end of the matter. Nick knew that. He also knew what he had to do before Selvage went off and said something to Kitty Anne.

On the positive side, he caught sight of several boys lugging heavy bags back out of the bungalow through the window as he stepped into his office. Nick smiled. Apparently all it took to get rid of Kitty Anne's mother was a firm tone and a few blunt words.

Chapter Seventeen

Kitty Anne sat down at her new desk and tried not to let her anxiousness show. It was time for her to meet her first student. As Dr. J had said, the only way to learn to swim was to jump into the pool. Kitty Anne didn't tell him that she didn't know how to swim. She didn't care to learn either, but this job was different.

This camp had a purpose. Her job had responsibilities. Kitty Anne had never had either one of those things before. It was a little unnerving, because if she screwed up, she'd screw some poor kid up. Just when she'd about talked her way out of the job, Kevin knocked on the door.

"Dr. J said I should come and see you." He stood there hesitantly, looking as nervous as she felt.

That helped to soothe Kitty Anne's own sense of insecurities as the sense of purpose she'd feared she would not feel rose up within her. Her job was to put this kid at ease. It started with a smile.

"Yes, please, come in, Kevin." Kitty Anne gestured for the boy to have a seat at the chair across from her desk, which was really just a big metal table.

"How'd you know my name?" he asked, skeptical and clearly reluctant to come much further into the room. "I haven't introduced myself yet."

"I saw you talking with your brother this afternoon at lunch. Don't you remember? I was sitting next to him."

Kevin shrugged at that and inched a little closer. Kitty Anne smiled and continued chatting away, hoping to tempt the boy even closer as she picked up the vanilla folder from the table.

"And even if I hadn't seen you there, I would have known your name because it is on your file. See?" She held the folder up for him to read the name typed in bold print on the tab. As Kitty Anne had anticipated, that had him stepping even closer.

"That's my file?" Kevin eyed the folder curiously. "And what does it say about me?"

"All sorts of things." Kitty Anne flipped it open and scanned through it. "That you're smart, quiet, and you don't get into trouble."

"That's a lie," Kevin stated without an ounce of reservation. "I'm always in trouble, one way or another."

"Really?" Kitty Anne lifted a brow and glanced back through the folder as she settled down into her seat. "There is no mention of disciplinary problems in your file. You want to tell me what you meant?"

"What are you? My counselor?" Kevin shot back, smacking his book bag down onto the table. "I thought you were supposed to be helping me with my writing?"

That was when Kitty Anne learned the first rule of dealing with her students. Don't push. So she backed off and nodded for him to have a seat. "Fine. Let's get started."

"I was supposed to be writing a story." Kevin yanked a notebook out of his bag and then dropped the bag onto the floor and his ass into his seat. "But I didn't do it."

He laid that down like a challenge, but Kitty Anne didn't take the bait. Instead, she calmly asked if there was a reason why he hadn't done his assignment.

"Saul quit." Kevin shrugged. "I didn't figure it would be due."

"Well, I guess we'll let that one slip," Kitty Anne allowed, not wanting to start their relationship off on any rockier of a footing than it already had. That didn't mean she could ease up on the kid. "But you're going to write me a story now."

"But I don't want to write a story."

She should have seen that one coming. Kitty Anne felt certain it had been planned, but she wasn't about to give up. She couldn't. This was her job and whether he liked it or not, Kevin needed her to do it well.

"Why not?" Kitty Anne pressed, deciding that the best thing would be to let the kid have his say before she shot him down.

"Because I don't know what to write about." Kevin just sounded frustrated now. "I mean I try but then there are characters and I don't know what they'd say or do."

"Who said you had to make things up?" Kitty Anne countered. "You can write about what you know. You can write about your life."

That seemed to give the kid pause. It also gave her one because she couldn't help but be struck in that moment how much his expression reminded her of Patton. Patton was smart, too. Not quiet, though. Definitely, stubborn. Kitty Anne had a sick feeling that so was Kevin.

"Nobody wants to read about my life," Kevin finally responded. "Trust me, lady, it's no fairy tale."

"And that's what will make it interesting." It was also what would give her insight to the world he came from and how exactly he'd ended up at Nick's camp, because right then Kitty Anne was really hazy on the details.

"It will?" Kevin eyed her doubtfully.

"It will."

Kevin didn't appear to be convinced but she was the teacher. That was a power that Kitty Anne marveled at for the rest of the day. That and the sheer audacity of teen age boys. She fielded more than one almost comical come-on and had a feeling she'd be fielding more over the coming days. The truth was that Kitty Anne had a feeling that she really didn't belong there.

She wanted to. She wanted to be doing something good with her life. She wanted to help. That didn't make her qualified to. At the end of the day, as she trudged back toward the cabin at the top of the hill, Kitty Anne couldn't help but wonder what she would do then if this didn't work out.

That wasn't what she should have been worried about.

* * * *

"What did you do?" Kitty Anne screeched, tearing through the closet that was now filled with full-length, high-necked, floral dresses. "*Where the hell are my clothes?*"

She'd been gone only a few hours. Hell, Kitty Anne had only stopped by the bungalow on her way to dinner to make sure her mother actually got something to eat. She'd been worried about Lynn Anne skipping lunch, but she should have been worried about what her mother was up to.

"I donated them," Lynn Anne answered primly, completely nonplussed by Kitty Anne as she clutched her chest and wheeled backward, certain she was about to keel over in shock at any second.

"You did what? Why? Oh, never mind, I don't care." Kitty Anne waved away her own questions as her shock soured into anger. "Go get them back. Now!"

"I can't. I took them down to the church's thrift store, but we all agreed they were...not suitable for sale, so we threw them out. But don't worry. I got you a more appropriate wardrobe for a teacher of young, impressionable boys."

Her mother smiled sweetly as she delivered that blow, seeming completely oblivious as Kitty Anne's fingers curling into fists, but she wouldn't strike Lynn Anne, and her mother knew it. Having accomplished her goal, Kitty Anne's mother turned and started for the bungalow's door.

"Hurry up, dear, I'm quite hungry this evening, and have you noticed that these little heathens demolish everything in sight? They're like rodents...actually, that's very fitting..."

Lynn Anne prattled on, her annoying commentary fading away beneath the roaring rush of the rage beginning to consume Kitty Anne. Her mother wanted war, then war it would be. That vow brought a smile to Kitty Anne's lips as she turned back into the closet and began gathering her mother's clothes up.

Damning the consequences to hell, she took the biggest armload she could hold. She chose the garments she knew her mother loved the best and lugged them right out the door to dump them on the very top of the hill, assuring everybody below would be able to see what she did.

Everybody included Lynn Anne even though she had already disappeared, but that was all right. She'd still get the message. Everybody would once she got the lighter fluid and matches Nick kept in the kitchen, along with the bag of charcoal. That was also where he kept the fire extinguisher. Kitty Anne brought that with her as well. It was showtime, and what a show it turned into.

Her mother came running at the first whiff of smoke, no doubt having already guessed that Kitty Anne had decided to take revenge. Lynn Anne tried desperately to stomp out the flames and save some of her pieces, but all she managed to do was catch her own clothes on fire. Kitty Anne reacted immediately, shoving her mother down and slapping out the flames as she rolled Lynn Anne in the grass.

By then Nick and several of the other instructors had appeared. They made the mistaken assumption that it was Kitty Anne's clothes going up in flames and that she'd tackled her mother in response. Before Kitty Anne could even begin to explain that the situation wasn't that logical, she found herself being hoisted up over Nick's shoulders while the other guys put down the fire.

It went out quickly, but that didn't stop the boys from gathering at the bottom of the hill below. Drawn by the smell and the commotion, they thickened into a large crowd. They didn't disperse either but remained fascinated by the scene playing out in front of them as Lynn Anne threw herself at Nick, knocking him down in her attempt to get at Kitty Anne.

That was when things really got out of hand.

* * * *

GD glanced around one last time, assuring nobody was around before he slipped into the back door of Lynn Anne's tiny trailer. The early evening light cast an eerie glow through the windows and painted the small place in creepy shadows that matched the psychotically feminine decorations.

It was no wonder Kitty Anne was so weird. GD shook his head at the thought and began doing what he did best—snooping. He was looking for some kind of leverage, something he and Nick could use to control Lynn Anne before things got out of control.

He had a suspicion that things were going to spiral in that direction pretty quickly. While Kitty Anne might be close to her mother, he didn't suspect that either one of them had a lot of patience for the other, which meant it would be best if Lynn Anne's stay was short.

GD kind of thought Kitty Anne would agree with that sentiment, but Kitty Anne's mother wasn't going anywhere until she got what she wanted, and he was pretty damn sure it wasn't to marry Kitty Anne off. It was to be bought off. The good news for Lynn Anne was that Nick and GD were willing to pay. So that was what he looked for, but what GD found was rather amusing.

The cigarettes hidden in an old vase was cliché, but the pot hidden in the vents wasn't, and neither was the bondage gear hidden in a small storage compartment built into the floor and tucked away from view by Lynn

Anne's bed. In some sick kind of way, all those telltale vices fit what he'd begun to suspect about Kitty Anne's mother.

The woman was a fraud.

Shit, she might even be a dealer given the quantity of reefer, not to mention the stash of pills. GD studied the labels on the golden bottles and wondered if Kitty Anne knew what her mother was up to or the fact that Lynn Anne had damn near ten thousand dollars hidden in a fireproof safe box stored in a false bottom of a large planter out on the patio.

GD recounted the cash quickly and wondered why, if Lynn Anne had so much money, she stayed there when it was obvious, given the papers he'd found on her desk, that she dreamed of living in a much bigger trailer. The answer evaded him, and he figured it didn't really matter as his phone rang.

It was Nick, and apparently all hell had broken loose, leaving GD repeating what was quickly becoming a new mantra for him. "You're kidding me, right?"

Cutting back through the woods toward where he had left his truck, GD kept his voice low but couldn't mask his shock as he listened to Nick describing a dinner, or at least an attempt at one, that was nothing short of tragically hilarious.

"Lynn Anne threw out all of Kitty Anne's clothes?"

"Including her underwear," Nick assured him.

"Then Kitty Anne set Lynn Anne's clothes on fire?"

"I think Lynn Anne actually caught on fire…briefly."

"Then Lynn Anne nailed you in the nuts?" It was hard, real hard, to say those words without laughing, but he tried. Tried and failed.

"I'm glad this is so damn amusing to you," Nick muttered. "I'm the one sitting here on a frickin' icepack."

"Yeah, well, it wasn't like the kids were going to be yours anyway." GD shrugged out of the last of the brush and checked both ways before crossing the highway to where his truck sat parked in the darkened ditch. "So then what happened?"

"The two of them tore into each other." Nick heaved a heavy sigh, and GD could all but hear the shake of his head. "I tell you what, man, we got three hundred boys in this camp and haven't had one fight until the two women showed up."

"I'm not sure it's right to judge the rest of the female population on Kitty Anne and her mother." In fact, GD knew it wasn't. "They're kind of special."

"They're kind of something," Nick grumbled. "So after we get them separated, Lynn Anne demands to be taken to the hospital to have her burns looked at, and I'm telling you, she wasn't even singed."

"She's probably planning on suing you, or Kitty Anne," GD tacked on as he settled into the cab and turned on the engine. He didn't bother to pull out onto the highway, not wanting to be distracted from his phone call. "Apparently, it's a family tradition."

"Great." Nick sounded downright miserable. "That's just what I need. At least, it didn't happen on campus or I'd probably lose my accreditation along with my insurance."

"Don't worry. I got the goods to keep Lynn Anne on a leash," GD assured him.

"Yeah? Well, what about Kitty Anne?" Nick shot back, unimpressed with GD's confidence. "You should have seen her when she finally did show up to dinner. I mean, my God, dude! It was terrifying!"

"What the hell did she look like?" GD demanded to know, certain there was no way Kitty Anne could be terrifying.

"Her hair…it looked like somebody electrocuted her, and she had like clown makeup on and her skirt tucked into like five pairs of old lady panties…it was something else."

"I can believe it. Kitty Anne's quite an actress."

"That was what it was, too, an act because the minute Kitty Anne found out her mother wasn't there she went back to the bathroom and returned looking…somewhat normal."

"And still beautiful enough to die for, right?"

"And still," Nick agreed as they shared a moment of silence and acceptance of what fate had given them, both good and crazy. "That reminds me, I think we have another problem."

"Another one?" They seemed to be swimming in them lately.

"When I caught up with Kitty Anne at lunch, she was sitting and talking with Seth." Nick paused, but GD wasn't certain what he was supposed to say about that.

"You think maybe she wants to add him to the roster?"

"No, dude! God!" Nick heaved an aggrieved sigh, proving Kitty Anne wasn't the only drama queen in their group. "You know how shy Seth is, so she had to be the one pushing the conversation and then Kevin comes over and she was all sweet to him..."

"...and you think she might be into younger guys?" Now GD was just having fun with Nick, and he knew it.

"I'm thinking more in line with the fact that Kitty Anne is besties with Rachel...Rachel who got her arrested and now got her a job. Are the pieces starting to add up for you yet?" Nick asked obnoxiously, but GD still wasn't completely impressed.

"Yeah, I guess you could be on to something," GD admitted reluctantly. "I could always swing by Rachel's work and take a look at her notes."

Nick's tone perked up as he jumped on that offer. "I like that idea."

"Yeah, well, not tonight." GD glanced at his watch and grimaced at the time. "I got another appointment to keep, and then I'll head out that way."

"Don't bother," Nick muttered. "I'm not in any kind of condition to have any fun, and Kitty Anne's sulking over her clothes."

"Then it's up to us to cheer her up," GD insisted. "I'll be there in an hour or so."

It would probably be more like "or so," but he didn't want to listen to Nick complain. Neither did GD want to head back out to the club, but right then, he was on the job, and he went where it took him. That evening it led him to Lana's office. He had to know the truth about the fire, had to know if her brothers really had started it and if he'd been blaming an innocent kid all this time.

Just the thought of how wrong he might be made GD a little sick.

He didn't find any evidence that pointed to Lana's brothers, not that he expected to. She was smarter than that, but he couldn't help but take note of her desk planner. It seemed as though every Tuesday she had a weekly meeting, but it wasn't for any club business. There really was no reason to be suspicious. He just was.

So GD headed the rest of the way into Dothan to the bar Lana had notated and waited for her to arrive. She was punctual. Gwen Harold was late. GD straightened up in his seat as he watched Gwen sashay into the bar and told himself not to jump to any conclusions, not that he could. He didn't have a clue as to what was going on, and he sure as hell couldn't go in there and find out.

Instead, he tested the waters the old-fashioned way and called Lana. She didn't answer. That wasn't a good sign. An even worse one was that she called him back ten minutes later, right after Gwen had sauntered out of the bar looking pleased as punch. Lana looked less so as she followed in the other woman's wake. GD eyed the two women as he flipped open his phone and called out a cheery greeting.

"Hey, Lana, what you got going on?"

"Not much. I was just seeing what you wanted."

"Oh yeah? I was just curious as to what you were up to tonight."

"You were curious about what I was up to?" That had Lana pausing in the parking lot and glancing around. She didn't spot his truck buried in the shadows of the alley across the street, but the fact that she looked told him she was guilty of something.

"Yeah. I was thinking of introducing you to my girl and seeing about getting her a membership," GD lied smoothly, watching as Lana relaxed and hurried on to her car.

"I'm not there now. I had some business to take care of, so…"

"Maybe some other time," GD filled in easily for her. "I get the message."

"You sure you want to get your girl a membership? You know the board hasn't changed the rules for members' significant others," Lana warned him.

"Yeah, you're right. I guess I ought to think about this a little more," GD agreed easily, knowing that would stoke her suspicions anew.

That didn't bother him. Just the opposite. It suited GD, and sure enough, Lana sounded as hesitant as he wanted her as she responded to that peculiar comeback.

"You do whatever you think is right."

That was just what he intended to do.

* * * *

Kitty Anne looked around the shed and sighed. It was small and sterile looking, but at least it was clean. There was even a cot tucked into the corner and Nick promised that tomorrow he'd have electricity run out to it and a hole cut in the side for a window. If that wasn't good enough, she'd have to return to the cabin and sleep with her mother.

That Kitty Anne would not do.

She was mad at her mother right then. Mad enough to once again consider throwing her mom out, but she still hadn't figured out how she was supposed to do that. Drag her out by her hair? Throw all her stuff away? Change the locks when she went out?

Every single suggestion that popped into her head left Kitty Anne both amused and a little ashamed. Her mother had sacrificed so much for Kitty Anne. Worse, Lynn Anne would be quick to remind her of that, making Kitty Anne feel guilty enough to not have the strength to confront her mother.

So, she nodded and accepted her fate. After all, she'd lived in worse.

"This will do." Kitty Anne sighed over that bit of faint praise and turned to smile at Nick.

Waiting in the doorway for the verdict, he appeared to relax at her acceptance. "I'm glad."

"And I owe you a thank-you." Sashaying up to him, Kitty Anne reveled in the now familiar thrill that twisted through her every time he was near.

He made her heart skip a beat, and she wanted to return the favor. However, when Kitty Anne wrapped her arms around his neck and tried to grind herself up against him, Nick laughed and stepped back away from her.

"You know I think you're just the sexiest thing," Nick started, and she could hear the "but" coming, "but I'm sorry. I'm sore."

Nick was definitely sulking, and Kitty Anne couldn't blame him. She and her mom really had put on a show, and unfortunately, Nick had kind of gotten caught up in the brawl. No doubt, he'd have claimed that was an understatement, given her mother hadn't accidently nailed him in the balls with her knee.

She'd done it on purpose. Worse, she probably wasn't done.

"I hate to tell you this…" Now it was Kitty Anne's turn to hesitate over the moment as the "but" built in the air until there was no escaping saying it. "But she's probably going to sue you."

"So I've been warned," Nick assured her, surprising Kitty Anne.

"You have?" She blinked in confusion. "By who?"

"By me," GD answered for Nick as he stepped up behind him. "Hey, beautiful, miss me?"

"All day long," Kitty Anne shot back as Nick let him pass so he could swoop her up in his arms.

He gave her a quick kiss that turned into a long kiss at Kitty Anne's insistence. Then she remembered Nick and his condition. That made this kind of cruel and anything more just downright mean. It was only Kitty Anne's concern over hurting him that gave her the strength to pull back.

GD let her go, smiling as he glanced around the small shed Nick had managed to tow up from the campus below. It clearly had been some kind of garden shed given the musty, dirt smell, but Kitty Anne had smelled worse.

"Nice pad." GD eyed the cot with a frown. "Did your boyfriend tell you that I was going to be sharing it with you?"

"You are?" Kitty Anne glanced over at the cot and chuckled. "Then I think we're going to need a bigger mattress."

"I think we're going to need a bigger shed." Nick sighed. "Because I don't think all three of us are going to fit in here comfortably."

"We could get a trailer," Kitty Anne suggested. "I know just where to find the cutest, little one."

"Now wait a minute," GD spoke up, clearly following the direction of her thoughts, but he didn't get a chance to lecture her before Nick's phone went off.

He looked at the number and swore before answering. It didn't take long to figure out what had him irritated.

Apparently, Kevin was gone.

Chapter Eighteen

"He's not at the Davis brothers' ranch," GD insisted, but he could tell that Nick was having difficulty accepting that fact.

GD had already been to the ranch and back while Nick and Seth had searched the camp for Kevin. They'd all come up empty. Seth was still out there looking, but GD and Nick had regrouped in his room to try and figure out something better.

"Are you sure?" Nick asked again, despite the absurdity of making GD repeat himself when he'd been perfectly clear the first time.

"I looked all over, man. Short of waking up everybody and searching high and low, all I can say is I didn't find Kevin. Now you got to decide if you want to wake everybody up."

"Damn it!" Nick snapped, flailing a fist into the air as he spun around and vented his anger with another deeply belted out curse. "*Damn it*! Where the hell else would he go?"

"Where else could he get to is the real question." At least to GD's way of thinking it was. "We're pretty secluded out here. He's probably lost somewhere in the damn woods. We'll be able to track him better in the morning."

"Morning? We don't know where he is, or what dangers he's facing. He could be dead by morning," Nick shot back, clearly not a fan of that idea.

"How?" GD scoffed, thinking Nick was overreacting more than just a little.

"Exposure to the elements."

"It's eighty degrees out there! He isn't going to freeze."

"He could get bit by a snake."

GD snorted and rolled his eyes, recognizing in that moment there was no reasoning with Nick.

"He could!" Nick insisted. "He could fall and break his leg and hemorrhage to death. He could be picked up by a pedophile and be tortured to death. He could—"

"But he's not," GD cut in, sensing Nick was working himself up to a point where he'd be totally useless. "There is no pedophile running around in the woods. The moon is full enough for him to see the holes and not fall down."

"And snakes?" Nick lifted a brow, all but daring GD to dismiss that possibility.

He couldn't. That could happen. GD just doubted it.

"Look, if anything happens to Kevin, I could lose this whole place," Nick stated, sounding suddenly rational.

He really was like a mother hen who liked to sit on his eggs and smother them. GD, on the other hand, was a little more reasonable in his reactions. The kid had traveled all the way over from Louisiana on his own, not but a few months back. That was a long way to walk and a lot of woods to survive. He could probably make it another night.

Nick might not, though.

Neither would GD if he went and told Kitty Anne he was abandoning the search. She wanted to be out there looking, too, but they'd put her on duty in front of Kevin's room, assuring that if he returned they'd know about it. That position also kept her conveniently out of the way, but that wouldn't last forever.

They really did need to find this kid.

* * * *

Kitty Anne sat with her back resting against Kevin's door, wondering if she was wasting all her time waiting there. When GD had explained that they needed somebody to let them know if the kid returned, it had sounded like a reasonable request, but an hour and a half later she was bored enough to reconsider the matter.

It felt as though the kid would never come back. With each passing second, Kitty Anne began to worry that he really had run away and hadn't just skipped out to go steal ice cream out of the freezer in the dining hall. That possibility grew dimmer as her worry grew greater.

In hindsight, Kitty Anne wondered if she hadn't really screwed up that afternoon. Perhaps Kevin had been offended by her wanting him to write about his life. Maybe he felt like it was minimalizing what had happened to him, but it wasn't as though she knew what the hell she was doing anyway. She didn't have a degree in either education or child psychology.

In fact, Kitty Anne was completely unqualified for her current position. That had become clear by the end of the day, as she'd constantly had to look things up. Shockingly enough, the ability to speak and read English did not actually equip a person to teach it. She'd have to have a talk with Nick about that. He was going to need to hire a real teacher, and she…hell, Kitty Anne didn't know what the hell would happen with her.

She didn't exactly have anywhere to go and that left her just where she was—sitting around doing nothing. That was the epitome of boring, and that could very well be the death of her relationship with Nick and GD.

Heaving a deep sigh over that grim thought, Kitty Anne glanced down at her watch and wondered just how long the two of them planned to leave her sitting there. She was just about ready to leave when the door behind her swung inward and she went toppling backward as a set of deep brown eyes blinked down over her.

"Oh…hello there." Kitty Anne smiled and tried not to sound as awkward as she felt scrambling around on the floor. The kid stepped back, his head tilting to the side as he watched her shove upward onto her knees and then her feet. "Sorry about that, didn't mean to almost clobber you there, but you caught me off guard."

"Why are you sitting in front of the door?" Neither accepting nor rejecting her explanation, the young boy asked that question with a seriousness that would have suited an adult better than a cherub-faced little kid still watching her as though she was some strange entity that had invaded his world.

"Well…" Kitty Anne hesitated, not certain if she should mention Kevin or not. Then again the kid had to know his roommate was gone. "I was waiting to see if Kevin came back."

"Kevin?" The boy snorted and rolled his eyes. "He always returns eventually."

"So he's done this before?" GD and Nick certainly hadn't mentioned that fact.

"Yeah." The kid nodded with easy acceptance. "He likes to go spy on his sister."

The kid nearly felled her with that off-handed comment. Kitty Anne stepped back, her mind racing with all the implications to finally settle on a simple question that needed to be answered before she could begin to sort through what the hell was really going on around here.

"He has a sister?" Kitty Anne didn't have to fake any shock over that question. All she had to do was use her confounded amazement that the kid knew about Patton.

"Yeah." The kid drew out the word. "So he says, but I think he might have made her up because…you know, his mom was such a whack-a-doo."

Actually, Kitty Anne didn't know, but she was interested in finding out and clearly this kid had the goods. Eyeing him as she considered the best way to proceed, she decided to treat him like she would an adult. After all, he kind of acted like one.

"My name's Kitty Anne," she offered along with her hand. "I don't think we've been properly introduced."

"Tyson." The kid shook her hand with a quick, firm grip that matched his serious personality. "And I know who you are. You're Mr. Dickles's girl. He already told us."

"Excuse me?" Kitty Anne blinked, sidetracked by that negligent comment. "He told you?"

"At dinner." Tyson paused as his lips quivered and he shot her a knowing look.

"That was just a little misunderstanding."

"Uh-huh."

"You know I don't have to explain this to you."

"Mmm."

"And what is that supposed to mean?"

"You know my mom had to go to anger management classes when she had her misunderstanding," Tyson stated with a pointed stare that assured Kitty Anne he considered her in the same boat as his mother. She was sure she wasn't helping that opinion by snarling at him, but he was kind of aggravating for a child.

"And did it help?"

"Do you think I'd be here if it did?" Tyson shot back, proving that he might be little, but he packed in a whole lot of attitude. "At least, my mom's not a whack-a-doo."

"I am not a whack-a-doo!"

"You set your mom on fire."

"It was an accident."

"Hmm-hmm."

Kitty Anne took a deep breath and prayed for patience because they had gotten way off track. This was supposed to be about Kevin, not about whether the whole campus thought she was a crazy lady. Perhaps they did. Perhaps she was. That didn't matter right then because Kevin was missing, and she needed to turn this conversation back to a safe course.

"And did Kevin's mom set him on fire?"

"Nah." Tyson shook his head. "Kevin's the little arsonist."

"Kevin?" Kitty Anne blinked. "He set a fire?"

"Apparently about burned up his sister." Tyson paused and then qualified that rumor. "Of course, he denies it, but who the hell is going to believe him? Who the hell believes any of us? Look at where we're at."

There was a grimness to that statement that cut through Kitty Anne's heart, and she couldn't help but feel a wash of shame over her recent, rather immature, argument with the kid.

"You could believe each other," Kitty Anne suggested. "That's a place to start."

"And you believe me?" Tyson asked, his gaze narrowing once again on her as he appeared to take her measure.

"Yes." Kitty Anne straightened up and took her stand. "Yes, I do."

* * * *

A half-hour later, Kitty Anne said good night to Tyson, who promised to give them a heads-up when Kevin returned. The kid seemed absolutely convinced that the other boy would return. Kitty Anne wasn't so certain. Given all that Tyson had told her, it wouldn't be shocking if Kevin had decided to run away.

After all, everybody was against him. That included his own brother, along with Nick, who Kitty Anne suspected thought he was doing right by the kid. After all, Nick had to know about the fire. According to Tyson, everybody did, though she suspected everybody did not include GD.

If GD knew, then the Davis brothers would have known and then Patton would have known and Rachel would have known and then Kitty Anne would have known. So, based on the fact that she did not know, Kitty Anne could assume that GD didn't know. That could only be because Nick hadn't told him, which meant he was protecting the kid, but the kid, apparently, claimed he was innocent.

Nobody believed Kevin. Not even Tyson. That was kind of why Kitty Anne did. Everybody needed somebody to believe in them. That was just what she would have told Nick but knew that if she brought the subject up it would endanger their fragile relationship because then the two of them would be conspiring to keep a secret from GD.

If he ever found out, that would probably devastate him. Kitty Anne couldn't betray one man over the other like that. So that left her, and Rachel, to help prove Kevin's innocence. Kitty Anne had no doubt that her friend would help...that is if she told her. Kitty Anne hadn't made up her mind on that one yet.

First, she needed to talk to Kevin. Actually, first, she needed to find Kevin. According to Tyson, Kevin normally skipped out to go watch his sister. Apparently, the boy was fascinated by her. Kitty Anne could imagine why. To a creature as reserved as Kevin appeared, Patton must have looked like a beacon of chaos.

Chaos and happiness, Kitty Anne qualified as she considered Patton's almost permanent grin. The woman lived to laugh, and maybe, that was just what Kevin wanted, too. Where would he get a laugh?

Kitty Anne didn't know the answer to that question because she didn't know the kid that well, but Tyson did. He'd pointed her toward a lake buried in the back woods and Kevin's stories about going night fishing with his brother back in Louisiana when he'd been little.

Apparently, those were fond memories for Kevin, and sure enough, as Kitty Anne followed the path Tyson had directed her to, she found a light glowing at the end of it as she came up on the pond Nick kept stocked for those who enjoyed casting a reel. Of course, he probably hadn't expected it to get used at night, but there was Kevin, floating a light off the bank's edge as he sat there holding on to a thin rod and staring out across the water with a blank expression.

He glanced her way as Kitty Anne approached, no doubt drawn by the glare of her own flashlight. He held a hand up, shielding his eyes from the bright light, and she clicked it off, forcing her eyes to adjust to the dim, nearly moonless, night.

"Who's there?" Kevin called out, apparently as blind as Kitty Anne in that moment.

"Hey, Kevin. It's me, Kitty Anne."

"Oh." There was a moment's hesitation as she sensed him shifting in the dark. "What are you doing out here?"

"Well, I heard there was some good fishing to be had and…I brought a rod." Kitty Anne could finally start to make out the kid's shadow and wondered if he could see her thrust the thin pole she'd snatched from the sports pen's inventory before heading down here. "Mind if I join you?"

"Suit yourself."

Kitty Anne could more than hear the shrug in his tone. She could see it, as finally her eyes began to dilate enough for the world to start to take form. There was the line of treetops on the other side and the cut of the pond's bank, along with the bright glow of the lantern Kevin had floated out onto the water's smooth top.

It was a perfect night, though not for fishing. Kitty Anne didn't know anything about fishing, but she didn't intend to let that stop her. In fact, she planned on using it to her advantage, and hopefully, she'd gain a little of Kevin's trust in the process.

"I'd love to, but I'm not exactly sure what to do with this pole," Kitty Anne confessed before asking slyly, "Maybe you could help show me?"

* * * *

"We're in trouble." Nick stared at his phone as he considered the implications of what Seth had just told him. It wasn't good. "Seth found Kevin, and you'll never guess who he was with."

"Kitty Anne?" GD asked, proving Nick wrong, though he'd made it kind of easy to guess. "Isn't she supposed to be watching Kevin's room? Did he return on his own?"

"No." That would be too easy and make life too simple. Life with these kids was never that simple. "Seth found them fishing in the lake out back."

GD blinked at that and then blinked again, clearly having difficulty comprehending Nick's revelation. "Fishing? Kitty Anne was *fishing*? Are you sure?"

"Seth said she caught three fish."

"No kidding." GD snorted as a smile began to spread across his face. "And here I was worried that she wouldn't make a good redneck woman, but she can kick ass and now she *fishes*? God is giving!"

"Will you focus?" Nick demanded, shocked and amazed at GD's cavalier attitude. "Kitty Anne *found* Kevin."

That earned Nick another blink as GD's smile faded back into a look of confusion. "So?"

"So, she's up to something." Nick could just sense it. Whatever it was, it wasn't good. GD clearly didn't get that as he shrugged once again.

"So?"

"So?" Nick repeated, amazed and outraged that GD didn't see the need to panic when it was clearly time to.

"Yes. So as in, so what?" GD shot back. "What do you really think she's going to do?"

"Tell Rachel about Kevin and Seth."

"Tell them what?" GD countered. "That they're brothers."

"That they're Patton's brothers!"

"And how would she know that? Huh?" GD pressed, taking up the argument before Nick could respond. "It's not like she knows Patton that well, and the only thing that she might have noticed is that they have similar colored eyes. That's hardly likely to be worth Rachel's interest."

"Okay, fine," Nick snapped, irritated by GD's reasonable points. "Then what the hell else could Rachel be up to?"

"Nothing," GD suggested with a shrug. "Why does she have to be up to anything? And even if she is, what makes you think Kitty Anne would rat Kevin out? You really think she'd do that to a kid? Especially not one she's bonding with by fishing."

"I'd still feel better if you had a look around Rachel's desk," Nick insisted. "Because while Kitty Anne might not mean to hurt Kevin, she might do so accidently."

"Whatever." GD folded with ill grace. "I'll take a look, but we still got a bigger problem than Kitty Anne, and that's her mother. Mommy needs to go because I'm not living in that tiny shed for the rest of my life."

Neither was Nick, but Lynn Anne wasn't his top concern right then. He made that clear in a way that had GD smirking.

"Whatever."

"You're a real snot, you know that?"

"Oh look, here comes Kitty Anne and Kevin." Nick ignored GD's question as he shoved past the big man and headed down the path lit by gas lanterns that had been dimmed at midnight.

They cast a molten glow over the cobblestoned way and painted Kevin's grin in an angelic halo that soothed a little of Nick's worry. Whatever bonding had happened over their fishing expedition, it was good for the kid's mood because he was clearly more relaxed and even a little excited as he babbled on to Seth about how he'd taught Kitty Anne to fish. She was a natural…or had beginner's luck. Kevin didn't know yet.

They'd have to go fishing again.

Kitty Anne agreed.

The happy trio swept past Nick without even really pausing, though they did gain a member. GD joined their ranks to enthusiastically "ooh" and "aah" over Kitty Anne's fish. That left Nick standing there watching them and wondering if they didn't have a problem.

Could he really be in love with Kitty Anne if he didn't trust her? And why didn't he trust her? Was he just that jaded or were his concerns justified? Nick didn't know, but he knew the answer was important.

Chapter Nineteen

Sunday, June 15th

Two weeks later, Kitty Anne stood in the lobby of GD's church and tried not to fidget. Religion really wasn't her thing. Like Nick, she believed in a higher-up but considered church to be more a social gathering than a spiritual one. That was exactly why she'd agreed to go when GD had asked her to because Kitty Anne knew how important a step this was for them.

She was meeting his friends, which consisted of just as many women as men. That didn't bother Kitty Anne, though his closeness with Heather was a little unnerving. It didn't help that Kitty Anne felt certain Heather didn't actually like her all that much. The other woman was more than a little uptight, and Kitty Anne prided herself on being loose.

Life was just more fun that way. That was true of these past two weeks. They'd been entertaining, enlightening, and frustrating. Casting a glance over at her big man, Kitty Anne felt the familiar warmth begin to heat her veins. She wanted him. She'd had him in almost every way accept for the two that counted the most, which was just aggravating in the extreme.

It made no sense that the man was willing to fuck her with anything and in any position except the twelve inches of thick dick she knew he was packing. He was being stubborn about the whole collar thing. If he didn't lighten up soon, GD was going to wake up one morning to find himself staked to the damn floor with her riding him and taking just what she wanted because Kitty Anne's patience was wearing thin.

Not just with him. Her mother was working on Kitty Anne's last nerve. Lynn Anne hadn't been amused when GD showed up hauling a tin can of a trailer with a borrowed tow-truck. She'd been even more outraged to learn that Kitty Anne planned to shack up in the trailer with her new man.

Technically she'd planned on shacking up with both her men, but that was a reality that her mother seemed oblivious to. It never appeared to dawn on Lynn Anne that GD and Nick were both always around. Of course, she'd grown really good at acting like GD didn't exist at all.

Obviously, Lynn Anne knew he did just as she knew that when she moved back into her trailer, Kitty Anne and Nick had moved back into the cabin with GD. The fact that Lynn Anne didn't want to talk about the matter was just fine with Kitty Anne. Not everything needed to be talked about and neither did everybody need to be talked to.

"Hey, Kitty!"

"Oh God." Closing her eyes with that groan, she turned slowly around and cracked them back open to find herself confronting not only Cole but his buddy Kyle and their girl Hailey, too.

"Hello." She offered that greeting tentatively, uncertain of just how things were about to go.

"We'd thought we'd stop by and thank you."

"Not me." Cole shook his head as he broke into a wide grin. "I just came by to gloat."

He would. As much as Kitty Anne was happy that Cole had turned out to be decent and loyal after all, she still thought Hailey deserved better. Then again that might be sour grapes on her part. After all, the plan had been for her to leave him chained to a bed while she called the cops. He would have been properly humiliated except that he was already working for the cops and she'd been the one who ended up doing the stripper's strut through the police station. Clearly, Cole had heard about those details. She could see the truth in his grin. That smile didn't even dip when Hailey jammed an elbow into his side.

"Ow!" Cole shot Hailey a sore look. "There isn't any need to get mean. The little Kitty knows she got beat."

"Bested." Kyle nodded.

"Outmaneuvered," Cole piled on, living up to his word and gloating. "But that's what you get when you mess with the best."

"Never underestimate a Cattleman," Kyle warned with a pointed look at both women, who just stared back at him for a long moment.

"Go." Hailey pointed toward the door as she issued that unflinching command. Both men went, chuckling between themselves as they obeyed.

Kitty Anne watched them leave and couldn't help but wonder again what Hailey saw in those two. They were like little boys, and Kitty Anne preferred men. She kept that opinion to herself though as Hailey turned back around with a smile tugging at her lips.

"Sorry about them." She apologized for the two men, even as she shrugged off their annoying tendencies. "They think they're funny."

"I'm thinking you do, too," Kitty Anne murmured, knowing she was right, despite the fact that Hailey didn't directly respond to that comment.

"I did want to stop by, though, and thank you…for everything."

"It was nothing," Kitty Anne lied and then immediately turned around and told the truth. "I had fun."

"Yeah? Then I'd say you got a strange definition of fun."

"Most people would." Kitty Anne didn't mind that either. Being different was just fine with her. "It looks like you're having fun, too. So I guess everything worked out?"

"Yeah…until my brothers showed up." Hailey's cheeks pinked to match the flame of her hair as she tacked that on.

"That sounds interesting." Kitty Anne could sense a story behind Hailey's look.

"I think you mean mortifying," Hailey corrected her before glancing around the vestibule. She leaned in closer, her tone dropping to a whisper as her eyes began to sparkle with a mischievous gleam. "But I got plans for revenge."

"On your boyfriends or your brothers?" Kitty Anne asked. "Because if you need help humiliating Cole, I would be *honored* to assist."

That had Hailey tipping back her head and laughing, a sound that echoed through the vestibule and had people glancing in their direction. That included GD, who caught Kitty Anne's gaze, and she could easily read the warning in his eyes. He didn't want her to get into trouble. Unfortunately, there was no trouble to be had.

"I'm sure you would." Hailey drew Kitty Anne's attention back to her as she offered Kitty Anne a sincere-sounding assurance. "And I'm sure you will get the chance to one day, but right now, I owe my brothers, and I have the perfect payback planned."

"That sounds ominous."

It hit Kitty Anne as she watched Hailey's smile take on a smug curve how lucky she was to have GD and Nick. The only games they played were ones that ended with her moaning and begging for more. They had enough drama in their lives between all the boys and her mother.

"Trust me, it's going to be tons of fun." Hailey snickered, but her smirk softened almost immediately as GD stepped up to join them.

"What's going to be fun?" he asked, clearly having caught the tail end of Hailey's comment.

"Nothing," Hailey answered instantly with a fake innocence that assured everybody knew she was lying.

"Mmm-hmm." GD eyed the little redhead for a moment before issuing a not-so-friendly-sounding warning. "You're not going to get my girl arrested again, are you?"

"No," Hailey shot back with a huff and a roll of her eyes. "And I'd point out that I didn't get her arrested. You guys did."

"Mmm-hmm," GD murmured again, sounding unimpressed.

"That's enough." Kitty Anne intervened, not wanting to be the cause of any kind of arguments. "I got myself arrested, so there is no need to glare at her, Mr. Davis."

GD flinched at the use of his formal name. "Well, you'll have to excuse me, Miss Allison, but I know how much trouble you girls get into in the name of fun."

That brought another laugh to Hailey's lips. "That's rich coming from the king of the Cattlemen."

"King?" Kitty Anne lifted a brow at that. They hadn't discussed his club, and as far as she knew, he hadn't been out there, but then again, she hadn't known he was king.

"She's exaggerating." GD dismissed Hailey's comment as if it were nothing, but Kitty Anne could see through his act. He was worried. "There is no king."

"You're the master of ceremonies," Hailey ratted him out, taking exception to his correction. "Cole told me so."

"And I'm retiring," GD shot back. "Did Cole tell you that?"

"No," Hailey admitted, but she wasn't about to go down in defeat. The little redhead was a fighter. Kitty Anne kind of admired that about her. "Did *you* tell Cole?"

"I don't have to tell Cole anything."

"No, but you do have to tell the guys out at the club," Hailey pointed out. "And one of them would have told Cole. So…"

Hailey batted her eyes patiently up at GD as she clearly waited for him to fill in the rest of the tale, but it was clear there was nothing else to tell because GD hadn't actually resigned…yet.

"Go away, Hailey," GD ordered, essentially admitting defeat and sending the redhead sauntering off with a victorious smile. He paid her no attention, turning instead to pin Kitty Anne with a serious look. "I really am retiring. I swear it. I don't have any interest in any of those women."

"Oh please." Kitty Anne rolled her eyes. "I'm more worried about how attached you are to Heather than that club full of sluts."

That was the truth, but it obviously struck GD as odd. He frowned in blatant confusion as he glanced back over to where Heather was standing with two men, who were clearly hovering over her.

"You don't need to worry about Heather." GD turned back to offer Kitty Anne a gentle smile. "She's just like a sister to me."

"One you slept with," Kitty Anne added on, causing GD to shrug.

"Okay, maybe not like a sister, but still—"

"She doesn't like me," Kitty Anne cut in, revealing her real fear because she knew how friends could sabotage a relationship. Their approval could be more important than the family's. At least, it was for her. Maybe not so much for GD.

"Well"—he paused as if to consider her concern but couldn't seem to take it too seriously—"then it's a good thing Heather's not dating you and I am, because I like you."

Those words soothed the bit of worry gnawing at her, and Kitty Anne couldn't help but step up and weave an arm through his as she pressed herself suggestively against his side.

"Just like me?"

"I might feel differently," GD allowed, a glint beginning to sparkle in his gaze as he wrapped an arm around her waist and tucked her in close. "That is if you were wearing my collar."

"How about I wear you instead?" Kitty Anne murmured huskily for his ears only.

"How about we find a private place where you can try and convince me to see things your way?" GD returned as his arm tightened around her in a subtle temptation that had her eagerly following him out the door.

After all, even if she didn't get dick, Kitty Anne knew she'd get something good.

* * * *

GD escorted Kitty Anne out into the bright sunlight and flicked his sunglasses down off the top of his head. It was hot out, and most of the other church patrons had already scurried off to find shelter from the heat. Most were probably headed toward Sunday brunch feasts, and he had to field off an invite from Heather and her men to join them back at Alex's parents' house for a spread that promised to be a lot less interesting than the one GD planned on making of Kitty Anne.

It sucked that Kitty Anne and Heather hadn't hit it off better, but he really wasn't surprised. They weren't much alike and had even less in common. Hopefully, that would change once they got Kitty Anne pregnant. Then they'd both be mothers.

More importantly, he'd be a daddy.

He couldn't wait, but of course, there wouldn't be any babies until he managed to convince Kitty Anne to wear his collar. That was turning out to be trickier than he'd assumed, mostly because the damn woman had dug her heels in. GD was pretty certain Kitty Anne didn't object to the collar in theory. She objected to the ultimatum.

He shouldn't have made it. GD admitted to that mistake, if only to himself. It was too late now to take it back, and he was bound and determined to out-stubborn the woman. Besides, it wasn't as if he wasn't getting served.

Already hard with the thought of what was about to come, he helped Kitty Anne up into his truck and headed back out toward the camp. A fact she took instant notice of.

"We're headed home?"

"Nick and I have a little surprise arranged for you." Actually it was a big one, and he couldn't wait to show her.

"Oh, I like surprises." Kitty Anne giggled with clear excitement.

Just the sound of her laughter had him smiling as he reached out to thread his fingers through hers. He held her hand all the way back to the cabin as they sat in a comfortable silence that held a deeper hint of contentment. He didn't want to lose that feeling and would do almost anything to hold on to it.

Anything was just what he and Nick planned on doing.

The other man was waiting by the front shrubs as GD pulled down the long drive that led to Nick's cabin. There was no assigned parking, so GD simply pulled his truck in next to Nick's beneath the shade of a trimmed cedar tree. Its big leafy branches twisted outward, forming a thick canopy that kept the heat of the sun at bay. Kitty Anne flashed him a grin as she pulled her hand free and reached for the door handle.

"You have my expectations up, so this better be good," she warned him as Nick appeared to assist her.

"Don't worry, it will be," GD assured her as he dug down into the pocket of his suit pants to pull out a length of black satin. "But first you got to put this on."

"Hmmm." Kitty eyed the fabric, ignoring Nick as he pulled open her door. "And what will you do to convince me?"

"No blindfold, no surprise," GD retorted as he held up the strip of satin.

Kitty Anne smiled and pointedly turned her back, allowing him to secure the blindfold into place. GD took extra care not to catch any of her hair as he tied the knot and couldn't resist the temptation to lean forward and nuzzle the graceful curve of her neck. Her skin was softer than the finest silks and her scent…GD's eyes closed for a brief second as he fought back the primal urges just being near her ignited in him.

"I think boyfriend number two needs a moment."

GD opened his eyes to pin a glare on Nick as he growled over Kitty Anne's shoulder back at the smirking man. "Well then, take one. Boyfriend number one will take our girl."

"There is no one or two," Kitty Anne interrupted. "Now stop arguing, or I'll have to get mean."

She sounded prissy as hell and looked it with her pursed lips, but GD knew the truth. Kitty Anne worried about Nick and him getting along. She was very sensitive and quick to interfere whenever she thought they were arguing over her, or too intensely over anything.

It was sweet, and totally unnecessary, though neither of them told her that. They kind of liked her worrying. Nick and GD shared a smile as Nick reached up to pull Kitty Anne down out of the truck.

"Don't sweat it, sexy. The big man knows what number he is." Nick tossed GD a wink, and he responded by flipping the other man off, but he was smiling.

GD's grin only grew as he hopped out of the truck and sauntered around the hood to take Kitty Anne's hand. Nick had a hold of her other one, and together they started leading her toward her surprise.

* * * *

Nick was nervous, more nervous than he'd ever been. Then again, very few things mattered as much as making sure that Kitty Anne was happy. Unfortunately, he had some bad news for her. He could only hope his surprise made up for that, but with every step they took, he grew more and more certain it wouldn't.

She was going to hate the idea. Worse, she was going to hate him because he was about to break her heart. That would break his, but it was too late to turn back now. Not that he could. Not that Mr. Selvage would let him. This was all that twerp's fault, and if Kitty Anne shed one tear, Nick would beat the crap out of him.

He laid down that silent vow as he brought Kitty Anne to a stop behind the cabin. To the right, the hill sloped downward toward the camp's campus. To the left, Lynn Anne's trailer sat nestled in by new garden beds that Nick took as an ominous sign.

Kitty Anne's mother was getting comfortable and Kitty Anne still seemed far from ready to tell her mother to get lost. Nick certainly wasn't going to risk pissing off Kitty Anne by doing it himself. He had hope that eventually Lynn Anne would push her daughter too far.

Right then, though, it was his own ass on the chopping block as he looked over the new shed he'd had installed that morning. It was bigger and nicer and already had three windows.

"You ready to see your surprise?" Nick asked, trying to force some cheer and enthusiasm into his voice, but he failed to fool either her or GD. The big man shot him a smirk as Kitty Anne scowled.

"Why are your hands sweaty?" Kitty Anne's nose wrinkled.

"He's just nervous." GD snorted as he reached for the ties to her blindfold. "So, be a good girl and try to pretend like you're pleased with his thoughtfulness because this is mostly on him."

Nick shot GD a dirty look for that one but was quickly distracted by Kitty Anne's reaction as the big man pulled the satin strap free. It took her a second for her eyes to focus. She blinked rapidly for a moment before her mouth fell open on a giddy gasp.

"That's my name!" Kitty Anne's smile lit up her face for a second, only to be replaced by a frown of confusion that quickly followed as she read the rest of the sign that was affixed to the shed's front door. "I'm a director...of *fundraising*?"

Nick swallowed hard, not certain if she were affronted or overwhelmed. Either way, it was time to sell his surprise and hope she didn't realize it was just a cover for correcting his mistake. Fortunately for him, he was good at selling, but then Kitty Anne was good at seeing through him. That was just what it felt like when her gaze turned on him as Nick took her hand in his and drew her attention away from the door.

"I know you're enjoying working with the boys, but—"

"I am," Kitty Anne quickly agreed, flashing him another quick smile. "They're a lot of fun."

"Well, so is fundraising," Nick quickly insisted. "You know, you have to travel and go to parties and galas and all sorts of events and hit rich people up for money and work on our online presence to raise awareness and money there, and then there's the annual Camp D for Delicious Dinner, where our boys cook and prep everything for a big blowout down around the Gulf Coast."

"You take the boys to the beach?" Kitty Anne pulled back, focusing on the smallest detail and completely ignoring his attempts to paint the job as something more than hustling up cash.

"The ones who earn the right." Nick shrugged. "Besides, everybody should have a vacation once a year, right?"

"Hmm." Kitty Anne nodded before sucking in a deep breath and letting it go in a sigh. "And every child should have a qualified teacher...right?"

"W–wh...what?" Nick stuttered, taken aback by the depth of her perception.

"I know, Nick," Kitty Anne assured him in a soft, conspirator whisper that had him blinking in confusion as GD snorted with amusement.

"What do you think you know, beautiful?" GD pressed as he smirked down at her.

"That you actually have to have a degree and be certified to teach," Kitty Anne shot back with a pointed look at Nick, who felt his cheeks flush with heat as his face went up in a rare blush.

"How did you…"

"Mr. Selvage explained it all…like two weeks ago," Kitty Anne admitted, her gaze going soft as her smile reappeared. "I was wondering how long it was going to take you to fire me."

"I—"

"I know," Kitty Anne cut him off again, placing a finger over Nick's lips and stopping him from apologizing. "It's okay. You didn't want to hurt me, and that is sweet, but you know you don't have to give me a job."

"I know," Nick agreed, causing GD to roll his eyes.

"He's been pissing his pants," the big man said, ratting Nick out. "Afraid as hell that you would be all heartbroken to be fired by your boyfriend, which actually is kind of ruthless. That really should drop him in the standing to boyfriend number two, don't you think?"

"Shut up, GD," Nick snapped.

He was trying to have a moment with their girl, and the big man wasn't helping, or maybe he was.

"I kept telling him not to sweat it. This is a hell of promotion, and you fucked him the last time he gave you a job, so…don't you think it's time to get naked?"

Nick liked the sound of that, but Kitty Anne just snorted and shook her head at him.

"I think it is time to hear all about my new job and check out my new shed, which is lovely by the way." Kitty Anne cast a sweet smile in Nick's direction as her eyes gleamed with something more than amusement. "And I'm hoping those windows come with curtains, because I'm assuming the director of fundraising has to take a lot of private meetings with the principal of the school."

Nick smiled, certain now that he was not only in the clear but also that Kitty Anne's clothes were coming off. Hopefully, she hadn't bothered with underwear today.

Chapter Twenty

Kitty Anne had never dreamed she'd have her own office...well, maybe she'd dreamed it, but she'd never thought it would actually happen. Admittedly, it was really a shed. Not an office, but that was a technicality she barely cared to notice.

After all, she had a large room. It had a beautiful natural view out the windows. They provided her not only with sunlight but a nice view of the gardens below and the activity fields beyond.

Those fields were filled with boys playing an impromptu game of soccer. The sight of them tugged at Kitty Anne's heart. She really did like working with the kids. She didn't want to give that up but was momentarily distracted by the chair tucked behind the very large, stately desk.

The desk alone was amazing, but now she had her own seat. Better yet, it was padded, very director looking. Kitty Anne couldn't help but squeal with her excitement as she rushed around the desk to throw herself into the fake leather upholstery with enough force to set the chair in motion. The room whipped around her as she spun with glee.

This was living...only she hadn't earned it.

That grim thought had her glancing back at the boys playing outside as her joy soured and her feet came down. Kitty Anne brought the twirling chair to a stop facing both GD and Nick. They were wearing matching grins, but while GD's was indulgent, Nick's was relieved. She hated to disappoint him, but if she wasn't honest, then there would be no hope for the future.

The truth was Kitty Anne didn't want to be the kind of girl who slept her way into a fancy title. That was that.

"Uh-oh," GD grumbled as he glanced from Kitty Anne's growing frown to Nick's fading smile. "I sense trouble."

GD had a good antenna for trouble. All three of them did, but he in particular was very good at guessing what was wrong with her. Today was no different.

"She's going to turn this job down," the big man informed Nick, causing his frown to darken into a true scowl.

"Why?"

"Because…" GD paused to study Kitty Anne, or maybe to give her a chance to fill in the rest, but she stayed silent, all but daring him to take a guess. "She hasn't earned it."

"And I'm not qualified," Kitty Anne added on just to make sure GD knew he hadn't been completely right.

"Oh please." Nick ignored the looks GD and Kitty Anne exchanged. Instead, he came around the desk to kneel before her and draw Kitty Anne's attention toward him as he took her hands back in his.

"Sexy, you are the three things that make a good fundraiser—hot, charming, and intelligent. Not to mention that you really care about these boys. The rest I can teach you," Nick assured her.

"That's so sweet." Kitty Anne sighed, pulling one of her hands free to cup the side of his face. Nick leaned into her touch, his eyes fluttering closed as his expression softened. "But—"

"No buts." Nick cut her off, his eyes snapping open to pin her with a pleading look. "Give it six months."

"And," Kitty Anne stressed, not about to give in completely, "if I'm no good, you fire me."

"Deal." Nick nodded his agreement without even taking a second to think about it.

He didn't need to, and Kitty Anne knew it was because he was lying. Nick would never fire her, but she could quit. That was just what she'd do if she failed to do right by both him and the boys. After all, a place like Camp D survived off fundraising. They needed her to do well. She'd give it everything she had.

Sealing that vow with a kiss, Kitty Anne leaned forward to brush her mouth across Nick's in a soft caress that left them both hungry for more. There was no good reason not to give in to that urge. Gentle and easy at first, it wasn't long before their lips were clinging to each other as their tongues began to tangle and duel.

Things were getting hot and heavy quickly and would have continued to grow even more so if GD hadn't interrupted by clearing his throat. Kitty Anne and Nick broke apart, their gazes locking as they shared a moment of both humor and understanding before they turned pointedly toward GD. He stood there on the other side of the desk, clearly biting back a smirk.

"Was there something you wanted?" Nick drawled out slowly, his accent, as always, thickening when he got turned on.

"I was just wondering when you were going to tell Kitty Anne that *I* picked out the chair." GD shrugged as if it weren't anything really to him, but the accusation in his tone was clear, even if it didn't sound sincere.

That didn't change the fact that he wanted his gratitude, and Kitty Anne was more than willing to give it to him. Maybe that was what he'd been waiting on all this time. It had been two weeks' worth of blowjobs. As much as she loved sucking his dick, she was more interested in taking it for a ride.

That thought had her smiling.

"If you'll excuse me for just a moment." Kitty glanced over at Nick, who held his hands up and scooted back.

"You do what you got to do, sexy."

"Thanks."

Kitty Anne stood up and ran a hand down the length of the skirt of the hideous dress her mother had deemed appropriate for church. Thankfully, Lynn Anne had not deemed GD's church as appropriate. She'd taken off that morning to go join her friends in their traditional Sunday routines. The boys also had a Sunday routine that would keep them busy elsewhere. That meant Kitty Anne had a little time with her men to herself. She wasn't about to let that opportunity pass.

With a sudden motion, Kitty Anne yanked the skirt up and out of her way as she went flying across the desk. Her feet barely touched the solid wood surface as she jumped up onto it and used the smooth platform as a launching pad that had her sailing through the air and slamming into GD. Instinctively his arms came up to catch her as he stumbled backward before crashing to the floor.

Before GD could offer any resistance, Kitty Anne had him pinned to the floor, and before he could even object, she was ripping at his clothes as she rained kisses down his neck and across his chest. GD didn't fight her, no doubt thinking he was about to get another blowjob, but she had a surprise for him. No sooner had she untangled his belt and freed the long, thick length of his cock from the folds of his suit pants than she was lifting up her skirt and mounting him. GD's expression tightened from a look of indulgence to a flash of alarm as the wet, swollen folds of her pussy slid down over his dick.

"That's right." Kitty Anne smiled smugly. "I'm not wearing underwear. Wanna see?"

Kitty Anne was aware of Nick rushing around the desk to slam the door to the shed closed. He threw the lock into place just as she whipped the oversized grandma gown off her head and tossed it to the side, leaving her wearing nothing more than a bra and two inches of the thickest dick she'd ever tried to mount.

Tried being the word, because GD was bent on driving her nuts. His hands came up to clamp around her waist and hold her aloft, refusing to allow Kitty Anne to fuck him. Apparently, he didn't see letting her fuck him as a compromise to his insistent, and stupid, stance of refusing to fuck her.

"Sorry, beautiful." GD smirked, sounding anything but apologetic. "But you know my conditions."

Yes, she did. She'd let him have his way for two weeks, but the man was being outright stubborn now. This was a loophole. She should be allowed to take what she wanted. If she wasn't, then he wasn't going to get what he wanted.

"Fine."

Kitty Anne jerked upward, completely unconcerned about her nudity. She didn't even pay Nick any mind as he stepped away from the blinds he'd just lowered to snap her bra free. It fell to the floor, like a gauntlet being thrown down. That attitude matched her tone perfectly.

"You want to be *technical* about everything, then no more blowjobs for you!" Kitty Anne stuck her chin in the air as she made that grand declaration. "After all, that is considered oral sex, and we can't have that…not until you wear *my* collar."

"Is that right?" GD scrambled off the floor, his hands working fast to tuck his big, flushed erection back into his pants.

Kitty Anne knew why he was putting himself away. He was afraid if he kept his cock out, he might put it to use. That was because he was close to breaking. He just had to be. She was pretty sure she knew how to break him.

"Yes. That's right. You can consider yourself cut off."

Kitty Anne refused to give an inch, even as GD paced slowly forward, backing her into Nick's hard heat. He was leaning against her desk, and his arms came up to cage her in, forcing Kitty Anne to settle back against him, even as GD pinned her into place with his large frame.

"And what about you?"

"Me?" Kitty Anne blinked innocently, even as she began to grind her ass against the deliciously hard bulge hidden behind Nick's zipper. "I think I'll survive. After all, I still have one penis to play with."

Nick chuckled behind her. His fingers dug into her hips as he helped her pump the plush globes of her ass down the length of his erection. It would have felt a lot better, though, if he'd freed himself first.

"Do you really expect me to make a choice between you and GD?" Nick murmured, the amusement in his tone assuring her he was far from distressed by the situation.

"No." Kitty Anne offered GD a smile before glancing back at Nick and hitting him with the truth. "I expect you to choose *you* over both of us. I mean, really? Do you want to get in the middle of this battle?"

"Hmmm." Nick cast a smirk in GD's direction. "She's got a point there, big man. What do you have to offer me?"

"I can offer you a promise," GD retorted without a hint of distress sounding in the dark growl of his tone. "I will have retribution."

"Don't you threaten him," Kitty Anne snapped, turning in Nick's arms to cuddle him close. Sliding a hand behind his neck, she pushed his head downward into the soft mound of her bosom. "He is allowed to do what is best for him."

"Yes," GD agreed easily, but the warning was still there in his words. "He is."

Kitty Anne's gaze narrowed on him, but she didn't have a response to that. She didn't need one. Nick's actions spoke for themselves as his lips molded around the puckered tip of her breast and began to suckle, nibble, and lick. He used his mouth, teeth, and tongue to tease and torment her nipple, leaving her gasping and arching into his mouth. Raining kisses down the gentle curve of one breast and up the side of the other, he captured her tender tit in a heated caress that had her twisting anew.

She couldn't help but smile as she felt GD press in even closer, his broad palms settling down over her ass as he began to roughly massage the two well-rounded cheeks. He rolled them up and apart, again and again until the callused tips of his fingers slipped down into the crease that divided her cheeks. Those blunt, callused tips hesitated to press ever so slightly to the entrance hidden between her cheeks.

Kitty Anne's breath caught as she tensed, wondering if he'd penetrate her now. He didn't. Instead, GD's bold touch slid down the slick trail to where her cunt was creaming itself in anticipation.

Not to be outdone, Nick curled a free hand around her breast to torment her swollen and wet nipple, even as he feasted on the other one. His hunger was a perfect match for the blunt, carnal exploration of GD's fingers. They traced over her swollen folds, plundering her intimate flesh before fucking themselves deep into her cunt and making Kitty Anne cry out with the pleasure that spasmed through her.

This was heaven, trapped between her two men, feeling their hands clutching at her, their mouths warm and hot against her skin. GD nibbled his way down the sensitive curve of her neck and spine as he slid to his knees. With a jerk, he yanked her hips back and her pussy down onto his waiting tongue.

Kitty Anne squealed and squirmed, delighted by the delicious pleasure of feeling his velvety tongue tickle up the sides of her sheath. She didn't even care that he'd pulled her free of Nick's ravaging kisses. She did, however, care when Nick slid up onto the desk and began fumbling with his belt buckle.

She had known that he would never choose GD's side. Nick was much more practical than that. Even if he wasn't, the pleasure was too intense to deny. It had been that way from the first time they'd laid eyes on each other, and nothing had changed in the past couple of weeks. Just the opposite. The hunger seemed to grow only stronger every time they came together.

Today was no different. Kitty Anne watched through narrow eyes as he freed his long, thick shaft. Already glistening with the proof of his own excitement, his blind eye pointed right at her in an unblinking invitation she couldn't deny. That didn't make it any easier to pull away from GD's tantalizing tongue.

He was tormenting her clit now and making her pant and mew. He twirled her pulsing bud around and around until she was light-headed and dizzy from the frantic bliss bubbling up her spine. She was aglow and alight with pleasure but nowhere near the rapturous release Kitty Anne knew awaited her if only she could find the strength to pull free of GD and crawl up onto Nick's lap.

It took a moment, and in the end, it didn't require strength so much as blind determination. With that, Kitty Anne managed to throw herself at Nick, pulling free of GD's kiss at the same time. Just as GD had fallen over when she'd crashed into him, Nick fell back as Kitty Anne plowed into him.

She took instant advantage, crawling up onto the desk and mounting him in a move just as she had GD. But unlike the big man, Nick didn't deny her. Instead, he let her take the full ride, his hands reaching up to guide her down the length of his dick as her pussy wept and pulsed in eager welcome. The hard thickness of his cock stretched her muscles wide, setting off fabulous thrills that fairly tickled a laugh right out of her. The joyous sound broke into a moan of pure, wanton need as GD stepped up to take command of the situation.

He knocked away Nick's hands as he claimed control of her hips, forcing Kitty Anne the rest of the way downward with a hard thrust that had her breath catching. The fizzy delight that had infused her sharpened into a piercing rapture that left her incapable of thought. All she could do was feel, and enjoy, as GD began to direct her motions, forcing her to fuck Nick with a rapid speed that had her breasts bouncing and the sweat building up along her spine.

Kitty Anne could feel the searing pressure of a glorious climax beginning to build within her. That was why it made perfect sense that would be the moment GD jerked her completely free of Nick's dick, leaving her cunt clenching around nothing but the painful emptiness. She cried out in dismay, flying into a wanton rage that ended with a squeal as she found herself slammed down over the meaty thickness of GD's dick.

He'd broken.

She'd known he would eventually. Not that GD would dare to admit to such a failure.

"Just a little taste," he snarled into her ear as he stumbled back into one of the guest chairs and pinned her down onto his lap. "So you know exactly what you are missing."

Kitty Anne smirked, not believing that was what motivated him for a moment. It didn't matter. What mattered was how good he felt. GD was definitely worth the wait, but she'd be a fool to hesitate a second longer. It was time to show him just what he'd been missing.

Planting her feet on the floor and her palms on the arms of the chair, Kitty Anne began to ride GD as fast as she could, given she was backward. He helped, his hands still clenching at her hips and guiding her motions as they grunted it out. The climax that had been cresting in her only seconds ago imploded on itself, fueling the inferno of pleasure consuming her.

Kitty Anne lost herself in the perfection of the moment. His dick was thick and long, its hard length stretching her muscles deliciously wide as the flared head of his cock ground against the sensitive walls of her sheath. Each pump of her hips ignited flares of pure-white rapture that had her twisting in desperation for more.

More was not on the menu, though. At least not for her. Her men, on the other hand, had plans. They involved tormenting her. Kitty Anne received that message loud as GD's fingers tightened around her hips, forcing her to a stop. To assure she stayed that way, he slid his knees slid out from under hers, trapping her legs between his and forcing her cunt to constrict wondrously tight around his dick.

It was almost too much but not nearly enough to light the release simmering in her veins. That pleasure boiled higher as GD slid a hand around and shoved it right down between her legs. His fingers unerringly found her clit. He began to slowly massage the little bundle of nerves, making Kitty Anne pant and melt against him as the bliss fizzling at the edge of her nerves intensified. Still, it wasn't enough, and he knew it.

"Well?" GD growled against her ear as his thumb rounded her clit, making Kitty Anne whimper. "You ready to put that collar on and finish this?"

The answer was forever yes, but Kitty Anne bit the words back. Instead, she responded by sliding her hand over his and down farther to the hot, heavy balls tucked up tight against her pussy. She treated GD to the same slow rolls that he tried to punish her with as she threw his words back at him.

"Are you? Because I could whip you up a collar and a leash in no time."

That earned her a laugh, though not from GD. Nick chuckled as he slid off the desk. He'd been watching them with a heated gaze that had only heightened the erotic thrill of the moment. Now, apparently, he was coming off the bench.

"You need a little help there, big man?" Nick smirked as he stepped up, drawing Kitty Anne's gaze up to his sparkling ones.

"This is a job for boyfriend number one," GD shot back with a snarl, not that he managed to intimidate Nick.

"Well then, I better get on it."

Kitty Anne couldn't agree more. With a smug smile that matched Nick's, she wiggled her ass as much as she could given her position and offered up a suggestion that had her heart racing with anticipation.

"Maybe we ought to move the big man to the backseat?" Kitty Anne all but purred as she leaned forward to lick her tongue out across the flushed and swollen head of Nick's cock as it bobbed just inches from her lips. Glancing up to catch his gaze, she was all but certain of victory. "Then maybe we can get this dick out of the cold into a nice, warm pussy?"

"You take my cunt, and I'll beat you bloody, boy," GD warned him with enough sharpness to make it clear he wasn't kidding. "You want to get fucked, then you can get sucked."

"I won't say no to that," Nick assured then both, proving who he was really loyal to because Kitty Anne knew he wasn't afraid of GD's fists. She'd never let him use them. They all three knew that.

"So, it's like that, is it?" Kitty Anne asked, going for a dry, condescending tone but knowing she failed to fool them. Both men knew just how much she liked to get a taste of them. That was just what was on the menu.

"Yeah, sexy, that's exactly how it is like." Nick matched his words with actions as he fisted a hand in her hair, but before he tilted her head down, he tilted it up, forcing her to meet his gaze. "And you're going to do right by both of us, or we're going to do something wrong to you. Understand?"

Kitty Anne didn't answer that threat. She just smiled and pulled free of his hold so she could take that taste he so desperately wanted her to have. That wasn't all Nick was desperate for, but it was all he was going to get. Poor GD, he wasn't even going to get that.

Chapter Twenty-One

"You know, they're just being difficult…refusing to have sex. What the *hell* is the point of that?" Heather demanded to know, not that she gave GD a chance to answer. "They're *Cattlemen*, for God's sake! They're supposed to use sex as a tool, not a weapon!"

"Weapons are tools," GD pointed out, earning himself a dirty look. He returned it with equal force, not in the mood to listen to Heather complain when he was aching himself.

Kitty Anne, that naughty vixen, had left both Nick and GD high and dry with erections that were painful to say the least. She thought she was teaching them a lesson. Well, it would be a lesson for her. He didn't give in. He got even. Kitty Anne was going to learn that the hard way.

GD had a feeling so was Heather.

"Fine." Heather held up her hands. "I can see you're not in the mood today to listen to me bitch about Alex and Konor, but what about Gwen? Huh? Can I complain about her?"

GD frowned at the mention of that name, all his senses going on alert. "Why? She been hanging around?"

Even as he asked that question, GD's gaze scanned over the nearly empty bakery. It was almost closing time, and he was only down here because he had to run a different errand. That, and if he'd stayed out at the Camp, he would have inevitably given in to Kitty Anne's charms.

As it was, he couldn't stop thinking about how gloriously wet and mind-blowingly tight Kitty Anne's little cunt had been. Sinking into her had been like sinking into heaven, and he could only damn himself as a fool for not taking complete advantage of her.

A prideful fool. That was GD, and he knew it. He also knew Heather wasn't far behind him, making them a matched set.

"No, she's not here now." Heather pointed out the obvious. "But she's been lingering about, and I know what she's trying to do."

"What?" GD asked because he'd really like a clue.

It'd been two weeks since his suspicions had been roused, but he hadn't followed through on them, too busy out at the camp to worry about the outside world. For a second there, he felt a twinge of guilt as he recognized he'd abandoned the friends he had out there, like Lana and the Davis brothers and, apparently, Heather.

"My men...or at least one of them," Heather huffed. "I mean, my God, GD, she snuck into his bed! That's like a blinking, neon sign reading 'psycho.'"

Yeah it was, but even psychos had motives. The question was, what was it? Or that was his question. Heather didn't seem to care about the answer. She just wanted Gwen gone.

"Of course, I'd feel a whole lot better about the situation if I was certain that I was taking care of his needs, but the damn man won't let me."

While she might sound pissed as hell about that fact, GD could sense the underlying hurt and insecurity. It bothered him not simply because she was one of his best friends and he hated to see her doubt herself but also because he couldn't help but wonder if he were inflicting the same kind of pain on Kitty Anne.

Maybe he was taking the wrong track here, or, maybe, he was just desperate.

"Why don't you just tell them how you are feeling?" GD suggested, knowing it was a futile effort because that was just too simple of an answer for women. It certainly was for Kitty Anne.

"Please." Heather snorted. "I know they're up to something. Probably trying to prove some stupid point about how good we'd be as a family."

"And that's a problem?" GD frowned, not following Heather's logic at all.

"Yes," she snapped back, as if he were the illogical one. "You can't prove that you're a good family in just a matter of days. It takes time. It takes *years!*"

"Well then, I guess you're going to be waiting for a while, huh?"

"Unless, of course, there is a way to accelerate the process," Heather muttered to herself as her eyes began to glint with a look GD knew all too well.

"You mean a way to make a bigger mess out of everything, don't you?" GD corrected her, knowing he was right. She knew it, too, and didn't deny it.

"Oh, shut up." Heather heaved a heavy sigh. "Don't think I don't know whose side you are on."

"Yours."

"Theirs."

"Isn't that the same side?" GD asked pointedly, earning himself another dirty look.

"Are you ready to order?" Heather snapped, intentionally ignoring his question.

"I'm not hungry." At least, not for food or anything else Heather could offer him. "I just stopped by to see how you were doing."

"Well, now you know. I'm horny."

There was a time, not but weeks past, that he'd have offered to help her with that problem. Today, though, they both just had to suffer through the pain.

"I know that look." Heather smirked. "You're in just as tight a spot as me, aren't you?"

"I might be," GD agreed, finding it a little odd to talk to Heather about Kitty Anne. It had never been an issue before, but something told him that Kitty Anne wouldn't appreciate him confiding too much in another woman, particularly Heather.

"Oh, I forgot," Heather muttered to herself before snickering down at him. "You're dating Kitty Anne. I don't know whether to celebrate the likelihood that you're about to get yours or pity you for what's coming."

"And what is that?" GD challenged her, bristling slightly at Heather's tone.

"Your downfall," she stated succinctly, making her opinion perfectly clear. "That woman's going to have you collared and leashed. I can already see it coming."

"Please." GD snorted, shifting uncomfortably. "No woman will ever leash me."

Heather's smile only grew at that as she turned and sauntered off to tend to the customer who came bustling into the bakery. GD recognized the older man as Mr. Wilkins, the manager of the local bank and a habitual Danish eater. He'd come for his fix, which meant he'd somehow escaped his wife. Everybody knew that Mrs. Wilkins ran a tight-fisted ship that was likely to keep Mr. Wilkins from eating himself into diabetes or an early death from a heart attack.

Lucky Mr. Wilkins. GD, on the other hand, was likely to be driven to an early grave by Kitty Anne. If not her, then by Nick, who was just as crazy as their girl. That left GD to be the sane one. More importantly, it was his job to assure that the two of them didn't spin completely out of control.

That was just why he headed out the bakery and turned to head for the entrance to the alley that ran back behind the row of buildings fronting Main Street. Every business along the way had a back door that fed into the alley, and he headed straight for the dented, metal door that belonged to the local newspaper.

GD had to figure that was where Rachel kept her notes, given she was living with two very nosy, very protective deputies. Killian and Adam were good enough guys, but the truth was they weren't much a match for Rachel. The girl was two steps ahead of them and headed for only God knew what kind of trouble.

One thing GD did know was that she wasn't taking Kitty down with her. He also knew that Kitty Anne wouldn't let anything happen to Kevin. They were tight. They were fishing buddies, and fishing buddies didn't betray each other. Still Nick would, no doubt, feel better if GD could assure him for certain that Rachel wasn't using Kitty Anne to work any angle.

So, he picked the lock and slipped into the back room that still housed an old-time printing press that had long ago been abandoned. Thankfully the lock had been just as old and comprised the entire security system for the offices that were still being used out front. GD slid through the shadows of the press toward the small rooms brightly lit by the sun shining through the windows that opened onto the main walk out front.

He was careful to keep an eye out for anybody passing by as he ambled over to the neatest desk in the room. Rachel's nameplate was clearly displayed, along with her sense of organization, which actually made everything easier for GD. He found what he was looking for in only a matter of minutes, but it wasn't exactly what he'd expected.

* * * *

Kitty Anne blinked back the tears as she read the sad tale of the little, lost boy and tried not to let how deeply upset she was show. The hero in the story had been neglected by his mom, picked on by his step-dad, and ultimately abandoned by his brother when he was thrown out of the house. That was when the kid had decided to go find his oldest brother, Patton.

Kitty Anne had to admit she was a little confused by that, but accepted that Kevin had probably altered a few details to fit the story narrative or to, maybe, mask the truth. She could see it anyway, though.

The kid was Kevin and he'd walked all the way from Louisiana, across Mississippi to end up in Pittsview, Alabama all for a sister he didn't even know. As amazing as that tale was, the story ended there. It just stopped abruptly, but Kitty Anne knew that wasn't the way life was.

So, she forced a smile for the boy anxiously watching her and decided to press for more. Kevin looked, as always, torn between fear and hope, and she knew him well enough now to know how desperately he wanted acceptance, wanted approval, and didn't need pity.

"Well?" Kevin pressed, bringing Kitty Anne's attention back to his worried scowl. "Do you like it?"

"It's very moving," Kitty Anne assured him before focusing on her job. "However, there are some grammatical mistakes that do distract from the power of the content."

"Power," Kevin repeated, blinking up at her as if Kitty Anne were some kind of angel. "You think my writing has power?"

"It *could*," Kitty Anne cautioned him. "If you put the time and attention into learning some rules."

Kevin snorted at that and glanced toward the window and the yard beyond where a large group of boys were still playing soccer. Kitty Anne could see not only his attention shift but his yearning, too, to be a part of the group. He just didn't know how, but she might have an idea.

"You like soccer?" she asked.

"I got asthma." Kevin shrugged as if that were some kind of answer.

"Kids with asthma can play soccer," she informed him, knowing that didn't make a difference. "But kids who like to write sometimes write about soccer."

"You mean a story?" Kevin glanced back at her with a frown as if the idea confused him.

"I mean like an article." Kitty Anne smiled, warming to her idea, even if Kevin still appeared less than convinced. "Like a sport's journalist...for a newspaper."

"I'm too young to work for a newspaper," Kevin informed her sourly, as if Kitty Anne weren't bright enough to know that fact.

"Well, what about a school paper?"

"There is no school paper."

"Then maybe we should start one." That was checkmate as far as Kitty Anne was concerned, but Kevin still looked far from convinced.

"And what are we going to put into a paper?" Kevin asked, clearly not thinking there was much of interest around campus to be worthy of reporting, but Kitty Anne didn't think that was really the point. She wanted a paper, and there was going to be a paper.

"For starters, we can have a sports champion segment."

"A what?"

"You go down there and watch the game. You figure out who you think the most valuable player is and interview him, and we'll put him in our champion segment."

Kevin blinked but didn't budge as he stared up at her with open doubt. "And what if who I pick doesn't want to be interviewed?"

"I'm sure any of them will want to be in our paper," Kitty Anne assured him, unable to fathom who wouldn't want to be.

"But we don't have a paper," Kevin pointed out once again.

Kitty Anne hung her head in defeat, though, only for the moment. Obviously, she needed to have a talk with Nick. She was sure he'd approve of the idea. There really wasn't much he didn't agree to as long as it kept the boys either mentally or physically active. He especially liked ideas that combined both, which was just why he should jump at the idea of a paper.

More than that, it would be a great marketing and fundraising tool. They could send it out to all the donors so that they could see what their money was being used for. Better yet, they'd see the faces of the boys they were helping. Kitty Anne might not know much about fundraising, but she had to figure that matching faces to the cause would help guilt more people into giving.

It would be good for the boys, too. It would give a chance to some of the kids who had a harder time getting involved, give them the opportunity to do so in a structured and safe way. Kids like Kevin. He wasn't alone in the shy camp, but Kitty Anne knew that wasn't a club Nick had ever belonged to. It was hard for him to understand how difficult a thing could be for more reserved kids.

They needed things like a little extra encouragement. All of them did. The paper could follow success stories of former students, giving the current ones something to look forward to and to work toward.

It was a perfect idea.

"Your story was very good." Kitty Anne lifted her chin and focused back on the real subject at hand.

"Thank you." That compliment was greeted with a relieved smile as he glanced down at the paper she was still holding. "I didn't know if it was...you know, too sad."

Sad wasn't the word for it. It was a heart-wrenching tale of a kid coping not only with his mom's mental illness but also his father's drug abuse. The hero of the piece really was his brother, who had protected him until their mother died and the father threw the older brother out, leaving the kid no choice but to run away.

"I think it just needs a part two," Kitty Anne declared as the quarter-of bell chimed across the campus below. It was a reminder to all that the hour mark was approaching. "I'm going to correct this, and you can pick it up in the morning. That way you can use it so that the next story you submit next week is free of these kinds of mistakes, deal?"

"Deal." Kevin nodded easily as he hopped out of his seat and began collecting his stuff. He paused to offer her a final smile. "I'm so glad that my story moved you. I didn't know I could be powerful."

"A strong voice is always powerful," Kitty Anne instructed him. "But it will weaken if it doesn't learn to speak correctly, understood?"

Kevin snorted and rolled his eyes as he heaved his backpack over his shoulder. "Understood."

"I expect to see you first thing in the morning after breakfast," Kitty Anne called out as he headed out the door of the shed, brushing past Nick, who paused to offer Kevin a quick greeting.

"Hey, Kev."

"Hey, Mr. Dickles."

"You headed down to play soccer."

"No, I'm headed down to watch." Kevin cast a quick look back at Kitty Anne before adding on, "And, apparently, interview one of the guys."

"Interview?" Nick frowned. "For what?"

"For the paper."

That had Nick's scowl deepening. "We don't have a paper."

"I know," Kevin assured him before disappearing down the hall and leaving Nick to cast his confused gaze in Kitty Anne's direction.

"Am I missing something here?"

"I think it would be great if we started a Camp D newspaper. I mean, I know you have to find a teacher to replace me, and I have a lot to learn about fundraising, but…it would be a great fundraising tool, and I'd love to help out getting the paper started."

Kitty Anne pulled herself up, both excited and expectant as she waited for Nick's response. She'd anticipated some amount of interest, good or bad, in the idea, but all she got was a grunt and a shrug.

"Whatever you want to do. I need—"

"What do you mean, whatever I want to do?" Kitty Anne frowned, disappointed with his response. He could show, at least, a modicum of excitement. "Don't you care what I do?"

"Of course I do, beautiful," Nick assured her all too quickly. "But I—"

"I'd believe you more if you would talk to something north of my breasts," Kitty Anne shot back huffily, venting her irritation on cleaning up the small classroom.

"I am not talking to your—"

"Hey, Mr. Dickles." Tony strolled in, confident and grinning as always. The kid was a charmer, and he knew it. He also aimed high, putting the moves on Kitty Anne more than once. "You joining Miss Kitty and me for a lesson?"

There was something about the way Tony talked that just made everything sound a little lewd, and Kitty Anne couldn't help but roll her eyes at the fifteen year-old's antics.

"Actually, I need to have a few private words with Miss Allison."

Nick put enough emphasis on her title to assure that his opinion of the kid's familiarity with Kitty Anne was understood. Just in case it wasn't, the dirty look he shot her made it clear that she'd overstepped her bounds. Maybe he was right. Tony might be harmless, but that didn't make him any less forward.

"Sure thing, Mr. Dickles." Tony nodded eagerly, appearing completely unfazed as he moved into the room to drop his bag by one of the desks.

"I'll just leave this and my...shirt"—Tony whipped his T-shirt off in a move that was clearly practiced and left Kitty Anne biting her cheeks to keep from laughing as he dropped it down on his bag— "right here and go play soccer till you holler for me."

With that, the kid strutted out of the room with the confidence of a man twice as old and three times larger. The sad thing was that Kitty Anne actually suspected Nick might be a little jealous. He certainly was annoyed. He watched Tony go with a look that had Kitty Anne smothering another round of giggles.

Heaving a heavy sigh, he looked toward the ceiling and shook his head. "This is exactly why I had rule against women working at the camp."

"Oh please," Kitty Anne huffed. "He's just teasing."

"No," Nick stated firmly with a shake of his head. "He's not, which is just why I have interviews lined up two weeks from now to find your replacement. Soon, the camp will be happily woman free again."

"How sexist can you be?"

"I might be sexist, but that doesn't mean you and your *mother* aren't causing me all sorts of problems," Nick stated pointedly as he rounded on Kitty Anne, who groaned.

"Oh God. It's going to be one of those talks."

"Yes. It is." Nick swallowed and braced himself in a gesture that was almost as comical as Tony's strut had been. "Your mother has to go."

"That's fine by me." Hell, it sounded better than that, but Kitty Anne knew there was a reason Nick was talking to her and not Lynn Anne. "Why don't you just go tell her that?"

"Because she scares me," Nick admitted with an honesty that had Kitty Anne's frown blooming back into a smile.

"Oh, don't be silly."

"She kneed me in the balls!"

"It was an accident."

"No." Nick shook his head, refusing to accept that lame excuse. "It wasn't, so I'm going to try something less painful and more effective."

"Yeah? And what's that?" Kitty Anne asked, unable to shake the smile his sore tone stirred in her. He was so cute when he got upset.

"I'm going to buy her off."

"What?" Kitty Anne blinked, her smile fading fast. "No."

Kitty Anne wasn't about to let her mother annoy her boyfriend into giving her money. That was too much.

"Absolutely not."

"Kitty Anne—"

"Nope." Kitty Anne shook her head, refusing to even talk about the matter. "Don't worry. I'll get rid of her."

"It's been almost two weeks," Nick complained. "I'm tired and sore, and I want to have sex in a bed like normal people."

"Oh please." Kitty Anne rolled her eyes at that. "We could have sex in a bed if we want to. Besides, we're not having sex, remember? You chose GD's side."

"I didn't choose any sides," Nick insisted, refusing to let Kitty Anne lure him out of his grumpy mood. "And I'm buying your mother off. I know what your mother wants, and I'm just going to give it to her and get rid of her."

"Well, if you're just going to do whatever it is you want, why are you bothering to tell me?" Kitty Anne demanded to know in exasperation.

"Because if I didn't tell you, you'd be upset with me for both doing it and not telling you. This way you're only pissed about one thing," Nick shot back as if that made all the sense in the world. He followed that indignant retort by snatching up Tony's shirt and shaking at her. "And I expect your pupils to stay *clothed*, Miss Allison, is that understood?"

"Kiss my ass, Mr. Dickles."

"Later," he promised her, sending a wicked thrill racing up Kitty Anne's spine. "After you put on GD's collar."

"Good luck."

He was going to need it, and maybe a little motivation wouldn't hurt. After all, as Nick had pointed out, it had been nearly two weeks and GD hadn't caved yet, proving that he was more stubborn than her. Now she had to wait on Nick?

No. He didn't have that kind of fortitude. She'd break him, and she knew just how.

"I'll tell you what." Kitty Anne smiled as she slunk across the room to rub up against Nick suggestively as she purred. "You get rid of my mom, and I'll put GD's collar on and celebrate...but if I get rid of her first, guess who wears the collar."

Chapter Twenty-Two

Monday, June 16th

"I am *not* wearing a collar." GD looked over at Nick, who was grinning like an idiot, and shook his head.

It had been a long, sleepless night. He'd stayed in town at his apartment last night, having worked late at the club. The Davis brothers refused to accept GD's resignation until he'd hired his replacement. They weren't going to waste their time interviewing people. GD suspected that was because each brother knew how hard it was going to be to find a replacement.

Any of the guys at the club would probably jump at the chance to claim the title of master of ceremonies, but that was sort of the problem. The master had to be laid-back and not out for either personal gain or vendettas. GD was considered to be very evenhanded and that was important because the other guys had to respect his opinions and rulings.

He had an idea of who to tap, but at the moment Hailey's brothers were both out somewhere in the Gulf of Mexico fishing. They wouldn't be back until the end of the month. So, some nights GD found himself crashing at his apartment instead of disturbing Kitty Anne and Nick by trying to slip into their bed in the middle of the night.

Besides, these quiet moments gave him a chance to think, normally about Kitty Anne. She was always in his thoughts and right then, his thoughts were focused not only on her but on how to get her to slip on his collar. He knew the woman didn't really object to wearing it.

She was just stubborn.

Kitty Anne was too bullheaded for her own good, and his. After all, she'd had a taste of what he had to offer, and GD knew she'd liked it, but yet…she still turned him down.

That hurt a little. It certainly didn't put him in a good mood.

"And if I'm going to be living out here, I'm really going to need my own office," GD grumbled, knowing he was repeating himself. He just didn't trust that Nick was actually listening.

"We'll attach it to the new house," Nick responded with what was becoming his standard retort. He shrugged, unconcerned about the matter, but then it wasn't his office.

"I'm serious, man," GD stressed.

"I know you are."

"I want to see these plans before they're finalized."

"Whatever."

That wasn't the firm agreement GD had been looking for, but he didn't think Nick was capable of being too firm right then. After all, the man had been getting laid for the past two weeks. That tended to put any man in a good mood. Kitty Anne's mother on the other hand tended to put most men into a bad one.

"That is after we get rid of Lynn Anne," Nick muttered, drawing GD's attention to his darkening frown. "If we *ever* get rid of her."

"It's going to be a week before the paperwork all clears."

"One more week of hell," Nick echoed.

"Yeah." GD frowned at the screen as he finally cleared the last hurdle and made it into Lana's bank account. "Well, shit."

"What?" Nick perked up, glancing over at the laptop GD had set up on Kitty Anne's desk. "Now that's a woman worth a lot of money."

"And if Gwen knew that, she'd probably ask for more," GD muttered to himself, wondering just why the hell Lana was paying her in the first place.

"Who?" Nick lifted a brow in open curiosity.

"Nobody," GD quickly assured him, backing out of Lana's accounts and closing down his laptop as he pointedly turned the conversation to the story Nick had shown him earlier. "What we really need to talk about is Rachel's investigation."

"Oh yeah. That." Nick's nose wrinkled as he settled back in his seat with a sigh. "I told you that woman was up to no good."

"She's just doing her job," GD corrected him for like the millionth time that morning. "More importantly, there was nothing in Rachel's notes that indicated that Kitty Anne had told her anything. She figured out the Seth's connection all on her own."

"And Kevin?"

"She doesn't know about him...well, not really. She's found his birth certificate, but hasn't put all the pieces together." It was only a matter of time before she did. "Right now, she's deduced that Seth came here to find Patton. Oh, and she thinks that *he* started the fire."

She was looking for proof, which was dangerous. Not just for Kevin and Seth. Alex and the district attorney hadn't pressed charges against Kevin for the Davis barn fire despite the evidence of his guilt. That was in their prerogative, but that didn't mean the voters would agree when the story ran in the paper.

Once that happened, all hell was going to break loose. It was tragedy upon tragedy. The girl—whose mother had abandoned her and whose father had been murdered by the father of the men who raised her and now claimed her as their own—had two brothers from her crazy mother that nobody had ever known about. That was the kind of drama the gossips waited a lifetime to kibitz over.

"And you suggest...what?" Nick waited pointedly, but he knew GD only had an old, well-worn solution.

"Telling the Davis brothers the truth."

And they could be the ones to tell Patton.

"That's up to Kevin and Seth," Nick insisted. "I'm not going to force either one of them to do anything. When they're ready—"

"What if Seth's never ready?" GD asked, loathing that cliché. Sometimes people were just too stubborn for their own good and needed a swift kick in the butt, but not literally.

"He will be. Even if Seth doesn't, Kevin probably will. Just look at how far he's come."

"Thanks to Kitty Anne," GD reminded him. "She's working wonders with him."

"Kitty Anne's got an ulterior motive."

"Oh come on," GD groaned. "What is it going to take to make you trust her?"

"What's it going to take to make you?" Nick shot back pointedly, but GD didn't have a clue as to what he was talking about.

"What is that supposed to mean?"

"When you wear Kitty Anne's collar...then I'll tell her whatever she wants to know about Kevin."

"I'm not crazy enough to let Kitty Anne put a collar on me." GD wasn't about to sink into that quicksand. Instead, he picked up his laptop and shoved his seat back. "Now, I got to go handle some business out at the club so...give Kitty Anne a kiss for me when you see her at lunch and tell her I'll see her later. Okay?"

"You can kiss me now," Kitty Anne cut in, speaking up from the doorway behind GD.

The doorway Nick could see clearly. His smile assured GD that he'd just been set up. If that didn't clue him in that she'd heard too much, Kitty Anne's own warning did.

"Of course I might bite, you never know. After all, you can't trust me, can you?"

"Thanks," GD whispered furiously at Nick, whose grin was growing wider by the second.

"Don't be snapping at Nick," Kitty Anne said, jumping immediately to his defense as she came wheeling around the desk to confront GD with her frown. "What is this? You won't wear my collar? What the hell do you think I'm going to do with you?"

That was a conversation he didn't want to have because he didn't want to give her any ideas. Instead, GD took the low road and pointed at Nick as he threw him under the bus. "He doesn't trust you with Kevin."

"What?" That had Kitty Anne wheeling around. "You don't trust me? Why the hell not?"

"We know you're working with Rachel on a story about Seth and Kevin," Nick warned her, cutting Kitty Anne off before she could blatantly lie. Of course, instead of responding with any sense of shame or embarrassment, Kitty Anne drew herself up indignantly.

"And just how do you know that?" Kitty Anne demanded to know.

"GD broke into the newspaper office and read her notes," Nick answered without any hesitation, drawing a glare from the accused himself as he growled out his displeasure at being betrayed.

"Thanks, man. That was a great help."

"You broke into Rachel's office?" Kitty Anne heaved a deep sigh as she shook her head at him. "You know that's illegal, right?"

"Only if you get caught," GD assured her. "And I'd love to continue this argument but—"

"You got to go to your naked girlie club," Kitty Anne filled in for him.

"I'm quitting. I swear."

"I guess I'll have to trust you then, huh?"

GD shot Kitty Anne a dirty look for that low blow and stepped around the desk to drop a quick kiss that spun out of control as she went all soft and easy in his arms. She was so sweet and sassy, and he'd have loved nothing more than to back her up against Nick's desk and have a little fun, but he really did have business to take care of.

Reluctantly lifting his lips, he gazed down into her eyes and cupped her gently curved jaw in his, allowing his thumb to stroke over the velvety smooth arch of her cheek.

"I'm not wearing a collar," he whispered softly. "But don't ever doubt that I'm your slave."

Kitty Anne's lips pulled into a satisfied grin. "I know, and you know I'm not going to do anything that might harm Kevin."

GD smiled. He did know, just as he knew it would irritate the crap out of her when he failed to agree. So he left her standing there, staring after him as he whistled his way out the door.

* * * *

Kitty Anne watched GD saunter away and couldn't help but sense that something else was up. He was moving too fast, not that she was really worried about him and the club. She knew all the signs of a cheating man, having gone through that before. GD was too attentive and way too horny to be straying just yet.

That thought gave Kitty Anne pause as it dawned on her that maybe GD and Nick weren't the only ones with trust issues. At least, though, she was trying. That was more than she could say for either of her men.

"You keep frowning like that and your face will get stuck," Nick warned her as he stretched forward to snake an arm around her waist and tumble Kitty Anne back onto his lap. "And you have such a pretty face. I hate to see it marred with such an angry scowl."

"So says the man who is worried I'm going to…what?" Kitty Anne looked up at him. "What is it you really think I'm going to do? Tell Patton that she has two brothers she doesn't know about? Or tell Rachel and let her write a story that blows up an entire family?"

Nick frowned over her questions. That was exactly what worried him. That and more, but he couldn't tell her that without revealing even more.

"Kitty Anne—"

"Nope." Kitty Anne held her up her hand in a pointed gesture for silence. "Save your lies, old man. I'm here for the truth!"

"I think you've been spending too much time with the boys," Nick muttered, making Kitty Anne smile as she took that complaint as a compliment.

"I probably do, and that's because I care." Kitty Anne sighed dramatically and shook her head at him was a sad slowness. "How could you think I would betray any one of them?"

"Then you're not going to tell Rachel anything?" Nick asked, neatly avoiding answering her question, though the answer was clear in his tone. He didn't trust her. Kitty Anne suspected that only time would soothe his worry. Time, and honesty.

"I might," Kitty Anne admitted. "But that's because I trust Rachel, and she wouldn't do anything to harm a child."

"She's a reporter," Nick retorted, as if that said it all.

"She has a conscience," Kitty Anne insisted. "Besides, I might need her help."

That darkened Nick's scowl as he grumbled defensively. "For what?"

"I'd tell you, but then I'd have to kill you."

"Kitty Anne!"

"You're going to have to trust me whether you want to or not," Kitty Anne declared magnificently as she shoved out of Nick's lap and rounded on him to wag a finger in his face. "Because families trust each other, and they stick together."

"Is that why you haven't chased your mother off?" Nick shot back as he caught her finger and brought it to his lips to nibble on the tip. He was trying to distract her, but she refused to be deterred.

"My mom is not so bad." Kitty Anne snatched her finger back as Nick hooted up a laugh.

"I'm sorry, sexy, but—yes. Yes, she is."

Kitty Anne couldn't argue that point. Still, she hesitated to agree. Her mother might be nutty and annoying, but she'd provided for Kitty Anne. She'd made sure she'd done well in school and didn't get into too much trouble. There had always been food and safety at her mother's house, despite how hard she'd struggled to provide those two basic things.

"I guess she is," Kitty Anne admitted slowly. "But you don't know what she's done for me over the years. It's not going to be easy to kick her to the curb."

"Nobody's getting kicked to the curb." Nick smiled slightly. "And I can see what she's done to you. Driven you a little crazy, hasn't she?"

"Just a little."

Then again Nick drove her a little crazy, too, but only in the best of ways. There was just something about being near to him that filled her with a warmth that always managed to make her feel better. Maybe it was his scent, which always heated her through.

Perhaps it was the feel of his body against hers. That always got her blood flowing in a rush. It got other things flowing, too. Kitty Anne sighed as her thoughts skipped away from her. They didn't get too far but were reeled back in by the sexy rumble of Nick's voice.

"You do accept that she has to go, right?" He sounded almost pained and a little afraid, making Kitty Anne smile.

"Yeah, I get that, but you got to understand I provide for her." Kitty Anne always would. That was just the way it was supposed to be. "So, she's never going to be too far away."

"We provide for her," Nick corrected as he used the hand he still had a hold of to tumble her back into his lap. "And Dothan isn't that far away…is it?"

"No." Kitty Anne wiggled into a more comfortable position, intentionally grinding her ass against the thick ridge of the boner pressing against her. "But we're not going to spend all morning talking about my mother, are we?"

"And what would you rather do?" Nick purred, his hand dipping down lower on her back until he was palming her ass. "Because I got a few ideas."

"I thought you were planning on holding out on me. Something about a collar?"

"Oh yeah." Nick smiled, keeping his hand right where it was. "Well, you know if I closed my eyes, then I wouldn't know if you were or you weren't wearing anything at all."

"I see." Kitty Anne couldn't help but smirk as Nick matched his words with actions, lifting his arms to thread his fingers behind his head and lean back.

"Then you could just have your dirty way with me."

"Well...I do have a few ideas," Kitty Anne admitted, already enjoying the thought of what came next.

* * * *

With the sun blazing down overhead, GD knew he didn't have to worry about Gwen being home. Despite the fact that she was accumulating a fortune in payoffs, she still had a job. So did all her neighbors. That made it a perfect time to go snooping.

That was just what he intended to do, and GD didn't even care what Kitty Anne might think of his tactics. It was necessary, and that was all there was to it because he needed to know what was going on between Gwen and Lana.

The only thing that was clear was that Lana was paying Gwen off, which could mean only that Gwen was blackmailing Lana. Given Lana wasn't skimming money from the club, there was only one other thing that GD could figure she'd pay to hide. Her brothers had started the fire.

That had to be it. Now he just needed to prove it.

Gwen had to have proof, and he was betting she kept it at home.

That wasn't all he was looking for, though. Given the amount of money Gwen was taking in, GD could only assume she'd made blackmail a professional career. Depending on who she was earning her butter from, her career could mean the death of the club. They couldn't afford to have Gwen ruin the illusion of security that GD had worked all these years to assure.

Beyond that, it was just a professional insult.

So, he had to know. He needed to figure out how far Gwen's scheme actually went and how many victims there were. He was hoping Gwen kept some kind of record or trophy trove at home, which, of course, she did. The woman didn't even have the sense to hide the evidence.

Instead, she had it meticulously organized and filed appropriately away, making it easy enough for him to find what he wanted. It would have been that easy for any of Gwen's victims to do the same, given she'd left more than one window wide open. Of course, she was probably relying on the fact that all the men she was blackmailing were too old to climb through a window without breaking a hip.

At least, GD assumed all the pictures of half-naked men tied to her bed were being blackmailed with them. Thankfully, none of them belonged to the club. Disturbingly, one of them was a preacher, and two were on the city council.

Most importantly, any of them could have been daddy dearest to the bun in Gwen's oven, and it looked as though she was baking something up. The doctors' bills and sonogram sort of proved the point. That was another problem the club wouldn't have to face.

Thankfully, GD was quitting, so it wouldn't be his problem.

"I thought I made it clear"—Kitty Anne's voice cut through the silent afternoon air and sent a shaft of honest fear straight down GD's spine— "breaking and entering is illegal...and I'm not real fond of dating criminals."

His heart froze as he glanced up to find Kitty Anne smirking at him across the room. She was there...in Gwen's house. GD just couldn't seem to accept those two facts, but when it did hit him, he exploded with the terror of his revelation.

"*What in the hell are you doing here?*" GD roared, charging at Kitty Anne with every intent of getting her the hell away from here.

"I followed you," Kitty Anne shot back as she quickly danced around Gwen's desk and away from GD. "And really I should be asking you that...once you tell me where here is."

"It doesn't matter where here is," GD snapped, lunging for and grasping Kitty Anne by the arm. "Because you're leaving. Now!"

"See? You don't want to date a criminal any more than I do." Kitty Anne latched onto the doorframe as GD tried to drag her past it and dug her nails in.

"Damn it, Kitty Anne! Let go!"

GD turned to try and pry Kitty Anne's hands free, but every time he managed one, she squirmed away from him, forcing him to redirect his attention and allowing her to clamp back down on the doorframe.

"Not until you explain to me what is going on."

"I'm working," GD snarled. "Now let go."

"Working on what?" Kitty Anne panted, fighting him with all her strength as he finally managed to free her from the door.

"None of your business."

That got GD tripped as Kitty Anne shifted her weight and used her legs to snarl his up and send him crashing backward into the hutch in Gwen's dining room, the hutch she used to display china that was way too nice not to be expensive. That made it all the more painful when they came crashing down. GD's patience shattered right along with each plate, platter, and serving dish as they all hit the hardwood floor.

"Oops."

"*Oops?*"

GD choked on that word, unable to believe that was all Kitty Anne had to say.

"Time to go," Kitty Anne declared, and then she went racing across the house to the bathroom and the window that opened into the backyard.

By the time GD got there, Kitty Anne was already gone. He caught up with her cutting through the woods to where she'd left her convertible parked behind his truck, one neighborhood over. GD let her run free, only striking when she'd reached her car. Then he pinned her up against it, using his entire body to flatten her along the curve of the driver's side door.

"What the hell do you think you're doing?" he demanded to know with a snarl that should have had Kitty Anne concerned, but the damn woman just ground herself up against him and wrapped her arms around his neck as she leaned up to nibble her way down his jaw.

"You're not really mad at me...are you?" Kitty Anne murmured softly between each suckling kiss she laid down his neck.

"This isn't going to work," GD warned her, stiffening up as he quickly reversed directions before she could feel how well it was actually working. "Return to the camp, and I will deal with you later."

"Oh." Kitty Anne perked up at that, her eyes taking on the same wicked gleam her smile did. "Am I going to get a spanking?"

She knew what those words did to him, knew the images his mind painted, and knew, too, how hard they made him. He was aching in an instant, and Kitty Anne was on him in the next one, her hand dropping down to cup the thick bulge of his erection as she rubbed the stiff peaks of her breasts tauntingly against him.

"Because, you know, I'd bend over and let you have a lick right here and now if you'd let me have one." There was no disguising just what kind of lick she was referring to as Kitty Anne squeezed his dick and shot him an eager smile. "And, maybe, even a little more than that."

GD caught her hand and pulled it away from his aching length, not about to be seduced when he was pissed. "I'll follow you back to the camp…and we can finish this discussion there."

"You mean you're going to yell at me," Kitty Anne translated. "And then spank me?"

"Kitty Anne—"

"We are getting to a spanking, aren't we?"

"This is not a joke!" GD snapped, his patience worn completely through by her flippant attitude. "Go. Now."

He managed to put enough force into those two words that finally, thankfully, Kitty Anne obeyed, though not before shooting him a dirty look and issuing her own threat.

"There had better be a spanking involved somewhere in this, or you'll wait another month for me to wear your damn collar."

With that, she had the audacity to turn and shake her ass at him before sliding into her seat and slamming the door. A second later, her engine roared to life. Her tires squealed against the pavement before catching traction and shooting the little convertible forward. The damn woman might have actually hit him if he hadn't jumped back.

That had him moving.

Chapter Twenty-Three

Nick knew there was going to be trouble, which was exactly why he hadn't gone with Kitty Anne when she'd set off after GD. He didn't know how she intended to find him but knew she would. It was inevitable, just as GD's reaction was sure to be bold and unpleasant.

So, he really couldn't be blamed when Kitty Anne came roaring back the dirt lane that served as his driveway to think that things had gone just as he assumed. No doubt, her tender feelings were undoubtedly bruised. Now he had to interfere because he couldn't let GD hurt her any further.

That was the only reason he'd dare to get into GD's way. The big man's truck came pounding down the rough road behind her. By the time GD brought the oversized vehicle to a stop and hopped out, Nick was there, blocking his path.

"Hold up, man."

"Hold up?" GD snorted. "I don't think so."

"But that doesn't mean you don't need to," Nick shot back, refusing to budge as GD simply walked into him. It actually wouldn't have been that hard for the big man to force his point, but he stepped back, choosing to pick an argument instead of a fight.

"Damn it, man, do you know what she did?"

"I don't care." And he didn't really. "I just think you need to—"

"Well?" Kitty Anne's taunting tone wafted over his shoulder like a sultry breeze. "Is it time for the spanking...or what?"

Nick blinked. GD growled. Everything was wrong. Everything was backward. That really shouldn't shock him. Turning slowly around to confront Kitty Anne's smirk, he couldn't help but ask the obviously stupid question.

"You're not upset?"

"I'm horny," Kitty Anne shot back. "But if you want me to be upset, I could be. After all, I have every reason to be pissed, don't you think?"

"Uh...no?" Nick was lost.

"More pissed than me?" GD demanded to know.

"Please," Kitty Anne scoffed. "You're not the one dating a criminal."

"You were arrested for prostitution!" GD snapped, a vein bulging out of his forehead that Nick had never seen pump like that.

"Trumped-up charges." Kitty Anne waved that point away, clearly unconcerned about GD's flush or the fists his fingers were clenching into.

"You broke into Gwen's house *and* broke her dishes."

"That was you," Kitty Anne shot back. "I'm the one who has come to find out that the two men I'm with don't trust me enough not to *investigate* me."

"That was his fault!" GD jammed a thumb in Nick's direction, who held his hands up instantly in surrender.

"Hey, don't drag me into this. I don't want to get cussed out."

"I did not cuss!" Kitty Anne took instant objection to that accusation.

"You're yelling," GD countered, matching Kitty Anne's steady stomp forward as the two of them began to close in on each other, catching Nick in the middle, pinned with a combatant on either side.

"I deserve equal measure, GD, even if I have to yell to get it."

"What the hell does that mean?"

"I want five questions."

"Five questions?" GD's frown lost its dark edge as his gaze narrowed on her. "Five honest answers? And I get?"

"Me wearing nothing but your collar." Kitty Anne smiled smugly, certain her offer would be accepted, and it was, without hesitation.

"Deal." GD stuck his hand out, reaching around Nick to shake hers as Kitty Anne nodded.

"Deal...you wanna do a little more than shake on it?"

"Don't you want to get your answers first?" GD's smile grew downright lecherous. "Then we can get around to settling debts."

"Fine." Kitty Anne's chin lifted into the air as her dismissive tone made it clear that she was far from intimidated. "You want to do it here or—"

"We're going to go with or and take this inside," Nick cut in, certain this conversation would be better conducted in private. While the hill he'd built his house on was decent sized, it wasn't high enough to afford them real privacy from the kids playing down below.

"We could take it down to my apartment?" GD countered, shooting another dark look in Kitty Anne's direction. "I got a bed…and cuffs."

Kitty Anne snorted at that and rolled her eyes. "How about the bungalow?"

"Your mother?"

"At the salon."

"Well, that's—"

"—perfect," Kitty Anne finished for GD with a smile that only a Venus would wear. It was full of welcome and suggestion, leaving no doubt of just what she really wanted.

"Nick, go grab some ropes, and we can tie her down to the bed. We'll make an offering out of our little Kitty Anne."

"You think you're all scary with these threats?" Kitty Anne laughed and shook her head at him. "I'm not afraid of you."

"That doesn't mean you shouldn't be."

"Okay. Enough." Nick imposed himself in the middle of their argument. "All fighters back to their corners. It's time for a time-out."

"He's a bossy one, isn't he?" Kitty Anne snorted as she shared a smile with GD, whose loyalties shifted in an instant.

"He's just trying to ruin our fun."

"I'm bossy because I'm the boss," Nick shot back at both of them, drawing another round of smirks.

Kitty Anne and GD eyed him like a couple of wolves who had spotted a cat, but Nick was no pussy. He straightened up under their mutual inspection and pinned each one with a glare as he issued his own commands. After all, he hadn't become a pimp because he lacked the ability to take control.

Actually, he'd become a pimp for the money and because the ladies liked him. Liked him enough to allow Nick to introduce them to erotic delights they'd never known. That kind of pleasure was more addictive than even heroin. His ladies had been insatiable, enough so that they'd wanted to sell themselves.

It hadn't even been his idea, but those girls had gotten their thrills and turned it into a lucrative business. It had also been a secure one because

Nick had been there to watch out for them. That, strangely enough, had been when he'd discovered his need to take care of other people.

Prison had defined that need better for him. That was when he realized that if he really wanted to make a difference, he needed to use his talents to help kids, help them before they ended up lost in a judicial system that sucked the life out of them. So, he'd built the camp from the ground up.

That made him the boss.

"You." Nick leveled a finger at GD, causing the big man to lift a brow, but he didn't issue a complaint as Nick ordered him to go find the rope before turning on Kitty Anne and more politely offering to escort her to the bungalow.

She stuck her tongue out at GD before allowing Nick to lead her away. Only once the other man had muttered over his complaints and turned to go do as he was told did Nick bother to offer Kitty Anne any real chastisement.

"I told you not to go chasing off after him." Not that it had done any good. Kitty Anne didn't tend to heed the advice of others. That was one of the things that made her so entertaining.

"Do you know where I found him?"

"I don't really care."

"He'd broken into somebody's house," Kitty Anne answered herself as if Nick hadn't even spoken. "That's just insane."

"No, what is insane is following him into the house," Nick corrected. "GD is a trained investigator."

"That doesn't give him the right to just break into people's house," Kitty Anne shot back with a half-laugh as if Nick had made a poor joke. "The man is going to get caught one day and then arrested, and I'm sorry, but I draw the line at taking my kids to jail to see their daddy."

"He's not going to end up in jail," Nick assured her.

"And how do you know that?"

"Because I can afford a lawyer to keep him out."

"Really?" Kitty Anne didn't sound impressed by that either. "Because you couldn't afford to keep yourself out."

"I was young." And he hadn't listened to his lawyers. "And not smart enough not to get caught."

"Neither is GD, or did you fail to notice that I caught him in the act?"

"Yeah? How did you find him?"

Kitty Anne's smile turned smug as she shrugged. "A woman's got to have some secrets."

"So does a man, beautiful," Nick warned her. "Especially one who is paid by others to keep them."

"GD's not paid to keep them," Kitty Anne contradicted him, pausing to step back as they reached the bungalow's doors. She waited until he followed her into the airy cabin before finishing that thought. "He's paid to find them out."

"He's paid to be suspicious, too," Nick pointed out. "So you might consider cutting him a break on having snooped around in Rachel's office."

"Especially since you sent him there?" Kitty Anne shot back.

"Kitty Anne—"

"Save it," Kitty Anne cut him off. "We all have our trust issues, including me."

"What do you mean including you?" That brought Nick to a stop as he cast a hard look in her direction. "Are you saying you don't trust us?"

"Does it smell like old lady in here to you?"

"Kitty Anne—"

"Not exactly a turn-on...is it?"

Nick waited another long moment before he pressed once again. "Are you done ignoring the subject?"

"Are you going to yell at me?" Kitty Anne retorted with an innocent stare that Nick didn't buy for a second.

"Are you saying you don't trust me?"

"Does it really matter?"

"Yes!" Nick shouted before catching himself. Kitty Anne might be the most infuriating woman, but he wouldn't allow her to break him. So, he took a deep breath and tried not to growl too much over his words. "If it wasn't, you wouldn't have been upset yourself earlier when you found out about our trust issues."

"Oh please." Kitty Anne waved that consideration away as she strolled over to pull a chair out from the table and arrange it just so. "Like I care about that."

"Excuse me?" Nick blinked in confusion, utterly amazed at her shift in attitude. "Weren't you just yelling at GD about that matter?"

"I was simply making a point."

"A point you don't even care about!"

"Well, I don't have to care about a point to make it, do I?" Kitty Anne asked with such sincerity he couldn't help but be confounded. The woman really was crazy, and the only thing to do with crazy was roll with it.

"Nope, I guess not." Nick let the matter go. "Though I don't know what you're planning to do now."

Kitty Anne didn't answer him.

She just smiled as the door opened behind him and GD sauntered into the bungalow, never realizing he was walking into a trap.

* * * *

Kitty Anne watched GD strut in through the front door, his swagger full of arrogance and his grin full of promise. He chunked the rope down onto the table and cast her a smug look that left no doubt of what he was thinking. He was certain of his victory, as certain as Kitty Anne was of hers.

"Don't give me that look," Kitty Anne shot back. "We'll get to your ropes after we get to my five questions. Now, have a seat."

"A seat?" GD snickered as he eyed the plastic chair she'd arranged in the middle of the room. "Is that supposed to intimidate me? Because I have no secrets."

"We're about to find out how true that is," Kitty Anne warned him. "Sit and answer. If you fail to, then you might as well get up and walk away because I'm done playing games. You want to be with me, you got to trust me. Understood?"

"Um, excuse me," Nick spoke up from where he'd leaned back against the front door. "Didn't you just say—"

"Shut up, Nick." Kitty Anne shot Nick a fleeting glare for that obnoxious interruption before turning back on GD. "Sit."

"Yes, ma'am."

GD saluted and plopped down in the chair that was clearly a little small for his frame. He slouched back, kicking out his legs and crossing his arms behind his head as he eyed her as if she was a cute little pet he was indulging. That big-man attitude had to go. Kitty Anne knew just how to wipe the smirk off his face. She came out hard, with a question she knew he wouldn't want to answer.

"What were you doing at Gwen's?"

It didn't shock her in the slightest when GD hesitated and then dodged her question with his serious tone. "There are *some* things that I *can't* talk about."

"Oh? You know, that's amazing because there are some *people* I can't talk to," Kitty Anne informed him, knowing she was putting everything on the line as she smarted off to GD. "Namely the people who won't talk to me."

"Kitty Anne."

"GD."

"Fine." GD held his hands up in defeat. "You want to know what I was doing? I'll tell you. Gwen Harold is pregnant."

"And you're the father," Kitty Anne whispered, feeling the earth shift under her feet. She wasn't ready for kids. She was still getting used to the boys at the camp. Not to mention having to put up with Gwen...whoever the hell she was.

"No!" GD snapped in exasperation. "The woman's slept with more men...and she's blackmailing almost every one of them."

"Really?" Kitty Anne's eyes rounded. Now that was interesting. "Hmm."

"And I'm trusting you not to run off and tell Rachel," GD pointed out, ruining Kitty Anne's momentary glow.

"I would never," Kitty Anne swore, though she knew she probably would have if he hadn't told her not to. Rachel would have loved that story, which caused her to have a sudden thought. "And why were you worried enough to search Rachel's office?"

"Nick—"

"No, not Nick." Kitty Anne cut him off, not about to be bullshitted by any easier answer. "You. You could have lied to Nick."

"That wouldn't be my style." GD dismissed that consideration, but Kitty Anne wasn't so convinced.

"You were worried about something, too."

"I wasn't," GD denied, but she wasn't listening to him anymore.

Kitty Anne's thoughts were churning, and she couldn't help but start to see a problem. "You found out Rachel knew that Seth was likely Patton's brother, and you know that Kevin is as well, but you're not concerned…which means you don't really care that she knows that."

"Kitty Anne—"

"No. No. No." Kitty Anne held her hand up, refusing to let Nick interrupt. "I think I'm on to something here because you're in a panic too."

"Of course, I'm panicked!" Nick snapped. "If Patton finds out about Kevin, she'll probably try to take him from the camp and this is where he needs to be."

"No." Kitty Anne shook her head. That might sound reasonable but that didn't make it true. "You're afraid of something else."

"What?" Nick asked as if the idea itself was absurd.

"You're afraid that Kevin set the Davis brothers' barn on fire."

There, that was it. There was no hiding the fact that she'd hit the nail on the head. Neither GD nor Nick appeared surprised by her declaration. Just the opposite. They exchanged a look that spoke volumes.

"And you both knew."

"Kitty Anne." Nick sighed but clearly didn't know what else to say.

"You know if you told me what was going on with Kevin, I'd have to keep it to myself, but if you don't…then I'm under no obligation to keep a confidence."

That was a threat that had the men sharing another look, but this time it was GD who spoke up.

"No, you aren't," he agreed. "But you will, and you know how I know that?"

"How?" Kitty Anne asked reluctantly, knowing she was about to get some pious lecture.

"Because *I* trust *you*," GD emphasized nobly.

"Then tell me the truth. Tell me what the big secret with Kevin is," Kitty Anne insisted, causing both men to exchange another look. It quickly became clear that GD was waiting on Nick to make his decision. When he came to it, Nick didn't appear pleased by it.

Heaving a deep sigh, he nodded. "Fine. You want to know the truth, I'll tell you. One of the sheriff's deputies picked Kevin up not but a few miles from the Davis ranch the day of the barn fire with an empty gas can."

"So, he did do it," Kitty Anne whispered, shocked to her core.

"No." GD shook his head. "That is not evidence. It's circumstantial. A point that Kevin's lawyer made to both the sheriff and the district attorney, which is why he's never been charged."

"Then what is the secret?" Kitty Anne demanded to know, completely confused by what they were trying to hide.

"Seth confessed to setting the fire."

"What?" Kitty Anne blinked, not expecting that quiet revelation from Nick. "So he set the fire?"

"We don't think so. He's just afraid—"

"—for Kevin," Kitty finished for Nick, seeing the logic now. "He's trying to cover for his brother."

"Yes."

"And?" There was still more, she could sense it but the tale did seem complete.

"And," GD began slowly, "the Davis brothers are very powerful. We're hiding not only the suspects from them but the brothers of the woman they're in love with. When the truth comes out, do you know how pissed they're going to be?"

Kitty Anne could, but she couldn't figure out why they were hiding the truth from the Davis boys in the first place. "So just tell them. They're going to find out eventually."

"Yes, eventually," Nick agreed. "And that time will be decided by Kevin and Seth. They're not ready to meet Patton yet and we're not pushing."

"And now you know the truth." GD pushed out of his seat as his phone started buzzing. "I've proven my trust in you, and when you trust me, you'll wear my collar."

With that grand declaration, he brushed past her as he reached for his phone. but Kitty Anne watched GD saunter away and rolled her eyes. She knew what he was doing. He was making a scene and a point. He didn't just want her in his collar. He wanted her on her knees.

Kitty Anne would go there for him, but she wouldn't chase after him. Instead she'd plot his downfall, so that when she finally slipped on his collar it would be a moment so magnificent Kitty Anne wouldn't be the only one humbled.

Right then, though, she had another man to humble. Turning her gaze on Nick, who was frowning at the door GD had disappeared through, Kitty Anne pinned him with a hard look.

"Kevin is innocent. You know that, right?"

That drew Nick's gaze in her direction. He offered her a quick smile before shaking his head.

"It's admirable that you believe that," Nick assured her with a patronizing tone that had Kitty Anne's teeth grinding together. "But you got to remember, beautiful, that these kids don't end up here because they're all angels."

"I know that." God, did Kitty Anne ever. It hadn't even taken two short weeks for her to figure out that a lot of these boys had some serious flaws, Kevin included, but this wasn't one of them.

"He's innocent," Kitty Anne insisted. "And I'm going to prove it."

"You really are such a sweet thing," Nick murmured, smiling at her in that special way that made her melt, and he knew it. He was there to catch her, crossing the room quickly enough that Kitty Anne didn't stand a chance of fending him off as he pulled her into his arms and waggled his eyebrows at her.

"What do you say we put the ropes to good use and go mess up the bed?"

That was an invitation Kitty Anne didn't have the power to resist. She wound her arms around his neck and lifted her lips to meet his as he stole her ability to object with a kiss that only ended after they'd stumbled their way through the bungalow. Desperate hands had clutched and torn at the clothes in their way until a trail of fabric led from the living room straight to the edge of the bed.

Kitty Anne felt the mattress bang into her legs, and then she was falling. Nick toppled down on top of her. All heated hardness and strength, he pinned her to the mattress with a hand capturing both of her wrists and his knees shoving her thighs apart. She spread them eagerly, twisting in his grip as she arched her back.

The motion had her breasts lifting in a blatant invitation he didn't hesitate to accept. Kitty Anne panted with the pleasure winding through her as he nibbled and licked his way from one puckered peak to the other. Nick treated each of her nipples to the same rough caresses, dragging her sensitive tips past the hard ridge of his teeth and into the warm, suckling depths of his kiss, but he was too eager to linger there for long.

Kitty Anne stilled, her whole body drawing tense as Nick's lips dipped over the curve of her breast to trace the quivering muscles stretched tight across her tummy. He paused there to tease her belly button before scraping the smooth plane of his cheek down over her mound to nuzzle the swollen folds of her cunt.

Unable to help but to laugh at the ticklish caress, Kitty Anne lifted her hips, offering herself up to his kiss. The one thing Nick did better than any man she'd ever had before was kiss. He had a wicked tongue and strong lips and was adventurous enough to put both to good use. Flicking, nibbling, sucking on her clit, he had her crying out and begging for more.

Nick didn't deny her.

Capturing her swollen bud under the heavy weight of his callused thumb, he continued to torment the sensitive bundle of nerves, even as he fucked his tongue deep into her cunt. Over and over again, one slow stroke at a time, his tongue danced up the walls of her sheath, tickling her with a light touch that made Kitty Anne only ache for a rougher one, but her cries had turned incoherent.

The words falling from her lips were melted into endless moans and mews by the heat of lust and want searing through her. Words, though, were not necessary. Nick knew exactly what she wanted, what she needed, because he needed it, too.

* * * *

Nick was in a frenzy, a desperate one that never seemed to fade no matter how many times he took Kitty Anne. He always needed her that much more. Without thought of anything other than the glorious rapture that filled him whenever he fucked himself into the tight clench of her body, Nick rolled her over and yanked her hips up, slamming the aching length of his cock into the molten depths of her cunt.

The velvety walls of her sheath sucked him deep, tightening around him as they spasmed. The feel of her pussy rippling down around his length was the most erotic massage Nick had ever experienced, and the ecstasy that flowed through his veins as he pumped himself in and out of her clinging depths was beyond any pleasure he'd ever known before…any pleasure that was but one.

He glanced down at the lush globes of Kitty Anne's ass bouncing beneath him. She rode him with the same eager franticness as he fucked her. Nick couldn't control the growl that rumbled through him as he palmed her cheeks and split them wide to eye the shadowed entrance to the greatest ride he'd ever taken. There was no hesitation in his motions as he pulled free of her pussy and lined the swollen, slickened head of his cock up with tight right of muscles guarding her ass.

Then he was sliding into heaven.

Nick's eyes fluttered closed as his back arched and he sank all the way into heated depths that only he had ever claimed. This was his paradise, and he knew how to make it even better. Clutching Kitty Anne's hips and pinning them against his, Nick rolled onto his back and settled her above him, allowing her weight to sink her down around him until his balls were tucked up against the plush curves of her ass cheeks.

Even though Nick could have died a happy man right then and there, he knew things could still get better, which was just why he released Kitty Anne's hips to capture her arms and take command of each one of her hands. Lacing his fingers through hers, he settled one over her breast and one over her cunt and began to torment her anew, only this time he got to enjoy all her wiggling and writhing from the inside out.

* * * *

"This had better be good," GD snapped into his phone as he stepped out into the bright daylight.

Ambling across the yard toward the shade of the cedar tree, GD glared back at the bungalow door, irritated that Kitty Anne hadn't come rushing after him to pledge her trust and vow to wear his collar. Of course, that would be too easy, and the woman was determined to make his life as difficult as possible. Otherwise, it would just be too boring.

"Hey, man." Alex sounded just as tense and annoyed as GD felt. He could guess why.

"Is this about Gwen?"

"Why do you ask that?" Alex shot back, making his own educated assumption. "Unless, of course, you were the jackass who broke into her place and smashed all of her mother's antique china."

"Actually, that was Kitty Anne's fault." GD wasn't going down for that one. So he threw Kitty Anne under the bus, mostly because he knew it wouldn't hit her.

"You took your girlfriend on a B&E?" Alex sounded torn between outrage and amusement.

"It's not like I invited her," GD retorted, a little insulted that Alex even considered such a thing. "Do you *really* want all the details?"

"No." Alex sighed. "But somebody's got to pay for the china."

"Gwen has the cash, and trust me, that ain't her mom's china." GD glanced up as a big, gold sedan came rolling slowly down the drive. It was Lynn Anne. She was back early.

"What's that supposed to mean?" Alex asked, drawing GD's attention back to their conversation.

"Man, that woman is blackmailing just about half the fucking county. You should see her accounts… Actually, you should see the pictures."

"Like I care," Alex sighed. "Just tell me this isn't about the club."

"Nope." GD paused to offer Kitty Anne's mom a smile as she pulled to a stop right before him, but the woman stuck her nose in the air and ignored him. She was good at that. "But I got to warn you, she's about to make somebody a daddy."

"Why the hell are you telling me that?" Alex demanded to know.

"No reason," GD answered too quickly, smirking as Lynn Anne stepped out of her car and shook out her skirt. Without a word to him, she shut her car door and headed to the cabin.

"I didn't sleep with that woman. I'm not no damn daddy," Alex snapped. "But you *did* break her dishes, and they will be replaced, right?"

"Whatever."

GD watched Lynn Anne disappear into the small bungalow and started counting the seconds. He only made it to five before her scream cut the quiet afternoon air.

"It's not whatever," Alex huffed. "If you're thinking it, the odds are so will Heather. God knows she's sensitive on the issue."

"Oh, really?"

That wasn't shocking. Neither were the hollers echoing out of the cabin. Nick was yelling at somebody to stop and GD could imagine it was Lynn Anne, given the things she was yelling at him.

"Yeah, so do me a favor and don't mention this to her," Alex pleaded.

"You want me to lie to Heather?"

"Yes!"

"Fine." GD wasn't all that interested in upsetting Heather, especially given he did think Alex was innocent.

Nick wasn't. He was a naughty, naughty boy, and he was being punished. GD broke into a grin as Nick came stumbling barefoot and in a rush out of the cabin. He had his jeans on and halfway closed, but he appeared to be having a hard time pulling he zipper all the way up. That might have had something to do with Lynn Anne chasing after him with a broom.

"Just let me know what kind of plates Gwen wants," GD murmured before clicking his phone closed on Alex's response without waiting to hear it.

He didn't care, not about the dishes, not about the blackmail, not about anything but the show being played out before him. Nick tore across the yard with Lynn Anne right on his heels, and Kitty Anne, looking like a complete mess, following behind them. That was worth a picture.

So, GD lifted his phone and took one.

* * * *

"You come back out here, you pervert!" By the time Kitty Anne caught up with her mother, Lynn Anne was pounding on the shed that Nick had locked himself into. Kitty Anne didn't blame him for hiding. She wished she could. "You're going to marry my daughter, and you're going to marry her now!"

"Mom!" Kitty Anne snapped, glancing all around and glad to see the fields below were empty.

"And you!" Lynn Anne turned on her, all flushed-faced and wild-eyed and shaking a broom at Kitty Anne. "Did we fail to have the sex talk? Because, unless you didn't know, you aren't supposed to stick *that* there!"

"Oh, for God's sakes, Mother," Kitty Anne muttered, feeling her face go up in flames. "Will you *shut up*?"

The answer to that question was no. Lynn Anne wasn't even listening to her but was caught up in the moment and in her own monologue, which Kitty Anne knew for a fact was nothing more than a pious act.

"You can't let a man stick his willy in whatever nilly he wants," Lynn Anne spat.

"Maybe I enjoy having his willy in my nilly," Kitty Anne shot back, pushed too far by her mother's self-righteousness. She happened to know for a fact that her mother didn't really object to a little nilly filling. That didn't stop her, though, from beginning to prod Kitty Anne back toward her trailer with her broom.

"Is that what has been going on here?" Her mom demanded to know as if the answer hadn't been obvious all along. "You been getting *stuck*? Well, that's over, young lady. There will be no more willys and nillys on *my* watch. You're moving back into your old room!"

"But, Mother—"

"Move!"

Lynn Anne wasn't asking. She chased Kitty Anne back into her trailer, sweeping the broom after her and poking Kitty Anne whenever she tried to stop and object. As she was forced across the yard, Kitty Anne could see GD sitting on the lowered tailgate of his truck, watching the show with a big grin.

She knew then that he'd seen this coming. Apparently, GD wasn't just going to deny her the pleasure of his own body but that of Nick's as well because there was going to be no more willy-nillying around according to her mother. From that moment forward, Lynn Anne swore she was going to keep both eyes on Kitty Anne.

Kitty Anne had a sick feeling she wasn't lying.

Chapter Twenty-Four

Monday, June 22nd

Nearly a week later, Kitty Anne sat at her desk, reading over the story before her while her mother knitted in the far corner. Just as she'd suspected, Lynn Anne had been dead serious about keeping both eyes on her. She was like Kitty Anne's shadow, following her every second of the day.

The only time she was really alone was when she went to the bathroom. She and Nick had tried to use that one little loophole to their advantage, but that had been the day they'd learned Lynn Anne wasn't going to give her more than five minutes to do anything alone, including showering. It had been an illuminating lesson that had ended with Lynn Anne chasing Nick across the yard once again, though this time she was outfitted with a three-foot-long shock stick that GD had given her.

That had made his position quite clear. There would be no sex for her, not with anybody, not until she put his collar on. Just to taunt the crap out of him, she had put his collar on and worn it to dinner, worn it to breakfast, worn it to her tutoring session, worn it whenever she knew he couldn't do a damn thing about it.

Kitty Anne could tell it was driving him mad. She could also sense that the lack of sex was beginning to drive Nick a little nuts, and he was the sane one in the group. Her mother needed to go, but that problem wasn't the one that had Kitty Anne worrying right then.

Right then, Kitty Anne had a bigger problem on her hands. It sat staring at her with wide eyes. Taking a deep breath and masking her reaction to the revelation in Kevin's story, she offered him a slight smile.

"Your work has a certain flow to it that is very touching, which is enhanced by the very details of the story *but*"—Kitty Anne paused, allowing

Kevin to get out a groan as he flopped back in his seat— "I'm still seeing some of the same grammatical errors. So we're going to go over them today, and you're going to write me a third part to this story."

"A third part?" Kevin frowned, looking confused by the very idea. "There is no third part."

"Because you haven't written it yet," Kitty Anne pointed out, knowing his objection had deeper roots than simple reluctance. That was too bad. She wasn't like Nick and GD. Kitty Anne wasn't going to sit back and let a family remain fragmented.

"I want to know what happens after the sister finds out about her brothers."

"But what if she never finds out?" Kevin countered, perking up in his seat. "What if the story ended there?"

"What if it didn't?" Kitty Anne insisted. "I want to know what happens."

"What if I don't know?" He sounded seriously confused, as if he really hadn't considered the matter.

"Then I guess you'll find out when you write it." Kitty Anne smiled and pressed forward with the conversation, certain that Kevin could waste what remained of their half-hour tutoring session arguing with her.

"And you won't be making the same mistakes when you write the next installment because you're going to pay attention now, and if you don't make any mistakes on this next installment…it can be your last one."

Kevin didn't appear appeased by that offering but focused nonetheless on Kitty Anne's instructions as they went over his story line by line. They'd barely made it to the end before the bell rang and Kevin went flying out the door. Lynn Anne watched him go with a baleful look.

"You got yourself a little arsonist there, Kitty Anne," her mother warned her, earning an eye roll from her daughter.

"Please, Mother."

"Don't take that tone with me," Lynn Anne grumbled. "I'm not the unreasonable one here. You're the naïve one if you believe that tale about the 'pretty, black-haired woman.'"

Her mother quoted from the story, proving that she'd been paying more attention than Kitty Anne had assumed. That was unnerving, and a subject best avoided.

"I believe it was a story." Kitty Anne shoved away from her desk. "And that I'm going to be late for lunch with Rachel if I don't get a move on it."

"You mean 'we,'" her mother corrected her as she gathered up her knitting and rose to her feet along with Kitty Anne.

"It's just lunch, Mother," Kitty Anne assured her, but Lynn Anne wasn't hearing it.

"It's just you and that pervert at the closest, cheapest motel doing something dirtier than the prostitutes in the neighboring room," Lynn Anne shot back.

"You watch too much TV," Kitty Anne complained. "And Nick would never take me to a cheap motel room. We'd do it in the back of his truck."

"Not until he puts a ring on it," Lynn Anne declared.

She'd made that her official stance, never seeming to realize that Kitty Anne might not want a shotgun wedding. Nick knew it, too. He had enough sense to realize that proposing to her with her mother's threat hanging over their heads would be a bad move, but that didn't mean Kitty Anne didn't sense that he intended to propose sometime in the near future.

If he didn't, it would be kind of shocking, given they'd already discussed plans for the house that Nick was building for them. He had an architect drawing up plans, and Lynn Anne knew it. That wasn't enough, though. Kitty Anne suspected that even a ring wouldn't be enough for her mother.

Her mother was not going anywhere. Not, at least, until she had a new and better home to move into. Until then, she was stuck to Kitty Anne's ass, and there was no point in arguing over it.

"Fine, you can come," Kitty Anne relented with ill grace. "But you can't sit with us."

"Still embarrassed to be seen with your mom?" Lynn Anne asked as she followed Kitty Anne out of the shed.

"Always," Kitty Anne assured her. "You're embarrassing, woman."

Lynn Anne smiled at that as if Kitty Anne had complimented her, and in a way, she had. After all, her mother worked on being annoying. Annoying and embarrassing, which was just why she ditched her mom the moment she walked into the Bread Box. The small bakery was no longer full of men but smelled just as delicious. Rachel, as always, was already seated and working on a glass of tea.

"Hey, Kitty Anne!" Rachel greeted with her typical enthusiasm.

"I'm so sorry I'm late," Kitty Anne apologized as she reached down to offer Rachel a quick hug before taking the seat opposite of her. "But it has just been a hectic day."

"I am sure they all are these days with all those boys you have to keep up with," Rachel teased her with a twinkle in her eyes.

The two friends shared a look and then burst out laughing. That set the tone for the rest of the lunch. They had a good time kibitzing about their respective men. Eventually the conversation turned toward Rachel's investigation of Seth, and Kitty Anne had no choice but to be honest with her longtime friend. After all, somebody needed to help Kevin prove his innocence. Kitty Anne couldn't do it alone.

"I just don't know." Kitty Anne sighed as she twirled her straw through her tea, coming to the end of her tale. "I mean Seth and Nick know Kevin well enough to know if he's capable of setting a fire, and obviously they think he is, but...I can't help but think the reason he's so sad is that they don't believe him."

"Maybe they shouldn't," Rachel spoke up, surprising Kitty Anne with that harsh critique, but when she lifted her eyes to meet her friend's gaze, Kitty Anne saw the truth.

"But we will." Kitty Anne smiled.

"Because everybody deserves to have somebody believe in them," Rachel finished for her with a nod. "So how are we going to find this black-haired beauty?"

Kitty Anne considered it for a moment before the obviousness of the solution hit her. "I know. We're going to hire ourselves an investigator."

* * * *

Nick watched Kitty Anne and her mother return from their lunch in town and had to smile. It was a good day. A good day because it was the last one he'd have to put up with that old hag. Everything was now in line. All the paperwork, all the money, all the taxes—everything was settled.

Now he just needed to go rock Lynn Anne's boat. He knew just how to do that. He sent one of the boys up the hill to the shed still serving as Kitty Anne's office and little classroom. He had the kid deliver a list of instructions to Lynn Anne that he knew would set her off. Sure enough, not five minutes later, Lynn Anne slammed through his door, waving a piece of paper in the air and demanding answers.

"What is this?" Lynn Anne tossed his letter back on the table. "Extortion?"

"I highly doubt making somebody do chores reaches the egregious nature of extortion," Nick responded dryly.

"Chores are for young boys who need the exercise," Lynn Anne retorted haughtily. "I, young man, am an old woman. I'm in no condition to be out there cleaning up after a bunch of heathens."

Nick didn't bother to argue over her choice of terms for his boys, having already learned that anything Lynn Anne thought annoyed him was something she would repeat readily. The woman was that kind of evil, and she needed to go.

"Chores are for anybody who is capable, and you, madam, are more than capable," Nick assured her.

"*How dare you?*" Lynn Anne drew herself up indignantly as she took a step forward and promptly slipped. She went down hard, but Nick didn't move. He didn't even blink when she cried out pathetically.

"Oh, my back!"

"You hurt?" he called out.

"I need an ambulance."

"Or, maybe, just some of that pot you got stored in your vent back at the trailer," Nick suggested, biting back a smile as Lynn Anne's head instantly popped back over the edge of the desk.

"What did you just say?"

"And it will probably be a while before you can fit back into your *leather* ensembles." Nick paused to let the weight of that revelation sink in before he continued smugly on. "So I guess it's a good thing you got all that *cash* to tide you over."

That had Lynn Anne rising slowly back up to her feet as she studied him with an intelligence that was normally hidden behind her outrageous persona. She retired the mask, though, for the moment as she finally responded to Nick's comments.

"So you know the truth," Lynn Anne began, her words slow and measured, a far cry from her normally shrill tone. "What are you going to do? Blackmail me?"

"Actually, I was thinking of bribing you," Nick admitted. "After all, you are going to be my future mother-in-law, and Kitty Anne seems fond of you."

"Saved by such faint praise." Lynn Anne smirked, though her gaze remained narrowed on him. "So what is the bribe?"

"First, you have to answer a question for me." Nick wasn't going to let go of the upper hand until he had what he wanted. Right then, there was one thing he was dying to know. "You make all that money whoring or dealing?"

"Don't be an ass," Lynn Anne snapped, instantly and honestly insulted. "That money's Kitty Anne's. I've been saving it for years."

"You've been saving Kitty Anne's money?" That didn't sound right, but there was no disguising the truth in Lynn Anne's tone.

"I just didn't want her to end up like me with nothing in her retirement years." Lynn Anne shrugged as if it were nothing. "As for the rest of what you found in your *illegal* search...that's personal. After all, my daughter is the one who was arrested for prostitution."

"Those charges were dismissed," Nick reminded her. He'd paid a very expensive lawyer to assure they'd never even seen the light of a courtroom.

"The damage to her reputation has been done," Lynn Anne insisted. "And her staying here isn't helping matters. So, if you expect me to sacrifice my daughter, you better be offering a very nice bribe."

"Trust me, I am."

* * * *

Happy to see her mom go, Kitty Anne quickly took off in search of GD, anxious to put Rachel and her plan into motion. She wished she could have talked with both him and Nick, but it was too important to wait for that miracle to happen.

In the past week, the three of them hadn't gotten a single opportunity to simply talk freely and privately. She missed that about as much as she missed the sex. They had fun together, and her mother had ruined that. It was just another reason she had to go.

That problem would have to wait. Right then she had a bigger one, finding GD. Kitty Anne searched high and low before she was pointed in the direction of the back pond. Apparently, he and Kevin had struck out to go fishing along with several other boys. He was, no doubt, chaperoning, meaning there was no private word to be had with him now.

There was just the chance to hang out, and she wasn't going to miss that.

Grabbing up a fishing pole, Kitty Anne headed out after them but didn't make it all the way down the path before she got distracted by the sight of several more boys crawling through the grass with shoeboxes that had small holes cut in. As she paused to study them, Kitty Anne recognized the chirp of crickets coming from the boxes when inspiration hit.

Knowing she didn't have a lot of time to see her plan through, Kitty Anne solicited the boys' help, which wasn't hard. Her mother hadn't exactly been winning over any fans among the boys. They lined up to not only help but also to peek through the window in the hopes of seeing Lynn Anne's reaction to the surprise they'd left inside her trailer.

At least they made it out in time.

Kitty Anne, on the other hand, got caught as her mother came sweeping in through the front door as though she was gliding on the air…and she was smiling. Kitty Anne blinked as she stared in amazement at her mother's grin.

Something wasn't right.

"There you are, Kitty Anne. I've been looking all over for you. I need to tell you that Mr. Davis is planning on towing my home back to its proper place this afternoon." Lynn Anne paused to smile down at her daughter, seeming completely unaware of Kitty Anne's wide-eyed stare.

"You're leaving?"

"I know you're worried about your reputation, but I've had a long talk with Mr. Dickles—"

"*Mr. Dickles*?" This really was too much. "What happened to warning me that I'd have to take that fleabag down to a free clinic for weekly shots given all the sluts he probably kept about the place?"

"What can I say?" Lynn Anne shrugged as she all but danced past Kitty Anne and into the closet. "At least he can afford to keep sluts."

"He bribed you."

And had won their bet.

"He really is a wonderful man," Lynn Anne insisted as she started to collect her figurines. "Do be a dear, honey, and go down to the camp and see if you can round up some boxes. I really would like to secure some of my belongings before they're knocked about again."

Instead of obeying, Kitty Anne trailed after her mother into the bedroom, where Lynn Anne started to collect her pictures and pack them into her dresser.

"Just what did Nick buy you off with? Jewelry? A new car? A vacation?"

"Try a house, honey." Lynn Anne cut her off with a smirk that assured Kitty Anne her mother felt no shame about accepting such an outrageous gift. "And I'm talking about a three-bedroom, two-bath, three-thousand-square-foot minimum…because, after all, those are the requirements for all homes built in The Oaks."

"*The Oaks?*" Kitty Anne gaped at her mother. "Are you insane? Those houses cost well over three hundred grand. You can't take that kind of money from Nick."

"And why not?" Lynn Anne paused to cast Kitty Anne a pointed look. "You don't turn down gifts, Kitty Anne. It's rude."

"That's when somebody is offering you a piece of pie!"

"Yes, well…Nick's offering me the whole pie, and I'm not fool enough to spite myself out of pride."

"Oh please." Kitty Anne rolled her eyes at that lie, completely disgusted by both her mother and her boyfriend. Both of them had clearly lost their minds.

"That's exactly right," Lynn Anne declared as she crossed the room to rest her hands on Kitty Anne's shoulders and looked deep into her eyes. "If you have any brains, you will do *whatever* it takes to keep that man pleased. Whatever he does to you—get over it. Whoever else he does—forgive him. As long as you're breathing…he hasn't gone too far."

Kitty Anne's mouth dropped open as she stared at her mother in blatant shock. Years ago Lynn Anne had taken a stand and kicked Kitty Anne's dad to the curb when he'd dared to raise a hand to her. The man had left and never returned. Kitty Anne had been raised to be glad he was gone.

No father was better than an abusive one…or so her mother had preached, but now? Years of struggling and suffering in different ways had clearly demented her mother. That was all Kitty Anne could think.

"I'm sorry, Mom." Clearly she needed to step in and put some sanity back into this situation because her mother had finally lost all of hers. "I can't let this happen."

"Excuse me?" Lynn Anne stepped back, releasing Kitty Anne as if she'd become hot to the touch. "Let? Did you say 'let' to me?"

Lynn Anne laughed as she shook her head and moved back toward where she'd left a pile of pillowcases she was clearly intent on taking with her. She paused, though, before continuing to fold them, tilting her head and frowning as she appeared to be listening to the air.

"Did you hear that?" Lynn Anne asked, turning to cast a concerned look in Kitty Anne's direction. "It sounded like something…I don't know. What is that sound?"

"Mother, focus," Kitty Anne snapped as Lynn Anne stepped back at the bed to stare at it in confusion. "You are *not* moving into The Oaks."

"And why shouldn't I?" she asked, abandoning her investigation of the bed to draw herself up haughtily and glare down her nose at Kitty Anne. "Don't you think I *deserve* to live in there?"

"What you deserve is not the point! The point is that Nick—"

"He wants to marry you. Did you know that?" Lynn Anne asked, cutting right through Kitty Anne's complaint and, no doubt, hoping to distract her. "He told me so himself, and if you have the sense that I hope you have, you'll say 'yes.' Then he'll be my son-in-law, and it is perfectly normal for a son to provide for his mother."

There was a strange and twisted logic to that point that made it hard to refute, leaving Kitty Anne uncertain of what to say. It would have been hard anyway to get the words out through the frustrated knot of tension balled in her throat. The exasperation needed an outlet, though, and she turned to bang her head against the wall as Lynn Anne glanced back at the closet.

"Did you hear that? I think there is something in here."

Lynn Anne followed her own comment over to the closet, leaving Kitty Anne standing there with her forehead pressed into the wall. She stared at the paint job, noticing that this close up it no longer looked as smooth as it did at a distance. In the background, she heard her mother continuing to comment to herself.

Those curious little questions erupted into a scream that fled all the way out the front door while giggles and chuckles erupted outside the window, proving the boys were still around. Her mother quickly took notice of that fact, and Kitty Anne heard her chasing them away while Kitty Anne just stood there, trying to figure out what she was supposed to do now.

There was nothing she really could do.

Nick had full authority over his money, and she had absolutely none over her mother. If the two of them conspired to be crazy, then, short of trying to find a judge to commit both of them, Kitty Anne was out of options. That didn't mean she was going to accept her defeat quietly.

Straightening up and starting after her mother, Kitty Anne decided that if Nick was going to pay that much then they should, at least, get the full package. There would be no more hiding the truth of their relationship, and neither would there be any judgmental comments from her mother if she wanted to stay on the payroll.

Kitty Anne found her mother panting outside with a hand flattened over her chest and her complexion pale in the sunlight. Her shock was obvious, but far from over.

"There are *snakes* in the closet!" Lynn Anne gasped out between panted breaths. "A whole *pile!*"

"Yes, I know." Kitty Anne smiled, giving in to the childish urge to taunt her mother. "I'm storing them there for the time being."

"You're storing them?" Now it was Lynn Anne's turn to gape at her daughter in wide-eyed shock. "They're snakes! You don't *store* snakes!"

"Some people do. Some people even keep them as pets." Kitty Anne stalked slowly up on her mother with each word, letting them roll off her tongue with a slow, dangerous drawl that had Lynn Anne backing steadily away from her. "Of course, some people like to be kept as pets while others like to do the keeping."

"And just what is that supposed to mean?"

"It means that Nick isn't going to cheat on me. He isn't going to beat me, and he's not in charge of this relationship because I'm not for sale and he knows better than to ask if I have a price."

"Oh please." Lynn Anne snorted and rolled her eyes in a gesture that was all too familiar. "You're talking like a naive ninny."

"I'm talking like a woman who is in love and is loved," Kitty Anne countered, refusing to allow her mother's cynicism to infect her anymore. She was free and unable to control the smile that thought spread across her face. "And not by just *one* willy."

Lynn Anne stilled at that clarification and slowly straightened up as her comically dismissive expression tightened into a very serious one. "And just what is that supposed to mean?"

"It means this nilly"—Kitty Anne jammed a finger into her chest, making sure her point was clear—"is a *two*-willy woman!"

"And just what is *that* supposed to mean?"

"I'm in love with GD, too."

There. She'd said it. It felt as if she'd walked off the edge of a cliff and was now free-falling, but Kitty Anne knew that she'd made the right choice. Even if she hadn't, it was too late to go back now and she had no reason not to nosedive into the battle roaring her way.

"It means that I love both of them…at the same time."

"You're kidding, right?" Lynn Anne narrowed her gaze on Kitty Anne, clearly having decided that was the only explanation for the things she was saying.

"Far from it," Kitty Anne assured her mother. "And just so you know, it's not all about the sex. We love each other, respect each other, trust each other. It's a relationship, and one that shouldn't have to be paid for, but since you feel a need to extort my future husbands—"

"Extort? Husbands? Do you hear yourself?"

"—then you're going to give something back."

"Give something back?" Lynn Anne continued to parrot Kitty Anne's words as if every other one was a new shocking revelation.

"Yes, you're going to give us and all the children we have…unconditional love."

"*Kids?*"

"Yes, kids!" Kitty Anne nodded, finally responding to her mother. "Probably lots of them, too. So what's it going to be? You going to take the house, shut up, and show up with a smile on your face when commanded, or you going to give in to that urge and say something nasty?"

Lynn Anne appeared to consider that for a moment, her gaze drifting over Kitty Anne's shoulder before returning as she gave her daughter a stiff nod. "Fine, but I might make some renovations to the house you picked out."

"Done."

It wasn't Kitty Anne who signed off on the deal, but Nick, who spoke from behind her, startling Kitty Anne into twirling around to find both him and GD smiling down at her. She didn't know how long they'd been there, but they'd clearly heard enough of what she had to say.

"And you..." Her mother turned her gaze back on Kitty Anne. "I'm going to leave you in charge of packing up my stuff since you decided to childishly infest my trailer with snakes. Trust me, if you don't get all those snakes out of my trailer, you will hear about it. Now go and fetch my purse and keys, and I'll leave you to your...men."

"Yes, Mother."

Kitty Anne bit back a smile and turned to demurely scurry back into the small trailer and fetch the items her mother had requested. She saw the story she'd dropped on the table while arguing with her mom and snatched it up, too. She returned the purse and keys to their rightful owner and stood there, watching her mother walk away, knowing that, despite her words, Lynn Anne was well pleased.

After all, her mother wasn't without her own kinks.

"Well done," Nick congratulated her, drawing her attention to the two men watching her like predators did prey. "You got rid of the wicked witch. Now how are you going to get the snakes out of her trailer?"

That brought a laugh to Kitty Anne's lips as she shook her head at Nick. "The same way they got in there. I'm going to ask the boys to round them up."

"You would." GD snorted with a roll of his eyes before narrowing his gaze on Kitty Anne, his smile taking on a lecherous turn. "You'll also be wearing my collar."

"I might." Kitty Anne returned his smile, knowing hers was tilted more toward a smug smirk that only widened as his grin dipped. Hers followed suit as she remembered the papers clutched in her hand. "But first, you need to see this."

All teasing aside, they needed to talk about Kevin.

Chapter Twenty-Five

GD took a deep breath and released it, but it didn't help ease the tension gripping him as he once again stared down at the words typed clearly on the page before him. The kid either had an active imagination or now he had his answer for why Lana was paying Gwen off—she'd started the fire.

It made a perfect kind of sense, except for how Gwen had come to know what Lana did.

"He might have made it up." That was all GD had to cling to. Given the frown that marred Kitty Anne's features, she didn't want him to have even that.

"Clearly he was there when the Davis brothers' barn caught fire," Kitty Anne admitted, but that was all she was willing to give. "But then so were a lot of people. So I'm not sure why you continue to blame Kevin."

"Because he was caught by the police with a gas can," GD shot back.

"So? *Lots* of people have gas cans!"

She wasn't wrong about that, and there was no point in arguing the matter with her. Lana was the one GD needed to be having a word with.

"I got to go."

"Go?" Kitty Anne blinked, glancing between him and Nick in confusion. "Where? I haven't even gotten around to hiring you."

"You're planning on hiring me?" That caught GD's attention. "To do what?"

"To prove Kevin's innocence. Duh!" Kitty Anne rolled her eyes as if that was obvious, but GD continued to stare at her as if she'd grown a second head. It wouldn't have shocked him if she had.

"Rachel and I—"

"Rachel and you?" That had Nick jumping in as his gaze narrowed on Kitty Anne. "You told her?"

"Yes, but—"

"I knew it!" Nick raised two angry fists into the air and flailed them about as he let out a shout of frustration. "Ah!"

"Are you done?" Kitty Anne snapped with obvious exasperation. "Because we have more important things than your obsession with Rachel."

"I am not obsessed."

"And she's not going to rat Kevin out," Kitty Anne retorted. "And just where are *you* going?"

Her attention shifted back toward GD as he inched toward the door. So much for his attempt to escape when she wasn't looking. Kitty Anne clearly was not going to let him escape without having her say first.

"We have to discuss this and figure out what we're going to say to Kevin. You know, this may be the very reason he didn't want to meet his sister because he thinks all of you think he's guilty."

"Then we need to know if he is," GD insisted. "And there is only one way to do that."

"You're not going to interrogate the kid," Nick warned him, his annoyance shifting along with his alarmed look. "Because I can't allow that."

Nick was Kevin's de facto guardian, and GD knew he wouldn't let anybody near the kid, at least not without a lawyer. As if he could get past Kitty Anne, who would probably try to smother the kid like a hen did eggs.

"You can rest easy, man, and you, too, beautiful," GD assured them both, unable not to be slightly insulted that they thought they had to protect Kevin from him. "I'm not looking to convict here. I'm looking for the truth."

"And how are you going to find it?" Nick demanded to know.

"I'm going to have a conversation with the blackhaired beauty Kevin mentions," GD swore, causing Kitty Anne to straighten up with a round-eyed look of amazement.

"You think you know who she is?"

"I have a pretty good idea of who she might be, and no, I'm not telling you who until I have more answers, but I will go get those answers now...if you let me."

"You're not going anywhere without me."

"Or me," Nick chipped in as he rose out of his seat.

"Oh, for God's sakes, you two." GD groaned, feeling very put upon in that moment. This was turning into a circus. "I have to go to the club."

"Fine." Kitty Anne nodded, clearly not about to miss this trip. "Let me grab my purse."

"Kitty—"

"I'm coming."

And that was that. GD could recognize the finality in her tone and caved with ill grace.

"Fine, but it's going to cost you…no more games, no more questions. It's time you wore my collar."

"Fine."

"And you can't be there when I talk to the other woman." He wasn't going to tolerate any arguments on that point and knew just how to assure he didn't have to. "Or she won't tell me the truth."

"Well then, I guess Nick and I will have to entertain ourselves." Kitty Anne shrugged, completely unconcerned by that threat. "I'm sure boyfriend number one and I will be able to find something to do at a sex club."

"Don't worry I'll keep her nice and warm for you, boyfriend number two," Nick tacked on with a smug smile.

"You two are a laugh a minute," GD muttered as he jerked the door open. "Best you both remember that, at the club, I'm king."

* * * *

Kitty Anne didn't know what she'd expected of GD's club, but it surpassed all the marks. She stood there in the luxurious entrance and stared around, marveling at the blatant wealth. Nick appeared to be in awe as well. GD, on the other hand, took it all in stride.

He wasn't kidding about being king, though Kitty Anne suspected there were a lot of kings lurking around. There were certainly a lot of guys acting like it as an endless sea of beautiful, naked women flowed around, headed in all directions.

There was the dining hall, the main hall, the men's den, the courtyard, something called the cube, and gardens that put Camp D's landscaping to shame. Kitty Anne saw it all as GD led her and Nick through an endless maze of writhing bodies toward a cabana that appeared to be floating in its own private lake.

The setting was nothing short of spectacular. The lake itself was clearly a pool, one laid out like a tropical lagoon. That matched the look of the cabana. The walls were made up of layers of sheer curtains that floated softly in the breeze. The floor was basically one big bed.

There were rings and posts and even a pulley system that she suspected was some kind of bondage tool. As far as she could tell from what she had seen of the club and its members, the Cattlemen liked their women naked and bound. The also liked them bent over, on their knees, legs spread, ankles behind their head, and that was just the beginning of a very long list.

Kitty Anne was impressed by just how long a list it was. That wasn't all she was. She also happened to be wet and more than a little turned on. She didn't think she was the only one. While GD cut through the crowds with a determined stride, dragging her behind him with a death grip on her hand, Nick followed at a slightly slower pace. Just as fascinated by the spectacle unfolding around them, he was all but tripping over his own feet as his eyes cut in all directions.

There was no mistaking the bulge growing bigger by the second beneath his jean's zipper or the looks Nick garnered from the women as they passed. Kitty Anne would have shot them dirty looks, but she was too busy staring in fascination. This place really was over the top, and GD was obviously king.

That quickly became clear from the nods he received, along with the constant pestering of questions he shrugged off. Now was clearly not the time. He had plans, and Kitty Anne could easily guess what they were. Even if she hadn't, it would have quickly become clear as GD pulled to a stop at the beginning of the floating walkway.

He turned toward her and stared down at Kitty Anne with a look that made her knees go weak. This was not her big gentle, redneck giant but a man who was not to be defied.

"As long as you are here, I am in charge," GD stated in a tone that brooked no argument, not that Kitty Anne planned on offering up any resistance. "I am the master. You will obey my every command without hesitation, or you will be punished. Understand?"

Kitty Anne just smiled. She understood. It would irritate him if she didn't agree, and she just might get that spanking after all, or maybe not. Before GD could respond to her disobedience, Nick spoke up, sounding more than a little irritated.

"What about me? Don't I get to be a master?"

"No." GD couldn't be any clearer than that.

"Hey!" Nick objected indignantly. "I want to boss Kitty Anne around, too, and I'd be good at it. Watch." Nick turned to her, scrunched his face all up as though he was constipated, and barked, "Strip! Now, wench!"

"That's not how you do it," GD objected instantly, which had Kitty Anne reaching for the hem of her dress, not that either man noticed.

"Well, maybe, that's not how you do it," Nick shot back. "But I ran an entire prostitution ring. I think I know how to boss women around."

"You didn't boss them around," GD snapped in exasperation. "You hooked them—"

"Look, she's naked," Nick cut him off, nodding to where Kitty Anne stood, wearing nothing more than a pair of panties and a bra that lifted her breasts up high.

Her dress floated across the pond like a forgotten talisman. Kitty Anne reached behind her and snapped her bra free, tossing it on to the gently waving water as both men eyed her with a hunger that left her feeling both emboldened and weak. She was their toy, and she couldn't wait to get played with.

With that thought warming the blood in her veins, Kitty Anne shoved her panties down to her ankles and kicked them off, allowing the heady scent of her wet pussy to thicken in the air as both men eyed her with a look that had Kitty Anne smiling. She didn't have to say a word. They knew who was in charge now.

To prove it, she turned and ran down the walkway, veering as she heard their footsteps pounding after her and leaping right off the edge into the pool. The cool water closed in around her, and she couldn't help but bite back a laugh.

This was living, and she wanted a membership.

* * * *

GD watched Kitty Anne float out into the pool. Like a siren, she'd lure him into temptation, and he so wanted to smash himself against her rocks...or her against his rocks, as the case may be. He wanted her, now and forever. That thought had him hearing again her own words of love.

It had been something else to watch Kitty Anne stand up to her mother and claim him as her own just as she had Nick. She loved them both, and they loved her. The future was set and couldn't be brighter or sweeter if he'd designed it himself. Of course, that future would have to wait a little longer because he had somebody else's to go ruin.

"Oh, it just sucks to be the king." Nick snickered as he tossed his shirt into the pool and bent over to start tugging at his boots. "Kings are always so busy managing their kingdoms. It's no wonder the queen tends to like to do the help."

"Are you the help?" GD quirked an eyebrow at that, not considering Nick helpful in that moment at all.

"Well, I'm certainly going to help myself." Nick chuckled, amused by his own wit. "And you got a raven-haired beauty to go harass, but don't worry, I'll keep Kitty Anne's pussy nice and wet for you."

GD's eyes narrowed on Nick's gloating smirk, but he couldn't deny that he had other things to do right then than Kitty Anne. That didn't mean he couldn't get a little revenge on Nick. Without a word, he shoved past the other man, pushing Nick straight into the pool still wearing his boots and knowing they'd be forever ruined.

Nick knew it, too. He hollered out at GD, calling him an asshole, but the laughter was still there in his tone. The deep-toned rumble was accentuated by the sweet giggles coming from Kitty Anne. She called out to him as well, urging him to come back quickly because she was in the mood for a sandwich.

As if he weren't hard and hurting bad enough, her words assured GD moved quickly as he cut through the Saturday night revelers filling out the Cattleman's Club. He looked high and low for Lana, frustratingly finding her nowhere. That wasn't right. He got a sick feeling in his stomach that something was really off, or maybe it was just the pain coming from his balls.

He didn't want to be wasting his time with Lana. He wanted to be back at the cabana, making more than just a snack out of Kitty Anne. He was going to make a whole damn meal out of her, and it was those thoughts that entertained him as he waited in a dark corner of Lana's office for her to return a half-hour later.

She stumbled into the small, well-organized room, appearing frazzled and upset. She didn't even notice GD sulking in the corner as she clicked on the desk lamp and dropped her purse into the leather seat tucked behind it. He waited till she had her back completely toward him before speaking up.

"So," he began, pausing for a second as Lana gasped and whipped around to cast a startled gaze in his direction.

The skirt of her dress arced in a perfect circle around her legs, and GD had to admit that she looked just as good dressed as undressed. That was something Kitty Anne wasn't anymore. He knew she wanted new clothes badly, but he and Nick also knew she wanted to make them herself.

He suspected that stubbornness would remain for the rest of their lives, but it was okay with him. Kitty Anne always looked beautiful to GD wearing anything and perfect wearing nothing. If the clothing her mother had provided her made Kitty Anne look anything less than gorgeous to the rest of the boys and men surrounding her every day, that was fine by him.

"GD! Oh my God, you damn near gave me a heart attack." Lana let her words weigh as she grasped her chest and staggered backward. "What are you doing over there in the corner?"

"Waiting for you."

"Really?" Lana frowned as she quickly moved around the desk, shifting her purse from the chair to the smooth, wooden desktop. "Is something wrong?"

"I don't know," GD admitted honestly. He'd considered just how he was going to handle this conversation for the last hour and come to only one conclusion. It was time to be blunt. "Did you set Chase's barn on fire, Lana?"

The answer was yes. He could see it in her eyes and in the way she hesitated before scoffing.

"Don't be ridiculous." Lana snorted and waved him away, but her act quickly crumbled as GD revealed the truth. "I would never—"

"There was a witness."

That was all it took to have Lana going still. Her gaze met his before her chin finally dipped and she gave up the charade. "I didn't know Patton was in there. Chase had told me…he'd made it clear he wasn't coming back. Not ever, you know?

"I just…" Lana shook her head as she sighed. "Everything just hit me. All the years. All the memories. That barn…it was just a symbol of everything, and I wanted to tear it down."

GD could get that. That barn was where the club had started, where the Davis brothers had honed their craft and their ideas. It was also where Lana had fallen in love with Chase. GD could understand why the thought of the place had probably pained Lana. He could even believe that she didn't know Patton was inside.

None of that changed anything.

"And Gwen saw you," GD took a guess at what had happened, but this time, he was wrong.

"No. Charlotte saw…" Lana's words faded as she appeared to realize she'd just been played. "I thought you knew there was a witness?"

"I knew Gwen was blackmailing you, and I figured out what she had on you." GD shrugged and quickly changed the conversation. "So Charlotte saw and told Gwen."

That made sense. Before Charlotte had been the Davis brothers' former housekeeper and bed warmer, she'd been tight with Gwen. They'd hung out at the club and even enjoyed each other's more intimate company.

"You have to prepare for this to become public knowledge," GD warned her, feeling the guilt for the light dimming in her eyes. Normally, he'd have protected her, but there was a kid involved. Kevin came first.

"You're going to turn me in?" she asked in disbelief.

"I have no choice."

Lana blinked that information in and then slumped back into her seat, recognizing the finality in his tone. "How long do I have?"

"How long do you need?" GD countered, not completely unsympathetic to her feelings and wishing he didn't have to sacrifice her.

"Give me a day."

"That's it?" That didn't seem like enough. After all, Lana co-owned a sex club with the Davis brothers, so saying things could get complicated was kind of an understatement. Lana, though, maintained her position.

"I'll tell them tonight." Speaking almost as if to herself, she whispered out that plan before glancing up and offering GD a half-smile and cold assurance. "I'll probably be gone by tomorrow."

"Then I'll miss you."

And he would, but that was life. It just kept going, and so did his. Certain that the issue was finally settled and his conscience free, GD lifted out of his seat to offer Lana a quick hug before heading back to the cabana and the comfort of his own future.

A future that wasn't exactly how he planned. By the time he'd gotten back to the pool, Kitty Anne and Nick had moved onto the bed...sort of.

Coming to a stop, GD blinked as he mouth fell open and the shock just popped out.

"Are you *kidding* me?"

Chapter Twenty-Six

"No." GD shook his head as Kitty Anne's lips puckered into a pout, but he refused to be moved. "No. Absolutely not."

"What?" Kitty Anne blinked as if surprised by his objection. "Don't you like my outfit? I found it in that little closet over there."

GD didn't glance at the corner column she pointed to. His gaze, instead, remaining riveted on her. Besides, he didn't doubt her words. He recognized the get-up, and she did look good in it, but still...the woman was also decked out in enough leather to make Catwoman jealous.

She even had a mask on, along with five-inch-stiletto boots that laced all the way up to her knees. As if her outfit wasn't preposterous enough, she had one foot propped up on the edge of the bedframe, opening up her cunt to Nick, who knelt at her feet with his head buried beneath the short skirt Kitty Anne was wearing.

GD had a pretty good idea of what the other man was up to. After all, he could hear how much fun Nick was having, and Kitty Anne was obviously swaying on her heels. A breathless smile lingered on her lips as she tried to cajole him into giving her what she wanted.

"Come on," Kitty Anne purred, pausing as her breath caught and her lashes fluttered. GD knew that look, knew Nick had just caught her clit up in some kind of kiss. He must have released it a second later because Kitty Anne picked right back up as if nothing had happened.

"I'm wearing your collar," Kitty pointed out with an innocent smile that GD didn't believe for a second.

"And that's *all* you are supposed to be wearing."

"Hmm." Kitty Anne appeared to consider that for a moment before tapping Nick on the shoulder.

At that silent command, he pulled back, releasing her pussy and glancing up as they exchanged a quick look before he shifted to the bed.

Settling back, Nick watched along with GD as Kitty Anne reached for her mask's ties. The bit of lace fluttered to the floor seconds later as her hand slid slowly down to the laces holding her corset together.

GD's gaze tracked the graceful motion of her hands as she began to unwind those laces, slowly allowing the full, rounded mounds of her naked breasts to fall free. The sight of those big and beautiful tits, tipped with the hardest, pink peaks, had him swallowing back the urge to growl.

Growl and strike because he'd waited long enough to feel her soft and wet and giving beneath him. The memory of that one little taste of her he'd gotten a week ago ate like acid at his control as he watched Kitty Anne's corset fall to the floor. It took all his strength to stand there and not touch. GD's hands clenched into fists as hers reached for the waistband of her skirt. A second later Kitty Anne was stepping out of it, leaving her wearing nothing but her boots and GD's collar as she came to a stop mere inches from him.

Kitty Anne held his gaze as she reached up and unlatched the collar. It fell to the floor with a soft thud that matched the solemn seriousness of Kitty Anne's tone as she lifted a hand and waved it before his nose.

"I'm not going to wear your collar, but I will wear your ring. Right here." She curled down every finger but her ring one. "Because I love you, and I'm going to marry you. You got me, George Davis?"

GD smiled. He got her, and he couldn't deny that she had him.

"Yeah?" Lifting a brow and playing along with her, GD cast a look back over at Nick, who was sitting there naked and grinning. "And what about boyfriend number one over there? Where's his ring going?"

"Beneath yours," Nick shot back. "She's going to get my name tattooed on her finger."

Kitty Anne didn't confirm or deny that claim. She didn't have to. Her smile said it all. "Of course, I'm not going to agree until you answer one last question honestly."

"And what is that?"

"How do you really feel about me, Mr. Davis?"

GD couldn't help but reach out and cup her soft cheeks in his big palms. Forcing her chin up, he dipped his head but hesitated to claim the kiss he knew she anticipated. Instead, he allowed his lips to brush against hers as he laid down his own vow.

"I love you, beautiful. Now pick up the collar and put it on because *I'm* in charge tonight."

"Is that right?" Kitty Anne leaned back to gaze up at him with a twinkle in her eyes. "And what do I get if I'm a good girl?"

"What do you want? A ring…or a spanking?"

* * * *

Kitty Anne wanted both. More importantly, she knew she would have both. GD wouldn't deny her. Not anything. Of that she was certain, which was just why she smiled and sank slowly to her knees. Holding GD's gaze, she slid down to her knees, putting her lips just inches from the thick bulge tenting his pants as she reached for his collar.

The hunger and possessive satisfaction flared in his dark gaze as she wrapped the piece of lace back around her neck and re-latched the little silver buckle, but when GD would have reached a hand out to stroke her cheek, Kitty Anne leaned back and offered him a warning.

"Married couples wear matching rings *and* collars."

"I'll tell you what, beautiful. We'll let that be the honeymoon surprise," GD suggested with a smile before nodding toward Nick. "Now be a good girl and go sit that ass down on boyfriend number one's lap. I want you good and comfortable while I explain a few things to you."

Kitty Anne could bet that wasn't at all what he had in mind, not with that smile curling at his lips. GD was up to something, and she couldn't wait to find out what. She got an idea of what was coming, though, when he pressed her back down to her knees as Kitty Anne started to rise up.

"Crawl, beautiful, and don't forget to stick that ass into the air."

Kitty Anne returned his smile and did as he commanded. Not only did she stick her ass into the air, she waved it at him, all but taunting him to spank her, but GD didn't take her up on the silent offer. Instead, he laughed and left Kitty Anne to content herself with the twelve inches of hardy goodness that Nick's dick had swollen to.

Licking her lips, Kitty Anne paused as she lifted up over the edge of the bed to consider taking a taste. No doubt that would get her spanked, but it would, also, be too easy. That didn't mean that she couldn't taunt them with the possibility of her disobedience. After all, Kitty Anne wasn't planning on behaving.

She made that clear as she crawled up between Nick's legs, intentionally capturing the heated length of his cock between the heavy press of her breasts. Plumping up her full curves in her hands, Kitty Anne treated both Nick and herself to a teasing massage that ended only when he groaned and pumped his hips in a silent demand for more. She gave it to him, rising until her cunt ground against the thick, heat of his erection.

He felt so good she forgot herself for a moment and shifted so that his engorged cockhead was brushing up against the swollen bud of her clit and setting off showers of sparkling thrills with every motion of her hips. Kitty Anne couldn't stay still.

Up and down, she rubbed herself against him with an increasingly frantic speed that ultimately ended with the flared head of his cock pressing up against the aching opening of her cunt. Then all it took was a little extra push and he was sliding into her, filling Kitty Anne with more than just a deliciously full sensation. She felt, in that moment, the love Nick had yet to confess to. He didn't have to. She could see it in his smile.

Kitty Anne could even sense the bond between GD and Nick was deep and rich, though she knew it would never be physical. There would never be any jealousy either, proven by the fact that Nick only laughed when GD jerked her off his dick so he could fuck his own deep into her cunt.

Kitty Anne couldn't help but moan in delightful surprise at just how magnificently thick GD's dick was. She'd forgotten how big he was, how well he filled her. Even then, there was remembering, and there was experiencing.

God help her, she'd never experienced anything half as good as the feeling of GD slamming into her…except maybe feeling Nick pound into her. Kitty Anne suspected that there would be truly nothing to compare to the feel of having both fuck her at the same time. She'd waited long enough to find out just how good that was going to feel, and she wasn't waiting any longer. Kitty Anne didn't care if she was wearing the collar. This was still her show.

So she jerked free, catching GD off guard and breaking his hold on her hips. Behind her, GD snarled, and Kitty Anne knew she had only seconds before he struck again. After all, she wasn't the only one who had been waiting all this time. Any concerns that Kitty Anne had harbored that GD might not want her as much as she needed him were dispelled by the savagely feral sounds grumbling out of him as his hands reclaimed her hips, his fingers biting into her flesh in an unbreakable hold.

He was too late.

Kitty Anne had already scrambled back over Nick's thighs, positioning the aching entrance of her pussy over the wondrously thick flare of his dick's head. Nick's own fingers curled around her thighs as he aided her and yanked Kitty Anne down onto his meaty length. He fucked a giggle out of her but not the thoughts out of her head. She knew what she wanted and bucked against Nick's attempts to force her to ride him.

Instead, she leaned forward and dangled the puckered tips of her breasts over his lips as she wiggled her ass at GD and tossed a sultry look back over her shoulder.

"If you're not going to spank it…will you, at least, fuck it?"

She must have been insane to taunt him that way, but Kitty Anne couldn't help herself. Neither did she regret teasing him for a second when he snarled and slid those big, heated paws of his around the curve of her ass to palm her cheeks in his rough grip. Kitty Anne had dreamed of this moment for weeks. Now that it was here, she couldn't help but smile and laugh.

That sound melted into a moan as Nick caught one of her nipples in a suckling kiss, sending a shower of sparkling delight raining down through her. Kitty Anne twisted with the deep, sensuous pleasure. It was filled with the wicked thrill of a nibbling bite of pain and pressure that radiated out of her ass as GD stretched her muscles wide around the thick, blunt press of his fingers.

There wasn't much room left thanks to the cock packed deep into her cunt. So it wasn't just her breath catching as GD ground his fingers down against her channel's sensitive walls. Even as Kitty Anne moaned and shivered with a sharp rush of rapture, Nick was snorting up a laugh.

"Man, I hate to tell you this, but…that kind of tickles."

"Shut up, Nick," GD snapped, clearly not in the mood to joke around. "I'm not here for you."

"Then what are you here for?" Kitty Anne tossed back. "Just to tease or take?"

GD answered that question with a quick thrust of his fingers as he began to fuck her with rapid, shallow strokes that didn't end until Kitty Anne was whimpering and rocking her hips in motion. Her desperation for more was blatant, just as his denial was pointed. He had her at his mercy, and Kitty Anne knew that GD didn't have much of that commodity left. She'd taunted it out of him weeks ago, or, at least, she hoped so.

With baited breath and eager anticipation, she waited to see what GD did next as he withdrew his fingers and left her achingly, painfully empty. His hand lifted to fist in her hair, and he used the silken strands as a leash to tilt her head back until his heated breath warmed the delicate curve of her ear.

"Are you sure this is what you want?" Just in case she didn't understand that question, he flexed his hips, pumping the thick, meaty length of his dick between the flushed cheeks of her ass. "Because I got to warn you, I'm not going to be nice. I need you, Kitty Anne, and it's going to be rough and hard all the way."

The softness of his tone added the weight of seriousness to his words, and Kitty Anne knew he wasn't kidding. This was no joke, but then again, it never had been. Not to her.

"Nice is just another word for boring," Kitty Anne panted out, glancing back over her shoulder at him. "And I really *hate* to be bored."

Her words lifted into a plaintive mew as Nick reached down to slip a hand between their bodies and cup her mound. While he licked, nibbled, and sucked his way from one breast to the other, his finger brushed the lips of her pussy farther apart so he could claim mastery of her clit. For several minutes, Kitty Anne lost all sense of time as Nick kept her entertained while GD methodically lubed up her ass in preparation for his penetration.

She heard the snap of a condom wrapper being opened, and then she felt the latex-covered crest of his flared cockhead pressing against the tight ring of muscles guarding her back entrance, and the whole world sharpened back into focus. A second later it shattered into a beautiful kaleidoscope of colors, smells, and sensations as GD forged forward and began filling her with his heat and hardness.

He was thick, and she was tight. Everything in the world was right. That was all Kitty Anne knew right then and there as she felt a pressure too great to be contained begin to expand out of her ass. It grew with every inch GD fed her, searing through her veins and flooding her with an intoxicating rush of rapture. Like a brilliant star, the amazing beauty of being filled by the two men closest to her heart held Kitty Anne captivated as GD finally settled the full length of his dick inside her.

The soft, heavy sac of his balls pressed against her, even as he reached around to pull her tit free of Nick's lips and force her to straighten back up until her back rested against his chest. The motion had her ass tightening down around his engorged cock and had her panting as he caught her nipples between his fingers.

GD treated Kitty Anne's tender tits to the same rough fondling Nick was tormenting her clit with, making Kitty Anne squirm and wiggle. With each shift of her weight, another round of pure, white-hot pleasure erupted out of her pelvis. The waves were tinged with the hint of the ecstasy to come. All that was needed was motion, but her two stubborn boyfriends didn't seem interested in moving at all. That could mean only one thing.

They wanted something.

"Please," Kitty Anne begged as she clawed at Nick's shoulder. She tried desperately to buck hard enough between the two of them in a desperate attempt to gain just a little more of the exotic thrill making all her nerve endings tingle. The need was damn near painful, and she couldn't endure it for much longer.

"*Please!*"

"Uh-uh-uh, beautiful," GD chastised her, his tone amused and thickened with something much more dangerous than lust. "You haven't said the magic words."

"I love you." That had to be it. That had to be what he wanted to hear, what *they* wanted to hear. Only it wasn't.

"Oh, sexy." Nick laughed up at her and shook his head. "We already know that."

"Then what?" Kitty Anne pleaded to know. "What do you want? Do you want to hear me say I trust you?"

"Not exactly."

"Then what exactly?" she shot back in exasperation, all but crying now with the frustration thickening through the rapture as it twisted into a painful ball of need.

"You know," GD insisted. "Go on and say it, Kitty Anne. Who's in charge?"

The love and laughter mixed into his tone broke through the frantic swirl of her thoughts and solidified them into one. It made perfect sense now. What they wanted, what they were really waiting for. Kitty Anne gave it to them. Lifting a hand to capture one of GD's and allowing her other to dip down and cover Nick's, she tipped her chin over her shoulder and offered her big man a smile.

"*I'm* in charge, and if you two need instructions on how to see things to the end...I'm always available to help." Kitty Anne relished that offer, knowing just what it would get her.

She didn't have to wait to claim her victory, either. Without hesitation, GD responded to that challenge with the same bold move as Nick. Both men released her intimate flesh to clutch at her hips and waist, holding her still as they flexed backward and pulled the thick, rigid lengths of their cocks down the sensitive walls of her sheath and ass until their flared heads barely kissed the inside of her body, and then they were slamming her back down, fucking a scream right out of her.

Together they took her, riding her hard and fast through one explosive peak after another. The ecstasy washing through her built and boiled until she felt on fire with the need for something so beyond words she could only express it by flexing against their motions and disrupting their rhythm.

Words, though, were not necessary. Not now. Not in this.

They knew what she needed because they needed it, too. Alternating their strokes, they sped everything up until the pleasure came in one endless tidal wave that drowned out everything but the blissful perfection of being claimed by both her men. As Kitty Anne felt the world come undone, she heard their whispers of love and adoration as both GD and Nick clutched at her. They were her anchors, just as she was theirs.

That thought had her lips curling into a smile, even as she passed out in the sweet oblivion of total unconsciousness, confident that her two men would keep her safe and sound, for always and forever.

Epilogue

It had been a long night, one that GD never wanted to end. That was why he couldn't seem to let it go and fall asleep. Instead, he lay there with Kitty Anne tucked into his side, running a hand through her hair as he enjoyed the moment of peace and contentment.

"I'm hungry," Kitty Anne murmured, proving that he wasn't alone in the moment, or, at least, he wasn't the only one awake.

GD's arm tightened around her as he turned his head to whisper a kiss across her brow and offer all that he could. "I got something you could snack on if you want."

That had Kitty Anne laughing as she levered herself up onto one arm. She shrugged out of Nick's hold as she glanced down at GD. The other man turned with a grumble and yanked at the sheet, paying Kitty Anne and GD no mind.

"I tell you what. You scour me up a real snack, and I might have enough energy to take care of you, my king."

"Done."

GD didn't even have to think about it. All he had to do was reach for the phone set in the small cubby beside the barely elevated bed. He didn't even have to dial. He just lifted up the receiver and demanded a double quarter-pound burger with cheese and all the fixings. Knowing his Kitty Anne as well as he did, GD added on an order of cheese-chili fries and a double thick chocolate milkshake.

He planned on exercising her good and didn't want any complaints about an empty stomach. Actually he didn't want her to complain about an empty anything, which was just why he rolled her on top of him as he hung up the phone. He didn't need to direct Kitty Anne any more than that. With an eagerness that was beyond sexy, she slid over him, her legs parting around his as she ground the wet, molten folds of her pussy over his growing erection.

She knew just how to turn him on and wasn't afraid to take what she wanted. With a smile fitting a Venus, Kitty Anne tilted her hips and lodged the swelling head of his cock against the heated entrance to her cunt. A second later she was taking him back into heaven.

Never before had GD ridden a woman bareback, but everything was different with Kitty Anne. She was his first true love. His only true love, and as GD stared up at her, he couldn't help but admire his good luck...even if she had issues with control.

Despite the collar wrapped around her neck, Kitty Anne continued to act as if she were the boss. Capturing both his wrists in her hands, she pinned his arms to the bed as she leaned over GD to taunt him with the sight of those big tits hanging dangerously close to his lips. He loved her breasts and loved the way she liked to flaunt them, right along with that lush ass of hers.

"Now that I've got you where I want you," Kitty Anne said, cutely acting as if she were actually in command, "I got a question for you, Mr. Davis."

"Yeah?" GD quirked a brow at that. "I thought we were done with the games, beautiful."

"Not until you tell me about the license plates. That first night, that *was* you, right?"

"Uh-huh."

"So...you either have two different trucks or a stockpile of tags," Kitty Anne concluded. "Which is it?"

"I'm sorry," GD apologized with a smirk. "That's a trade secret, but I might let you in on it if you tell me how you managed to find me at Gwen's house."

Kitty Anne just grinned, not answering. Not that he expected her to. Instead, she began to pump her hips, riding him with a slow deliberation GD knew was meant to drive him insane. He let her go, enjoying the ride as the pleasure and the pressure built back up to insatiable levels. Then he could no longer remain passive.

Primitive instinct demanded GD take control. That was just what he did. Shaking off her hold, he clamped his hands down around her waist and directed her motions until the whole bed was bouncing and Nick was muttering complaints once again. Neither GD nor Kitty Anne paid him any mind. They were too lost in the beauty of the moment.

Kitty Anne's cunt clung to his dick, milking his sensitive length in a velvety fist that was beyond beautiful. It was beyond perfect, and GD never wanted the pleasure to end. He strained to hold back, but the white-hot bliss beginning to sear through his veins couldn't be contained, and with a shout, he gave himself over to the release pulsing out of his balls. Flushed and shuddering with her own intense climax, Kitty Anne wavered over him before collapsing down onto GD's chest.

They stayed like that for several minutes before Kitty Anne finally broke the heavy silence that had thickened around them like a comforting blanket.

"We have to do that more often." Sliding her cheek over his chest, she lifted her chin to pin GD with a pointed look. "No more holding out on me, right?"

"Not in a million years, beautiful." He wasn't that crazy or masochistic.

Fucking Kitty Anne was way too much fun to bench himself again. That didn't mean life wouldn't interfere on occasion. Right then it intruded with the shrill ring of the phone. It wasn't the club phone, and despite GD's attempts to ignore it, the damn thing just kept going off.

"That sounds serious," Kitty Anne murmured, shifting off GD and making him groan as she pulled free of his dick, but all she offered him was a frown. "It could be the camp. You better get it."

Muttering to himself that somebody had better be dead or bloody, GD rolled out of the bed and reached for his jeans just as Nick cracked an eye and shot him a dirty look.

"Are you going to get that?"

"Yeah, yeah, yeah." GD grumbled as he fished his cell phone out of his pocket. It stopped ringing the second he touched it, and GD was half torn about bothering to see if he had a message.

"I swear, between the two of you," Nick complained as he grabbed a pillow and pulled it over his head, "I'm never going to get a good night's sleep again, am I?"

Kitty Anne smirked and then pounced, bouncing all around Nick as she yanked the pillow out of his hand and started to beat him with it. GD watched Nick snarl and launch himself at Kitty Anne. They wrestled about as his phone went off again. He'd have ignored it but glancing down he saw Alex's name flashing across the screen and knew it was bad news.

"Hey, man, what's up?"

"Gwen's dead," Alex retorted with a grimness that assured GD he wasn't joking. Not that he would about that kind of thing, but still, it took GD a moment to process that declaration. Even then, he still couldn't accept it.

"What?"

"We found her body, but it looks like it happened sometime earlier tonight. It doesn't look natural or accidental either."

"Crap!" GD spat, feeling his plans to take things easy and work on helping out at the camp slide away.

"I got to tell you, man," Alex murmured into the phone, his voice dropping with a heavy hint of panic. "It's bad. Real bad."

Alex didn't know how right he was.

THE END

WWW.JENNYPENN.COM

ABOUT THE AUTHOR

I live near Charleston, SC with my two biggies, my dogs. I have had a slightly unconventional life. Moving almost every three years, I've had a range of day jobs that included everything from working for one of the world's largest banks as an auditor to turning wrenches as an outboard repair mechanic. I've always regretted that we only get one life and have tried to cram as much as I can into this one.

Throughout it all, I've always read books, feeding my need to dream and fantasize about what could be. An avid reader since childhood, and as a latchkey kid, I'd spend hours at the library earning those shiny stars the librarian would paste up on the board after my name.

I credit my grandmother's yearly visits as the beginning of my obsession with romances. When she'd come, she'd bring stacks of romance books, the old fashion kind that didn't have sex in them. Imagine my shock when I went to the used bookstore and found out what really could be in a romance novel.

I've worked on my own stories for years and have found a particular love of erotic romances. In this genre, women are no longer confined to a stereotype and plots are no longer constrained to the rational. I love the "anything goes" mentality and letting my imagination run wild.

I hope you enjoyed running with me and will consider picking up another book and coming along for another adventure.

For all titles by Jenny Penn, please visit
www.bookstrand.com/jenny-penn

Siren Publishing, Inc.
www.SirenPublishing.com

Lightning Source UK Ltd.
Milton Keynes UK
UKHW02f0312200318
319683UK00009B/959/P